HOOSIER
Crossroads

Jennifer Johnson

BARBOUR
PUBLISHING

Cover Model Photography: Jim Celuch, Celuch Creative Imaging

Published by Barbour Publishing, Inc., P.O. Box 719, Uhrichsville, Ohio 44683, www.barbourbooks.com

Our mission is to publish and distribute inspirational products offering exceptional value and biblical encouragement to the masses.

Member of the
Evangelical Christian
Publishers Association

Printed in the United States of America.

Dear Readers,

I cannot even begin to tell you the excitement and humility I feel as I write this letter. Why God would allow me, Jennifer Collins Johnson, to pen stories that demonstrate His love and its reflection on humanity, I will never know. I am proof of what the Bible says in I Corinthians: "He chose the lowly things of this world and the despised things—and the things that are not." There is absolutely nothing special about me, except that I am covered by the blood of my Lord and Savior, Jesus Christ, which makes me a wonderful being indeed!

These stories, *Picket Fence Pursuit*, *Pursuing the Goal*, and *In Pursuit of Peace* are set in my original home state of Indiana. (For all you Hoosier fans, when I was a little girl, I was going to marry Steve Alford. Many of us were, weren't we?) The stories are all about the Andrews family; a blue-collar, coal-mining family who worked hard, loved the Lord, and loved each other. The family as a whole was developed in honor of my best friend, Robin Ratliff. The mother and father characters, Lorma and Richard, are named after my grandparents. I didn't make them look alike, but these characters certainly honor the spirit of my grandparents.

As you will see, *Picket Fence Pursuit* is dedicated to my oldest daughter, Brooke. I made the main character of that story, Kylie Andrews, look just like her, and she shares many of my daughter's traits. The same is true with *Pursuing the Goal*; the main character, Chloe Andrews, is just like my middle daughter, Hayley. However, if I were true to Hayley's character, I would have made Chloe a lot messier (a constant inside family joke). Lastly, I made the main character, Lydia Hammond, from the story *In Pursuit of Peace* look like my youngest, Allie. I'm not sure if Allie can concoct the delicious apple desserts that Lydia could, but we'd be happy to let her work on it.

Thanks so much for reading my stories. I pray God uses them to bless your heart and draw you closer to Him. I would love for you to visit my Web site, www.jenniferjohnsonbooks.com. You can also email me at jenwrites4god@bellsouth.net. God is so good!

Sincerely,
Jennifer Johnson

PICKET FENCE PURSUIT

Dedication

To my oldest daughter, Brooke. What a treasure you are! I'm so proud of your desire to live your life for the Lord. May you never cease to pursue Him.

Thank you, Rose McCauley, for your continual faithfulness in critiquing my work and for being such a sweet friend.

Thank you, Albert, Brooke, Hayley, and Allie, for your constant support for and patience with your loony wife and mommy.

Robin, you are such a dear friend. I thank God for you.

Lastly, praise You, Jesus, because You guide every breath I take and because You take broken vessels and make them whole. May I never stop yearning for You!

Chapter 1

"This is what I want out of life." Kylie Andrews lifted the handle of the ice-cream machine and twirled the cone beneath the flow of the creamy, chocolate treat.

"What's that?" Robin handed Kylie a napkin.

Wrapping the napkin around the bottom of the cone, Kylie turned and handed it to the small, black-haired boy in front of the counter. He licked his lips in animated anticipation.

Kylie smiled at the urchin, then winked at her friend. "A little guy like this." Turning back to the boy, she said, "That'll be two dollars."

He pushed the money across the countertop, then shoved the tip of the ice cream between his lips. Kylie covered her mouth to avoid a giggle as the boy's eyes grew big as saucers and he shook his head. Brain freeze, no doubt. He closed his eyes and mouthed a slobbery thank-you, then turned and ran toward a man and a woman who held a baby girl.

"Kylie." Robin playfully shoved her. "You're not married. You don't even have a boyfriend."

"Yeah, but look at them. They're the perfect little family. Beautiful parents. Adorable kids. Little vacation."

Robin propped her elbows onto the counter and rested her chin in her hands. "He is a cute little guy, huh?"

Kylie looked at her longtime friend and burst into laughter. "I thought for sure he was going to pass out after taking that huge bite. I bet his head still hurts."

Robin chuckled. "Bet you're right."

Kylie swiped a wet towel out of the compact, aluminum sink and wiped her hands. "This job is a lot of fun. I'm glad you thought of it."

"Holiday World was always my favorite vacation spot as a kid. I figured if we're going to live near Santa Claus, Indiana, we might as well spend the summer working somewhere fun."

"It was really nice of your uncle to let us live in one of his apartments free of charge."

"Not exactly free. We still have to mow and keep the flowers alive."

Kylie laughed. "I'll gladly do the yard work. I've lived in a University of

Evansville dorm room long enough. Mowing will be bliss."

"What about the drive?"

"The one-hour commute will be cake. We can share gas and enjoy each other's company. Even with gas prices as high as they are, a free apartment and lengthy drive is cheaper than a dorm room."

Robin nodded. "True."

"And this job is perfect—simple and stress free. One more semester of college for me, a few more for you, and we're done. *Fini.* Then it's *sayonara*, baby!"

"Yep." Robin looked at her watch. "We get off in half an hour. What do ya want to do?"

Kylie shrugged. Her happy-go-lucky mood plummeted, and she sighed. "Check my e-mail for sure."

"You gotta let that drop. You know Professor Nickels is going to give you an A. You earned it. He'll review your grades. Everything'll be fine."

"What if he doesn't?" Kylie cringed. Besides her desire to graduate with highest honors, she had to have a 3.5 grade point average to keep her academic scholarship. She'd gotten a B in Biology and couldn't afford a B in Accounting. Accounting, for crying out loud. Accounting was her major. Kylie never dreamed that Professor Nickels would be so difficult. Anyone else would have given her an A. But not Nickels the knucklehead.

"Robin, if I lose my scholarship—"

"Then you'll get a loan. Besides, you're not going to lose your scholarship."

Kylie turned away from her friend. She didn't want any more loans. She needed to be as debt free as possible when she started a job so she could help her parents.

Robin nudged her shoulder. "Let's just have fun, okay?"

"You're right." Kylie turned toward her friend just as a spoonful of ice cream launched from a pink plastic stick. She gasped when the cold, sticky goop smacked her mouth, cheek, and strands of loose hair.

"Oh, yeah." Robin danced back and forth. "I gotcha good."

"You think so, Ms. Reed?" Kylie grasped the ice-cream machine's handle, lifted, and poured a golf-ball-sized glob into her hand. She glanced at Robin, who was filling a cup from the second machine. Before Robin could finish, Kylie smacked the frozen treat onto the back of Robin's head and swooshed it around.

"You're such a good friend." Kylie rubbed her hands together and grabbed Robin in a bear hug, wiping the goop all over her friend's back. "I love you so much, Robin."

"Oh, yeah?" Robin dumped the cup over Kylie's head. "Mmm. What's that new perfume you're wearing? Chocolate drops?"

"Am I interrupting something?"

Kylie jumped at the masculine voice. Her heart beat faster and heat rushed up her neck and to her cheeks when she turned toward the man wearing a pale blue uniform that looked very much like the one she wore. A stream of cold, melting ice cream streaked down her cheek and pooled above her collarbone. She glanced at Robin, who looked as petrified as she. "I'm sorry. It won't happen again."

Wishing to crawl under the counter, Kylie grabbed several napkins from the container and wiped her cheek, neck, and hair. *Yuck. Disgusting.* She imagined the brown shade sticking to her blond hair in straight, sticky spikes around her head. She glanced at Robin, whose coal black curls were sticking straight up on the left side.

"You're not bothering me."

Kylie looked back at the man. A slow smile spread across his face, and he lifted his hands in surrender. "I just didn't want to get caught in the crossfire. My shift is about to start."

"You sure?" Robin giggled as she lifted the handle and poured a new stream into her cup. "This shade of brown would complement your red hair quite nicely."

Kylie gaped at her friend. "Robin, hush." Through gritted teeth she added, "This could get us into a lot of trouble. Ix-nay the lay-pay."

"Yeah, nix the play." He pointed at Robin, then interlocked arms with Kylie. Leaning toward her, he whispered, "I think I'll stick close to you. You must be the levelheaded one." He looked at her and cocked his head. "Actually, your hair is anything but level."

Kylie pulled her arm from his and grabbed her purse from the cabinet beside the ice-cream machines. No doubt she was a fright. Robin looked atrocious with sticky hair and chocolate handprints all over her back. "Let's go, Robin. We need to get cleaned up."

Without another glance at their relief, Kylie grabbed Robin's hand and guided her out of the cramped ice-cream concession.

"Bye. Hey, what's your. . ."

Kylie held tight to Robin's arm as she picked up the pace away from the entirely-too-cute guy and headed toward the parking lot. They had to get out of there before anyone else saw them.

"Weren't *you* in a hurry?" Robin huffed as she slid into the passenger seat, then fastened her seat belt.

Kylie stuck her key in the ignition, turned, and willed her aged Ford to start. It growled in protest, but finally it complied, and Kylie pulled out of the parking lot.

Robin popped a piece of gum into her mouth. "That guy was kind of cute. You know, in a curly-haired, hippie-looking, Richie Cunningham kind of way."

"You would think that."

"What's that supposed to mean?"

"Robin, you have to pay attention."

"Attention to what?"

"You and I both come from poor backgrounds. We want more for our children, right?"

Robin scrunched up her nose. "What's that got to do with ice-cream man?"

"Didn't you notice that he's not some young college boy? He looked like a man—older than eighteen, like closer to thirty. And, he's working at Holiday World?" Kylie looked at Robin, lifted her eyebrows, and shook her head for effect. "In my book that spells L–O–S–E–R. We can't marry losers."

"Did I ask you to marry him? I don't even remember mentioning dating him." Robin touched Kylie's shoulder. "Look, girl, you've got to get over this I-gotta-have-everything-my-way-or-no-way-and-my-way-is-perfect complex."

"What?"

"You heard me."

"So I'm a snob? Look, Robin, if I remember right, you've got to have money to be a snob."

"No you don't."

Kylie huffed. Stopping at a red light, she tapped the steering wheel and stared at a brand-new Explorer that pulled up beside her. Two girls sat in the backseat. One was trying to hit the other. A woman turned in the driver's seat and leaned around the DVD player suspended from the ceiling to scold them. Kylie took a deep breath and exhaled. "You think I'm a snob?"

"At the moment, yes."

"Marriage is a big step. Living on love is rough." She should know. With seven siblings and a father whose income came from the coal mines, she knew all about living rough. *Even if we did have a lot of love in our home.*

Robin tapped Kylie's head. "Earth to Kylie. I didn't hear any proposals back there in ice-cream land. In fact, we don't even know his name."

"You're right. I do get crazy sometimes." Kylie sighed. *Judging. I always prejudge people. Forgive me, Lord.*

"He was cute, though."

Kylie pushed the accelerator as the light turned green. "Yeah."

"Gorgeous blue eyes. Looked like the ocean."

"Those light reddish curls were awfully cute, too."

"I totally agree."

Kylie smiled as she turned into their apartment parking space. "He wasn't too tall, but definitely not short. Not too thin, not too heavy."

"I'd say, *Goldilocks*, he was just right." Robin hopped out of the car then poked her head back in. "Race you to the door."

Kylie shook her head. "You're nuts."

"Fine, but I get the shower first."

"Wait!" But it was too late. Robin had already made it to the door and run inside.

"Great, now I get to wait, sticky and sweaty, while Robin takes her notorious forty-five-minute shower. I won't have any hot water." Kylie got out of the car and shut the door. She pried a strand of hair away from her cheek and chuckled. "Robin hit the nail on the head. He was just right."

∾

Ryan Watkins walked through the bank doors and pushed the raincoat's hood from his head. Drops of water splattered the wall and floor. Slipping out of the coat, Ryan hung it on the rack beside half a dozen other wet garments. He walked toward the teller. "Good afternoon, Mr. Richards."

His friend Michael Richards smiled. "Hey, Ryan. Gramps didn't come with you?"

"Not in this weather." Ryan opened the candy jar on the counter and scooped up three peppermints. "But I promised him a few of your goodies."

"Take as many as you'd like." Michael turned to his computer and punched several numbers. "You want your interest transferred to your checking account?"

"Yes."

"Do you want another CD like the one before?"

"Yes."

"Good. I have it ready."

Ryan grinned. "Well, Michael, aren't you on top of things?"

"I try. So, how did your grandfather's appointment go?"

"His blood pressure is still up. They had to switch his medication." Ryan grabbed the papers and pen. He was praying the new medicine worked. Gramps had already lived through one heart attack. Ryan didn't want to see him go through another. *God, You're in control.* He signed the documents, then pushed them back toward Michael. "Are you coming to the game Thursday?"

"Wouldn't miss it. Church softball is my only recreation right now."

Ryan laughed. "Are you hinting that your sweet little baby girl is keeping you up at night?"

Michael furrowed his eyebrows and shook his head. "That kid has more air in her lungs than Candy after a day of being cooped up in the house."

"Ouch. You better not let your wife hear you say that."

"Don't worry. I still love her. Both hers." Michael grinned and took the papers from Ryan. Separating the pages, Michael handed Ryan's copies to him. "I'd say our missions trip meetings will start up pretty soon."

"Yep. I'm heading to Hope to pick up some stuff today."

"I'm not sure if Candy and I will both be able to go this time. We may have to take turns until Suzanna's a little older."

Ryan nodded. "It would be hard to make a trip with a baby, especially a missions trip."

"True, but we want to take Suzanna to her birth country every chance we get. We want to be up front about her adoption."

"I'm sure you and Candy will have that girl back in Belize several times in her growing-up years."

The phone rang. Michael reached for it. "I'll see you Thursday."

"See ya then."

Ryan grabbed his raincoat and put it on. He glanced at the receipt Michael had paper-clipped to the top of the papers. His next stop was Hope Community Church to pick up several boxes of clothes, toys, shoes, eyeglasses, and other items. It wouldn't be long before he'd be on his third missions trip to Belize.

His heart sped up at the thought of wearing the clown suit and making balloon animals for the children he'd visit who had almost nothing. Remembering young Alberta's prayer of salvation on his last trip brought a smile to his face. He couldn't wait to go back.

The afternoon sped by as Ryan collected almost more than his truck could hold. He deposited the donated items at the missions team leader's house, then stopped off at a fast-food restaurant to swallow some food before work.

Having changed quickly in the staff locker room, little beads of sweat gathered on his forehead as he strode toward the small ice-cream concession. Not much larger than a child's playhouse, the place was just big enough to hold two ice-cream machines and a worker or two.

"It's like this. I'm not interested in any yahoos."

Ryan stopped at the woman's words. That sounded just like the lady from yesterday who'd been covered in chocolate ice cream. He sneaked a peek around the corner. It was her; and the same dark-haired girl was with her.

"I don't want a yahoo, either, but you're too picky," the black-haired woman answered.

"Robin, you have to have priorities."

"And I don't?"

The blond smirked, then smiled. "Did I say that?"

"All right, Ms. Hoity-Toity, what are your priorities?"

"First," she said and lifted her finger, "he must be a Christian."

Ryan smiled. He agreed with her first.

"Duh," responded the one the blond called Robin.

"Second, he must love me and want a family, but not too big and not too small."

"Here we go again, Goldilocks."

The blond stomped her foot. "Do you want to hear my priorities or not?"

"Go ahead."

"He has to be strong but gentle, kind but firm, athletic but homey—"

"Homey?"

"You know, not be afraid to do the dishes, clean the toilets, and all that stuff."

"I *totally* agree with you there."

Ryan held a chuckle inside. This conversation was classic. What does a woman want? Ryan Watkins was getting the privilege of learning firsthand.

"Of course he has to have a good, stable job. Secure. I will not even consider a yahoo. Looks mean nothing."

Robin frowned. "Nothing?"

"Well, maybe a little bit. I don't want ugly kids, but gorgeous, blue eyes are at the bottom of the list."

"Let me get this straight. You want a successful, Christian husband, your own great job, and 2.5 kids. Do you also want the dog and white picket fence?"

The blond leaned against the counter. "The dog is open for discussion, but the picket fence is crucial, and yes, it must be white."

Robin flung back her head and laughed. "Why is that?"

"What perfect, established, successful family do you know that doesn't have a white picket fence?"

"You need serious help."

Red scoured up the blond's neck and flushed her cheeks. Ryan decided he'd better announce himself or the black-haired gal may end up covered in ice cream...again. Opening the concession door, Ryan stepped in and bowed. "One certified yahoo reporting for duty."

Chapter 2

Kylie watched in horror as Robin jumped toward the stranger from the day before, wrapped him in a bear hug, and said, "Hey, Richie, what's up?"

The man chuckled. "Richie, huh? That's original. I've never heard that before."

Robin cocked her head. "Really? But you look so much like a young, long-haired Ron Howard."

"I think he's being facetious," Kylie spat behind clenched teeth. She hated when her friend acted ridiculous in front of people they didn't know. It would be one thing for her to do it alone, but Robin always chose to do it when she was with Kylie. "Robin, I think our shift is over. We need to get going. No scenes."

"Name's Ryan Watkins." The man thrust his hand toward Kylie's friend. "You must be Robin."

She giggled and grabbed his hand. "Yep, Robin Reed." Pointing toward Kylie, she added, "This here's my friend Kylie Andrews." She leaned toward him. "She's a bit on the grumpy side."

Kylie scowled at her, but Ryan threw back his head and laughed. "I think you're right. Maybe she needs a hug, too."

"Don't even think about it, you. . .you. . .curly-headed mops."

Ryan frowned and looked at Robin. "Did she just insult us?"

"I think she did."

"Your curls are lovely."

"So are yours." Robin twirled a strand of hair around her finger. "You and I must go to the same barber. I believe we have the same haircut."

Ryan gasped. "I believe you may be right. I mean, aside from the fact that yours is a bit longer."

"Oh, but your curls lie so perfectly. Maybe we should make an appointment to go together."

"That's it. I've had enough." Kylie grabbed her purse from the drawer. Robin knew she hated to be embarrassed, but her *friend* was determined to make a fool of her with a complete stranger. "Find your own way home. Maybe your Bobbsey twin will give you a ride."

"Wait! That was really jerky of me, and you don't even know me." Ryan grabbed her arm. "I was just teasing. I'm a notorious teaser. I'm sorry."

"Me, too." Robin looked at the floor like a scolded puppy. "You know I'm uncontrollably silly sometimes. I wasn't trying to be mean."

Swallowing hard, Kylie forced a grin. "Of course you were teasing. I know that. I love a good joke." She choked up a laugh.

Ryan extended his hand. "Forgive me?"

"Of course." Without looking at him, Kylie accepted his hand for an instant, then grabbed her purse tighter. "Robin, are you ready to go?" She tried to sound light, but she knew this Ryan Watkins had seen to her soul. He knew he'd bruise her ego, and he was genuinely sorry.

How she wished to be more like Robin—free and glib. Instead, Kylie was sensitive and sentimental and entirely too vulnerable. She didn't like that Ryan had seen that in her.

Walking toward the car, Kylie fought to keep her chin up. She focused on trying to find her keys in her purse.

"I'm sorry, Kylie. Usually you go right along with the teasing. You know I'd never intentionally hurt your feelings. You're my best friend."

"I know. I don't know why I'm being so sensitive."

"You must like him."

Kylie gasped and gawked at her friend. "What? I—I don't even know him."

"Either that or you're worried about your accounting grade."

"The latter, I'm sure."

Kylie found her keys and gripped them in her hand. The truth was, she had gotten more upset than normal. Usually when Robin teased, Kylie laughed it off. Today, it hurt. Maybe it was Ryan's teasing that hurt.

<hr />

Ryan sat in the church pew, pulling miserably at his shirt collar. A dress shirt and sport coat were not his favorite attire. He'd wear them only to Sunday morning church services. And only for Gramps. Many of the congregation opted for a more casual attire, but Gramps was from the old school. A person dressed up on Sundays, and until Gramps decided otherwise, Ryan would respect that and dress up, as well.

Ryan pulled at the shoulder of his sport coat. The thing was too small. He needed to buy a new one. He sighed. *For Gramps, dressing up is a small price to pay.* At least most times it was. Today, Ryan felt as if he were suffocating.

"Why, Ryan, imagine seeing you here."

Ryan looked toward the voice that sounded very much like Robin Reed's. His mouth fell open when he saw her. "Hi." He stood and shook her hand. "I didn't know you came to church here."

"Actually, we're visiting. We attended church in Evansville for the last three years, but now that we're living near Santa Claus, we're looking for something closer. We never joined the church near school. We're hoping to find a home church now that we're getting closer to graduating."

"So you're both from Evansville?"

"Otwell, actually. Our fathers are coal miners. We've been best friends since birth, so we decided to go to college in Evansville together, too."

"How did you end up here?"

"My uncle owns an apartment building. He's letting us live in one of the apartments in exchange for keeping up the yard work." Robin smacked her hands together. "The deal was too good for two college gals to pass up."

Ryan nodded. "That's for sure. Where is Kylie?" He still felt bad for the way he'd teased her at work. Though a kidder at heart, he wasn't usually cruel. Something about her drew him, and he hadn't expected it, hadn't known how to handle it.

"Restroom."

"Oh."

"Ahem." Ryan glanced at his grandfather, who had grabbed the pew in front of him and was getting ready to stand.

Ryan grinned. "I'm sorry. Gramps, this is Robin. Robin, Gramps."

Gramps grabbed her hand and winked. "I reckon you can call me Gramps."

"I'd love to."

Kylie walked toward them. She was fumbling through her purse. "Robin, I found a couple of seats on the other side." She looked up. Her light skin flamed red. "Oh—um—I didn't see you." She looked at her bag again. "Hi, Ryan."

Ryan's heart sped up. Yes, something about Kylie definitely drew him. He could tell she had confidence, yet she seemed so vulnerable. Maybe that was what beckoned him. He'd always fought for the underdog. But Kylie wasn't an underdog. And what about the way her creamy cheeks and neck shaded crimson? He found it endearing, almost inviting.

Gramps pushed past him and grabbed Kylie's hand. "Hi, sweetie. I'm Gramps."

"Kylie." She smiled and lifted her chin. "It's wonderful to meet you."

"Won't you two sit here beside me?" Gramps pulled her hand toward him.

"Well. . ." She glanced at Ryan. He could see her confidence wane again.

"Of course we will." Robin scooted past all three of them and sat, leaving a space for Kylie to sit by Gramps.

Kylie nodded and followed Robin. Ryan inhaled cocoa butter as she passed and longed for his sunglasses, swimsuit, and a beach.

After they sat, Ryan sneaked a peek at Gramps. He patted Kylie's hand. "After the services, Ryan and I will treat you to the best Italian food you've ever tasted."

Gramps hadn't requested. He'd simply made a decision. Ryan glanced at Kylie. She smiled and nodded, but Ryan would have given a hundred bucks to cruise the inside of her mind. He had a feeling agreement wouldn't be there.

Kylie lifted her purse strap higher on her shoulder as she walked through the door of Marinelli's. A blast of air-conditioning blew through her hair, and she shuddered. *That's just great.* Because of her nerves, her body was already shaking of its own volition. She didn't need a second excuse.

The Sunday afternoon lunch crowd gathered around them. Ryan's grandfather and Robin moved to one side, chatting about weather conditions. Kylie knew the conversation could go on for hours since meteorology had once-upon-a-time been Robin's major and obviously the older man's favorite pastime.

Kylie moved to the other side. Something poked her in the back. She turned around to find Ryan shifting his arm around her as another couple squished through the door behind him. "Sorry."

"That's okay." Kylie shuddered again. Aggravated, she folded her arms in front of her chest. She had absolutely no reason to feel insecure, shy, or anything else in front of Ryan. He was simply a guy, a loser, in fact, according to her list of who could be considered potential date material.

She glanced at him. His light auburn curls lay softly around his head. The shaggy style appealed to her more than she'd have thought possible, in a silly, kind of goofy way.

He caught her looking at him. Heat flooded her cheeks and she averted her gaze, but not before Kylie noticed his eyes could challenge the ocean for beauty rights. She felt him looking at her. The knowledge stirred her insides, making her shudder a third time.

"Are you cold?"

"A little." She wanted to crumble under the concern in his voice.

"Here." Ryan took off his sports jacket and dropped it over her shoulders.

Why had she chosen to wear a sleeveless dress? A light sweater would have been appropriate for the middle of May. The uncommonly warm weather had her brain fuzzy. The smell of men's Obsession cologne was making it worse. She needed to sit down.

"Are you all right?" Ryan touched her arm.

She looked up at him, praying the earth would just open and swallow her whole. "I'm—"

"Watkins. Party of four."

"That's us. Take my hand."

Before she could respond, Ryan grabbed her hand and led her toward the hostess. His hand felt warm, a bit rough—and safe. Kylie focused on putting one foot in front of the other. She was determined not to think about his strong hand, his firm grip.

Once they reached the table, Ryan pulled out her chair and Kylie sat. Looking around she realized Gramps and Robin were already seated. Robin raised her eyebrows in obvious question, and Kylie looked away from her. Ryan's coat still hung from her shoulders. Kylie pondered taking it off but knew she'd shake through the whole meal. *If I act natural no one will think anything about it.*

She tried to act natural as she pushed each arm through the sleeves. Smiling, she looked around as if nothing was wrong. Her left hand knocked a glass. *Oh no.* She spied the water and tried to grab the glass. It teetered and wobbled before spilling all over the table.

Utensils clinked against the table as Ryan yanked up his cloth napkin. Robin lifted the tablecloth to keep the stream of water from landing on her, but succeeded in altering its way toward Kylie. Before Kylie could stop it, the frigid liquid poured onto her lap.

"Ah!" She jumped up, knocking her chair against the person behind her. Turning to him she shook her head, willing back tears. "I'm so sorry."

"It's okay, Kylie." Ryan stood and grabbed her arm. She faced him, and he placed a clean napkin in her hand. "It's okay."

His voice was soft and soothing, like a gentle caress. His gaze was sweet and sincere. A single tear threatened to slip down her cheek. She blinked it back as she looked at her dress. *What is wrong with me?*

Ryan gently swiped her cheek with his back of his hand. Stunned, Kylie looked up at him. Surprise washed his face, as well. He stepped back and sat in his chair.

"I'll go to the restroom with you, if you want."

Kylie stared at Robin. Realizing she still stood, she brushed her dress and shook her head. "It's just water. It'll dry."

Determined to regain control of her body and emotions, Kylie replaced her chair in its place, smiled a second apology at the man behind her, and then sat. Grabbing her menu, Kylie studied it. The words blurred, and heat rushed up her cheeks as she thought of what she must have looked like only moments before. *Stop it.* She scooted in her chair and focused harder on the menu. When the words continued to jumble, Kylie closed her eyes. *I'll just order spaghetti. Every Italian restaurant has that.*

"Do you guys know what you want?" Robin studied the menu. She opened the inside flap, then shut it again.

"My favorite is veal parmesan," answered Ryan.

"I'm getting lasagna. I always get lasagna." Gramps nodded at Ryan. "Don't I?"

"You sure do." Ryan smiled and picked up his glass of water. He took a drink. "What did you think about Pastor Chambers's sermon today?" He placed the glass back on the table.

"Good. Good. Did you see Elma's hair? The woman dyed it blue. Can you believe that? Was pink. Now blue." Gramps snorted and shook his head.

Kylie settled back in the chair. She concentrated on keeping her breathing steady. She'd never before been such a bundle of nerves in front of a guy. Ryan wasn't even her type. He was a hippie wannabe with that shaggy haircut, or rather lack of cut. And red. She'd never liked redheads. Well, truth be told, his was a bit more of an auburn, but still it had quite a bit of red in it.

And his clothes. His red and navy blue plaid shirt was definitely a size too small and obviously uncomfortable. His khakis had seen better days, as well. Kylie had always envisioned herself with a man in a wrinkle-free, high-dollar suit that fit to exemplary perfection.

She sneaked another peek at Ryan. *And yet I'm attracted to him. Like a bee to honey. A moth to light. A magnet to metal. A poor girl to a loser.*

She sighed.

Growing up in a household of eight children with her daddy as a coal miner, Kylie knew the truth of the phrase "feast or famine." When the coal industry was going well, the Andrewses had lots of food, clothes, and fun. When the industry was down, it was free lunch at school and beans for dinner—every night.

Two of her sisters had already married coal miners. They lived the life she knew all too well. No, she wanted more. This poor girl would have nothing to do with a loser, attraction or not. God had blessed her with a good deal of intelligence and some common sense to boot. Losers were not on her list.

Who ever said being poor made one a loser? "Blessed are the poor. . . ."

Kylie shook the thought away. She would never—could never—consider living a life of poverty.

The waitress stopped at their table. "What can I get you all?" She pulled a pen from behind her ear then dropped it. Ryan reached over, picked it up, and handed it to her. "Thanks."

"You're welcome." Ryan folded his menu and then looked at Kylie. A sweet smile warmed his face, and Kylie's resolve melted. Her palms began to sweat and her heart beat faster.

"Are you ready, miss?"

Kylie looked at the waitress, determined not to think of the adorable scattering of freckles she'd noticed beneath Ryan's eyes. "Yes." She cleared her throat and clasped her hands to keep them from shaking. "I'll have maghetti and speatballs."

That's it. No more outings with the redhead.

Chapter 3

The next day Ryan grabbed his cell phone and wallet off his dresser and walked into the living area where Gramps had already opened the front door. His grandfather folded his arms in front of his chest. "I don't need my grandson holding my hand at the doctor's office."

Ryan blew out his breath, determined not to get aggravated with his hard-headed grandfather. "I'm going with you."

"I'm fine, I tell you." Gramps placed his newsboy cap on his head and picked up his car keys.

"Gramps, you're all the family I have left. I want to go with you."

Gramps grunted and pulled his polyester pants higher around his waist. "Fine, but I'm driving."

"Sounds like a plan."

Ryan buckled his seat belt as Gramps pulled onto the street. Gramps's bluegrass music filtered through the speakers. The older man leaned over and snapped it off. "So tell me about those girls from church."

"What about them?"

"Where'd you meet them?"

"At work."

"Mmm."

Ryan shifted in his seat. He knew his grandfather. He wanted more information than that, but Ryan didn't know what to tell him. He found himself attracted to Kylie, but he was pretty sure she was hung up on money and wanting things her way. He'd already gone down that relationship path, and he had no intentions of taking that road again.

"Tell me about the blond one." Gramps interrupted his thinking.

Ryan shrugged. "What about her?"

"A little jumpy, don't you think?"

"Yeah, she's definitely jumpy."

"A little clumsy, too."

Ryan remembered the water spilling on her dress. "Maybe, but I think she was just nervous."

"Nervous about what?"

"She was cold. I put my jacket on her shoulders—I don't know."

"If she was cold, why would wearing your jacket make her nervous?" Gramps glanced at Ryan, then back at the road. "Unless. . .she likes you a bit."

"No way. I'm a yahoo in her book."

"A what?"

Ryan shook his head. "Never mind."

Gramps pulled into the doctor's office parking lot. He took the keys from the ignition. "Well, let's get this over with."

Ryan followed his grandfather into the office. Gramps signed in and was taken back to a room within no time.

"So how are we feeling today?" A young, petite nurse took Gramps's blood pressure and pulse.

"Fit as a fiddle."

"That's good." She wrote down his numbers, then winked at him. "Dr. Hurst will be in to see you in just a moment." She opened the door and shut it behind her.

Ryan shoved his hands into his pockets. "I didn't hear her say what your blood pressure was."

"That's because she didn't."

"Don't they always tell you when they take it? Every appointment I've ever been to the nurse always tells me my weight, my temperature, my pulse, my blood pressure—"

Gramps huffed and pointed to the chair. "Would you have a seat? You're raising my blood pressure with all your worrying."

Ryan sat and crossed his arms in front of his chest. *That man is as mule-headed as a. . .as a mule!* "I just worry about you, Gramps."

"I know, but worrying won't lower my blood pressure."

Ryan leaned back in his chair. "You're right."

The doctor opened the door, looked at Gramps's chart, and then checked him. "Well, Mr. Watkins, the new medicine seems to be doing the trick. Your blood pressure is better than mine."

Ryan sighed in relief. *Thank You, Lord.* The doctor gave Gramps his prescription and left. After Gramps buttoned his shirtsleeve, they walked to the desk, paid the bill, and headed for the car.

"Feel better?" Gramps asked.

"Much."

"I reckon I do, too."

Ryan chuckled. Gramps would never admit he'd been concerned as well. Ryan slid into the passenger's seat and buckled his seat belt.

"I'll say one thing for sure," said Gramps.

"What's that?"

"She sure is a cutie."

Ryan frowned. "The nurse?"

"No, the blond."

"What blond?"

"The gals that went to lunch with us. What was the blond's name?"

"Kylie."

"Yeah, her. 'Course the black-haired one was cute, too, but there was something about the blond. What do you think?"

Ryan shrugged. "She's all right."

"Just all right?"

"No. She's beautiful." Ryan looked out his window. "And there is definitely something special about her."

◈

"Thanks for taking Robin's shift. It's probably going to be a busy day with several schools bringing their students."

Ryan smiled. "It's definitely a busy day, but I love watching all these kids. Makes me feel young."

Kylie chuckled. "Spoken like a man with experience."

"It's my fourth year working summers here."

Four years. Why would any grown man want to work here for four years? A teenager, sure. A college student, sure. She peeked at Ryan. Though he wore his hair in a younger style, Kylie felt sure he was past college age.

"I don't know if I've ever seen Robin so sick." Kylie avoided making eye contact with Ryan as she wrapped the apron around her waist.

"I hope it's nothing serious."

"Just a stomach bug, I think." She grabbed a rag and wiped off the ice-cream machine. "I was afraid you might have a daytime job that would keep you from being able to cover for her."

"Nope." He stepped in front of her, forcing her to look up at him. "This is the only place I work."

There goes that hope. She couldn't stop thinking about Ryan Watkins, from the moment she woke up to the moment she went to bed. She hoped, dreamed, prayed even, that maybe, just maybe, he had a good, solid day job and simply worked at Holiday World in the evenings because he led an otherwise boring and uneventful evening life. She turned toward the counter and began wiping it off. *Yep, one dream right out the window.*

It doesn't matter. I am the decider of my fate.

A soft voice nudged at her heart. *"I thought I was."*

She shook her head. Of course, God was the most important thing in her life. She would follow Him anywhere. She had chosen accounting as a major because He had shown her He wanted her to be there. Her life belonged to

24

Him. She was clay in the Potter's hands.

Even in poverty?

Grabbing the broom, she squelched the thought. *I'm being silly. God wants only the best for His children. He's shown me the way, and I'm to follow it. I'm just getting a little freaked out because I'm so close to graduating—so close to finally reaching the goals He has set up for me.* "Yes, that's all that's wrong," she whispered.

"What did you say?"

She looked at Ryan. The sun seemed to glisten in his reddish hair. How could she be so attracted to Richie Cunningham, as Robin called him? "I was just mumbling to myself."

"Oh." Ryan grabbed the broom from her hand and set it against the wall. "I think you've made this place spotless." He crossed his arms and leaned against the counter. "We're going to be here awhile. Why don't you tell me a bit about yourself?"

Okay, I can do this. Small talk. No big deal. In fact, the more I learn about him, the less attractive he'll become. She smiled, grabbed a stool from beside one of the machines, and hopped onto it. "I'm an accounting major at the University of Evansville. I only have one semester left. I can hardly wait to graduate."

"That's great. What made you decide on accounting?"

"The Lord."

"The Lord?"

"Yeah, I was taking a Bible study class, asking God what my major should be. I've always loved to work with numbers. I'd kind of narrowed it down to accounting or teaching math, and I don't know how to describe it—I just felt He told me to go into accounting. Probably because I have a better chance financially with an accounting position."

"I see."

A perplexed look crossed Ryan's face, and Kylie wondered what she'd said that confused him. "Where did you go to college?"

"I didn't."

Kylie nodded. "I see." *There you have it. He already looks less attractive. One step down the "Perfect Man" ladder.*

"Hey, can we get an ice-cream cone?" A preteen girl with braces on her teeth placed her money on the counter.

"Sure can," Ryan responded before Kylie had a chance. "What can we get you?"

"I want a chocolate cone." She looked at the boy a full three inches shorter—her boyfriend, Kylie presumed. "He wants a chocolate and vanilla cone."

"You got it." Ryan smiled at Kylie. "I'll get the swirl if you'll get the chocolate."

"No problem."

They fixed the cones and handed them to the pair.

"Thanks," the youngsters said in unison and walked away. Kylie watched as the girl grabbed the boy's free hand.

"So tell me about your Lord."

"What?" Kylie looked at Ryan.

"You said the Lord led you to accounting. I was just curious about your Lord."

Kylie frowned. She'd never heard such a statement and wasn't sure what kind of response he wanted, but she'd tell him the best she could. "Well, I grew up in a large family. We attended church from as far back as I can remember. When I was eight, I felt the Lord drawing me to go forward in church. I asked Jesus into my heart and was baptized the next week." She looked up at Ryan. He seemed enthralled with every word she spoke. She swallowed as a wave of heat washed over her. "Is that what you mean?"

"Absolutely. I would have loved growing up in a big family. My parents died in a car accident when I was a teenager. That's when I moved near Santa Claus to live with Gramps. I received Christ after that."

"Where did you live before?"

"Alaska."

"Alaska?"

"Yeah. My dad had a bit of an adventurer's heart, and when he and Mom visited Alaska for their honeymoon, he fell in love with the state. I was eleven when I had to move. I still visit sometimes."

"Do you want to live there again?"

Ryan shook his head. "Not really. Sometimes I get nostalgic about it, but Gramps is all the family I have now, and I want to be near him."

"It's good you live so close that you can take him to church."

Ryan chuckled. "First of all, the man hardly ever lets me take him anywhere. He loves to drive. Second, we live in the same house. So like it or not, and sometimes he does make me crazy, we are definitely close enough to go to church together."

He's so poor he has to live with his grandfather. Getting to know each other was the best idea Ryan Watkins ever had. She smiled up at him. His hair didn't glisten all that much, and his eyes didn't seem quite so swimming. Another step down the ladder.

"That teen over there. He's been lurking around awhile, hasn't he?" Ryan nodded to the adolescent standing beside a bench. His hair was unkempt and looked dirty. His clothes, worn and torn in places, were worse than his hair. The teen looked in his wallet, then at the ice-cream stand, then back at his wallet.

"I don't know." Memories of being sponsored for school trips washed over

Kylie. She remembered friends' parents who'd generously spotted her a few dollars for lunch or snacks. They never seemed to mind, but Kylie had.

"Hey, buddy." Ryan held an ice-cream cone in one hand and motioned with his free hand for the boy to come to the stand.

The adolescent sauntered over, his face hardened, and his hand tightly clutched his wallet. "What?"

"I've got an extra ice-cream cone here. Just wondered if you'd like to have it."

The teen's eyes lit for a moment and then clouded. "Don't need no charity. If I want an ice cream, I'll buy an ice cream."

Ryan shook his head. "Ain't charity, man. I just thought you might like an ice-cream cone."

"Everyone else has to buy one. Why not me? Sounds an awful lot like charity."

Kylie tried to swallow the knot that formed in her throat. She knew exactly how the boy felt. She hated charity. Loathed it. How could Ryan do this? The ice cream wasn't worth it to the teen. He'd rather go without than always be beholden to one person or another.

Ryan leaned against the counter. "I'm not going to lie to you, man. Everyone else does have to pay, but sometimes in life people like to give a little gift to other people. I'm not seeing you as charity. I just simply bought an ice-cream cone." Ryan grabbed money from his pocket, opened the cash register, and dropped it in. "And I want to give it to you. Now, are you going to take it or not?"

The teen seemed to search Ryan's expression. Finally, he exhaled. "Sure, I'll take it."

Kylie watched as the adolescent walked away, licking his ice-cream cone. She looked back at Ryan, who'd already turned away to wipe off the machines. Ryan's heart was as genuine as the mop of reddish hair atop his head.

That's just great. The guy falls two steps down the ladder and hops three steps up.

Chapter 4

This is going to be fun." Robin hooked arms with Kylie.

"Fun," Kylie mumbled as she picked a wisp of hair out of her lipstick-covered lips and pushed it behind her ear.

"Come on, Kylie, have a little fun. You got your grades today." She wiggled and bumped her hip against Kylie's. "Professor Nickels gave you the A."

Kylie smiled. Pure satisfaction filled her heart. "I earned that A, my friend."

"Yes, you did. Now, loosen up and let's have a little fun."

"You're on."

Kylie quickened her step, and Robin fell in line with her. The twosome pushed open the church's recreation center doors. A banner on the far wall read SINGLES' GAME DAY. Queasiness filled Kylie's stomach.

"Don't get nervous," Robin whispered in her ear and squeezed her arm for reassurance. "This will be a blast."

"You know me too well."

"Yep, and you'll be fine." Robin let go of Kylie's arm and winked at her. "Let's go sign in."

Kylie placed her name tag on her shirt and listened as a large, brown-haired man announced different groups. "In group three," the man's voice boomed over the speakers, "Kylie Andrews, Mike Dickerson, Cami Longman. . ."

Kylie listened, praying he would announce Robin Reed in her group. She clutched her purse strap.

"Sandy Osborne, Zane Sanderson. . ."

Kylie's heart plummeted. He was reading in alphabetical order. Robin wouldn't be in her group.

"You'll have fun," Robin whispered and squeezed her arm once more.

"And Ryan Watkins." The announcer stopped and pointed to a group of chairs in one corner. "Group three will meet right there."

"Hey, somebody I know," Ryan's voice sounded from behind her.

Robin laughed. "I'm glad you're here. Kylie gets so nervous. She'll already have a friend in her group."

"Robin," Kylie spat through clenched teeth. She was a great friend, but she had precious little tact.

"I'm glad to have a friend in my group, too."

Kylie looked up at her male "friend." His gaze spoke nothing but sincerity and kindness, and she willed her nerves to calm. "Let's go, then."

They walked to the group and sat beside each other on metal folding chairs. The group's leader, a tiny brunette, bounced around the circle, introducing herself to everyone. She stopped, clapped her hands, and exhaled. "I've already told you my name is Macy. We're going to have a great time today. I know we will build lifelong friendships—and who knows, maybe our perfect, God-intended match." She looked at Ryan and winked.

She did not just wink at him. Kylie peeked at Ryan, who simply grinned and leaned back in his chair. *What do I care if she winked at him?* She placed her purse under her chair, then crossed her legs. *What do I care if he grinned at her wink?*

Kylie sneaked another peek at Ryan. This time he glanced at her and winked. She forced a smile and looked away. *The nerve of him. Flirting with me after the cute little group leader flirted with him.*

"Okay, the first thing we're going to do is get to know each other," bubbled Macy. "I've copied Bible verses onto slips of paper. I'll pass them out, you'll read the verse silently, and then tell us your name and what the verse means to you in your walk with Christ."

Kylie trembled at the thought of sharing such personal information with a group of twelve strangers.

"I'm sorry. Putting the cart before the horse." Macy smacked the side of her leg and snorted at her mistake. Even her snort sounded cute. "I'm going to pair you up for this activity, then we'll go to a group game." She walked around the circle. "You and you. You and you." She pointed to Kylie and Ryan. "You and you."

Ryan turned toward Kylie. "This is great. We already kind of know each other."

"That's true." Kylie wasn't sure she was quite as thrilled to be paired with a man whose cologne made her weak in the knees and whose too-long, wavy hair attracted her in the weirdest of ways.

"You want to go first or you want me to?"

"I think I want to get it over with." Kylie read through her verse and smiled. It fit her life perfectly. She looked at Ryan. "You ready?"

"Whenever you are."

Kylie shifted in her chair. "Okay. You already know I'm Kylie. My verse is Proverbs 21:21. 'He who pursues righteousness and love finds life, prosperity and honor.'"

"That's a great verse."

"Yes, and it's perfect for me to share. I think I've told you I was raised in a large family, eight kids to be exact."

Ryan's eyes bulged. "You're kidding."

"Not kidding. We were pretty poor most of the time. My dad was a coal miner. He and Mama grew up in eastern Kentucky, and for the first few years of their marriage, Daddy worked in Pike County. By the time Mama was pregnant with me, times were pretty rough. He was offered a job in Otwell, and they've lived there ever since. Still, if you know anything about coal mining, you'd know life is feast or famine, and with ten mouths to feed, it was often famine."

"But what a blessing. You never lacked a playmate."

Kylie laughed. "That's true. I also never enjoyed some peace and quiet or the ability to have a few personal items that no one messed with, but as a kid I *wanted* both!"

"I bet it was hard to keep your siblings out of your stuff."

"Definitely. Anyway, even as a small girl I knew God wanted me to pursue more than the life I led." She uncrossed her legs and rested her elbows on her knees. "Two of my sisters have already married coal miners, and life is hard for them. Well, now I'm about to graduate from college. I plan to get a good job and marry a man with a steady income. I will pursue righteousness for the love of my family. I'll be able to help them."

Ryan's brows furrowed into a deep frown. "I don't understand how you're getting 'be rich and marry rich' from that verse."

"Don't you see—the verse says 'He who pursues righteousness and love'— I'm getting my degree to get a good job. It's a righteous pursuit for the love of my family." Kylie read the rest of her verse. " 'Finds life, prosperity and honor.' God will give me prosperity, because my pursuit is to help my family."

"So, your family resents the coal mining business?"

"Well, no."

"Then they hate the poverty that goes up and down with it?"

Kylie remembered the many times her mother had made a game out of the unusual concoctions of dinner menus, like beans and corn bread with a side order of pancakes. As kids, they'd loved to guess what their mom would conjure up. "Well, not really."

"So, is your pursuit really from God?"

How dare he challenge her walk with the Lord! Ryan Watkins hardly knew a thing about her. He had no idea what her life had been like. He obviously had family willing and ready to let him mooch off them. She was not and would never again be a charity case. God gave her a capable mind and two capable hands with which to provide work—hard work. She could hardly wait to help her family, to buy food during the down times, and to buy clothes for her siblings and nephews. "Yes, my pursuit is definitely from God."

"Kylie, I really like him."

"Robin, you don't even know him."

Ryan didn't mean to eavesdrop, but the two were only a few feet away from him. He twisted in his chair in an attempt not to listen.

"But I feel an instant connection," Robin responded.

"You always move too fast. You don't think things through. What do you know about him?"

"He's a Christian. A youth minister, in fact. He has a small son."

Kylie gasped, and Ryan couldn't help but pay attention now. "He has a child?"

"It's not like that. Tyler's wife died from leukemia when their son was three."

"Oh, Robin, haven't you heard of serial murderers who pick up young women at functions like these? They fill women's heads with garbage."

"Lots of people know Tyler." Robin scanned the room and then poked Ryan in the back. He cringed. Tyler was a great guy, but there was no way Ryan wanted to be in on this discussion. "Ryan, do you know Tyler Pettry?"

"Uh, yeah." Ryan took a slow drink of his pop.

"Is he a serial murderer?"

Ryan choked back his laugh. "I hope not. He leads our youth."

Robin patted Kylie's back. "There you have it. Probably not a serial murderer."

Kylie crossed her arms in front of her chest. "Fine. At least the utilities are paid this month, so if you don't come home because"—Kylie unfolded her arms and pointed to her chest—"*I told you so*, then at least I won't have to pay them by myself."

Ryan smiled at Kylie's dramatics.

Robin punched Ryan's arm and then hugged Kylie. "I'll see you tonight, girlfriend."

Ryan watched as Robin walked out of the building with Tyler. He gazed back at Kylie, whose expression was sour as a lemon drop.

"I think I'll head on home," Kylie muttered. She opened her purse and searched inside. "Oh, no."

"What is it?"

"Robin drove today, and she didn't leave me her car keys."

"I'll see if I can catch them." Ryan raced out the door as Tyler's Camry turned onto the main road. He walked back to Kylie. "They're gone."

Kylie placed her cell phone back in her purse. "Robin doesn't have her phone on." She slouched into a chair and placed her hand on her head.

"I'll take you home, Ki."

"What did you call me?"

Ryan tried to replay what he'd said. "I don't know."

"You called me Ki. I haven't heard that since before my granny died."

"I'm sorry." Ryan shoved his hands into his pockets. "I didn't mean to offend you."

"It's all right." Kylie picked at a chip in her fingernail polish. "It was kind of nice to hear it again."

Ryan grabbed her hand and helped her up from the chair. Her skin, soft beneath his, felt nice and warm. "I'll take you home."

"I'd appreciate it."

She'd softened somehow. Despite their disagreement about the verse, despite Robin's leaving with a serial murderer/youth minister, Ryan found himself drawn to this side of the woman.

Kylie was smart. She was beautiful with her long, silky blond hair, sprinkling of freckles beneath blue eyes, and the cutest dimple in her chin he'd ever seen. She was loyal to family and friends, and he could sense her love for the Lord, even if her understanding of scripture seemed quite misguided.

Which is exactly why I must keep up my guard. The last thing I need is another well-meaning woman like Vanessa Bailey in my life and heart.

Yes, he'd have to stay alert when it came to Kylie Andrews. Ryan had believed Vanessa to be his one and only, and she was sweet as honey until she learned of Ryan's true material worth. Ryan had no intention of lording his wealth over others. After spending his preteen years watching his dad slave away at a logging company, God gave Ryan the machine idea that made cutting logs less strenuous for the workers and still more efficient for the owners. God also allowed him to sell the blueprints to an Alaskan company. And it was God who blessed him with the revenue that could have been squandered in a year or two's time had it not been for his investing-savvy grandfather who'd put chunks of money in several good stocks and bonds and taught Ryan how to manage his assets and make them grow.

Ryan wasn't rich, but he would never want for anything, either. Because he loved giving to others, he took small jobs like at the amusement park and as a Santa at the mall in Evansville during Christmas. He didn't want others to know. The gifts, the ministry trips—they were between him and God.

"You want to grab a bite of dinner on the way?"

He watched as Kylie tensed as she seemed to contemplate the offer. "Robin and I desperately need to go to the grocery, so I think I'll take you up on that."

They began to walk toward his car. "Mind if I drive by the house and pick up Gramps?"

Kylie smiled and relaxed. "That would be great."

Ryan opened her door. As she slid into the passenger seat, Ryan caught a whiff of her hair. The floral scent was nice. He imagined running his fingers through the length of it. *Get a grip, man.* He shut the door and moved to the driver's side.

"I don't live too far away." He put the keys in the ignition and started the car. "Gramps will enjoy having someone besides me to talk to."

"You don't get along?"

Ryan laughed. "We just see a lot of each other."

He turned onto the secluded road that led to his house. Anxiety welled inside him as he drove nearer. What would Kylie think of his home? Why did it matter what she thought?

Within moments, the top of his white, colonial-style house came into sight. It wasn't overly large, but Ryan had built a good-sized home, one that would, hopefully, be filled with children someday. Full-grown trees dotted his property. Flowers and bushes, strawberry vines and blackberry bushes, even a vegetable garden spotted the front and backyard. Gramps loved to work with nature.

His wraparound porch sported a swing, wicker furniture, and rocking chairs. Gramps sat in one of the chairs, reading a science-fiction novel as he rocked back and forth.

He glanced at Kylie. An expression of pleasant awe covered her face. "This place is amazing. It's beautiful."

"Thanks." Ryan relaxed in his seat. He had no choice but to admit it. What she thought meant a whole lot.

❦

Kylie hesitantly waved at Ryan's grandfather as she stepped out of the car. The man smacked his book shut and hopped up from the rocking chair.

"Well, hello there, Kylie. It's great to see you. Wonderful evening, don't you think?" Gramps covered the distance between them and shook her hand.

"Yes. The weather's very nice." She looked from him to Ryan. "You have a beautiful home."

Ryan's gaze fell to the ground, then back up to hers. "Thank you."

His eyes seemed to penetrate her soul, sending tingles through her body. "You're welcome."

Ryan turned toward his grandfather. "Gramps, we were heading to town for a bite to eat. Thought you might like to go."

"I just fixed up a big pot of vegetable soup. The corn bread'll be done in about ten minutes. Why don't you two just stay here and eat?"

Kylie grinned at the older man. *What a sweetie.* She'd fall flat on her face if she ever walked into her parents' house and found her daddy or one of her three brothers fixing a meal. Of course, Ryan and Gramps did live alone. "I'd love to stay."

Ryan lifted his eyebrows. His look of surprise made Kylie realize she hadn't been her true self around the man. She'd remedy that today.

"Great." Gramps grabbed her hand and led her into the house. "Ryan, take her on a tour, and I'll get the corn bread out of the oven."

For the first time embarrassment and uncertainty wrapped Ryan's features. He motioned for her to follow him into one room after the other. She loved the homey feel of the house, although it definitely had a bachelor's edge. He took her into a room upstairs. Pictures from a tropical-looking region sat on a table and hung on the walls. She leaned down and looked at a picture of a family standing in front of a small home.

"That's a family from Belize." Ryan picked up the frame and handed it to her.

"Belize?"

"Yes, it's a small country in Central America. I go there with a group on missions trips."

"Oh." Kylie studied the man before her. He gave away ice-cream cones and went on missions trips. What other secrets would she discover about the man?

"Our group fixed their home. It had been damaged by a storm."

"That's really neat. I've always wanted to go on a missions trip."

"We're having a meeting next week. We'll be going again in January."

"Really?"

"I'd love to have you go with us."

"I think I'd like to go." She peered up at Ryan, realizing there was more to him than she'd originally thought. *I'm actually looking forward to getting to know him better.*

Chapter 5

Kylie watched as the missions trip video showed a doctor examining a small boy's mouth. She listened as the speaker shared about the multitude of children in Belize who received medication and vitamins from the ministry's effort.

A single tear slipped down Kylie's cheek before the picture switched to show a clown making animal balloons for a group of children. Her heart pounded within her chest when a boy jumped up and down, then smiled fully for the camera when the clown handed him a red giraffe.

Ryan leaned close and whispered in her ear, "That's me."

"That's you?" She turned toward him and studied his profile. *Who are you, Ryan Watkins? I've never met anyone like you.*

She watched wrinkles form at the corners of his eyes as his smile grew. Pleasure in serving "the least of these" surrounded his face and seemed to seep from his very pores. "Yeah. I love to see the children's faces light up when I make balloon art for them."

"I'm sure it's wonderful."

"The children have almost nothing. They get so excited over the smallest gifts."

She looked back at the video. In the film, Ryan the clown turned toward the camera, making a honking noise as he squeezed his oversize, red-ball nose. He waved as he lifted a toddling child in his arms. The child squeezed his nose, as well.

God, I want what Ryan has. I've loved and served You for as long as I can remember, but there's something different about him. Something—more.

The video ended and Kylie listened as a pastor from a sister church talked about ministry opportunities available for people who would like to join their trip to Belize. "Of course, the people need to be examined by nurses, doctors, and dentists. We need carpenters, electricians, and plumbers to help with home and church needs."

The pastor grabbed a packet filled with crayons, glue, scissors, and other items. He held it up before the group of potential short-term missionaries. "But we also hold a vacation Bible school. If you can color with a child, help a mother by holding her baby so she can teach Bible school, or even dress up like a clown—"

Ryan clenched his fists over his head and pumped his arms as if he'd just won a race. Kylie giggled and pushed him with her shoulder.

The pastor laughed. "As I was saying, you could dress up like a clown as our good friend Ryan does on every trip."

Kylie looked at Ryan. "You've gone on every trip?"

He nodded. "Every one."

The pastor continued. "Anything you can do is a huge help. Simply telling others what Christ has done for you is the greatest ministry you can give."

Kylie leaned back in her chair. She couldn't remember the last time she'd shared her faith with someone. The idea of it sent nervous but excited tingles through her body.

The pastor's voice interrupted her thoughts. "Remember in scripture when Peter and John went to the temple in Jerusalem. There was a lame beggar sitting in front of the gate called Beautiful."

Kylie crossed her legs and touched her chin in contemplation. There were several beggar stories in scripture. She wasn't sure which one he referred to.

The pastor went on. "Peter told the beggar he didn't have any silver or gold." He lifted his finger in the air. "But Peter said what he could give, he would. So he healed the man in Christ's name that very moment." The pastor spread his arms open. "Friends, God has given us different talents and abilities. What we can give, let's give."

Kylie's stomach turned and her heart raced. She wanted to go on this missions trip. She didn't have any medical or construction talents, but she could definitely hold a baby.

A middle-aged woman walked to the front of the group. "Understand, friends, funding has to be raised on an individual basis. Our ministry is not supported by any federal or state missions boards." She showed a presentation that broke down the cost of the trip.

Kylie gasped when the woman reached the final total. *Money!* Her heart plummeted. *It's always about money.*

⌘

"Well, what did you think?" Ryan started the car and pulled onto the road.

"It sounds wonderful."

Ryan could hear the hesitation in her voice. Why, he wasn't sure. He saw the lone tear slide down her cheek during the video. Her excitement was evident, magnetic even.

"But?" Ryan took in the look of frustration wrapping her features. "There's a problem, huh?"

"I don't know."

"It can't be school. You'll graduate in December."

"That's true."

He pulled into her apartment building's parking lot and turned off the car. Shifting in his seat, he looked at her. She'd pulled her long hair into a ponytail. The wind allowed several blond strands to escape around her ears and the nape of her neck. Baby hairs, he'd once heard someone call them. Her skin, so light, looked almost porcelain, like the sun had never touched it. She was a true beauty on the outside. The more time he spent with her, he saw it on the inside, too.

So, why wouldn't she want to go? The truth hit him in an instant. "Is it the money?"

"It's always the money." She didn't look at him but kept her gaze focused on the windshield.

"No prob—" Ryan stopped. He longed to tell her he'd pay her way, to tell her money was not an inkling of an issue. But he couldn't. Not yet. "I'll help you raise the money."

Kylie huffed. "What about yours? Don't you have to raise your own?"

"God always provides."

"I wish I had your faith." She grabbed her purse off the floorboard and opened the car door. "Look," she said, turning back toward him, "I really want to go. And you *are* right. If God wants me there, He will provide."

She shut the door. Ryan watched as she walked up the sidewalk. She unlocked the door, then waved back at him. "Thanks for taking me, Ryan."

She disappeared into the apartment. Ryan sat for several seconds. Kylie wasn't like any other woman he knew. Her love for the Lord was there, evident, and that quality meant more to him than anything else. She also had a wonderful personality, and she cared—truly cared—for the people in her life, like her family and Robin. And her looks? There was no question he was physically attracted to her.

But the money. He knew she'd grown up poor. Knew she had a passel of sisters and brothers. Knew life had been tough for her. She'd shared as much with him, but what was her hang-up? Many people grew up in financially difficult situations, but they didn't resent their pasts or gear their futures on account of it. Ryan growled at the steering wheel. "She stated the problem from her own lips. For some people, it's always about the money."

Chapter 6

I can't believe you landed an interview at Miller Enterprises." Robin grabbed Kylie's arm and shook it in excitement.

Kylie laughed. "I know. It's my dream job. I didn't think I'd have a chance for an interview like this until I'd worked ten years or more."

"And you're not even graduated!"

"I know! I figured I'd do the books for some mom-and-pop store for a while, get some experience, then maybe land a good interview somewhere. But Miller takes care of all the accounting for several major businesses in Evansville." Kylie's hand shook as she took her lipstick from her makeup case and applied it to her lips. "I think you need to pinch me or something."

"No, I just need to borrow your pink flip-flops." Robin raced into the other room.

"What?"

Robin held up Kylie's hot pink, daisy-covered sandals. "These."

"Okay, but why?"

"Tyler and I are taking Bransom on a picnic."

Kylie studied her friend's reflection in the mirror. "You've been spending a lot of time with Tyler."

"I know." Robin combed her curls, then fluffed them back into place.

"A lot of time."

Robin turned toward Kylie. "I'm going to be honest; I like Tyler—a lot. A lot, lot."

"You know when school starts back you won't have as much time for—"

"I'm not even thinking about when school starts back. I haven't been as focused as you. I still have a full two years ahead of me *if* I figure out what major I want."

"What are you saying?"

"I'm not saying anything."

"It sounds to me like you're saying something."

"Kylie, I'm not thinking about school. I'm not as gung ho as you. I'm taking life one day at a time." She wrapped her arms around Kylie. "I don't want to talk about this. You go to that interview and knock their socks off."

"But, Robin—"

Robin pulled away, grabbing both of Kylie's forearms. "It's not the time for us to talk about this. You go to that interview and show them what a wonderful person you are."

Kylie let out a long breath and smiled as she squeezed her friend in a tight hug. She let go and grabbed her keys from the bathroom counter. "You're right, but we *are* going to talk later."

As she bounded through the apartment, she grabbed her briefcase off the couch and headed out the door. "God," she whispered, "You know all things. You know how much I want to help my family. This feels like my chance."

⟨⟨≈⟩⟩

"Come on in," Gramps's voice sounded from the entry.

Ryan grabbed an oven mitt, opened the oven door, and lifted out the yeast rolls. Whoever had stopped for a visit was in for a treat. Ryan had grilled thick T-bone steaks and aluminum-wrapped potatoes, green peppers, and onions mixed with butter and garlic salt. Gramps had boiled corn on the cob and tossed a salad.

"Take off that little sweater you got on. We're about to have supper, and you're staying," Gramps's voice boomed through the house.

"Really, I didn't mean to impose. I didn't realize you'd eat this early."

"Kylie?" Ryan pulled the oven mitt off. *That sounded just like her. What is she doing here?*

"Girl, you're not imposing on anyone. You're going to stay right here and eat." Gramps nudged Kylie into the kitchen.

"Don't you look nice." Ryan drank in her blond hair, soft and loosely pulled up. Her cheeks flushed, making her eyes a deeper blue. Her navy suit didn't look half bad, either.

"Thanks." She cupped her hand over her mouth. "I like your apron."

Ryan glanced down at his pink polka-dotted apron with lace fringe. His face burned as he untied the strings around his waist. "It's a joke between me and Gramps."

"I have no idea what he's talking about." Gramps inhaled and shook his head. "It embarrasses me each and every time he puts that thing on."

"Gramps!"

Kylie giggled. "I think it's great. How does the saying go—'Real men wear pink'?"

Ryan pounded his chest with his fist. "Yep, and I'm a real man." He laughed. "Okay, enough of that." He grabbed another plate from the cabinet. "Let's eat and you can tell us why you're here."

"I really didn't mean to impose."

"Do you think we can eat all this ourselves?" Ryan waved his hand across the counter.

Kylie grinned. "You are two grown men, and my brothers could do it."

Ryan lifted his eyebrows. "Probably true, but we want to share. Now eat."

He moved closer to her, shoving the plate in her hand. Her perfume lingered as she moved over to the table. Ryan relished it for just a moment longer than necessary as he fixed his own plate. Once Gramps was ready, Ryan blessed the food.

He looked up as Kylie took a sip of her pop. *I like seeing her here, Lord. This feels right.* She crinkled the napkin in her hand, and Ryan glanced up to find her blushing. *She knows what I'm thinking.* Ryan continued to stare into her eyes. He couldn't deny it. He was falling for her.

"So what brings you out here?" said Gramps.

Ryan blinked, grabbed his knife and fork, and began cutting his steak.

"I have wonderful news." Kylie placed her napkin in her lap.

"What is it?" asked Ryan.

"I had a job interview at Miller Enterprises today."

"What's Miller Enterprises?" asked Gramps.

"A large accounting firm in Evansville. They handle the books for several businesses. It's like my dream job."

"That's terrific." Ryan smiled. Her excitement was contagious.

"Mmm-hmm, and it went great, too. I've got the job. I start at the end of January."

"Congratulations." Gramps stood and shook her hand.

"Thanks, and I should be able to go on the missions trip with you." She looked at Ryan with such anticipation he thought his heart would burst.

"I'm really happy for you. It's just what you've wanted."

"Yes. Isn't God amazing?"

"He's definitely amazing."

Ryan listened as Kylie chattered about the interview, the position, and how God had given her the desires of her heart. Contentment welled in his own heart as he thought of sharing excitement and sadness, success and failure, up and down on a daily basis with her. The more she spoke, the more Ryan wanted to hear, and the more he wanted to know.

God, I'm falling hard, and I like it. He closed his eyes for a brief moment. *I'm going to trust You with my heart.*

"Let me help you with those dishes." Kylie stood and stacked the plates.

"You don't need to do that." Ryan took them from her hand.

"It's the least I can do." She gazed up at him and puckered her lip. "Please."

Everything in him wanted to draw her close and kiss her. He swallowed and turned toward the sink. "Okay, you can help."

Pretending to focus on getting the water to the right temperature, Ryan stilled his anxious thoughts.

"You're a pretty good cook." Kylie picked up the salad bowl and the dressing bottles. She had taken her hair out of its knot and let it flow down her back. Its softness called to him, and he had to look away again.

"I'll have to return the favor sometime." She walked toward him. Once again her sweet perfume sent his senses into overdrive.

"Sounds good." Ryan plunged his hands into the soapy water.

"I can't believe you don't have a dishwasher. Two bachelors doing manual dishes." Kylie winked and smiled, sending his brain into a frenzy.

"Look, Kylie." Ryan yanked his hand out of the water, sending bubbles through the air. Several hit her face. She scrunched her nose and spit them away.

"Yeah?" She wiped them away, smudging bubbles across her cheek.

She couldn't possibly look any cuter than she does right now with bubbles streaked across her face. "I'm sorry." He grabbed a paper towel and wiped her cheek. Allowing his hand to linger, he gazed into her eyes. "What I'm trying to say is, would you like to go out to dinner this Saturday?"

"As a date?"

"As a date."

Kylie blinked. "O–kay."

Ryan cupped her chin in his hand. "I can't wait."

Chapter 7

What was I thinking?" Kylie stared at her closet. Nothing looked appealing.

"You were thinking that Richie Cunningham is quite the cutie. That you'd love to run your fingers through that long, curly mop."

"Ugh." Kylie pretended to gag. "You make his hair sound disgusting."

"You and I both know it's not disgusting. He has the most unique color and style I've ever seen." Robin wiggled her eyebrows. "And it's adorable."

Kylie grabbed a bright orange T-shirt and an aqua polo shirt with pink and white stripes from her closet. She turned toward Robin. "Which one?"

"Definitely the aqua. It brings out your eyes and complements your fair skin."

Kylie leaned against the dresser and studied her face in the mirror. "I hate my coloring."

"Don't get me started on that again. Do you know how many people would kill to have your perfect complexion? And that sprinkling of the cutest freckles across your cheeks and nose to boot? I spent my entire teenage life fighting pimples and blackheads."

"Oh no, here we go."

"Here we go is right." Robin hopped off her bed and tugged Kylie's arm. "I spent years in a dermatologist's office—"

"And my skin still doesn't look as good as yours." Kylie finished Robin's sentence and stuck out her tongue. "Fine. I won't complain about my skin color."

"Thank you." Robin crossed her arms in front of her chest and feigned frustration. One side of her mouth lifted in a grin. "So, where's Richie taking you?"

"Dinner, I think."

"Casual?"

"He didn't say, so I'm going with khaki capris and a nice top. I figure I can wear that to fast food or to a halfway decent restaurant."

"Sounds like a plan." Robin grabbed Kylie's arm and squeezed. "Listen, let yourself have fun. I want to hear all the juicy details tonight." She picked up her purse, then slid on her sandals.

"Where are you going?"

"Out."

"With Tyler?"

"Yep."

"Robin, you've spent a lot of time with him, like almost every waking hour for the last few weeks. You even got Ryan to cover for you at work one day."

"Yep."

"We need to talk about this. What are you going to do when school starts?"

"I told you I'm not worried about that. One day at a time."

"Robin—"

"Look, Kylie, Tyler is a wonderful Christian man. Bransom is a super kid. I love them." Robin faced Kylie. "Both of them."

Kylie sat on the edge of the bed as her stomach tied in knots. "Are you saying—"

Robin nodded. "Yes, I am." She kissed the top of Kylie's head then headed for the door. "I'll see you later."

Before Kylie had a chance to respond, Robin was gone. "Oh, my. What is she thinking?"

She stood, grabbed the aqua polo, and pulled it over her head, then slid into her capris. After applying a touch of blush and mascara, she brushed her hair, deciding to let it fall straight and silky down her back.

She looked at her alarm clock. "I still have forty-five minutes until he gets here." While puttering around the apartment, straightening magazines and fluffing pillows, she noticed her bank statement on the coffee table. "Might as well balance my checkbook before he comes."

After scooping it off the table, she grabbed her purse from the counter and searched through it for her checkbook. "This probably isn't the best of ideas." She opened the cupboard and picked up the calculator. "This always makes me grouchy."

After sliding into a dining room chair, Kylie spread her papers on the table. It didn't take long to figure the numbers and discover she had ten dollars less than she thought in the account due to a subtraction error. "Not too bad of a mistake." She wrote her current balance in the ledger and then flipped her checkbook pages to find the calendar. "Don't have much to live on 'til payday, though."

Exhaling, she smacked the checkbook shut, collected the statement and calculator, and put them away. "I hate being broke."

Her mind wandered to Robin. What was her friend thinking? She needed to keep her head, to finish school, not to fall head over heels for the first guy she dated. Kylie didn't deny Tyler being a great guy. She didn't even have a problem with Robin falling in love with him, marrying him, and having children with him, but her friend needed to finish school first. She needed to be able to support them if something tragic happened.

Of course, Tyler won't be getting black lung from his job. Kylie closed her eyes and thought of her parents. Only four of her brothers and sisters still lived at home. Two of them worked to support the family until Daddy's disability claim could be settled. Coal mining had sucked the life from her family.

Her mind skipped to Ryan. He was a true gem, the kind of man she would want to marry, have a few kids with, a dog, and a white picket fence, but he wasn't a provider. "He's an ice-cream-cone clerk at an amusement park." She smacked her thigh. "I need a provider."

She looked at her watch again. He should arrive in fifteen minutes or less. She walked into the bathroom and brushed through her hair one last time. After pulling her lipstick from the drawer, she put some on and smacked her lips together. "Tonight, I'll tell him we can only be friends."

Ryan couldn't remember the last time he'd felt this way. He was downright giddy. Truly unmasculine, that was for sure. He squelched the excitement inside him as he opened the restaurant door for Kylie. The host seated them, and Ryan picked up the menu.

"Do you know what you want?" Kylie asked before he'd had a chance to read what they offered.

He chuckled. "Not yet."

"I always get the shrimp platter."

"Good, huh?"

"Yeah."

"I'll trust your judgment and just go with that."

"Oh, I didn't mean. . ."

Ryan frowned. Kylie was nervous, and he couldn't figure out why. Maybe just because this was their first date. One of many, if he had his way. "I love shrimp. I'm sure it will be great."

He put down the menu. He watched as Kylie played with her silverware for several moments then scanned the room, looking anywhere but at him. Small talk... think of something to say. "So, how do you like working at Holiday World?"

"It's good."

"Great." Ryan fiddled with the tip of his napkin. Strike one. *Think of something else, Watkins.* "What about school? You ready to go back?"

"Oh, yeah. I can hardly wait to graduate." She flipped her hair over her shoulder and watched the family beside them.

Strike two. *This is like pulling teeth. She acts like I'm not even here.* "Have you heard anything else from your job?"

"I go for a physical next week. If it goes well and my criminal record comes back clean, I'm hired."

"Uh-oh." Ryan tapped the top of her hand. "Your speeding tickets are going to come back to haunt you."

"I don't have any speeding tickets."

"I was just kidding."

"Oh."

Ryan sighed. Strike three. No doubt about it, he had struck out. They ordered their food and ate in near silence. Ryan watched Kylie focus on everyone in the restaurant except him. Something was wrong. Sure, Kylie hadn't sent tons of signals suggesting her interest in him, but she had shared her job offer with him first thing, even before she'd told Robin.

He smiled. "I've got an idea."

"Yes?"

Ryan furrowed his eyebrows. He hadn't meant to say that out loud. "When was the last time you went to Frosty's Fun Center?"

"Never."

"Never?"

She shook her head.

"Not even as a kid?"

Her expression clouded, and Ryan knew he'd said the wrong thing. He pulled cash for their dinner from his wallet and laid it on the table. "Well, I'm going to take you."

"I don't know. I'm a little tired."

"Come on, Ki."

A faint smile lifted her lips, and a glimmer shot through her eyes. "Something about you calling me that. . ." She shook her head and waved her hand. "Never mind."

Aha. It was there. He hadn't imagined it. She was attracted to him. He just had to convince her to let it grow. "Come on. We won't stay long."

"Okay."

Ryan led her to the car, opened the door for her, then walked over to the driver's side. He slid inside and drove to Frosty's. "Arcade or miniature golf first?"

Kylie's tenseness seemed to fade. "I'm afraid I'll be terrible at either."

"That's okay." He grabbed her hand and squeezed. "I'll just rub your face in it every time I beat you."

Kylie's expression charged with competition. "I'm going to take you down, Ryan Watkins."

Ryan wiggled his eyebrows and winked. "Bring it on, Ki."

She hopped out of the car and raced to the front of the building. Ryan followed her inside. She pointed to the pinball machines. "Arcade first."

He purchased tokens and escorted her to a racing game. "Okay, you'll control one car. I'll control the other. We'll race around an obstacle course. Understand?"

Kylie lifted her eyebrows. "No speeding tickets?"

Ryan laughed. "Nope."

She batted her eyelashes. "Good. I don't want to risk my job, you know."

"Just play."

They raced, and Ryan beat her easily, even with his effort to let her catch him. "We can go on to miniature golf."

"Let's play again." Kylie's eyes lit with pleasure.

"I didn't know you were so competitive."

"I'll beat you yet."

They played again, and Ryan still beat her despite slowing down at many places.

"One more time."

Ryan chuckled. "Okay." The cars raced down the arcade freeway. He shifted his gears and turned his wheel with his car easily taking the lead. "Ready to call it quits?"

"Never." Kylie giggled, then leaned over and tickled his ribs.

"What are you doing?" He swerved and his car plunged into the guardrail.

Kylie's car moved slow and steady but stayed on course. He turned his around and hit the gas again. She leaned over and tickled him once more.

"Kylie!"

She laughed as her car passed the finish line first. "I won! I won!" She pumped her fist in the air.

Ryan growled and grabbed her waist, pulling her toward him. She lifted her gaze to meet his, and Ryan longed to lean down and kiss her lips. He grazed her cheek with the back of his hand, and her eyes closed for a brief moment.

"You cheated," he whispered as he lowered his lips toward hers.

A push from behind knocked him into her, severing the moment. "Sorry!" a boy yelled, as he chased another child to one of the games.

"Ready for me to beat you at miniature golf?" Kylie smiled like the Cheshire cat as she reached up and twirled the bottom of his hair with her fingers. Surprise welled in her eyes. "I can't believe—I'm sorry. . . . I've wanted to feel your hair—oh, my."

She turned away from him but not before he saw her neck and cheeks blaze red. He grabbed her hand. "Let's go play." He led her to the shack where they picked out their golf clubs and ball colors. She put her ball on the tee, and he strolled up behind her. "You can play with my hair anytime you like."

She gazed up at him and wrinkled her nose. "You're trying to break my concentration, aren't you?"

Ryan touched his chest and tilted his head as if he had been wounded. "The things you accuse me of. I'm hurt."

Kylie rolled her eyes and swung her club. The ball launched through the air and hit the green of the second hole. She covered her mouth. "I guess I hit it too hard."

"You think?" Ryan laughed. He retrieved her ball and showed her how to hit it. By the time they'd finished, Kylie had beaten him. They walked back to the car, and Ryan relished the great time they'd had.

"It was pretty hard playing bad enough to let me win, wasn't it?"

"I'd say."

Kylie giggled. "The mark of a true man." She laid both hands on her heart. "He lets the lady win."

"It's true." Ryan pulled into her apartment's parking lot and walked her to the front door. "I had a really good time, Ki."

Kylie closed her eyes. Her tense stance had returned. Ryan brushed a wisp of hair behind her shoulder. "I'd really like to do it again sometime."

"Ryan." He watched her take a few quick breaths. "We can't."

"Why?"

"I need. . ." She looked up but not at him. "I need more. I just want to be friends." She turned away, opened her door, and slipped inside.

Ryan looked at the front door knocker. *I should just barrel in there and tell her to quit being silly.* He stared at the rusty spot at the bottom of the brass knocker. *I could tell her I am able to support her and she'd never have to worry about money again.*

He shook his head and walked back to his car. "Then I'd never know if she wanted me for me." Sliding into the driver's seat, he hit the steering wheel. "Why is it always about money? First Vanessa. Now Kylie."

Ryan looked at the passenger's seat and thought of Kylie sitting there only moments before. He wanted Kylie. He needed her to want him, with or without his money.

Chapter 8

W ell, hello there, big sis." Kylie's twenty-year-old brother pulled her into the house and smothered her in a bear hug.

"You're not missing any meals are you, Dalton?" Kylie broke free and patted her brother's rounded gut.

A monster of a smile bowed his lips. "Nope. When Mama's not feeding me, Tanya is."

Kylie's mouth fell open. "Tanya? Little Tanya Burns?"

"The one and only."

"You two are seeing each other?"

"I bought her a ring."

"You're kidding."

"Nope." He laced his fingers through his jeans belt loops. "I'd imagine we'll all be married before you."

Kylie squinted her eyes. "That doesn't hurt my feelings. Are you still going to the technology school?"

"Nope. Got a job at the mine."

"Why?" She smacked her hip. "Why would you do that, Dalton? Just—just look at Daddy."

Dalton frowned. "Yeah. Look at Daddy. He's raised eight children. Every one of them loves the Lord. Every one of them watched him work hard—"

"Dalton, you know what I mean."

"Let me finish." He pointed to his chest. "We've watched him love our mama, watched him come home from a hard day and sit on the porch and play his guitar and sing hymns to us." He pointed toward her. "When are you going to figure out what's important, big sister?"

"You know he had to have wanted a better life, an easier life. He's sick now, little brother." She clenched her teeth and stared at him for several moments. Finally she exhaled. "I didn't come here to fight."

"Dalton, did I hear the door?" Mama walked up behind him. She clapped her hands when Kylie peeked around her overgrown brother. "Kylie, come here, girl! How was your drive?" She opened her arms and wrapped Kylie in an embrace.

"Hi, Mama." Kylie kissed her mother's cheek. "It wasn't bad. Just took a little over an hour." As always, Mama's hair was rolled in a large knot on top of her head. It was as close to being a beehive as she could get it without it actually being one. Her bright blue eyes sparkled, overshadowing the wrinkles that lined her face. Mama wore the same type of outfit she always wore: a pair of stretch-waist jeans and a blouse with a big floral pattern.

"Get yourself in this house. We don't see enough of you. First you go off to college an hour away, then you get an apartment that's an hour from the college and still over an hour from your family." Mama grabbed her arm and pulled her farther into the living room. The same burnt orange couch and light brown, oversize chair sat upon the same dark brown, worn carpet. The same old cuckoo clock rested on the wall above the television. Everything was clean but as aged as her parents' anniversary, thirty years.

"How's Daddy feeling?"

"He has good days and bad days. The good news is his disability starts next month."

"It's about time. Where is he?"

"Taking a nap." She looked at Kylie. "How long are you staying?"

"I have to work tomorrow afternoon."

"I'll tell you what. Let's call your sisters and your brothers-in-law and get their families on over here for dinner. I'll fix some fried chicken, and we'll whip up some mashed potatoes and baked beans—"

"Mama, you know Kylie's nothing but a nuisance in the kitchen."

Kylie looked back, scrunched up her nose, and stuck out her tongue at her brother.

"Now, Dalton, don't go picking on Kylie. Why don't you call Tanya and have her come over, as well?" She opened the freezer and grabbed several packages of chicken. "Your daddy will be tickled pink to see all of us here when he wakes up."

Kylie wrinkled her nose when her mother handed her a ten-pound bag of potatoes and a paring knife. She hated peeling potatoes. Trudging to the trash can, she pulled it beside the table so she could throw the peels into it. "I can't wait, Mama."

Later, as Kylie placed the last dish on the dining room table, she had to admit helping Mama in the kitchen felt wonderful despite the nick on her thumb from cutting some apple slices and the cut on her finger from dicing the onion.

"You helped Mama with all of this?" Sabrina, Kylie's oldest sister, set up the card table for her three boys and Natalie's son.

"Yes, I did."

"I'm impressed." Natalie smiled. "We thought you were only good at schoolwork."

"Ha-ha. I'll have you know—"

"Is that my Kylie?" Daddy's deep voice sounded from just outside his bedroom door.

"Daddy!" Kylie ran and hugged him. "I've missed you."

"And I've missed you." He looked past her. "Looks like the whole family's here."

"Yep."

He turned his head and coughed several times. He looked back at her, then wrapped his arm around her shoulder. "Well, let's eat. I'm starved."

His cough and the weariness in his eyes tugged at her heartstrings. She loved her daddy and couldn't imagine life without him. Soon God would provide her with the income to help her parents.

As everyone gathered around the table, Kylie walked her father to his seat. Soon the adults settled at the big table, and the four grandchildren sat at the card table.

"Are you ready for me to bless the meal?" asked her father.

"Yes, Daddy, let's hurry it up." Twenty-one-year-old Amanda snorted. "After all, I am eating for three."

"What?" Mama stopped arranging the serving dishes to make room for the butter dish and gawked at her fourth child. "Did you say three?"

"Me and my big mouth." Amanda hit the table. "I wanted to surprise you guys after dinner."

Kylie watched as tears glistened in her daddy's eyes. "I remember when Chloe and Cameron were born." He looked at his youngest children, the twins. "We had the best times, didn't we Mama?"

"It was an adventure, that's for sure." Mama walked over to Amanda, patted her shoulder, and kissed the top of her head. "The Lord just keeps on blessing us."

Kylie placed her napkin on the table. "Excuse me."

"Are you okay?" Daddy's face was etched with concern.

"My stomach's just hurting a bit. Must have been all the taste testing Mama made me do." She tried to chuckle. "You all start without me."

Kylie shut the door to the bathroom and dropped onto the pink toilet seat. Same pink toilet. Same pink tub. Same pink sink. Same single bathroom. Nothing had changed. They didn't have the money to change any of it. She bit her lip and willed the tears to stay away.

How could her parents possibly be happy that Amanda was having twins? Her sister was a baby herself, a baby married to a coal miner. Natalie, pregnant with her second child, married to a coal truck driver. At least Sabrina had the good sense to marry a man with a safe and stable job. Although she wasn't sure if being a high-school principal was exactly safe, but at least it was stable, and he had a good income. One that provided consistently for his family.

She remembered her father coughing when he got up from his nap. Coughing again when he sat down for dinner. She didn't know how many more years she'd have with her father. All because of the coal mines. She hated the feast or famine they'd endured as a family at the hands of her daddy's employer. She hated seeing her daddy sick.

Two brothers-in-law working in the mines. Now, her flesh-and-blood brother would join them. One grandchild after another, and none of her sisters had an education above high school. Yet her parents, her sisters, her brothers— they all seemed content, happy.

She stood and stared at herself in the mirror. "Am I missing something here?"

Yes.

She squelched the answer that popped into her mind. Yes, she was missing something all right. She was missing the fact that no one in her family had a lick of sense. No one except her.

❦

Ryan gazed out the window of the airplane. Kylie's rejection of him had hurt more than he initially realized. Trying to escape, if only for a few days, Ryan had booked a flight to see his old friend in Alaska. He sucked in a deep breath and blew it out slowly, willing the Dramamine to kick in. Though he traveled by plane at least three times each year, flying still made him nervous.

He closed his eyes and leaned back in his seat. A vision of Kylie peering up at him at the arcade just before the boy ran into them filled his mind. He visualized lowering his lips to hers. They were soft and sweet beneath his.

His mind shifted to the remembrance of the pain in her eyes when she told him she needed more. More. Why did women always want more? Why couldn't they be content with love, with knowing a man cared about them?

He turned his head. He didn't care what women wanted. Only what Kylie wanted. His heart was filled to the brim and spilling over with her, and he couldn't stop the overflow. *I think I'm falling in love with her.*

Darkness surrounded him for a brief moment. He jolted at the voice of a woman instructing him to remain seated as the flight landed. He rubbed his eyes and looked at his watch. "Wow, I've been out for three hours." He smiled. Dramamine was God's gift to the fearful flyer.

The plane landed, and Ryan snatched his carry-on bag from the overhead compartment. Holding in a yawn, he made his way past the attendant and into the airport. He stopped at a coffee shop and bought an extra-large black java. After a few quick puffs to cool the coffee, he sucked down a large gulp.

He rented a pickup then headed for his hotel. After checking in, he drove

51

to the Alaskan Logging Company. He yanked his cell phone from his pocket and dialed the owner's number.

"You don't get to surprise me this time, buddy."

Ryan snapped his phone shut and turned at the sound of Jim's voice behind him. "You take all the fun out of things, Jim." He grabbed Jim Thompson's hand and shook it as he patted his friend on the back. "How are you and your ladies doing?"

"Good. Callie's working part-time in a florist shop now that all three girls are in school. What about you?"

"I'm doing good."

"Any special lady in your life?"

Kylie's face popped into Ryan's mind. He swept the image away. "No."

"Wouldn't you say it's about time?" He punched Ryan's shoulder. "Aren't you pushing thirty?"

Ryan forced a laugh. "Yeah. I'm just waiting on God's timing."

"Maybe you just need to make a move to cooler climates." Jim nodded for Ryan to follow him into the office. "You know I would welcome your help here. Your dad was one of my uncle's best workers, and the machine you invented—why, production has nearly doubled in the last several years."

"I'm glad to hear it." Ryan settled into the plush couch that sat opposite Jim's desk. The phone rang.

"Just a sec, Ryan." He picked up the receiver and his pen at the same time. "Thompson." A grin lifted his mouth, and he laid down the pen. "Hey, doll, how's your day going?" Jim's attention stayed on his desk as he shook his head. "Sorry 'bout that, but don't worry. I'll be home at six, and I'll call them. No, you don't have to worry. I love you. I'll see you tonight."

Jim replaced the receiver, and Ryan started to stand. "I'll come back tomorrow. Sounds like you need to get home."

Jim shook his head and motioned for him to sit. "No. It's fine. Callie had to take the SUV to the shop. She feels like she's getting the runaround. She just needed to know I'd take care of it."

Jim's words echoed in Ryan's mind. Callie wanted security. Kylie wanted security. Maybe Kylie's wants were less about money and more about her need to feel cared for. Ryan would do anything to ensure that Kylie was safe and taken care of. Somehow he had to prove it to her.

Maybe I need to take Jim up on a job here. Maybe she needs to know that I go to work each day and come home each night. Help me, Lord. I love the freedom I have to serve You in any way You lead. Now that Kylie's entered my life, show me how I'm to follow.

⟨⟩

Having spent a never-ending dinner with her future supervisor, Kylie led Brad

Dickson to the exit of Marinelli's. If she had to spend another moment listening to Brad praise himself for his business abilities or brag about the many women who fell at his feet, Kylie felt sure she would vomit. She glanced at her watch. *We've spent forty-five minutes in the restaurant—it seemed like hours.*

She looked back at Brad, noting his exquisite pinstriped navy suit, starched white shirt, and red, silk tie. A power outfit, for sure. She wondered what he thought of her not-so-elaborate attire of a good pair of khakis and a fitted sweater. She'd thought their dinner would be a get-to-know-each-other-a-bit kind of thing. Obviously, he'd expected something a bit more formal. She pushed open the door and walked outside.

"That was a quaint place. Do you go often?" Brad peered down at her with a condescending smirk plastered on his face.

She recognized the tone. His intent was to make her feel inferior. Marinelli's was beneath him. Well, where did the man usually eat? A five-star restaurant? She agreed with Gramps. Marinelli's had awesome Italian food.

"Yes. It's probably my favorite restaurant."

"Really?" He wrinkled his nose. "I'm surprised you would take your future boss to such a second-rate place. I thought the meat was overcooked, the noodles pasty, and the bread had hardly any garlic taste to it at all."

What an arrogant, self-righteous baboon! Okay, so he didn't like the place. But why act as if she'd purposely tried to displease her boss? Anger surged through her veins. Taking slow breaths, she remembered who dwelled within her heart. *Help me turn the other cheek, Lord.* She closed her eyes for the briefest of moments. God called His children to love, to tell others about Him. *You never said it would be easy. Give me patience with him, Lord.*

"Hi, Kylie." She turned at the sound of Gramps's voice beside her in the parking lot.

"Hello, Gramps." She hugged the older man, then nodded toward Brad. "Gramps, allow me to introduce you to Brad Dickson. He'll be my supervisor at Miller Enterprises."

"How do you do, Brad?" Gramps grabbed Brad's hand and shook it firmly, then pulled Kylie close and patted her back. "You've got a good one here."

"I couldn't agree more, Gramps." Brad's smug tone made Kylie want to punch him in the jaw. She couldn't fathom how she would stand working with him on a day-to-day basis.

Gramps leaned toward Kylie. "Did you see Elma's hair this morning at church?"

Kylie shook her head. She watched as Brad's eyebrows lifted in humor. He cupped his chin with his finger and thumb, then smirked at her and Ryan's grandfather.

"The woman's hair was pink! Silly woman can't make up her mind." Gramps chuckled and nudged her shoulder, knocking her back a step.

Ryan walked up beside them. A knot formed in Kylie's throat. She hadn't seen him in two weeks, and she'd missed him more than she expected. Heat rushed to her cheeks. She didn't want Ryan to think she was dating Brad. "Ryan." She touched his arm. "This is Brad Dickson. He's my future supervisor."

Hurt flickered in his eyes before he nodded to Brad and grabbed his hand. "Nice to meet you."

Brad lifted his nose and grunted an acknowledgment. He released Ryan's hand and wiped his palm on his pants. The unbelievable arrogance of the man! He was nothing like this in the interview. He had been kind, more than civil, but then Mr. Miller had been sitting there, as well. She looked up at him and willed her dinner to stay in her stomach. How would she make it through each day on the job?

◈

Ryan studied this Brad Dickson. The man's dark blond hair had been high-lighted with lighter streaks. Clean-shaven and groomed to a tee, the man would definitely be considered good-looking. He walked behind Kylie with his nose so high in the air, Ryan wondered if he would trip from not watching where he was going. Ryan had seen men like this before. Power hungry. Their main objective was to make others feel of little worth. *So this is what Kylie wants in a man?*

He huffed as he followed Gramps into the restaurant. He'd missed Kylie something fierce the two weeks he'd spent in Alaska. However foolish he'd been when he fell head over heels for Vanessa, Ryan wouldn't make the same mistake again, even if it ripped his heart to pieces.

Chapter 9

Having spent the evening before preparing food for the singles' get-together, Kylie placed the bowl of spinach dip and the plate stacked with homemade bread on the cloth-covered table. Robin laid home-made macadamia nut cookies next to the other desserts. Scanning the recreation room, Kylie inhaled a long breath, then rubbed her hands together. Ryan was nowhere in sight. Surprised by how much she missed him, her heart plummeted at his absence. She hadn't seen him for two weeks—outside of their brief encounter at Marinelli's.

"It's a little sad, isn't it?" Robin whispered in her ear.

Kylie frowned, fearing Robin had read her thoughts about Ryan. "Sad?"

"Yeah, it's the last singles' get-together of the summer."

"Oh, yeah. I guess it's sad." Kylie searched her mind for something encouraging to say. "But it also means school is about to start."

"Yeah." Robin looked away. "That's true."

With the thought planted in her brain, a seed of happiness sprouted in Kylie's heart. "The sooner it starts, the sooner it's over with." She linked arms with Robin. "We'll get up in the morning, drive the one-hour commute to campus, hit the coffee shop for a cappuccino, then head to class."

"Uh, sure." Robin gently unlinked her arm and pointed to the man waving to them from the far corner. Robin's face lit up and she waved back. "There's Tyler. Come on."

The sprout of happiness withered in Kylie's chest. She'd hardly seen Robin in the last few months. "We could hang out together. Just you and me. Talk a bit."

Confusion wrapped Robin's features. "Without Tyler?"

"Well, we haven't seen much of each other."

"Um. . ."

Kylie watched as Robin's face scrunched in uncertainty with how to respond.

Kylie swatted the air then pushed her friend in Tyler's direction. "No. You go on." She lifted her purse. "I think I'll freshen up in the restroom then grab a bite of all this good food."

"You sure?"

"Yeah. You go on."

"Okay, see you later."

Kylie watched as Robin walked away without so much as a backward glance. Sighing, Kylie made her way to the bathroom. So much of her life seemed to be changing. Getting rocky. Unstable. First, her daddy's illness. Then Dalton's engagement. Amanda's announcement of twins. Now Robin's dating. It made her feel out of control.

She laid her purse on the sink and rummaged through its contents. Finding her lipstick, she opened it and applied the watermelon color. She smacked her lips together. Ryan had been right where she needed him all summer. Consistent.

What am I thinking? Ryan was a grown man working at Holiday World. Sure, he was godly and generous and fun to be around, but when the electric bill came due or the pantry emptied—then what? He'd take a side job as a lifeguard at a pool? No, Ryan's picture would not be the one displayed in the dictionary beside the definition of "consistent."

And yet he was just that.

Trying to forget the thought, she leaned closer to the mirror and brushed away an eyelash that had fallen on her cheek. "I wonder where he's been."

She stood straighter and brushed invisible wrinkles from her sundress's hem. "Classes will soon begin. Life will go back to normal. I will not worry about Ryan Watkins." She squirted some blackberry-scented lotion into her palm and rubbed her hands together. "I'm going to mingle"—she zipped her purse shut and exited the restroom—"have a bit of fun, then head home and go to bed early before work tomorrow."

A purposeful bounce had formed in her step by the time she reached the recreation center. "Only two more weeks of work at Holiday World." She pushed open the door. A groan sounded from the other side. She gasped, covered her mouth, and peered around the door.

"Ryan!"

"You pack quite a punch." Ryan touched each side of his nose.

"I'm so sorry. What were you doing right behind the door?"

"Reaching for the handle."

Kylie grimaced and moved his hands from his face to see the damage. "I'm sorry. You're not bleeding. A little red, maybe."

He sniffed and wiggled his nose. "I'm fine. How are you doing, Ki?"

Flutters filled her belly when he shortened her name. Wow, she had missed him. "I'm good."

"How's Brad?"

She shrugged. Why would he ask her about Brad the Baboon? She almost chuckled aloud at the thought of the pet name she'd made up for the man. "Good, I guess."

Taking in his cool blue gaze and sun-kissed nose and cheeks, she acknowledged how cute this Richie Cunningham was to her, more attractive than she wanted to admit. "I haven't seen you at work."

"I had some other things I needed to get done."

She furrowed her brows. "Don't you. . .don't you need to work? I mean, you said you didn't have a day job." She swatted the air. "It's none of my business."

"You want to get some food?"

"Sure."

Ryan led her to the table. She picked up a plate and loaded it with country ham biscuits, potato chips, fruit salad, crackers and cheese dip, and an oversize double chocolate brownie. After grabbing a can of pop, she sat at a vacant round table. Ryan sat beside her. "You want me to bless our food?"

"Sure." She bowed her head and closed her eyes.

"Thank You for our food, Lord. Thank You for this time of fellowship. I pray You will draw us closer to You, that our lives will be filled with joy and contentment. Amen."

She looked up at him, then down at her plate. Was her life joyful? Could she say she felt contentment? The thought of working with Brad Dickson made her feel nauseated. Her brother barely grunted at her every time she called her parents' house. Robin was preoccupied with Tyler. "Joy" and "contentment" were not words she would choose to describe her life right now. She bit into her sandwich.

"Excuse me. Can we have your attention for a moment?"

Kylie turned at the sound of Tyler's voice. He stood in the middle of the room, with Robin holding tight to his side. An indeterminable queasiness overtook Kylie.

"Robin and I have an announcement to make."

"No," Kylie whispered and barely shook her head.

Tyler's bottom lip quivered. "God blessed me once with a wonderful wife. When Cheryl died, I thought my whole life belonged to my son and the youth." He peered at Robin, and tears filled his eyes.

"No, this is not happening." Kylie gripped her fork.

Robin pulled a tissue from her front pocket. She handed it to Tyler, leaned close, and whispered something in his ear, then kissed his cheek. Tyler continued, "Well, God had other plans."

Kylie's heart sped up. "No."

"He blessed me to love again." He gazed at Robin. "I'm humbled and honored to share with you that Robin has agreed to be my wife."

Kylie smacked her fork on the table, stood, and started to walk away.

"Kylie." Ryan tried to grab her hand.

"No, Ryan." She pivoted and gawked at him. "She does things on a whim. She never thinks things through. She needs"—she smacked her hip for emphasis—"to finish school." She peered at the ceiling, nearly hidden by red and blue helium balloons. "Am I the only person on the planet who believes in being sensible?"

She turned and walked to the restroom. The words of Ryan's prayer flooded her mind. Everything about Robin exuded joy and contentment. She'd practically floated on clouds each time she was with Tyler.

Kylie made her way to the mirror in the ladies' room and peered at her reflection. "Everything's going wrong, Lord."

Ryan waited at the end of the line of people that had formed to congratulate the newly engaged couple. Two weeks he'd spent away from Kylie. He'd purposefully tried to get the woman out of his mind, out of his heart. Time away would squelch his feelings. Seeing her with Brad and again tonight proved his plan hadn't worked. When his turn came, Ryan hugged Robin and shook Tyler's hand.

"Where's Kylie?" Robin leaned close and asked.

"In the restroom."

Robin turned toward her fiancé. "Tyler, I'll be right back." She yanked Ryan away from the crowd. "Let's talk."

"What is it?"

"Kylie."

"I think she feels you've moved too fast."

Robin bit her lip. "Look. I love Kylie. We've been the best of friends for as long as I can remember, but she has issues."

"Issues?" Ryan frowned. He knew she wanted a good job and a steady husband and that being financially secure seemed to be the most important pursuit of her life.

"Not like that. She just can't loosen up. Can't trust. Can't let herself—she's just so worried about having the perfect life she can't see when God's best is right in front of her."

"What are you saying?"

Robin huffed. "You." She poked his shoulder. "You, Richie Cunningham, are perfect for her. She's so consumed with her perfect husband, perfect kids, perfect dog running along her perfect white picket fence, that she's blind to what God has provided that is actually perfect for her."

"Aren't you being a bit dramatic?"

"No, I'm not." She stomped her foot then giggled at her reaction. "I'm always dramatic, but that doesn't change what's going on with Kylie. Being poor as a girl and now with her dad fighting black lung, she needs to feel safe." Robin cocked her head and stared at him. "What do you do for income?"

Ryan's collar tightened around his neck as Robin's scrutinizing gaze peered into him. "I work at Holiday World."

"And that's all?"

"I'm a Santa at the mall in Evansville at Christmastime."

Robin raised her eyebrows.

Ryan cleared his throat. "That's all the work I do that comes with a paycheck."

"Hmm. I think there's more to it than you let on." She pointed her finger at him. "Look, I don't want you to give up on her."

"What about Brad Dickson?"

"Brad?"

Ryan rolled his eyes. "The guy she's going to work with. The one who took her on a business dinner a few days ago. Mr. Clean-Cut, Nose-in-the-Air—"

"Wow. I think the green-eyed monster's been paying Mr. Watkins a visit."

"Humph."

"He sounds cute, though." She laughed and punched Ryan's shoulder again. "I'm just teasing. I haven't met this Brad Dickson."

"You haven't?"

"Nope, and she never talks about him."

"Do you talk to her much now that your schedule is full with Tyler and Bransom?"

"You got me there." Robin bit her lip thoughtfully. "Look. Don't give up on her, okay?"

"Who says I'm pursuing her?"

Robin snorted. "I've been preoccupied, but I'm not blind. It's obvious you like her. Pray she can see past her fears. She wants you. She just hasn't admitted it to herself yet."

Ryan watched as Robin scurried back to Tyler's side. *It's obvious I care about Kylie, huh? And Robin thinks she cares about me—just doesn't know it.* In his peripheral vision, he saw Kylie sit down at the table. She scooped some fruit salad on her fork and took a bite.

But what about Brad? Robin didn't have an answer for him—didn't even know who he was. He looked at Kylie. He longed for her to be his. No matter what he did, his attraction wouldn't dissipate, wouldn't even budge. He made his way toward her.

"Hey." Ryan sat beside her.

"Hey." She smiled at him, but he could see the hint of red around her slightly swollen eyelids. "Are you still going to Belize in January?"

Ryan lifted his eyebrows. Her question surprised him. "Yes. We have a meeting this Friday."

"You guys have fund-raisers and other things to raise the money to go, right?"

"Yeah."

"I'd like to go to the meeting."

"Sure. I can pick you up at seven."

"That would be great." Kylie stood and picked up her plate and cup. "I'm pretty tired. I think I'm going to head back to the apartment, but I'll see you then."

Stunned, Ryan sat as Kylie threw away her food then headed out the door. She hadn't congratulated Robin and Tyler. Sadness gleamed from her eyes. Robin was right. Brad wasn't the problem. Kylie needed to trust God with her future, with her family's future. Yes, everything would work out as soon as Kylie put her full trust in God.

Chapter 10

A few days later, Ryan walked Kylie to the front door of her apartment after another missions trip meeting. "School starts tomorrow, huh?"

"Yep."

"What did you think of the meeting?"

"I'm looking forward to the trip. I want to hold the babies." Her eyes flashed with excitement as a smile warmed her lips. Ryan found himself wanting to touch the dimple on her chin. It was the deepest he'd ever seen; yet it added the neatest beauty to her face.

"You'll make a beautiful baby-holder." Ryan's voice sounded huskier than he'd intended. He cleared his throat as Kylie's cheeks blazed pink.

She jingled her keys. "I'm thinking of making hair bows for the fund-raiser."

"That sounds great."

"It's a lot of money to raise."

"God always provides."

Kylie peered up at him. She studied him with an intensity that would make a bear cower back into the woods. "You really trust Him completely."

She hadn't asked, simply stated. Ryan swallowed, pondering if the declaration was accurate. Did he trust God? Completely? Kylie struggled with trust in poverty. What about his wealth? The greed and power that had filled Vanessa's eyes when she learned of his worth flooded his mind. He remembered the way she had spoken with disdain to his friends who had less. Since then, he hadn't been able to risk letting others know his true financial status. His intentions had been to live humbly, but had it really been for pride? "I—I try to trust Him."

Kylie touched his cheek. "I'm thankful for your faith." Before he could respond, she thrust her key into the doorknob, unlocked it, and scurried inside.

Humbled, Ryan walked back to his car, contemplating if he trusted his Lord as much as he thought.

❧

Kylie settled into the wooden school desk. Her drive had been a long and lonely one. She was thankful that Robin planned to stay in the apartment until the wedding and that Robin's uncle offered to let Kylie keep the apartment until she had graduated and was gainfully employed. But she still missed Robin. The semester just wouldn't be the same without her best friend.

She shuffled her folders, then placed all but the one she'd designated for the accounting course under her desk. Retrieving two pencils from her purse, she checked to make sure they were well sharpened. She pulled her schedule from her pocket. Only four classes this semester. Since she'd attended summer courses the first two years, Kylie was able to finish all necessary accounting content except this one fall semester class. The other three courses she took simply to keep her academic scholarship.

Ms. Jones. She read the instructor's name for the class. Kylie had heard wonderful things about the fairly young professor. According to the buzz on campus, Ms. Jones was dynamic and an out-of-the-box thinker, yet she stayed abreast of the current business expectations. Kylie bit the eraser of her pencil. *It seems I heard she was expecting.*

Kylie dropped her pencil when Professor Nickels trudged through the door. His salt-and-pepper hair, a mass of wiry curls, swayed with each step he took. "I know you're expecting Professor Jones."

Nickels plopped his briefcase on the teacher's desk. "I'm not looking forward to teaching this class any more than you're interested in taking it." He scanned the room. His gaze landed on Kylie. He scowled.

He jerked a stack of papers from his case and walked to one side of the room. "Professor Jones is having complications with her pregnancy." He counted students and syllabi, then handed several to the first person in each row. "So, I'm filling in."

A small, dark-haired lady raised her hand. "Will Ms. Jones and the baby be all right?"

"How would I know?" Professor Nickels shrugged and turned toward the chalkboard. "Look at page one in your syllabus. . . ."

Kylie slumped in her seat. Perfect. This was just great. This semester was supposed to be cake, and now she had Nickels to deal with—again. She frowned at the packet in front of her. Robin, her ever-consistent pick-me-up friend, wouldn't be keeping her company on the long drive to campus. She wouldn't be walking to the coffee shop with her each morning to encourage Kylie to make it through his class.

Robin's eyes had shone like emeralds when she'd returned from the singles' get-together just a few weeks before. Her countenance had been a mixture of adrenaline, bliss, and contentment. "I'm not going back." Robin's words echoed in Kylie's mind. . . .

"What? But you have to. You want to graduate. You want to get a good—"

"No, Kylie." Robin had rested her hand on top of Kylie's. "I never wanted it like you did. Don't you see? That's why I still don't have a major." She looked at the engagement ring on her finger, then back at Kylie. "I'm twenty-three years old. All

I've ever wanted was to be a wife and mom. Think about it. When you wanted to play business, I wanted to play house. When you wanted to play school, I wanted to play house. When you wanted to play store, I wanted to play—"

"House," Kylie finished.

"Yes. This is what I want. God has given me such peace, such confirmation. I want you to be happy for me." She grabbed Kylie in a hug. "And I want you to be my maid of honor."

Kylie had wiped away the threat of tears that filled her eyes. "Of course I'm happy, and I'd better be your maid of honor."

The chalk screeched against the board, and Kylie snapped from her reverie. She glanced at the syllabus on the desk of the guy sitting beside her. Nickels was on page five. She flipped her pages over. Gazing at his scoring guide, she cringed. To be able to graduate summa cum laude, with a 3.85 grade point average or better, she'd have to have a B in this class. *I can do it.*

She looked at her watch. Five more minutes. Her cell phone vibrated in her front pocket. Discreetly, she pulled it out, as no one ever called her during the day once school started. Her phone's display read her parents' number, and her heart plunged into her gut. Quickly, she gathered her things and slipped out of the room. *Please, God, let Daddy be okay.*

She pressed the button. "Hello?"

"Hi, honey," her mother's voice sounded over the line.

"What's wrong?"

"Nothing serious."

Kylie let out her breath. "Mama, you scared me to death. I was sitting in class, and I thought something happened to Daddy."

"I'm sorry. I thought your classes started next week."

"Mama." Kylie bit back her frustration.

"Listen, I do have something I want to tell you, something for you to pray about."

"Okay."

"The lady handling Daddy's disability claim called and said there's been a bit of a delay. Seems his checks won't start for another couple months."

"Are you all going to be okay? Dalton and Gideon are still helping out, right?"

"Well, Dalton's had a bit of an injury."

Kylie's heart sped up. "At the mine?"

"No. Playing basketball with his buddies. Seems he went up for a block and fell on his foot and broke it."

"Oh, my."

"I want you to pray for us. God has always provided. In fact, I love to see how creative He can be. He's already blessed us in that Dalton's boss is holding his job, and your daddy is feeling quite well."

"I'll be praying, Mama."

"Oh, did I tell you Chloe was selected for some sort of special soccer team?"

"No."

"You know how that girl is always dribbling the ball around the house. Well, she's really pretty good. It's a lot of fun to watch her games."

"Maybe I can get down to see one."

"I hope so."

"I love you, Mama. Tell Daddy I love him."

"I will. I love you, too."

Kylie snapped her phone shut as the students exited the classroom. Professor Nickels trailed behind them. *I don't know what it will take, but I will get an A in his class. I'll make sure Miller Enterprises is happy to have selected me. They have to be. My family needs me.*

⤜∞⤛

"Here, Ryan." Gramps shoved several boxes into his hands. "Stack these cereal boxes on that far shelf."

"Yes, sir." Ryan clicked his heels and marched like a soldier toward his destination.

"When you're finished, I need you to stack these rice boxes beside them. I'll start setting the vegetable cans on this shelf."

Ryan saluted then picked up the rice. "Aye-aye, captain."

"All right now, smarty-britches, we only have fifteen minutes before God's Pantry opens."

Ryan stacked the fruit cans beside the vegetables. "All done. What do we do when they get here?"

"Just follow me at first. I'll show you." Gramps patted Ryan's back. "I'm glad you're here with me today."

"I am, too, Gramps."

Gramps walked over to the door and unlocked it. Already two women stood outside. He looked at Ryan. "The place is too small. We let one person at a time come in." He turned to the second woman. "We'll be with you in just a moment."

Ryan watched as Gramps took a pink slip from the first lady. Because people were referred from the health department and could only come twice a month, they had to bring a slip with them. Gramps checked it off and wrote her name in a ledger then pushed a grocery cart over to her.

"Come on." Gramps motioned for the lady to follow him. He handed her peanut butter, beans, and several other items. They reached the cereal, and

Gramps let her pick three different kinds. Ryan noticed the woman never actually touched the foods.

"Do you go to church anywhere, miss?" Gramps asked, his voice tendered in a way Ryan seldom heard.

"Not really," the woman answered.

He placed a gallon of milk in the basket. "We'd love for you to visit our church."

"I don't know."

"Have you heard of Jesus?"

"Sorta." The woman stared at the items in the basket.

Gramps opened the freezer and let her pick three dessert items. Once finished, he transferred the food into bags. He pulled out a tract and one of their church pamphlets from his shirt pocket. "Miss, I'm glad you came today. I'd love to talk to you about Jesus anytime you'd like. I hope you'll consider visiting our church. You can sit with me and my grandson. Right, Ryan?"

"Yep."

"Thanks." The woman averted her eyes and picked up two bags. "I'll be right back."

"Ryan and I will help you out." Gramps lifted two bags, and Ryan grabbed the remaining three. They followed her to an aged Chrysler. Ryan noted two car seats in the back as they filled her trunk. Gramps slammed it shut and walked to the front of the car. "Remember what I said, and bring your babies."

The woman smiled slightly. "I don't know. Maybe." She slid into the driver's seat and stuck her head through the window. "Thanks, Mr. Watkins."

"I'll see ya." Gramps waved as she backed out of the parking lot.

"You know her?"

"I see her every two weeks. Have the same conversation. Get the same response. But one day. . ." Gramps lifted his finger in the air. "I believe we'll see her in church."

"Why didn't she touch any of the food?"

"Not allowed."

"Not allowed?"

"There's a lot of people in this county who benefit from God's Pantry, people who use it for what it's meant to be—help to those who need it." Gramps's face clouded. "But we still get a few who abuse it, who try to take more than we can supply. Because of them, the rules are strict."

Ryan watched the woman turn the corner. "It's worth it, isn't it, Gramps?"

"Helping others is always worth it, even if only one of ten had a true need. I'd rather err on the side of being taken advantage of than miss helping those who can't help themselves."

Ryan's thoughts drifted to Kylie. She didn't physically need food like those he'd see today, but she had other needs. She needed peace, needed the ability to completely trust God with her finances and her future.

Lord, everything in me wants to tell Kylie I can provide for her for the rest of her life, yet I'm afraid.

Ryan scratched his jaw. Afraid? Of what? He no longer believed Kylie to be a money-grubber. He didn't think she'd fall in love with him the moment she found out he could provide, yet he needed to know she'd love him for him, only him.

"Trust in the Lord with all your heart." Did he trust the Lord enough to share his secret with Kylie? He shook the thought away.

Instead, Ryan thought of her compassionate expression as she watched the Belize missions trip video. He remembered the concern etched on her face as she spoke of her family. He knew her pain with Robin's decision not to return to school was founded in care and worry for her friend. Kylie loved. There was no doubt in his mind that her heart was filled with a want to see those around her happy and at peace.

She just wants to control how they get it. Ryan sighed. Patience was not his strong suit. Loving Kylie required nothing less. "She wants control. I want her to give it up right now so I can tell her I'll provide for her and her family for the rest of our lives," he mumbled. "We're a great pair."

"What's that?"

"Nothing, I'm just mumbling to myself."

"Well, let's get on in there. We've got work to do."

Ryan smiled as he followed Gramps into the building. Though usually a bit rough around the edges, Gramps was sweet as sugar to the people he met at God's Pantry. This was Gramps's missions arena, and Ryan felt privileged to be a part of it.

⬥

Kylie gazed at the two bridesmaid dress pictures Robin placed in front of her. "Which do you like better?"

"They both seem a bit warm."

"Well, yeah, it'll probably be cold in December."

"You're getting married in December? That's less than three months away."

"We don't want to wait. We want to spend Christmas as a family."

"Oh." Kylie stared at the pictures. "Either is fine with me."

The phone rang, and Robin hopped up. "I bet that's the florist."

Kylie turned away from the magazine. She didn't want to think about Robin's wedding. She didn't want to think about her injured brother, her sick father, or her younger sister pregnant with twins. She didn't want to think about why God seemed so distant despite her continual pleas for help.

"I'm doing the right things, Lord. I'm finishing school. I've already lined up a great job. I'm doing what is good. So, why am I so miserable?"

"What good is it for a man to gain the whole world, and yet lose or forfeit his very self?" Scripture from the pastor's sermon pierced her heart.

She huffed. "He was talking about those who don't know Christ. I know Jesus, and I love Him with my whole heart."

"Trust in the Lord with all your heart." One of her favorite Proverbs verses slipped into her mind.

"I do trust You, Lord." A weight fell on her shoulders and dropped harder into her chest. "At least, I try."

Chapter 11

Kylie glared at the numbers before her. Professor Nickels had assigned a project that she'd almost finished. Except the numbers wouldn't match up. Grabbing her calculator, she typed in the first row and tallied them. She flipped through the pages of the project to be sure she'd deducted all expenses, then she tallied the second column. She slammed the calculator on the table. "I'm still $9.53 off!"

She raked her fingers through her hair then trudged to the refrigerator and grabbed a pop. Unscrewing the cap, she took a long drink then wiped her lips. "If it was off by a double zero number, I could find the mistake easily." She slunk back into her chair. "But this could take forever to find."

A knock sounded at the door, and Kylie glared at the clock. "Who could that be?" She walked over and peeked through the peephole. "Ryan?" She unbolted the door and opened it. "Hey."

"Ya ready?"

"Ready for what?"

"Ready for the missions meeting." He furrowed his eyebrows. "You didn't remember we had another meeting tonight, did you?"

Kylie smacked her hip. "I completely forgot. I'm working on this project for my accounting class."

"Oh."

"But. . ." Kylie slipped on a pair of flip-flops and grabbed her purse. "I could use a break." After stepping outside, she dug through her purse, found her keys, and dead-bolted the door.

She followed Ryan to his car and slid into the passenger's seat. As he pulled the car into traffic, Kylie opened the visor mirror to apply some lipstick. She gasped. "Ryan."

"What?"

"I'm a mess." She stared at her face, clear of all makeup, of all color. "I forgot I washed my face when I got home."

"I think you look pretty."

"Pretty! I'm a ghost. I can't go looking like this." She scoured her purse for some blush, some powder, anything. Nothing. She couldn't even find her lipstick.

Ryan pulled into the church's parking lot. He shut off the car and turned toward her. Placing one hand on hers, he cupped her chin with the other and turned her to face him. "You're beautiful, Ki."

The intensity of his voice gripped her. His gaze devoured every inch of her face. Her heart fluttered at his attraction, and she couldn't tear her gaze from him. Her eyes widened as he leaned closer. *He's going to kiss me.*

Excitement tingled through her veins. *I want him to kiss me.* She closed her eyes and lifted her chin.

He kissed her cheek.

Stunned and a bit disappointed, she opened her eyes as he reached for the door handle. His hand shook as he pushed the door open. *He wanted to kiss me.* The knowledge surged through her in a satisfaction she couldn't describe. *I wanted him to kiss me.*

Digesting the truth of it, Kylie slipped out of the car and followed Ryan into the church. "Tonight we're splitting into groups." Ryan didn't make eye contact with her. "One group is made of medical people. One of manual labor or repair people. And the last are those who are going as Bible school workers or general helpers. We'll go to that group."

"So, they break up to. . . ?"

"To talk about the items we need to collect for our specific purposes—so that we can plan what we want to do and how we want to go about doing it."

"Oh, okay."

Kylie found a seat in the already made circle beside a large woman with an infant on her lap. "Hi."

"So, what are you going to be doing in Belize?" the woman asked.

Kylie shrugged. "I don't have any special talents. I can hold a baby, though."

"Ya want to start now?" The woman's face broke into a large grin. "I'm supposed to be making coffee for the group, but my husband couldn't get off work in time to watch Suzanna."

"Sure." Kylie reached for the baby then turned Suzanna around to face her.

"My name's Candy." She pulled up the baby's falling shoe. Suzanna smiled up at Kylie. "I think she likes you. You'll do just fine."

Kylie peered down at the baby. "I have four nephews and three more babies on the way." Of course, Kylie had hardly ever held any of them. She'd been too busy to visit much. A pain stabbed her heart as Suzanna reached for her necklace. Sudden longing for her family nestled inside her as she inhaled the sweet scent that belonged only to babies.

"She's a cutie, isn't she?" Ryan sat beside her.

"Yes."

"She's such a blessing for Candy and her husband. They had five miscarriages.

Candy couldn't seem to carry a baby to term."

"Really?" Kylie caressed the baby's soft, chubby hand.

"Yeah. Candy and Michael looked like the perfect couple. Great jobs. Nice home. Both loved the Lord. But they hurt on the inside because they wanted a child so badly."

"I'm happy God allowed Candy to have her."

"Suzanna's adopted."

"She is?"

"Yeah."

A man at the front of the circle motioned for the meeting to begin.

Ryan leaned over. "Sometimes God gives us a different route. It may not be the one we expect, but it's still perfect."

Kylie kissed Suzanna's cheek. She tried to focus on the plans the group started to make, but she hashed over Ryan's words in her mind. She'd marked her destination as a high-school teen. Mapped out the perfect route and followed it to exactness. She was sure God had guided her decisions. Logically—practically, her plan made sense.

She glanced at Ryan. Not only was he fun to be around, his heart was also big, so generous—she'd never met anyone like him. And integrity. He didn't kiss her when she gave him the chance. She knew he wanted to. Her destination—graduation and a good job—was so close, only months away. Studying Ryan, she knew her heart longed for a detour.

God, my route is a good one. I want to be able to help my family. Surely I am following Your will. She glanced down at the Suzanna. Her heart wasn't convinced. Even her mind couldn't form solid confirmation. And peace evaded her completely.

❧

Ryan stuck a french fry into his mouth, then swallowed a gulp of pop. "So, whaddya think about Belize?"

"I can't wait to go."

"I'm telling you, Ki, there is nothing better than to see those children's eyes light up when we come. They know we're bringing balloons and candy and toys, and they know more about Jesus than a lot of churchgoing adults I know."

"I don't think I could dress up like a clown or anything like that."

"Hold the babies, huh?"

"Yep." She grinned, and crimson flooded her cheeks and neck. "Or help in any way I'm needed."

"You'll do wonderful taking care of babies." He thought of Suzanna, wiggling in her arms. Contentment had flooded her face, and for a moment, Ryan imagined Kylie holding their child, their daughter.

He longed to take Kylie in his arms. Before the meeting, he'd almost done it. She'd closed her eyes, welcomed his kiss. But she wasn't ready. He knew she wasn't. He didn't want to risk her shutting him out completely.

He shoved another fry into his mouth as Kylie nibbled on a piece of salad. They really were different. Kylie ate a chicken salad with light dressing while he devoured a hamburger and french fries drenched in ketchup. She was a classic beauty sitting with a Richie Cunningham look-alike. She was steady; he was fly-by-night. Quiet Kylie. Outgoing Ryan.

And yet, she was right.

Everything about her drew him, especially their differences. He just had to wait for her trust issues with God to be resolved. God, in His perfect, humorous way, chose to work on Ryan's lack of patience at the same time.

"Have you already raised the money for the trip?" Kylie's question interrupted his thoughts.

Now would be the perfect time to tell her the truth. Vanessa's face flooded his mind. The expensive outfit she'd bought and handed him the receipt for the day after he'd shared the truth with her. She'd fawned on him, tried to manipulate him, and his heart had shattered. No, he couldn't tell Kylie. Not yet. "Uh, I haven't raised any money."

"Well, what kinds of things can we do? I just don't know how I'll ever come up with enough."

"You know about the craft fair in early November. That always goes over well."

"Yes." Kylie twirled a piece of salad with her fork. "I'm making Christmas-colored hair bows for that, remember? Do we do anything else as a group?"

"A bake sale, I know."

"That sounds good." She pushed a cherry tomato to the side of her plate. "Money. It's a constant pain in my side."

"God always provides."

"Yes. That's true." Kylie pinned him with her gaze. "But it's a lot easier for some than others. Like you. How in the world do you work for an amusement park and not think anything about the cost of doing this type of thing?"

Tell her now. This is your chance. Trust God with her response. "Well, I—"

"Does your grandfather pay for it? I guess since you live in his house, you can save up or something. Are you still working at the park on weekends until it closes?"

She thinks I'm a moocher. I need to tell her right now. Ryan sat still, unsure how to say the truth. "Just spit it out," Gramps would tell him, but it wasn't that easy. He probably did appear irresponsible in her eyes. Jim's words about a woman needing to feel safe and settled replayed in his mind. "The truth is—"

"I'm sorry, Ryan." Kylie pushed her salad away. "That was so unkind of me. And not my business at all. I have a big project due and a test coming. Brad called last night wanting to have another 'getting acquainted' dinner. I—I think I'm just stressed. Could you take me home?"

Brad Dickson. Just the mention of his name sent a wave of revulsion through Ryan. He remembered the way Brad had looked at Kylie as if she were dessert after the main course. The man had been condescending and rude, but Ryan hadn't missed that Brad also viewed Kylie as a physical beauty. Ryan also recalled Kylie's kindness toward the snake. "Sure, I'll take you home."

Ryan drove back to her apartment. He watched as she went inside, waved hesitantly at him, then shut the door. He couldn't fault her for believing he depended on Gramps. In her eyes, he worked at Holiday World. Soon he'd be unemployed.

His heart stung at the thought of her feeling he took advantage of others, but he had to put his pride to the side, had to wait until she loved him for the man he was and no other reason. His ego had to step aside and wait.

He turned the ignition as thoughts of Vanessa and Brad whirled inside his mind. *Maybe it is about my pride—only in a different way.*

<hr>

I'm such a jerk. Kylie flung herself onto her bed. *I can't believe I said those awful things.*

A tear slid down her cheek. *How can I be so attracted to him?* She cuddled her pillow. *This is worse than falling for a man who works in the coal mines. Ryan doesn't even have a real job.*

She allowed the spilling of tears. She needed a pity party. Ryan Watkins made no sense. Her love for him didn't either. She sat up. "I can't love him."

Her perfect job destination, her graduation route flooded her mind. She didn't want to take a fall-in-love-with-Ryan-Watkins detour. She'd end up worse than her twenty-one-year-old sister, Amanda, who was married to a coal miner and pregnant with twins.

A vision of herself barefoot and pregnant, kissing Ryan—clad in his Holiday World uniform—filled her mind. Gramps sat on the front porch holding a red-haired toddler while another child played at his feet.

God, that is not the detour You want me to take. I don't believe it. I won't.

Chapter 12

Ryan held up the blond-haired fashion doll adorned in a pink princess dress. *Dana will love this.* He picked up the dark-haired male doll that wore a tuxedo and laid both in his cart. On Ryan's birthday his favorite present was to buy for his godchildren.

Moving down the aisle, he took in the massive assortment of dolls. *Little Heidi will want a baby.* He selected a box that advertised a doll that could eat and soil its diaper. *Yuck.* He laid it back down. Another boasted its doll could do flips. Ryan shook his head. *I want to get her something soft.* He moved down and found a baby that looked real, even had downy skin. *Perfect.* He placed it in the cart beside the fashion dolls. *One more stop.*

He strolled to electronics and chose a handheld car racing game. *I'm set.* Getting into the checkout line, he knew he had two more stops. One to a favorite local restaurant, and one to the mall. He paid for the toys, headed into parking lot, then loaded the car. He yanked out his cell phone and dialed Kylie's number.

"Hello." Her voice sounded light, happy.

"Hey, Ki."

"Um, hi." It changed to quiet, unsure. Ryan didn't know if that meant she didn't want to talk to him or if she still felt bad for what she'd said.

"Today's September twenty-first."

"You're right."

"It's my birthday."

"Happy birthday." Her sincerity sounded in the inflection of her voice. "How old are you?"

"Twenty-nine."

"No way."

"Yep."

"You're six years older than me."

"I'm older than a lot of people think."

"I just thought—I mean. . ."

Ryan wanted to groan. His age made her think him even more of a loser. "I was wondering"—he interrupted before she said something they'd both regret—"if you would go out to dinner with me to celebrate."

"You really want me to?"

"Yep. Can you be ready in about three hours?"

"Sure."

"Okay, see you then." He snapped his phone shut, drove to the restaurant, and picked up a gift certificate for Neal and Melissa. Afterward, he made his way to the mall in Evansville. He finished at the service center then walked past a glass shop. From the window, he spotted a single, long-stemmed, yellow rose. He thought of Kylie.

What would she think if I bought her a small gift? The desire to buy her the rose grew. *It's my birthday. She can't say a thing.*

He smiled as he lifted it off the shelf and took it to the clerk. The college-aged woman rang up the price. "This is my favorite piece," she said as she wrapped it in tissue.

"It is?"

"Yeah. Yellow roses are my favorite. They mean peace and friendship."

"They do?"

The lady laughed. "I think so. I get the colors and their meanings all confused sometimes, but I'm almost positive I'm right."

Ryan laughed out loud. "We'll just say you are."

She put the wrapped rose in a bag and handed it to him. "I hope she likes it."

Ryan lifted his eyebrows. "I never said that this was for a woman."

"What man buys a rose for himself? At the very least it's for your mom."

Ryan laughed out loud again. "Not my mom, and I hope she likes it, too."

⬦

"Kylie, this is Neal and Melissa Nelson."

Kylie offered her hand in greeting at Ryan's introduction. She skimmed the room, laden with aged furnishings. Three children sat on the floor beside an enormous, panting mutt.

Ryan leaned over and petted the dog's head. "This is Mutt."

Kylie didn't squelch her giggle in time.

Melissa shook her head. "The kids couldn't agree on a name, so we didn't give him one. Now he's just Mutt."

"It fits him well." Kylie bent down and petted the dog's head.

"Me." The youngest girl pointed to her chest.

Ryan grinned and tickled her chin. "This is Heidi. How old are you, Heidi?" She held up three fingers.

"You're a big girl," Kylie chimed in.

"I'm Dana." The older girl stood, grabbed the hem of her skirt, and twirled it back and forth. "I'm five, and I'm in kindergarten."

"Hello, Dana." Kylie turned toward the older boy. "And you are?"

"Evan." The preteen's cheeks turned scarlet as he grabbed her hand.

"It's nice to meet you." Kylie smiled then quietly clasped her hands in front of her. She had no idea why Ryan had brought her here. He said they were going to dinner for his birthday—not that she minded meeting this family. They were nice, but she didn't know what she was supposed to do.

"You're pretty." Dana grabbed a wisp of her hair and shoved it in her mouth.

"Thank you."

"Today is Neal and Melissa's thirteenth wedding anniversary."

"Lucky thirteen," Neal bellowed in an exasperated tone, then wrapped his arm around Melissa's shoulder.

"You're lucky I'm with you." Melissa poked him in the ribs.

"Yes, I am." Neal kissed her forehead.

Kylie smiled at their banter. Their love for one another was evident. She nudged Dana. "Are they always like this?"

Dana pursed her lips and shook her head. "Always."

They laughed at the seriousness in Dana's tone. Ryan smacked his thighs, then knelt eye-to-eye with Dana. "I have a surprise for you guys."

"Yea!" Dana jumped up and down, clapping her hands. Heidi watched and then mimicked her sister.

"Yes." Evan made a fist, pumping his elbow next to his side.

"I'll be right back. Kylie's going to help me."

Kylie followed him to the car. He popped the trunk, and she gasped at the gifts filling it. "All of those are for them?"

"Yep. It's the best birthday gift I could get."

Kylie studied Ryan as he placed several presents in her hands then filled his own. Her parents were generous. They'd give the shirts off their backs to help someone in need. She'd never met anyone as giving as they were. Until Ryan.

Speechless, she followed him inside and helped distribute the presents. She watched in awe as the children squealed over their toys and as tears filled Melissa's eyes when she opened the restaurant and mall gift certificates.

"When do you want me to come get the kids so you can go?"

Kylie's mouth dropped open. Ryan actually watched the children when they went for their date that he'd paid for. *He's perfect. He's sickeningly perfect, and he doesn't work.* Her gaze skimmed the room. *Who paid for these things?*

"Kylie, will you come, too?" Dana peered up at her with doe-like eyes.

"Uh. . ." She gazed at the urchin. She couldn't say no. "If Ryan is okay with it."

"You know I am." He smiled and grabbed her elbow. "Kylie and I better go. We're heading to dinner. How 'bout two weeks from Saturday?"

"Sounds good to me." Melissa wrapped Ryan up in a hug, then embraced Kylie as well.

They said good-bye and walked back to his car. Unable to speak, Kylie stared out the windshield as Ryan drove to the restaurant. Once there, he grabbed a small, white bag from the backseat. *Another surprise, I'm sure.* Kylie opened her door before Ryan could do it for her.

Once settled into the booth, Ryan asked, "What did you think about the Nelsons?"

"They're a lovely family."

"Melissa and I lived on the same street when I moved in with Gramps. She's a good five years older than me. Growing up, I always had a crush on her." He chuckled. "I'd follow her around, and she'd fuss and push me away."

"And you're still pining for her," Kylie teased.

Ryan threw back his head and laughed. "Not exactly. Oh, don't get me wrong, when they married on my sixteenth birthday, I felt as if she'd done it on purpose just to spite me."

"They seem to be very much in love."

"They are. I'm the children's godfather."

"That's really neat."

Kylie bit her lip when the waitress brought their pops. She felt comfortable with Ryan, yet weird at the same time. Physical, emotional, and spiritual attraction for him churned within her. Logic sent her mind into a tailspin.

"Ki, I have something for you."

"Ryan, it's your birthday and all you've done is buy for everyone else."

"I don't need anything, and this is more fun." He fumbled with the bag. "I hope you like it."

"You shouldn't have bought me anything. I was so mean the last time I saw you." She clasped her hands in her lap. "You're too nice."

"Probably why I've never married. You know what they say—girls don't like the nice guys." He shoved the bag closer to her. "Please take it."

"Smart girls do like nice guys, and they marry them, too." Embarrassment filled her when the statement slipped from her lips then smacked Kylie in the face. Was integrity worth more than stability? What was wrong with wanting both? Kylie dismissed the questions and lifted the tissue-wrapped object from the bag. Gingerly, she pulled off the paper and gazed at a yellow glass rose. "It's beautiful."

"The clerk said it meant peace and friendship, but she wasn't sure."

Kylie noted the nervousness etched in his voice.

"Friends?" She gazed into his eyes, searching them for honesty.

"I was thinking more along the lines of peace."

He wanted more than friendship. The truth of it was written all over his face. She couldn't take it anymore. "Ryan, are you a drug dealer?"

His eyes bulged and he frowned. "No."

"Did you win the lottery?"

"Never played in my life."

"Is your grandfather some wealthy landowner or businessman or something?"

He scrunched up his nose. "He's a retired military man. What are you getting at?"

"Where do you get your money? You buy presents for entire families. You take me out to eat and never let me pay. I don't understand."

She trailed the rose with her fingertips. "I worked all summer to pay for my gas and utilities and whatnot. I'm living off scholarships and loans, but for the life of me, I can't figure out what you're living off of."

Ryan took her hand. "Okay, the truth is—"

"Kylie, well, imagine seeing you here." Brad Dickson rubbed the top of her arm in a possessive, overly familiar manner. Kylie recoiled as Brad turned his attention to Ryan. "I forgot your name."

"Ryan Watkins." Ryan extended his hand to Brad, who acted as if he didn't notice and looked back at Kylie.

She swallowed, willing ugly, spiteful words away from her lips. She wanted to be a witness to the baboon. *Oh, God, help me see him as You do. Someone who needs You.* "Hello, Brad. Are you here with a date?"

"No. Business dinner." He touched her shoulder again, and Kylie shifted in her seat to make his hand fall. He looked at her in a way that made her feel uncomfortable. "Something I'm sure we'll have to do. . .often."

Ryan leaned across the table. "Well, Brad." His voice, laced with protection, sounded thick and strong. "We'll let you get back to your business."

Kylie gazed at Ryan. He'd always shown her nothing but respect. Even now he would allow nothing less from someone else. She looked back up at Brad. "Yes. I'll see you later."

Brad huffed and walked away without another word. Kylie smiled at Ryan. She couldn't deny it. She was falling for him, even without a job. "You were telling me that you weren't a drug dealer or a lottery winner or a—"

A shadow fell across Ryan's eyes. He shook his head. "I was just going to say God always provides."

"Yes, He does, but that still doesn't tell me how you bought all these things. Did someone give you money for your birthday?"

"Please, just believe me when I tell you I'm not a criminal. My life is surrendered to God and His work."

Kylie peered into Ryan's eyes. She knew he spoke the truth, but it still didn't make sense. And in her thinking, things had to make sense.

"I was going to tell her, God. It was right on the tip of my tongue when Brad Dickson interrupted us." Ryan walked in his front door and slammed it shut. "The way he looked at Kylie. God, how can she even speak to him? He's a snake."

"What?" Gramps walked into the room. "You saw a snake?"

"Sure did," Ryan growled under his breath then looked up at his grandfather. "No. There're no snakes out there."

"Good." Gramps shuddered. "I hate them slithering creatures."

Ryan laughed when Brad's face came to mind. "I'm not too fond of them, either."

Chapter 13

Kylie twirled her pencil as Professor Nickels passed out their graded exams. Though she'd studied for a solid day before, the test had been more difficult than she expected. Too much of her time over the last few weeks had been spent planning the Belize trip.

I know I did well on the essays. They were simple enough, but the multiple-choice section was killer, and it was worth half. Nickels passed by her the fourth time but still didn't give her the test. She laid her pencil down and bit her lip. There can't be that many left. He ambled toward her and finally laid her test facedown.

"I can handle a C," she whispered to herself. "My grades are high enough that I could still pull off the B." Closing her eyes, she turned the paper over. She peeked open one eye and shut it tight again. "No."

Flipping her test facedown again, she gazed at the board where Professor Nickels wrote the results of the test: 3 As. 4 Bs. 12 Cs. 8 Ds. 3 Fs. "It's not possible."

She turned it back over and stared at the oversize, red F. "There has to be some mistake." Skimming the first page, she hadn't missed any of the multiple-choice questions. She turned the page, noting two questions she'd missed. The third page revealed one wrong answer. She flipped to the essay questions. In bright red, the words "Answer irrelevant to question" screamed at her. "Lacks supporting details" blared from the next essay.

"He's failed me on my essays." She scoured the questions and her answers to both. Digging through her folder, she found the notes she'd taken applying to both questions. "These are good answers. Solid."

Through her peripheral vision, she saw fellow students leave their seats. Nickels must have dismissed class, but Kylie couldn't move. She yanked her calculator from her purse and tallied her grades. An F on this test gave her a high C in the class. It wasn't possible. It wasn't fair. Her answers were well thought out, well written. Nickels had some sort of vendetta against her that she didn't understand.

A briefcase shut, drawing her attention. Nickels walked toward the door. *I have to talk to him about this.* She swallowed, dreading any kind of confrontation.

"Professor Nickels." She stood and met him by the door. "Can I ask you about my test?"

"I wouldn't be able to say if you can."

Kylie sighed, feeling as if her second-grade teacher had just reprimanded her. "May I speak with you about my test?"

He nodded. "Yes, you may."

"I don't understand why my essay grades are so low." She pulled out her notes. "My answers look very much like the notes I took from your presentation."

"You didn't explain yourself well. Look." He pointed to his personal scribbling. "I told you, you lacked details."

Kylie cleared her throat. She had no intention of being disrespectful, but something wasn't right. He'd taken too many points away. "Professor Nickels, you gave me almost no points, and I identified each area with a minimum of a paragraph of explanation."

"I can't help it that you have poor writing skills. I could not make heads or tails of your support. Besides, essays are subjective."

Kylie gawked at him. It was personal. There was nothing she could say to him, probably nothing she could do to get the grade she needed from this class, except go to administration. She wasn't sure she had the desire to do that. "I'm sorry I took up your time." Kylie headed out the door.

"I hear you have an offer from Miller Enterprises."

Kylie turned on her heel. "Yes, I do."

"That's quite an accomplishment for a soon-to-be grad. Most new accountants start out working for a small business, doing some income tax work and whatnot. Miller handles several upstanding business accounts."

"I agree. It's my dream job."

He lowered his head, peering at her from above his bifocals. "You're not ready for that."

Kylie straightened her shoulders. "I will work hard for them. Give my best."

"Hard work is a good thing, but you don't have what it takes, Kylie Andrews."

Kylie stared at him. His disdain evident, she had no idea what caused it. "I hope your personal beliefs have nothing to do with my grade."

He lifted his head and pushed his glasses up on his nose.

Kylie pivoted toward the door. "I'll see you Monday, Professor Nickels."

❧

"I've never seen you two before. Are you new to the community?" Gramps asked the older woman and young, pregnant lady as Ryan placed canned beans in the cart.

"We're not really from around here—a county over. My husband worked in the coal mines. He's gotten sick with black lung. His disability will start in a month or so, but we need to take what the Good Lord provides until it starts."

Ryan took in the woman's salt-and-pepper hair. Her skin was wrinkled from age and what he suspected to be a hard life, but her eyes shone with laughter and happiness.

"I'm just here to help Mama." The obviously pregnant younger woman smiled. Her light-colored, straight hair reminded Ryan of Kylie's. Her eyes kind of did, as well.

"Well, we're glad to help," said Gramps. "How is your husband?"

"He's doing well. Rests quite a bit but picks up his energy whenever the grandbabies come around."

"How many grandbabies do you have?"

"We have four grandsons and three babies on the way. Amanda, here, is giving us twins." She laughed and her face lit up. "I'm hoping for at least one granddaughter. I'm anxious to buy a dress or two."

"Sounds like you have a wonderful family." Gramps pushed the cart toward the refrigerated items.

"Oh yes, Jesus blessed us with eight children, and every one of them is serving Him."

Ryan perked up. Eight children? And this pregnant lady looks a lot like Kylie.

The woman continued, "My third daughter is getting ready to graduate from the University of Evansville, then she's heading on a missions trip in January."

Gramps smiled. "My grandson is going to Belize in January."

The woman peered up at Ryan. "Belize is where my girl is going."

Ryan cleared his throat. "What did you say your name was, ma'am?"

"I'm Lorma Andrews. This is my daughter, Amanda."

"Andrews?" Gramps smacked the counter and grinned. "Is your daughter Kylie?"

"Yes."

"Well, it's a small world after all. Ryan and I know Kylie. She's been going to our church since she and her friend moved near Santa Claus. We've had dinner with her a few times. Ryan worked with her at Holiday World." He looked at Ryan and winked. "Special girl, wouldn't you say?"

"Are you Ryan Watkins?" asked Amanda.

A shot of excitement zipped through his veins. Kylie had talked to her family about him. "Yes."

"You're the Ryan my Kylie talked about?" Lorma Andrews poked Amanda's arm. "What time is it, dear?"

"Eleven thirty."

"Amanda and I brought some lunch for the trip over here. I'd love it if you two would join us."

"We've got turkey and ham sandwiches, potato chips, and sliced veggies. Pickles and homemade chocolate cake, too," Amanda added.

Gramps rubbed his stomach. "Sounds wonderful. We'll be happy to join you, but our lunch doesn't start until twelve."

"That'll be fine. Amanda and I will get it all set up on that picnic table I saw around back."

Ryan carried the cooler to the table for Mrs. Andrews and Amanda to set up their lunch, then he busied himself with stocking the shelves and breaking down boxes. Half an hour seemed to never pass. He could hardly wait to learn more about Kylie's family.

At twelve exactly, Ryan and Gramps headed out to the picnic table. Ryan filled his plate then bit into his sandwich. "This is wonderful."

Gramps wiped his mouth. "Best lunch we've had in a while."

"Thank you." Mrs. Andrews smiled then took a bite of her pickle.

Gramps elbowed Ryan then cleared his throat. "Ryan and I adore Kylie. Tell us about your family."

"Well, my oldest is Sabrina. She's married to our high-school principal. They have three sons. Next is Natalie. Husband's a coal truck driver. They have a son and another on the way. Then there's Kylie. Then Amanda here, whose husband works in the coal mines, too. I told you she's having twins. Next is our first boy."

She laughed. "Took us five times to get us a son; now I can't seem to get any granddaughters. Anyway, Dalton's next. He and Kylie love to argue. When they were little they'd wrestle around on the floor until something was broke or spilled."

Her eyes glazed at the memories. "Then we have Gideon. He's getting ready to go to Indiana University; wants to work in agriculture. Last, we have the twins, Cameron and Chloe. Chloe might as well have been a boy. She loves to run and tumble and fight with them. I guess that's what happens when your sisters are all several years older and your brothers are about the same age. She was just selected to a special soccer team."

"Sounds like a lot of fun." Ryan raked his fingers through his hair. "I didn't have any brothers or sisters."

"God blessed us with a full home." She patted Ryan's hand. "Maybe He'll give you a passel of kids of your own to raise someday."

Ryan envisioned several stair-stepped, blond-haired girls and boys scampering around his front porch. Kylie sat in a rocking chair, cuddling another over her shoulder. His heart warmed. "Maybe."

They continued to share until it was time for Gramps and Ryan to reopen God's Pantry. Mrs. Andrews walked around the picnic table and wrapped Ryan in an embrace. "It was nice to meet you. I need you to do me a favor."

"Sure."

"Don't tell Kylie we were here. She worries herself sick over her daddy and me. I try to tell her God always provides, but Kylie's a fixer. She loves Jesus with all her heart, but she wants to take care of things."

"Yes, I know."

"I bet you do." Lorma Andrews studied him for a moment then patted his hand. "Hang in there. We're praying."

❦

Robin flipped through pages of the bridal magazine. "You know you could complain to administration."

"I know." Kylie replayed Professor Nickels's words in her mind. He said what she'd been feeling—"not ready." All through college she'd been on fire to get her degree—single-minded, focused. Now she was confused. Her passion had waned. She felt drawn to something different.

Gazing at Robin as she wrote down different menu options, Kylie picked up her test once more and scowled at it. "I'm just tired because the end is getting close."

Robin slipped out a photo from inside her purse. "Look, I took a picture of Bransom in the tux he's going to wear."

Kylie grinned at the small, dark-haired boy who looked so much like Tyler. Robin knelt beside him with one arm around him and both hands cupping his shoulders. His head was tilted as he focused on his soon-to-be mother. The image tugged at Kylie's heartstrings.

She knew her pursuit to get her degree was a good one. Her heart had been in the right place—at least she thought it had been. But that little slip of paper from the University of Evansville had been her sole purpose for more than three years. Lately, she longed for more.

"He's adorable, Robin." She handed the photo back to her friend. She lifted her exam. "I'm going to put this away and get my pj's on."

Once in her room, Kylie plopped the exam on her dresser and knelt next to her bed. "God, I'm confused. I can hardly fathom that I've spent this long doing the wrong thing when I've always tried to seek You. But it's Your will I want, not my own. Show me, Jesus. Give me strength no matter what that means."

Her cell phone rang. Kylie picked it up and read Candy's number in the window. She pushed the TALK button. "Hello."

"Hi, Kylie," Candy's voice sang over the line. "I wanted to ask you about interviewing for the missions ministry position."

"There's a missions ministry position?"

"It's going to be a new job—the only paid position the ministry will have. Whoever gets the job will keep track of missions trip dates, the travel fares, the accommodations, and other stuff. He or she will keep the books, as well as stay on top of what needs to be bought or collected from different churches or locations, keep up with volunteers—just a whole bunch of stuff."

Kylie bit her bottom lip. "It sounds interesting." She and Robin had only joined the church as members about a month ago, and now she was being asked to interview for a paying position.

"And you'd be more than qualified. . . ."

Chapter 14

Kylie had no idea what she was doing. After walking into Candy's family room, she peeked around the dining room door and saw all five of the missions ministry's leaders sitting in a semicircle around a lone chair. Hers, she presumed. They chatted amongst themselves and hadn't realized she'd arrived. "I'm so glad you accepted the interview," Candy whispered behind her.

"I can't believe I'm here," Kylie whispered to her new friend. Baby Suzanna cackled and kicked her legs. Kylie tickled the baby's chin and heightened her voice. "I've already got a job, don't I, Suzanna? Yes, I do."

Suzanna wiggled in her mother's arms, and Candy kissed her head. "Sometimes what we think we're supposed to have isn't what's meant for us at all. God has a different plan."

Kylie took a deep breath. "That's what Ryan said when he told me about you and Michael adopting Suzanna."

"You know, if we'd had a biological child, we probably would have never gotten Suzanna." She cradled the child closer to her chest. "And what a blessing we would have missed."

Kylie allowed Candy's words to seep into her heart. Ryan. The man had infiltrated her every waking, even sometimes sleeping, thoughts. He touched her to the very core of her being. She adored him. Heat rushed to her cheeks as she remembered how she'd drilled him about money at dinner the other night. She didn't understand it, and she needed to—desperately. Her head had to believe he could provide for her, because her heart didn't seem to care.

Clearing her mind, she pushed the dining room door open all the way and walked inside. She nodded at the ministry leaders and sat in her seat. "It's nice to see you all today."

Pastor Chambers smiled and scratched his nose. "We're glad you're here." He leaned back in his chair and drummed his fingers across his potbelly. The vision almost sent Kylie into a fit of giggles—she'd watched her pregnant sisters do the same thing. "Kylie, we understand you've already been offered a position at Miller Enterprises."

"Yes, that's true." *And it's a great position,* she wanted to add. Any accounting major would be ecstatic knowing Mr. Miller had even looked at his or her résumé and overwhelmed to be considered for an interview, but to actually get the job? It was unheard-of.

"But you're willing to consider interviewing with us?" asked Pastor Foster. He pressed his fingers against his overgrown eyebrows. Being color-blind and unmarried, Pastor Foster's clothes rarely coordinated. Today was no different. He wore a pair of khaki-colored dress slacks, a nearly lime green dress shirt, and a deep red tie with a black paisley design. Sometimes she thought he mismatched his clothes on purpose as a means to get people look at him, at which point he'd run up and introduce himself. She loved his personality, the way he didn't mind what people thought of his appearance.

She crossed her legs. "I guess I am willing to interview. I'll be honest with you; I'm not sure why I accepted. The position at Miller Enterprises is one I've always wanted." She uncrossed her legs and flattened her hands against her thighs. She didn't want to sound ungrateful, but she wanted to be truthful. It wouldn't make any sense for her to take a different job offer. She looked at the leaders sitting across from her. "When Candy asked me to come, I—I just felt I should."

Pastor Chambers bent over and picked up a folder. "We'll level with you. This is a full-time position, but the pay is probably substantially less than what you've been offered. Volunteers have kept the business and accounting aspects of our missions running, but it's becoming too big of a job." He handed her the folder. "Look it over."

Kylie opened it and looked at the job's duties. Everything seemed within reason. In fact, she wondered if the position really would require a forty-hour workweek. She flipped the page to find the salary and benefits. It was almost half what she'd been offered from Miller.

The logical response was to decline. Now. Before she left. Before she even got up from her seat. Yet, she paused. The income was enough for her to live modestly, and she'd have time to spend with her family. She longed to see them more, to hold her nephews and maybe one day soon her nieces, to cherish the last bit of time she'd have with her daddy. The last few family get-togethers they'd shared had been a lot of fun. She felt close to her siblings again, in the same way she had when they were little.

Looking up at the ministry leaders, she thought of how easy it would be to work with these men and women. Ease at the office was not something she expected at Miller's. She shut the folder and held it to her chest. "May I pray about this for a few days?"

Pastor Chambers grinned. "Absolutely. You didn't join our church until God showed you the time was right." He paused. "Tell you what. I'll give you a call in two weeks. We're not in a rush, and we want you to be sure of your decision."

"Thank you."

Glad Kylie had agreed to go with him to help take care of his godchildren while their parents went on their date, Ryan glanced at Kylie in the passenger seat then looked in the rearview mirror at Evan, Dana, and Heidi. Kylie had no idea what he had planned for the day. Simply telling her to wear tennis shoes and something comfortable for outside, he'd hoped it would be a surprise for her as well as the kids. Now he wasn't sure he should have kept it a secret. The day would be quite eventful—and exhausting.

He turned onto the road leading to Holiday World. Signs greeted them from every side. Kylie looked at him. "Are we—"

"We're going to Holiday World!" Evan shouted from the backseat. "Ryan, thank you, thank you, thank you."

"I've never been to Holiday World." Dana's eyes grew big with excitement. "Mommy said I'll get to go one day soon enough, when I'm in fifth grade. That's when the school—"

"What Howiday Word?" Heidi asked from the backseat.

Ryan pulled into the parking lot and turned off the car. He turned toward Kylie. "Are you okay with this?"

A full grin lit her face. "This will be great."

Relief flooded his heart as he turned toward the children. "Now, you know it's October. That means Splashin' Safari is closed."

"What Spashin' Sari?" Heidi asked.

Evan leaned toward her. "The water rides."

Ryan nodded. "Yes, but we'll still be able to get on the other rides."

They filed out of the car and walked toward the entrance. Through peripheral vision, Ryan watched as Kylie scooped Heidi into her arms so the girl wouldn't have to walk as far. *I never even thought of bringing a stroller. We'll just rent one.*

"Can we ride the Raven first?" Evan rubbed his hands together as they entered the park.

"What's the Raven?" asked Dana.

"It's the best roller coaster in the whole world," Evan proclaimed. "Can we?"

"That sounds fine with me. First, let's rent a stroller." Ryan looked at Kylie. She smiled and nodded in agreement.

Moments later, Kylie strapped Heidi into her stroller, and they headed toward the roller coaster.

"Look." Dana pointed toward the dog character with HOLIDAY WORLD written on his chest and on a blue cap that sat on his head. She clutched Ryan's hand.

"That's the park's mascot. His name is Holidog. You want to go say hello to him?"

Dana's voice quieted. "I—I guess."

Ryan motioned for Holidog. As the character ambled closer, Heidi broke out into screams of terror. Stunned, Ryan watched as Kylie turned her away and unbuckled her from the stroller. Within a moment, Kylie had Heidi out and nestled against her chest. Kylie whispered quiet words of comfort to the child.

Dana gripped Ryan's hand and half hid behind his leg. He hadn't been prepared for this. Evan saved him when he shook Holidog's hand and said, "See, Dana. See, Heidi. He's nice."

A hesitant smile lifted Dana's lips as she gripped Ryan's leg with one hand and shook Holidog's hand with the other.

"You want to say hi?" Kylie asked Heidi, but the child shook her head and wrapped her arms around Kylie's neck. "Okay." Kylie's voice was soothing as she stroked Heidi's hair. "That's okay. You can stay right here with me."

Ryan's heart nearly burst with adoration for the woman as they walked away. She knew exactly what to say, what to do to calm Heidi. A natural love for his godchild spilled from within her. She'd make a wonderful mother.

The hours passed, and Kylie still held Heidi everywhere they went. The poor child was completely overwhelmed by all there was to do and see at Holiday World. Dana relished riding the Hallow Swings. Evan had even convinced her to ride the Legend roller coaster as she just made the height cutoff, but Heidi remained as close to Kylie as her little body could get. After enjoying pizza for dinner, Ryan took them to the souvenir shop and let the children pick out a candy and toy. To his surprise, Heidi selected a stuffed Holidog. She gripped it in her hand and nestled back into Kylie's chest.

Walking back to the car, Ryan wondered what Kylie thought. She had to be exhausted. Heidi wouldn't let him take her, though he'd tried many times. He knew Kylie's arms had to ache. After Evan helped secure Dana's seat belt then latched his own, Ryan watched as Kylie lowered Heidi into her car seat and fastened it. Kylie slid into the passenger seat, laid her head back, and closed her eyes. *What was I thinking taking the children to Holiday World? I've worn Kylie to the bone. She'll never want to do anything like this again.*

He drove to the Nelsons' house and stopped the car. Evan and Dana jumped out of the back and raced inside, yelling about the great day they'd had. Kylie stepped out of the car and unbuckled a sleeping Heidi. She picked her up and nestled the girl into her shoulder. After kissing her cheek, she handed Heidi to Melissa, then got back into the car.

"Thanks for taking them." Melissa smiled at Ryan.

"Did you and Neal have fun?"

"We had a great time. You're too good, Ryan Watkins." She kissed his cheek. "I better take this girl inside. She's plumb tuckered out."

"Yes, she is." Ryan got into the car. He looked at Kylie. *That one is plumb tuckered out, too.* He drove to her apartment. Silence filled the car. Peeking at her, he noticed her head resting against the window, her eyes closed. *I've killed her, Lord. I should have told her my plans, given her the chance to say it would be too hard of a day.* He pulled into the parking space and turned off the car.

He gently touched her cheek. "We're here, Ki."

Her eyes fluttered open and she inhaled a long breath. "I'm sorry. I must have fallen asleep."

"No, I'm sorry. I should have told you where we were going. I never dreamed Heidi would—"

Kylie placed her hand on his. A single tear slipped down her cheek. "That was the best day I've had in a long time. Thank you for taking me."

Stunned, Ryan watched as she opened the door and made her way to her apartment. She waved and then slipped inside and shut the door.

<hr>

Kylie fell onto the couch in utter exhaustion. She allowed the tears to fall down her cheeks as the sweet smell of Heidi lingered about her. She could still feel the girl's embrace about her neck. Probably had the marks to prove it. *God, I've missed so much with my family, with my own nephews. I've been so preoccupied. Give me the chance to love on them. To go to the park. To read them a story. To hold them and tell them how much they mean to me.*

The folder from the ministry leaders lay on the coffee table in front of her. Her heart screamed to take the position. She'd have time to spend with her family, but what about Miller Enterprises? It was her dream, her means to help her family. Surely it was God Himself who'd provided her with the position. She sat up and kicked off her shoes. Yes, she was just being emotional. She was tired from the long day. Without a doubt, God had blessed her with a wonderful opportunity and the perfect job.

Chapter 15

After several knocks, Kylie opened the front door. Wearing a pinstriped brown suit and yellow silk tie, Brad smiled down at her. She'd pegged him sly as a fox, but there was no denying he'd been hit by the handsome stick.

"Kylie, you look surprised to see me."

"I am. You know where I live?"

Brad smirked. "It would be on the résumé." His gaze roamed up and down her body. "Cleaning today?"

Feeling violated, Kylie squinted as her lips formed a straight line. She tugged the bottom of her white T-shirt farther down her jean shorts. "No. As a matter of fact, I'm getting ready to go to an informal meeting."

"'Informal' being the key word." He snorted and tilted his head to look past her and into her apartment. "Good manners would insist you invite me in."

"No." Kylie stepped outside and shut the door behind her. "Not necessarily. Especially not when the weather is as lovely as it is right now and we have two comfortable chairs to sit in and enjoy it." Kylie sat in one of the lawn chairs on the apartment's small front porch. She motioned for Brad to sit in the other. "Now, to what do I owe the privilege of this visit?"

He dusted the chair's seat, then sat. "All right then." He clasped his hands. "Miller's been trying to get in touch with you for a week."

"He has? My answering machine's been giving me fits. One moment it works, the next it doesn't."

"Well, he planned to cancel a meeting to make a trip over here, but I told him not to worry. I could handle this."

Queasiness churned inside her. "What's up?"

He handed her a memo. "It seems the position you were hired for isn't needed."

Kylie tried to skim the content. Heaviness filled her heart, and tears welled in her eyes. She took long breaths to hold her emotions at bay in front of Brad. Standing, she lifted her chin and extended her hand. "Thank you for coming personally."

He stood and took her hand. "That's the breaks, kid." He winked, turned, and walked toward his car.

Kylie stepped inside the apartment. After shutting the door, she leaned against it and allowed the dam inside her to crumble. *I guess You're telling me to take the job at the ministry, God. I thought I was keeping the one at Miller's.*

Arms full of Chinese takeout, Ryan kicked Kylie's front door with his foot. His heart had plunged when she'd called him crying, saying she couldn't attend the missions meeting. He couldn't make heads or tails of her reason. He could only distinguish the word "Brad."

If there was a person on the planet Ryan felt distrust for, it would be Brad Dickson. Christian feelings did not surface when Ryan thought of that man. The fact that Brad often sweet-talked Kylie didn't help matters.

Kylie opened the door. Her eyes, bloodshot and swollen from crying, glanced at his packages. She sniffed and offered a weak smile. "Come on in, Ryan."

He set the bags on the table, then pulled out a box. "I've got sweet-and-sour chicken, sweet-and-sour pork, some General Tso's, two kinds of rice, crab rangoons. . ."

Kylie rested her hand on his. "Thanks, Ryan." She disappeared into the kitchen and returned with two plates, forks, and cans of pop. They filled their plates. "Let's go sit on the couch."

Ryan picked up his drink with his free hand and followed Kylie. They ate in silence except for Kylie's occasional sniff. Ryan peeked at her, unsure what to say and when to say it. He took another bite and swallowed. She sniffed. He couldn't take it anymore. "You want to talk about it, Ki?"

She let out a long breath. "I don't have a job in January."

Ryan laid his plate on the coffee table and scooted closer to her. He wrapped his arm around her shoulder. "I'm sorry."

Tears formed and spilled quickly from her eyes. "It was the perfect job, and Miller sent Brad over here to tell me. Mr. Hoity-Toity himself."

"I thought you liked Brad."

Kylie scrunched up her face. "Ugh. He's an uppity snob if ever there was one." Kylie's expression loosened. "I shouldn't have said that. I try to pray for him. He just makes me so—so mad."

Ryan scratched his jaw. Here, he'd believed Kylie liked Brad, but if he thought about it, Kylie never flirted. She was polite, courteous, but she didn't lead Brad on. He peered at the woman beside him. She wasn't like Brad or Vanessa. She was goal-driven, determined, but she wasn't money hungry.

Deep down, he knew that. His own fears of not being accepted for himself had kept him from seeing Kylie for the woman she was. *What a fool I am.*

"Thanks for the Chinese, Ryan." Kylie interrupted his revelation. She looked at her watch. "The meeting starts in about twenty minutes."

"You feel up to going?"

Kylie shook her head. "I think I'll stay home tonight."

"You want me to stay with you? We can rent a funny movie or just hang out."

"No. You go." She picked up her Bible from the shelf under the coffee table. "I think I'm going to spend some time in this tonight."

Ryan stood and kissed her forehead. "I'll be praying for you."

Kylie opened her Bible. A slip of paper fell onto her lap. "It's the verse from the singles' fellowship." She read it. " 'He who pursues righteousness and love finds life, prosperity and honor,' Proverbs 21:21."

The phone rang, and she laid the paper and the Bible on the coffee table. She answered the call, and a man with the invitation company asked to speak with Robin. "She's not here right now, but I'll tell her you called."

Kylie laid down the phone, then started to clear the table. The proverb swam through her mind. Life, prosperity, and honor—she'd wanted them since she was a small girl.

She wanted a life free of financial worry. Her mother always said she was silly and too sensitive, but Kylie hated feeling bad for asking her parents for money for a movie or for a snack after school. She knew everything she asked for would be a hardship for them. Sure, her sisters and brothers didn't seem to have qualms about asking, but Kylie didn't want to add any strife.

Prosperity. Her parents never had it, but God had given Kylie a smart mind. She was a clear thinker; school came easy to her, especially math. "I know writing isn't my strength." She opened the refrigerator and stuck the leftovers inside. "But despite what Professor Nickels thinks, I won an award in high school for my persuasive letter about the dangers of strip-mining, and I did well in all my college English classes." No, her parents had never prospered, but God had given Kylie the necessary talents to help her family.

Her mother's eyes, gleaming with pride when Amanda announced she was having twins, slipped into Kylie's thoughts. A vision of her daddy hugging Mama and thanking her for supper followed swiftly behind. They'd always said God had blessed them beyond measure. Kylie never quite understood them.

And honor. If she had anything to do with it, Kylie would never have a child of hers receive a free lunch. Her son would never be sponsored for field trips or extracurricular sports. Her daughter would never wear someone else's prom dress. Instead, Kylie would be the one to give those things to someone who needed it. She'd pay back all that she'd received as a child. "Isn't that what God calls us to do? When we've been given, we pull ourselves up, and then give more than we've received."

Something sounded wrong with her words. They felt funny. She couldn't put her finger on it. After throwing the food wrappers in the trash, she scraped the plates and placed them in the dishwasher. She wiped off the counters, then grabbed a bottle of water from the refrigerator and headed back to the couch.

She picked up the slip of paper and read it again. "'He who pursues righteousness and love finds life, prosperity and honor,' Proverbs 21:21." Flipping to the reference in her Bible, she added, "My reasons for working hard have always been driven by righteousness and love. I don't know why this verse keeps tripping me up."

Kylie devoured the chapter. Each verse, a nugget of wisdom from Solomon, spoke of many things from the wicked to the mocker to the ill-tempered wife. Verse two pricked her heart and she read it again. "All a man's ways seem right to him, but the LORD weighs the heart."

"My ways seem right to me, Lord." She gazed out her window, past the parking area, past the other homes, and toward the horizon. The land was flat, but she could see the tips of trees in the distance. A clear, blue sky blanketed their tops. "What is the weight of my heart, Lord?"

Her parents, her siblings, they seemed to line up in her soul, displaying their peace in good times and bad times. The Nelsons, gracious and thankful, spilled into her mind. Contentment gleamed from their faces.

Sweet, kind Ryan flooded her thoughts. She had no idea where he got his means, but he always gave of all he had. His heart overflowed with generosity. She relished every moment with him. He never despaired over financial gain, for right or wrong reasons.

It wasn't financial stability they needed. It was God, plain and simple. Their walk with the Lord made them rich, not poor. Proverbs 22:2 screamed at her from the page. "Rich and poor have this in common: The LORD is the Maker of them all."

Kylie fell to her knees in front of the couch. "Forgive me, Jesus. My pursuit has been my own. In my pride and self-centeredness, I let the world's standards dictate my worth. I have been a fool."

A tear, warm and refreshing, slipped down her cheek. She clasped her hands and lifted her eyes toward the ceiling. "My life belongs to You. My past. My present. My future. In poverty or wealth or somewhere in between, I don't want to live another moment concerned about the wealth of this world."

Scriptures from Matthew filled her. "God, I don't want to store up treasures from this earth. You are my treasure, Lord. Weigh my heart, and find me full of You."

She stood, walked to her room, and grabbed her cell phone from the shelf. Searching her directory, she found Candy's number then pushed it. Candy's voice sang, "Hello," over the line. Kylie inhaled as peace enveloped her soul. "Candy, I'm going to take that position with the ministry."

Chapter 16

Ryan couldn't get Kylie off his mind as he stocked cans of green beans and corn on the shelves at God's Pantry. She'd changed over the last few weeks. Eager to raise money for the missions trip, she'd participated in a bake sale and a parents' night out with members of the team. Her eyes danced, and smiles warmed her lips on a regular basis, and Ryan longed to be with her more. He'd been watching for the right time to tell her about his reasons for not working, but he hadn't had a moment alone with her.

Welcoming a couple, Gramps opened the door, and a gust of cool November wind swept through the small building. "Awful cold to not even be Thanksgiving," Gramps's voice boomed.

"Sure is," a man responded.

"Hello. How are you?"

A familiar female voice said, "Did your grandson come today?"

Ryan strolled down the aisle to find Kylie's mom and a man standing beside Gramps. "Mrs. Andrews, it's so good to see you again." Ryan extended his hand. She grabbed him in a hug instead.

"It's good to see you, too. This is my husband, Richard." She patted the man's shoulder.

"You must be Ryan." Mr. Andrews shook his hand, then turned his head to cough. The slump in his shoulders gave away his fatigue and illness. Ryan could tell he'd been a strong man, but black lung was taking its toll on him. He stopped coughing and looked back at Ryan. "Lorma can't seem to stop talking about you."

"How's Kylie?" she asked. "We seem to be playing phone tag."

"She's great. Working hard to raise money for the missions trip and going to school."

"The last I talked to her, she found out she wasn't getting that job she wanted. We've been praying for her." Mrs. Andrews clucked her tongue. "Kylie worries something fierce over having things all laid out nice."

Mr. Andrews cleared his throat. "Life just isn't always like that. Praise the Lord, He's in charge."

"Amen to that." Gramps patted Richard's back.

Mrs. Andrews handed a sack to Ryan. "We came to give back the cans and boxed foods we didn't use."

"You didn't need to do that." Ryan tried to hand it back to her.

She lifted her hand. "No. The good Lord blesses us with what we need each time we need it. Richard's disability checks are coming in now."

"That's right," Mr. Andrews interrupted. He reached into his shirt pocket and pulled out a check. "There's a time to give and a time to receive. We needed to receive from this pantry for a while. Now God's allowing us to give a bit back."

"You're a wonderful couple." Gramps accepted the check.

"I'd like to ask one thing in return." Mrs. Andrews looked up at Ryan. "Can I have another hug?"

Ryan laughed as he leaned down and embraced the older woman. She whispered, "Take care of my Kylie."

"Always." He released her, and she smiled and nodded her head.

Ryan watched as the couple made their way to their car. Though Mrs. Andrews was the driver, her husband opened the door for her and then walked to the passenger side. She leaned over and kissed his cheek before buckling her seat belt and starting the car.

"Kylie has a great family," said Gramps as he sat to write down the donation in the ledger.

"Yes, she does."

"Did you notice that Richard's coat has seen better days?" A sparkle lit Gramps's eyes.

"You know, Gramps, I hadn't noticed, but now that you mention it, Mrs. Andrews's coat wasn't in too great of shape, either."

"Hmm." Gramps hunched over the desk and calculated some numbers.

Ryan pushed a cart filled with laundry detergents that needed to be placed on the shelf. "We'll just have to take care of that."

⤸⤷

"God," Kylie mumbled, "I'm trusting in You." She arranged the Christmas-colored hair bows on the table for the craft bazaar. Having raised only a third of the money she needed for the missions trip, Kylie was depending on a good turnout today to even consider making the missions trip.

"Hey, Ki." Ryan walked toward her, his arms weighed down with wooden poles.

"What are these?" Kylie took a couple from his hands.

"They're Christmas poles to put in your front yard." He grabbed one. "This one's for you."

Kylie looked at the pole painted white. At the top was a piece of red-painted wood that stuck out like a street sign, reading KYLIE'S KOTTAGE. A smiling cardinal sat perched on top, wearing a Santa's hat.

"This is adorable."

"Thanks. Gramps and I love to make them."

"How much are you selling them for?"

Ryan scratched his jaw. "I haven't thought about it."

"Haven't thought about it?" Kylie furrowed her eyebrows. "Aren't you worried at all about raising enough money for the trip?"

"Not really. You see, I need to talk to you—"

"We open the doors in five minutes." Candy scanned the room. "Is everyone ready?"

"Sure are!" a man yelled.

Kylie poked Ryan's arm. "You were saying?"

Ryan furrowed his eyebrows, looked at his poles, and mumbled, "It's never the right time."

"Right time for what?"

"Oh, nothing. I don't worry about the money. God's already provided." Ryan stared into Kylie's eyes as if he were trying to tell her something.

Kylie squelched the urge to rationalize and crunch numbers in her head. She knew God used practical means. She'd also learned He cared more about the heart than the way the money was provided. Her heart had no doubt. For this missions trip, God wanted her to trust Him. She smiled. "You're right."

Kylie placed her signs displaying the cost in front of the different-sized bows. She counted her change drawer one last time.

Customers filtered into the building. A woman with two daughters walked to her table. "These are pretty, Mom." The younger, dark-haired girl touched one of the nicer, silk ribbon bows.

"They are adorable." She picked up several. "I'll take all of these."

Kylie quoted her price, placed the hair bows in a bag, then took the money. "Thank you so much."

The woman moved toward Ryan's side of the table. "This is so cute." She picked up a pole similar to Kylie's except it had four cardinals on top of the sign.

"Look." The older, red-haired girl pointed to the birds. "It's a daddy, a mommy, and two kids. It's just like us."

"Yes, I believe you're right." Ryan picked up the pole. "How 'bout if I do this?"

Kylie watched as Ryan picked up a paintbrush, dipped it in green, then painted a bow on the mother cardinal and the two smaller birds.

"Now, they're girl kids." Ryan laid down the smaller brush and picked up a bigger one. "What's your last name?"

"Sims," the girls answered in unison.

Ryan painted the name on the sign and handed it to the mother. "Be careful. It won't be dry for a while."

"How much does it cost?" The woman reached into her purse.

"Not a thing." He winked at the girls. "Have fun."

Within moments, several people flooded their table, having heard the tall redhead was giving away free decorative poles. Ryan directed them to Kylie's side of the table as he personalized signs for different customers. Two hours before the bazaar ended, Kylie had sold every bow, and Ryan had given away all his signs.

"That was a productive day." Ryan closed his paints and wrapped his brushes.

"For me." Kylie shut and locked her money box. "Did you make anything?"

Ryan shrugged.

"Well?"

"No, but you sold all your bows."

Kylie studied Ryan. Not an ounce of concern for raising enough money etched his face. She now had enough to cover a little more than half the trip's expenses, but as far as she could tell, Ryan hadn't raised a penny.

He leaned closer. "If it makes you feel any better, Gramps and I always make those to give away. We love it."

A smile tugged at her lips. "God always provides for you."

"Every time." Ryan drew closer still until a wisp of his hair caressed her cheek. Her heart sped as goose bumps covered her skin. "Let's grab a burger."

She swallowed, unable to speak. If she tilted her head just slightly she'd be able to kiss him. The idea sent a wave of excitement through her veins. Instead, she nodded.

"Come on." He stood and grabbed her hand. "We're heading out, Candy."

She looked up from her table. "Out of stuff to sell?"

"Yep."

"Okay. See you later."

Kylie slipped into Ryan's car. The urge to kiss him still made her knees weak. She noted the stubble on his jaw and wondered at its roughness. His lips, probably soft, would contrast. . . . She shook her head. *What am I thinking?*

"You want a burger or a sit-down meal?"

"Oh, no." Kylie looked at her watch. "It's Saturday."

"Last time I checked."

"With the bazaar and all, I completely forgot. I'm supposed to try on my gown for Robin's wedding in an hour."

"Not a problem. We'll grab a burger and head over there."

"Thanks, Ryan."

Ryan tried to make himself comfortable in the boutique's stiff chair. The thing was small enough, he felt sure his over-six-foot, two-hundred-plus-pound frame would break it in pieces.

"Honey," the gray-haired woman with a tape measure draped around her neck called into the fitting room. "I'll be right back. I've got another customer who's ready for me to set up her alterations."

Ryan scanned the room. Dresses of every color and style hung from the walls. Several mannequins sported different ones, as well. Headpieces and shoes and other sparkly things sat in nearly every crevice of the shop. The place was completely overwhelming. He couldn't imagine anyone finding what they wanted.

"Where did the seamstress go?"

At the sound of Kylie's voice, Ryan turned toward her and sucked in his breath. The dark red dress, bare of straps, exposed her small neck and the curves of her collarbone. The material flowed down her frame, hugging her perfect shape. It looked soft, and he yearned to touch it. "Wow."

When her cheeks and neck flushed, Ryan knew his mouth gaped open. She was beautiful! Standing, he couldn't stop himself from walking to her. "I thought all eyes were supposed to be on the bride on her wedding day."

The crimson color on her skin deepened as she looked down.

Ryan cupped her chin in his hands. "I know I won't be able to take my eyes off you."

Not able to tear away from her eyes, he watched as her gaze traveled from his jaw to his mouth, up to his eyes, then back to his mouth. She lifted her lips, ever so slightly, and Ryan could take it no more. He lowered his mouth and claimed his first kiss. Her lips, soft and sweet, welcomed his.

Pulling away, Ryan swallowed the desire raging within him. He touched her cheek. "Oh, Ki, you are so beautiful."

"Okay, let's have a look at the dress," the seamstress's voice sounded from across the room. Ryan stepped away as the woman scurried toward them. "Oh, honey." The woman placed her hands on her hips. "That dress fits you like a glove. You're gorgeous."

"I'd say." Ryan sat back into the chair. All the stuff in the shop faded. Everything except Kylie.

Chapter 17

K ylie crept into her mother's kitchen. Mama, testing the turkey, was bent over with her head practically stuck inside the oven. Her oldest sister, Sabrina, peeled potatoes, her back facing the door. Amanda sat at the table, chopping celery. Kylie wrapped her arms around her younger sister. "Amanda, you are absolutely glowing."

The blond dropped her knife and gasped. "Kylie Andrews, you scared the life out of me." She stood, and Kylie's jaw dropped. Amanda punched her arm. "Hey, I am carrying twins."

"But you're huge!"

Amanda clamped her lips together and crossed her arms in front of her chest. "Mama!"

"Kylie." Her mother hustled over to her. "Women in the family way don't like to be addressed like that." She grinned. "Come here, and give your old mama a hug and a kiss."

"Yeah." Amanda stuck her tongue out, then smiled. "Wait 'til you see Natalie."

Natalie waddled into the kitchen, holding a casserole dish of banana pudding. She brushed a dark wisp of hair away from her cheek. "What about Natalie?"

Kylie reached out both hands and touched each sister's belly. "I don't know who's bigger."

"Har, har, spinster sister. Your day will come—eventually." Natalie smirked.

"Good one." Amanda gave her a high five.

"Mama, Amanda called me a spinster," Kylie squealed.

"Girls, you're acting like toddlers." Mama grabbed a dishrag and wiped her hands. "We've got work to do. Sabrina, Amanda, go back to your potatoes and celery. Kylie, you chop up some onion. Natalie, I want you to whip up those brownies."

Kylie grabbed a knife and a cutting board from the drawer. Grabbing an onion from the sink, she peeled off the outer layer and rinsed it. "Why did I get stuck with the onion?"

"Because Natalie and I will throw up," Amanda answered.

"Did you see Mama's new coat?" Sabrina asked, as she scraped potato shavings into the trash can. "It's the nicest thing I've ever seen."

"Your daddy got one, too." Mama scurried out of the kitchen like a child on Christmas morning. When she returned, she carried in one hand a long, chocolate-colored London Fog trench coat with a thick, plush lining. A full-length, lined, navy coat with a multicolored matching scarf hung from the hanger in her other hand.

"They are beautiful." Kylie fingered the soft material. "Where'd you get them?"

"We don't know. The pastor said someone bought them for us. He couldn't say who."

Bile rose in Kylie's throat. Charity. She hated when people felt sorry for them. If she'd been able to have that job at Miller Enterprises, her parents would have never wanted for anything again.

"I better put these away before we get food on them." Mama walked out of the kitchen.

"We hoped you'd have a guest with you this year," said Natalie.

"Yeah, all this talk about some man. What was his name?" asked Sabrina.

"Ryan," said Mama as she walked back into the kitchen.

Talking about Ryan lifted her spirits some. "I thought about inviting him." Goose bumps covered Kylie's arms when she thought of the last time she'd seen Ryan. At the boutique. She'd never felt so scared and alive all at the same time. Her reaction to his kiss had surprised her.

"Why didn't you?" asked Mama.

"I don't know." Kylie walked to the sink for another onion. "Mama, there's no more in the sink."

"There's some in the drawer of the fridge."

Kylie opened the refrigerator. "Uh-oh, Mama. Someone's been in your deviled eggs."

Mama jumped up and hustled to Kylie. "That daddy of yours. He can't ever wait until suppertime. Richard!"

Dalton ran into the kitchen, his face white as an eggshell. "Mama, come quick!"

"What is it?"

"It's Daddy."

Kylie followed her mother and sisters to the living room. Her daddy sat in his brown chair, gasping for breath. He held his left arm. "Lorma, something doesn't feel right."

"Oh, sweet Jesus, help my Richard. Where are you hurting?"

"My chest. My arm."

"I'll get an aspirin." Sabrina ran into the kitchen while Kylie grabbed the

100

phone and dialed 9-1-1. Mama coaxed the medicine down Daddy's throat. She held his hands and prayed over him.

Please, God. Please don't take Daddy yet. An eternity seemed to pass while they waited for the ambulance. Finally, it arrived, and Kylie watched as the paramedics loaded him into the back. Mama jumped in beside Daddy.

Loading into two vans and a car, Kylie, her sisters and brothers, and their families followed behind. The hospital came into view, and Kylie watched as the ambulance pulled into the emergency-room entrance. Her father was unloaded from the back and rushed inside.

Dalton parked his car, and everyone filtered out. Kylie couldn't move. "Go on." Kylie motioned when Dalton extended his hand to her. "I'll come in a second."

She watched as her family disappeared into the hospital. Fear mounted inside her. Tears welled in her eyes. *Not on Thanksgiving, Lord. Please, don't take Daddy yet. We still need him.* She pulled her cell phone from her front jeans pocket and dialed Ryan's number.

"Hello."

"Ryan." Kylie's voice caught in her throat.

"Ki, what's wrong?"

"I—I need you."

"Where are you?"

"At the hospital in Petersburg. My daddy's having a heart attack."

Breathless, Ryan ran into the hospital's emergency-room waiting area and spied Kylie. He rushed to her and wrapped his arms around her. "I got here as quick as I could."

She nestled her face into his embrace and tightened her arms around him. "I know. I need you here so much."

His heart melted. He'd scale a mountain, swim an ocean, fight a lion—anything he needed to do to take care of Kylie. "Have you heard anything yet?"

She pulled away but grabbed his hand. "Not yet."

A large, young man approached and offered his hand. "I'm Dalton. You must be Ryan."

"It's nice to meet you. I wish that it were under different circumstances."

Dalton tried to grin, but his eyes remained weighted and dull. "We're going to keep praying."

Kylie peered up at Ryan. "I won't introduce you now. I'll just point out my brothers and sisters. The boy and the girl at the pop machine are Chloe and Cameron. The pregnant lady on the phone is Natalie. The one on her cell phone is Sabrina. Amanda is the other pregnant one. You just met Dalton. Gideon's the tall, thin one leaning against the wall. The boys are my nephews and the other men are my brothers-in-law—oh, I'll introduce you later."

The doors leading to the back burst open. Mrs. Andrews walked out and clasped her hands. "He's going to be okay."

Ryan rushed over with Kylie and her family as they surrounded her mother. "What's wrong with him, Mama?" one of the siblings asked.

Mrs. Andrews cupped her nearest child's jaw with both hands. "Indigestion." She released her youngest son and wrapped her arms around Amanda. "Your silly, silly daddy ate half a dozen deviled eggs and gave himself a bad case of indigestion."

"Thank You, Lord," whispered Kylie. Ryan squeezed her hand.

"Ryan!" Lorma grabbed him in a hug. "I'm so glad you're here."

Kylie frowned. "You know Ryan?"

"Yes, we met at God's Pantry. He and his grandfather volunteer there."

Ryan felt Kylie's grip loosen. *Don't pull away, Ki.* He tried to squeeze her hand, but she pulled away.

"Why were you at God's Pantry, Mama?"

"We went a few times before your daddy's disability checks started." She looked around at her family. "Who wants to see Daddy first?" Before anyone could respond, Mama grabbed Chloe and Cameron and guided them back through the door.

"You help at God's Pantry, too?"

"Gramps has for years. I've just been helping him the last few times."

"My family paid you a couple visits, and you didn't tell me?"

How could he tell her his mother asked him not to? She hadn't wanted Kylie to worry. He should have never agreed to keep it from Kylie, but he didn't want her to be upset, either. Her self-imposed embarrassment about the times her family lacked financially was ridiculous. He wanted her to get past the money—with him, with her family. He thought she had.

"Someone bought my poverty-stricken parents brand-new coats. Did you know that?"

Ryan swallowed. She couldn't possibly know he bought those coats. He'd sent them through the family's pastor. The man himself didn't even know Ryan's name.

"Is there anything else I can share with you? Any charity you'd like to give?"

"What is the matter with you?" Ryan tried to grab her hand. "An hour ago you needed me because you thought your dad was in serious condition; now you're mad because I saw your parents at God's Pantry? I don't care about your family's lack of wealth. I care about you." He touched her cheek. "I love you, Ki."

Contentment glazed her eyes. For a moment. She shook her head. "I'm sorry, Ryan." She moved her face away from his hand. "I shouldn't have called."

Chapter 18

Kylie hugged her father longer than usual. Willing herself never to forget it, she inhaled his scent, a musky, sweet mixture of aftershave and butterscotch. "Daddy, I—"

"I'm okay, honey." He squeezed her then held her at arm's length. "Just one more month and this family has its first college graduate. I'm proud of you."

She tore her gaze from his. The sincere pride in his eyes made her want to cry—again. "Daddy, I'm going to help. . . ."

He lifted her chin with his thumb. "Now you listen to me. The best help you can give me and your mama is to follow the Lord. He will lead you in the right way."

"I will. God will give me a job where I can make sure you get your medicine and—"

"Kylie." Her father clasped her hands in his. "God has always provided for your mama and me. Always. It's not your job to provide. You, honey, you have to follow God's plan for your life."

"Okay, Daddy." She kissed his cheek and walked to her car. After starting the ignition, she pulled onto the country road leading to the interstate.

It's not okay. God, I want to trust You, but seeing Daddy taken by stretcher into the hospital. . . She shuddered. *There was nothing I could do to help him. Nothing.*

Glancing to her right, Kylie saw the old abandoned church she and her family used to attend. The congregation had long ago outgrown it and built a new one. She drove into the lot and shut off the engine. Envisioning her sisters, baby dolls in tow, standing beneath the large oak tree, she could also see her brother Dalton trying to coerce Gideon into eating a bug.

Smiling, she left the car and walked toward the swing that hung from one of the oak's limbs. Sitting on it, she swung back and forth, allowing the cool November wind to whip through her hair. She looked toward the church's door and remembered Chloe and Cameron toddling around her mama's legs and Daddy shaking hands with the preacher.

Hopping off the swing, she made her way to the back of the property. A small creek was barely recognizable with the grass and weeds grown up all around it. A giggle welled in her throat. "We used to hunt crawdads here."

She looked past the creek at the forever-flowing land before her. In summer, rows of corn would grace it. She remembered a time when Daddy got mad at her, Sabrina, and Natalie because they'd chased Amanda into the rows, then left her there. *We were so ornery.*

Glancing at her watch, she realized it would be dark before she made it back to her apartment. She ambled back to her car and got in. She looked at the church again. "We had a lot of fun."

She pulled back onto the main road. "Even when we didn't have anything."

<hr />

"That woman is without a doubt the most infuriating person on the planet." Ryan smacked his keys onto the cabinet.

Gramps sat at the kitchen table, whittling a piece of wood. He didn't even look up. "Ya love her, huh?"

Ryan kicked off his shoes and slid into a chair beside Gramps. Ryan raked his fingers through his hair. "Yes, I love her. I even told her so."

"What did she say?"

" 'I'm sorry. I shouldn't have called.' " Ryan snipped the words in a mocking tone.

"Hmm."

"One moment she's all flustered about me. 'What does Ryan do for money? Is he a thief, a moocher off his grandpa?' The next moment she's all mad because her parents saw us at the pantry when they got food there."

"Hmm."

"I don't know why I even care. How could I fall in love like this again? Vanessa—"

Gramps laid down the piece of wood and his knife. "Kylie is nothing like Vanessa."

"I know." Ryan rested his head against the table. "She's making me crazy. I don't know how I can convince her—"

"How you can convince her?" Gramps huffed and swatted the air. "Seems that's the problem with both of you. It's all about you."

"What do you mean? I'm not doing any—"

Gramps lifted his hand to stop Ryan. "Sometimes God wants us to sit still and listen—to Him. Kylie is so worried about taking care of her parents and making sure she never lives poor again that she can't see what God is giving her."

"I agree. But you said both of us. I'm trusting God."

"Are you, son? Are you really? You're so worried about her being like Vanessa that you won't give Kylie a chance. Worse yet, you won't give God a chance to show you that Kylie is not after your money."

"But—"

"I'm too old for all this." Gramps pushed himself up out of his chair. "Why don't you sit still a second and see what God tells you?"

Ryan watched as Gramps made his way up the stairs. *I have been trusting You, God. I've tried to tell her several times.*

The Holy Spirit spoke to his heart. *"Then why didn't you?"*

He slipped his shoes back on and walked out onto the porch. Lowering into a rocking chair, he watched the sun sink into the horizon. Yellows and deep oranges blanketed the earth. Ryan couldn't help but wonder at God's creativity and brilliance.

"You painted this picture, Lord. The heavens and the earth proclaim Your majesty. Why am I afraid to tell Kylie about the wealth You've given me?"

He walked back into the house and grabbed his keys from the counter. He made his way back to the car. "Because I haven't completely trusted You. Forgive me, Lord."

Pulling out of his driveway, he drummed the steering wheel. "Now what should I say, God? 'Um, Kylie, I know you think I'm living off Gramps, but really I'm loaded.'" He shook his head.

"What about, 'Kylie, I'm sorry I never told you, but I have the means to provide for you for the rest of your life.'" He groaned. "God, I feel like a total idiot."

An idea sprang to mind. *Thank You, Lord.* He raced to the bank and withdrew the money he needed from the ATM. A smile lifted his lips as he made his way to Candy's house. Glancing at the clock on the dash, he sighed. "I don't think it's too late."

He pulled into Candy's driveway and hopped out. His heart sped up when he rang the doorbell. Footsteps sounded inside, and Ryan feared his heart would pound through his chest at any moment.

With Suzanna planted on her hip, Candy opened the door and grinned. "Hey, Ryan. Come on in."

Ryan stepped inside. "Thanks. I won't stay long."

"What can I do for you?"

"I want to pay for the rest of Kylie's trip. How much does she need?"

Candy's eyes bulged as a smile formed on her lips. "That's wonderful. What a load off her shoulders! Here, take Suzanna; I'll go find out."

Before Ryan could say otherwise, Candy placed the wiggling baby in his arms. Suzanna grabbed his hair with one hand. She laughed when she yanked a few strands from his head. "Aren't you a little spitfire?" Ryan pried her fist open and wiped his hair away from her slobbery hand.

"This is what she owes." Candy returned, took the baby, and handed him a slip of paper. Ryan handed her the money. Candy's eyebrows lifted as she looked up at him. "She's going to want to know who paid for it."

"Yep, she will. Don't tell her it's me; just say this exactly: 'The person who paid for the rest of your trip wants you to know God always provides, Ki.'"

" 'God always provides'?"

"No." Ryan shook his head. " 'God always provides, Ki.'"

Candy shrugged. "Okay. You got it."

Ryan waved before Candy shut the door behind him. He jingled his keys as he headed toward his car. The sun had set. God graced the sky with the moon and a sprinkling of stars. "I pray Kylie gets it, too."

Chapter 19

Kylie trudged up the sidewalk toward her apartment. She unlocked the door and walked inside. Exhausted from her trip, she plopped her suitcase and purse on a chair. After kicking off her shoes, she trailed into the kitchen for a pop. She glanced at the answering machine on the counter. "Eight messages! Has Robin even checked this thing?"

Probably not, she realized. Robin spent precious little time at the apartment as she planned her wedding and spent time with Tyler and Bransom. *Three days, and I won't have a roommate.*

The finality of it hit hard. It had taken time, but Kylie had come to believe her friend would be content as a wife and mother. Still, the change stung. Maybe it wasn't the change, but the glimmer in Robin's eye, the lilt in her voice, the bounce in her step.

Brushing the thoughts aside, Kylie pushed the MESSAGE button on the answering machine.

"Message one," the English-accented recorded voice announced.

A click sounded. Someone hung up on the machine. Kylie pushed DELETE, then listened as the next two messages were the same. "Why do people wait until they hear the entire 'Leave a message' spiel and then hang up?"

"Message four." Kylie always smiled at the computerized pronunciation of the number.

"Hey, Robin," Tyler's voice boomed through the room. "I'm running late."

Kylie deleted the days-old message.

"Message five."

"Hi, Robin," her own voice, as well as muffled activity from her parents' home, spilled from the machine. "I wanted to wish you a happy Thanksgiving."

She pushed the DELETE button. She'd called before her father's rush to the hospital. *I miss them so much already.*

"Message six."

"Hi, Kylie." Candy's voice held a hint of laughter. "I have the best news for you. Someone has paid for the remainder of your trip."

"What?" Kylie leaned closer to hear better as excitement welled within her.

"The person didn't want me to come out and tell you who he was, but to say, and I quote, 'God always provides, Ki.'"

"God always provides, Ki?" She furrowed her brows. "The only person who would say that, who calls me Ki is—"

"Message seven."

"Hello, Kylie, this is Brad Dickson at Miller Enterprises."

Kylie sucked in her breath at the sound of his voice. What could he possibly want?

"It seems we have another opening in our office. Mr. Miller would like to offer you the position, but he needs you to begin as soon as you graduate, mid-December. If not, we'll need to get someone else in here. We're in a bit of a crunch, and there're a few other qualified candidates to choose from. Call as soon as you get this message."

I can have the job again?

"Message eight."

"Hi, Robin. This is the florist. . ."

Stumbling from the kitchen, Kylie's messages churned in her stomach. She plopped on the couch, laid her head back, and stared at the ceiling. "I can go on the trip. I can have the job."

She blinked. "But not both."

Candy's message from Kylie's benefactor swam through her mind. *"God always provides, Ki."*

"No one but Ryan calls me Ki." She sat up and stared at the wall. "But how could he possibly afford to pay the rest of my way? He hasn't even earned money for his."

She stood and ambled to the bathroom. Resting her hands on the vanity, she stared at her reflection. "I can have a job at Miller's again. I'll make enough money there to provide well for my family and me."

But the job is demanding, and I won't be able to go on the missions trip.

Her heart sank. She thought of the hours Mr. Miller expected of his employees. Well above the forty-hour workweek. Financially, she could help her mama and daddy, but she'd rarely have time to see them. She stared at the mirror. "I miss them so much, and I just saw them earlier today."

The goals she'd set for herself were finally coming to fruition. She could easily tell the ministry leaders she had reconsidered and decided to work at Miller Enterprises. This was her chance, but she didn't feel happy. Not even excited. Nothing. . .but heaviness.

She grabbed a towel and washcloth from the linen closet and turned on the shower. "I just need to rest a minute. Let all this sink in."

After feeling to make sure the water was hot, she pulled the ponytail from her hair. "God always provides, Ki." The words slipped into her mind. She closed her eyes. "Oh, sweet Jesus, guide me."

Ryan strode into the jewelry shop. Clear glass counters adorned each wall. Deep red and green fabric hung like fancy curtains above the counters. A covered display of possible Christmas gifts "for that special someone" sat on a circular, center table.

"May I help you, sir?" A short, balding man approached.

"Yes. I've come to pick up my order. For Ryan Watkins."

The man nodded. "Very good. I'll be right back."

Ryan walked to a counter, pulled his wallet from his back pocket, and dug through it for the receipt. The gift cost too much for any dispute over whether it had been paid for.

"Here we go." The man rested the box on the counter.

Ryan handed the man the receipt, then opened the side and pulled out the silver plate with Tyler's and Robin's names as well as their wedding date engraved into it. Joshua's proclamation, "As for me and my household, we will serve the LORD," scrolled across the center in calligraphy.

To him, this was a silly, frivolous gift. But Gramps insisted. Every wedding he always insisted.

"It's a tradition," he'd say. "When your grandma and I married, her favorite gift was her silver plate. For every wedding we attended, she bought the same for the newlyweds."

Ryan slid it back into the box. "It looks nice. Thank you."

"Is there anything else I can help you with?"

"I don't believe so."

Ryan turned to leave, when he saw a young woman trying on a ring. She extended her hand and gazed at it. The man beside her leaned down and whispered in her ear. She stood on tiptoes and kissed his cheek.

A sudden longing for Kylie stirred him. No more games. No more waiting. He knew he loved her. Knew he wanted to spend the rest of his life with her. *God, I've already given the whole money thing over to You.*

The time had come.

He glanced back at the clerk. "I may look around a bit."

"Very good. Let me know if I can help you with anything."

Ryan looked in the case that held the engagement rings. So many round diamonds in varying sizes shone back at him. Some rested in yellow gold settings. Some in white, and still others in platinum. He moved farther down and noted the different settings. The rings seemed much the same as the round ones, only now the stone had a marquise shape.

Moving still farther down, he came to a section of multiple-stoned rings. Many were large and gaudy. One in particular with three huge stones caught his eye. He huffed. "Vanessa would have wanted that one."

Ryan shook his head. Kylie was nothing like Vanessa. *Thank You, Lord.* Another ring caught his eye. The white gold band had a center, circular diamond, resting in a square setting. It wasn't overly large, but it was a nice size. Smaller diamonds adorned both sides, with even smaller stones outside of them. The ring had an antique appearance. Somehow it made him feel the commitment, the longevity of the promise it held.

Ryan motioned to the man for assistance. After showing the one he wanted to view, the man placed it in Ryan's hand. He pushed it onto his pinky. *It's perfect.* "I'll take it."

Kylie glanced to the left, then right in the church's foyer. Empty. She adjusted the top of the strapless bridesmaid dress, then quietly peeked around the corner of one door.

Family and friends filled the small church to capacity. Deep red rosebuds and baby's breath arrangements adorned the side of every third pew. Just beyond the altar rested an elaborate wedding arch dressed in crimson velvet and white satin. Full-bloom roses wrapped around the unity candle.

Tyler and the groomsmen had already taken their positions in the front. They looked handsome in their matching black tuxedos and red cummerbunds. Only Tyler wore black with a white vest.

She scanned the crowd. If Kylie didn't hurry and get back to the wedding party, Robin's mom would faint for sure. Kylie had never seen a mother so frazzled. *Where is Ryan?*

"Kylie."

Kylie jumped, then placed her hand on her chest to calm her heart. "Ryan, you scared the life out of me. I was just looking for you."

"You were?" His eyebrows rose in interest.

Heat raced up her neck and cheeks. Seeing him now, she knew she missed him more than she'd realized. His eyes, honest and compassionate, bore at her soul. The playful, stray curls at the base of his neck begged to be touched. "Yes, well. . ."

"You're absolutely gorgeous."

"Thank you, I—"

He bent down toward her. She lifted her chin, willing his kiss. Instead, his breath brushed her ear. "I better find a seat. I'll talk to you at the reception."

"Okay." She blinked. What just happened? *I just felt an attraction I've never experienced in my life.* Opening her heart and mind to God over the last few days, she'd felt a peace she hadn't known in years. She'd been trying to get hold of Ryan to ask him about the missions trip money and tell him about her job decision. He hadn't been home. But the electricity she'd just experienced at his closeness had wiped all that from her mind.

At the quiet chattering behind her, she hurried back to Robin and the bridesmaids. They hustled into their line as the music began. When it was Kylie's turn, she began her slow ascent to the altar. Peering to her left, she found Ryan. He watched her with such longing her knees grew weak. Tearing her gaze from him, she focused on putting one foot in front of the other.

What is happening, Lord? This feels like more than attraction. She took her place as maid of honor. *I've said time and again I'm falling for him, but I could always rationalize myself through.*

She sneaked a quick peek at him. He smiled, and she knew he hadn't stopped watching her. *I don't want to rationalize, Lord, and it feels right.*

Gripping the bouquet tighter, she listened as Tyler and Robin recited their vows. She wanted more than the perfect husband, the perfect kids, the perfect dog, the perfect white picket fence. The perfect job. She needed more. She needed love. "The pursuit of righteousness and love."

Looking at Ryan again, she smiled when their gazes met. Yes, love.

⌘

Ryan touched Kylie's hand. "Have I told you how beautiful you look?"

A blush crept up her cheek, adding to her innocent beauty. "A few times." She shrugged, then nudged his shoulder. "But then a girl never tires of hearing it."

Ryan laughed. "I've been trying to reach you."

"I've tried calling you, too."

"I think we're playing phone tag."

She nodded.

"How is your dad?"

"He's doing great. I—I wanted to apologize for how I treated you at the hospital. I was under a lot of stress then. I've been doing a lot of praying this week. Someone told me that God always provides...." She stopped and winked at him.

She got it. She knows it was me who paid for her trip. This is my chance, Lord. You've shown me the time.

"Kylie, I—"

"Kylie." Tyler's best man grabbed her arm. "I've been looking everywhere for you. I want to pray a blessing for Tyler and Robin before they cut the cake."

"Okay." Kylie stood and smiled at Ryan. "I'll be back."

Ryan's heart sank as she walked away. He yearned to finish their conversation, but as the evening progressed, her duties continually called her away.

After several hours passed, Ryan noticed her step slowed and her shoulders slumped ever so slightly. Once the newlyweds were nestled into their car and

112

headed to the airport, Ryan touched Kylie's arm. "You want me to take you home?"

"I'm going to help clean up. Plus, I drove." She stepped closer to him. "But I still want to talk."

Every manly urge within him wanted to grab her into his arms, to caress the exhaustion away from her face. He swallowed and shoved his fists into his pockets. "How 'bout I take you to dinner and then the Festival of Lights tomorrow night?"

"Oh, I love the lights. That sounds wonderful."

He kissed her forehead. "I can't wait."

Chapter 20

Kylie plopped onto the wooden chair. "It's early in the morning, the weekend, and I'm at school." She slipped the book bag from her shoulder and dropped it to the floor beside the computer station. Clicking the computer mouse, she waited for the machine to wake up. Glancing around the university library, she sighed. "But this may be my last time in here."

The bittersweet reality pricked at her heart. For four years her focus had been on the pursuit of this prize—her degree. Not just a degree but one with the highest of honors. Summa cum laude. She figured the better the grade point average, the more likely she'd be to land a good, solid accounting position.

University of Evansville scrolled across the screen. She clicked the school's icon, moved through the system, then typed in her screen name and password. Once the computer recognized her, she scrolled down the options until she came to Grades.

She took a deep breath. There was no way she could get an A in Nickels's class this semester. She may not get a B. Failing her first test and doing only fairly well on the project, her grade depended on the final exam. Which had been excruciatingly difficult. If she received a C, she wouldn't receive highest honors.

Tapping the bottom of the mouse, she couldn't seem to make herself click the screen. A bit of trepidation sailed through her veins, but not what she would have expected. Just a few short months ago, during the summer, she'd been stressed to the max about a possible B in Nickels's class. Now the possibility of a C didn't truly faze her.

So much had happened this last semester. She thought her daddy might die of a heart attack. Miller Enterprises offered a job, took it back, then offered one again. Robin got married. Ryan—

The thought of Ryan brought a smile to her lips. Kind. Considerate. Gentle. Handsome. Godly. He was everything she'd ever wanted in a man. But without a steady job. She chuckled and shook her head. Of all the requirements for a mate she'd ever had, her top two had been that he love the Lord and that he have a good, steady income. Ryan met only one.

Somehow, I'm all right with that.

Studying the options before her on the computer screen, she shrugged.

"Might as well get it over with."

She clicked for her grades. The class courses popped on the screen. Within a second the grade followed. She bit her lip and grinned. "Three As and one C."

After closing her account and then the screen, she picked up her bag and slung it over her shoulder. She had several books she needed to return in hopes of getting some kind of refund. Glancing one last time at the library, she grinned as peace flooded her soul. "I'm not summa cum laude, and it's okay."

❧

Ryan unbuckled the oversize black belt, then folded off the Santa suit and extra padding. The air had been nippy for the town's annual Christmas in Santa Claus Parade, but sweat still beaded on his forehead due to the mass of padding. He didn't mind. Seeing the children of the community's faces light up when his sleigh approached them had been priceless. As he passed, he tried to make sure each one received a candy cane from Santa.

He peeled off the white beard, mustache, and eyebrows. Rubbing the now-tender places, he hoped his face wouldn't be red for his date with Kylie.

"Tonight's the big night, huh?" Gramps, adorned in a bright green shirt and candy cane suspenders, strolled into Ryan's bedroom. Large, red pointy shoes with bells stitched at the tips covered the man's feet. A matching hat sat on his head.

Ryan shook his head and chuckled.

"Oh, so it's okay for you to dress up like Santa Claus, but I can't be an elf."

"Are you kidding? You look great. Heading to Santa's Lodge for the concerts?"

"Yep, then St. Nick's Restaurant for dinner. Wouldn't miss the gingerbread decorating for the world."

"Hmm. I'm not sure if it's the decorating or seeing Elma that you like so much."

"Tosh, son." Gramps swatted the air. "That woman drives me crazy. Did you see her hair at church on Sunday? It's back to blue! Blue, pink, blue, pink. You'd think the woman would make up her mind."

Ryan laughed out loud.

Gramps moved closer to him. "I think you're avoiding my question."

Ryan cleared his throat and glanced at his closet. "What question?"

"I asked if tonight was the night."

"The night for the Festival of Lights? Yep. It sure is."

Gramps shook his finger. "Don't play coy with me. If you don't want to say, then don't say."

Ryan smiled. "I'm just teasing. Yes. Tonight's the night."

A sparkle lit Gramps's eyes. "I'll pray for you."

"That would be great."

Kylie gazed at her reflection in the full-length mirror. The shimmering blue dress flared at the skirt as she twirled around. In truth, it was a bit fancy for a simple dinner and tour of the lights date. Flutters filled Kylie's stomach as she prayed Ryan had something more in mind.

"I can't believe I want to marry the man." She touched her cheeks when they began to blaze with the desire that filled her whole being. She closed her eyes. "Please, Lord, let him ask me tonight."

Bending over, she picked up her high-heeled black shoes. She sat on the bed and put them on. Standing again, she twirled once more in the mirror. Her feminine instinct yearned for Ryan to find her breathtaking.

The doorbell rang, and Kylie glanced at the alarm clock on her nightstand. "He's a full half hour early." Kylie walked to the front door and peered through the peephole. "Brad?"

Turning away, she leaned against the door, contemplating if she should pretend not to be home. Her heart pricked. "I know, God; that would be wrong." Taking a deep breath, Kylie unlocked and opened the door. She plastered a smile to her face. "Hello, Brad."

Brad whistled and eyed her up and down, again making her feel cheap. "Where are you going, babe?"

She inhaled a deep breath and bit back a retort regarding his lack of manners. "Did you need something, Brad?"

He leaned against the door frame. "You want to invite me in?"

"I don't have much time." She planted her feet firmly in the doorway.

He leaned closer to her, and Kylie didn't budge. He lifted his hands in the air. "Okay, okay. I quit. I just came to see if you were going to take the job."

Kylie frowned and folded her arms in front of her chest. "I've already talked to Mr. Miller."

"Oh." Brad snapped his fingers. "He may have mentioned that."

"What did you come for, Brad?"

He shrugged and slinked into one of her chairs on the porch. "I don't know. Thought you might want to go out sometime." He peered up at her, and for once Kylie saw a hint of sincerity in his eyes. "I haven't met anyone like you, Kylie. Most girls fall all over me."

Kylie bit the inside of her lip. Even his attempt at honesty was laced with his inflated ego. Still, it was the first attempt at truthfulness she'd seen from him since her first interview when Mr. Miller had been present. "I can't go out with you, Brad."

"It's that Ryan, isn't it?"

Warmth flooded her heart at the mention of his name. "Yes."

Brad stood and started down the sidewalk. "Well, it was nice meeting you, Kylie."

A twinge of guilt filled her. "Brad." She walked toward him. "I would love it if you would come to my church sometime. We have a really great singles' group. You'd probably enjoy yourself."

Brad half grinned. "I might do that."

Ryan gazed at Kylie from across the booth in the restaurant. She was a vision of beauty with her hair held away from her face with a clip. Small wisps distracted him as they caressed her neck with each move of her head. Her bright blue dress enhanced her eyes, which shone against her creamy skin. "You're stunning, Ki."

Her cheeks reddened as a smile of pleasure bowed her lips. "Thank you."

"I think you'd make a garbage sack beautiful."

"Ryan." She smacked his hand. "You're silly."

He inwardly growled at her playfulness. She had no idea how much he yearned to take her in his arms and kiss her sweet lips.

She grabbed his hand. "I have some news for you."

He relished the softness of her skin. "I have something I want to tell you, too."

She removed her hand, and he missed her warmth. "Okay. You first."

Ryan shook his head. "No. Go ahead."

"Okay. First, I got a C in Nickels's class. No highest honors for me."

He grimaced, knowing how much her grades meant to her. "I'm sorry."

"It's okay." She shrugged. "It's really okay." Her eyes glistened with the smile that graced her mouth. "I got another job offer with Miller Enterprises, but it starts in December."

"That's. . .great." Ryan tried not to frown as his heart fell into his stomach. She wouldn't be going on the missions trip, and that job would be so time-consuming.

"I turned it down."

"You what?"

She giggled. "Yep. I turned it down. This person, who remains nameless, paid for my missions trip. He said that God always provides. Well, I've been praying and searching, and I know God wants me to go on that trip. More importantly, He wants me to trust Him with my life. I was offered the position with the missions ministry, and I'm taking it."

"Oh, Kylie."

"I know you paid my way, Ryan. I've wanted to thank you—to tell you that I have deep feelings for you. I've—I've struggled with a lot of things, but I—I. . ."

Ryan's heart swelled. Excitement coursed through him. "Kylie." He placed his finger across her lips. "I have to tell you something first."

He took her hand in his, caressing her palm with his thumb. "About eight years ago, I fell in love with a woman. I thought she was everything I was looking for. Until she found out about. . ."

Ryan took a deep breath. This wasn't the way he wanted to tell her. Ryan cleared his throat. "Let me start over. There's a reason I don't work a nine-to-five job. When I was in high school, I developed a machine to make logging easier. I sold my blueprints to a company in Alaska. I made a good amount of money from the sale, and then Gramps invested big chunks of it into different stocks and bonds."

He watched as her eyes widened. "I don't understand."

"Vanessa, the woman I mentioned before, she loved my wealth, not me. I swore I'd never tell anyone about the money again. If God ever placed a woman in my life, she'd have to love me for me."

"You thought I'd love you for your money?"

"When I first saw you, you were talking to Robin about yahoo men, and you were so focused on getting through school to get a good-paying job."

He watched as her shoulders slumped a bit as she let out a breath. Her gaze lowered to the table, and she moved her hand from his. "I see."

"No, you don't. I was wrong. I wasn't putting my trust in the Lord or you. I was too worried about what Vanessa had done. Ki." He grabbed her hand again. "I love you."

She gazed up at him. Uncertainty filled her eyes. In a rush, Ryan reached into his pocket and pulled out the ring box. He knelt beside her and opened the box. "Please, Ki. You're the perfect woman for me. The one God intended. I love you. Marry me."

Tears filled her eyes as she slowly shook her head. "I don't think I can."

Chapter 21

Kylie bit into her hamburger. The stale bun and overcooked meat stuck to the roof of her mouth. She sighed as yet another mall-going, happy couple walked past her.

"What is the matter with you? You've acted all day like you lost your best friend." Amanda swiped a fry from Kylie's tray. "Our annual Christmas shopping trip is supposed to be fun."

Kylie halfheartedly gazed at her more-pregnant-than-ever little sister. Amanda's hair looked fuller and healthier as it framed her sickeningly glowing face. She rested a protective hand on her belly as she drowned the fry in ketchup then shoved it into her mouth. A drop fell on the top arch of her stomach. Amanda giggled as she licked her napkin and wiped it off.

Amanda's happiness made Kylie's stomach whirl. Kylie wrinkled her nose. "Just grouchy, I guess."

Amanda eyed her. "I'd say you're more than grouchy. Remember, big sis, we shared a room far too long for you to play games with me. What gives?"

Kylie twirled her straw in her now-runny chocolate shake. "Ryan asked me to marry him."

Amanda's mouth popped open and her eyes glistened with excitement. "That's great! Please, Kylie." She placed her hand on Kylie's. "Please tell me that you have realized that you love this man. It's so obvious to the rest of us."

"I do love him." Kylie tried to sip the milk shake, but it pooled in the back of her throat, making her feel nauseated. Her gaze found a teenage couple walking by hand in hand.

"But—"

"But I told him no."

"What?" Amanda smacked her napkin onto the table. "Kylie Andrews, why?"

"He's been lying to me all this time."

"Lying to you? About what?"

"He's rich, Amanda." Kylie pushed the tray away from her. "I don't know how rich, but enough that the man doesn't even have to work."

"Okay." Amanda furrowed her eyebrows. "So Ryan is rich. He didn't come right out and tell you, but now he wants to marry you. I'm not following the problem here."

119

"Some girl he used to love wanted him for his money or something like that, so he didn't tell me because he didn't want me to want him for his money; he wanted me to want him for himself." She flailed her arms and shook her head. "Oh, he just didn't trust me to tell me, okay?"

"Kylie."

"He knew how much I wanted to help take care of Mama and Daddy. He knew I was trying so hard to get a good job. He knew how afraid I was of ending up married to a coal. . . miner." Kylie lowered her gaze. "I'm sorry, Amanda."

"Kylie." Amanda placed her hand on Kylie's arm. "I love my coal-mining husband. So, so much. And he loves me. And he loves the Lord. I wouldn't trade my life for all the financial stability in the world." Amanda let go of Kylie's arm, then folded her hands on the table. "I'm sorry for you, Kylie."

Kylie frowned at her sister.

Amanda closed her eyes. "God's given you a wonderful man with the financial stability you've always dreamed about." Amanda opened her eyes and let out a deep breath. "And you still don't see it."

<hr>

Ryan grabbed a bag of potato chips from the pantry then opened the refrigerator and took out a can of pop. After snatching the remote control from the coffee table, he fell into the oversize recliner. Restless, he flipped through stations. Nothing interested him. He stopped on a station showing a commercial and dropped the remote on the end table.

"Still sulking?" Gramps's voice sounded from the couch where he lay facing the cushions, arms around a pillow.

"I thought you were taking a nap."

Gramps turned around and pushed the pillow behind his head. "I reckon a man can't sleep with the racket you're making."

"Sorry." Ryan shoved a potato chip in his mouth, then washed it down with a swig of pop. The commercial ended.

"*It's a Wonderful Life* is on." Gramps sat up. "I love this movie."

Ryan groaned. *Great. It's a Wonderful Life. Oh, yes. Mine is absolutely terrific.* He crunched another chip. *Like I haven't seen this a million times anyway.*

"You're becoming unbearable to live with." Gramps reached over and grabbed a handful of chips from the bag.

"I'm not even saying anything."

"It's what you're not saying."

"What?"

"You asked Kylie to marry you a week ago. Now you're not saying much of anything." Gramps looked at him. "Tell me what happened."

Ryan shrugged and watched the screen as Jimmy Stewart threatened to throw himself off the bridge. At this moment, Ryan understood Jimmy's need, his feelings of complete failure. "She said no."

"Just like that." Gramps folded his arms in front of his chest. "No."

"Just like that."

"Did she say why?"

"She didn't want me when I didn't have money. Now she doesn't want me because I do. Now, in my thinking, that means she flat-out just doesn't want me." Ryan leaned back in his chair and looked at the ceiling. "I thought she was about to tell me she loved me, but—what does it matter now?"

"You're probably right." Gramps stretched his arms over his head. "Think I'm going to head over to St. Nick's for a cup of coffee. You wanna come?" He swatted the air. "Nah. You oughta stay here and watch some television." He stood and patted Ryan's shoulder. "You haven't done much of that lately."

"Are you making fun of me?"

"I'd never do that." Gramps grabbed his coat off the rack and slid into it. "I'll see you in a bit."

Ryan watched as Gramps stepped out and shut the door. He offered no "I hate that for you, son." No "I'm so sorry." Ryan frowned as he looked back at the screen. Jimmy Stewart raked his hand through his hair in grievous frustration. Without the money, his place would close and so would his life. *Money. It's always about money, and I'm sick of it.*

❧

"Just a minute!" Kylie called through the apartment when the doorbell rang. She grabbed an oven mitt then pulled the Christmas cookies from the oven. "I'm coming." After taking the mitt off her hand, she brushed a few wayward wisps of hair behind her ear.

She peeked through the peephole. "Gramps?" After opening the door, Kylie motioned for him to come inside. "I haven't seen you in a while. How are you?"

"Good."

She pointed toward the couch, then sat in a chair. Wringing her hands, her heart sped in nervous anticipation. She had no idea what Ryan had said and if Gramps was mad or hurt or what. "Have a seat. How's—how's Ryan?"

"Miserable." Gramps didn't move. Instead, he crossed his arms in front of his chest.

Kylie looked at her hands. She picked at a chip in one of her fingernails as a mixture of relief and sadness filled her spirit. "Oh."

"Is that all you have to say? 'Oh'?"

She gazed up at the older man. He'd cared about her from the moment she met him. He was the perfect gramps, a little rough around the edges, a bit of a spitfire, too, but with a heart filled with love, generosity, and loyalty. Her grandparents died when she was young, and she'd enjoyed Ryan's grandfather as if he were her own. "I don't know what else to say."

"All right. Let's figure this out, because I'm thinkin' your feelings for Ryan run deeper than you want to admit."

"Well. . ."

He scratched his gray-stubbled jaw with his fingers and paced the floor. "When you met Ryan, you thought he was a bit of a yahoo—"

Kylie's mouth dropped open. "How would you know—?"

He raised his hand to stop her. "Ryan mentioned it."

Her cheeks blazed hot at the memory, at the thought of what he must have felt when he heard her talking. People never ceased to surprise her. As soon as she was sure she had someone pegged, she'd learn there was more to them than she realized. "I judged him wrong."

Gramps clucked his tongue. "Which is why God tells us not to judge people."

Kylie nodded, feeling the swell of emotion in her throat. "You're right. God and I have talked a lot about that over the last few days."

Gramps smiled as he paced away from her. "You thought Ryan was a poor guy, one who didn't even work a full-time job. Can't say I blame you for not wanting to jump into a relationship with him. He was a bit silly not to trust God with you from the very beginning."

Kylie smiled. At least Gramps understood why she'd been blown away.

Gramps sat on the couch across from her. "But now you know the truth. You know he has the means to provide for you. You know he didn't tell you because of what happened in his past. I believe you know he loves you with all his heart, and you love him. It's nothing more than pride and arrogance that keeps you from him."

"You're right."

"Huh?"

Kylie giggled. "You're right. It's been pride. I've had my mind on one goal for so long. The one I know God did give me. I just wasn't prepared for how God planned to bless me with it. I thought He would give me a job in a prestigious company with a business-oriented husband all wrapped up in a neat package." She stood, walked to the table, and picked up the handmade Christmas card she'd made for Ryan. "But God had a different plan. A better one. Ryan."

Gramps leaned back in his seat. He tapped the arm of the couch as he bit his lip, then chuckled. "You were heading over to the house to talk to Ryan, weren't you?"

Kylie nodded. "Just as soon as I got up the courage."

"I'd be happy to go with you."

"I think I'd appreciate that."

Gramps stood and walked toward her. He wrapped his arms around her, and Kylie savored his hug of understanding and acceptance. "That boy's been unbearable. I'd like to get you on over there just as quick as I can."

Kylie laughed and squeezed him tight one more time. "Let's go."

"You can ride over there with me, then Ryan'll have to bring you home." A twinkle lit Gramps's eye, and he winked at her.

Nervousness filled Kylie's gut as she slipped her shoes on and grabbed her coat, and they headed toward the front door. Ryan may be miserable to live with, but that didn't mean he was ready to welcome Kylie into his heart with open arms. She opened the front door and ran into a mass of man. "Ryan?"

※

"Kylie." Ryan lowered his hand from the doorbell. Deciding he couldn't take it anymore, he'd turned off *It's a Wonderful Life* and headed to her apartment to talk with her one more time. He looked past Kylie. "Gramps? What are you doing here?"

Gramps buttoned the top of his coat and moved past Kylie and out the door. "I reckon it's time for me to go on home."

"Gramps." Ryan glared at his grandfather. "What were you doing?"

"Go on in there." Gramps practically pushed him into Kylie. "Talk to the woman." He hustled down the sidewalk. He mumbled, "Didn't I say I was too old for all this? Young people these days. . ."

Ryan turned back toward Kylie. Her eyes sparkled, but he couldn't decide if that was from happiness at seeing him or nervousness that he was there. "Can I come in?"

"Oh, yeah, yeah." She stepped backward and tried to pull off her coat all in one motion, then tripped on the rug. Her arms flailed in an attempt to catch herself.

Ryan tried to grab her arm to stop her fall. Instead, he gripped the coat sleeve and her arm slipped through it. She landed with a thud on the floor. Ryan stepped forward to help her. "Oh, Ki, are you—"

His foot caught on the rug and he launched forward, landing on his hands and knees beside her. "Ouch." He turned over and sat beside her, rubbing his knees. "You didn't have to drag me down here. I've already fallen for you."

"Ryan, are you okay?" She took his hands in hers and rubbed the red spots on his palms.

Ryan clasped both her hands in his. "I came over here to tell you I love you. I'm not letting you get away from me. I'm going to sit right here in your living room until we talk everything out and I've convinced you that we belong together."

She lowered her gaze and slipped her hands from his. "Do you mind if we sit somewhere besides here?" She pointed to the open front door. "It's kind of cold outside."

He hopped to his feet, shut the door, then reached down and helped her up. He held her close and peered into her eyes for the briefest of moments. "I love you, Ki."

Letting go of her hand, he walked farther into the apartment. "It's like this. I was convinced you had feelings for Brad. I was afraid you were like Vanessa. Yes, my heart told me that wasn't true, but I was so focused on the past that I wasn't listening to God clearly."

He walked toward her again. "I should have told you from the beginning. Of course, you were afraid I couldn't provide for a family. I was—"

"Ryan." She grabbed his hand in hers, caressing his palm with her thumb. Fire raced through him, blazing a trail of desire to convince her to be his wife. After all, God had brought them together.

"You have to understand—"

"Ryan." She lifted up on tiptoes and brushed her lips against his. She lowered to her height and gazed into his eyes. "You gotta hush a minute."

Ryan swallowed. The sweet softness of her lips took him by surprise. He was hushed. Stunned to utter silence better described it. "Kylie." He leaned toward her to claim another kiss, one that he could enjoy without surprise.

She pushed a paper into his hand. "I was coming to your house to give you this."

Ryan looked at the homemade card that had a photo of himself dressed as Santa in the Christmas parade. In it, he held a small candy cane in his hand, offering it to a child. Opening the card, he saw pictures cut from magazines. First of a chocolate ice-cream cone, then a clown suit. Next was a cutout of canned foods and cereal boxes, then a winter coat. She'd taken a picture of her Christmas pole and glued it on there as well. Around the edges of the card were crayon-drawn, stick-figure people holding hands.

Kylie cleared her throat. "I'm not overly crafty. Look at the back. That's what I was getting at."

The back contained no pictures, just Kylie's handwriting. She expressed her journey over the last several months with him—how she'd found him to be the most generous, loving person she'd ever known. She shared how God had showed her to pursue Him, not specific goals. Ryan's heart warmed as she wrote how she'd fallen in love with him, the man, before learning he could provide for her.

"I still love the man." Kylie quoted the last sentence of her letter. Her face flushed and she lowered her gaze. "It's kind of a silly thing, a full-grown woman making a man a homemade card, but I—"

Ryan closed the card, laid it on the table, then wrapped his arms around her. "It's the best present I've ever received. Only one could be better."

He reached into his jeans pocket and pulled out the ring box. After popping it open, he lowered to his knee and took her hand in his. "I love you. Marry me."

Her eyes lit with merriment as she knelt beside him. She wrapped her arms around his neck and kissed him on the lips. "Absolutely," she replied after she pulled away.

Ryan huffed as he placed the ring on her finger. "You've kissed me twice today. I have yet to kiss you."

"You take too long." She claimed his lips again.

"Never again." He stood and helped her up. Wrapping his arms around her, he lifted her up and kissed her with the fullness of his love. He lowered her to her feet, then brushed her hair away from her face. He caressed her soft cheek with his thumb. "I'm holding on to you for the rest of my life."

Chapter 22

May

Ryan felt the buttons on his tuxedo jacket to be sure he hadn't missed one. He raked his fingers through his hair.

"Nervous?" Gramps, his best man, poked Ryan's side.

"A little."

"No cold feet." Dalton leaned over past Gramps. He nodded toward his other brothers, Gideon and Cameron, as well as Tyler. "We'll take you out if you even consider leaving our big sis at the altar."

Tyler laughed at Ryan. "I believe they could take you, friend."

Dalton winked and showed his newly covered ring finger. "Nah, seriously. It's a piece of cake."

Ryan watched as Dalton waved at his bride, Tanya. She blushed as she fidgeted with one of Amanda's twin sons. The other started to fuss, and Amanda's husband picked him up. The only baby girl in the family, Natalie's new daughter, sat contentedly on her daddy's lap.

A laugh formed in Ryan's gut as he thought of the ever-growing family he was marrying into. He and Gramps had lived so long with only each other. Both of them relished becoming part of Kylie's family. "Don't worry, Dalton. I'm not going anywhere."

"We're about to begin," the minister whispered to them.

Ryan straightened his shoulders, watching as one of their ushers escorted Kylie's tearful mother to her place in the audience. She smiled at Ryan as she scanned the row of groomsmen—his grandfather, all three of her sons, and Tyler. Ryan knew Mrs. Andrews thanked God for each of her children and their choices in spouses. Ryan felt blessed and honored that she and Mr. Andrews approved of him.

The music began and Chloe, Kylie's youngest sister, made her way to the front. Next came her oldest sister, Sabrina. "Mommy!" her barely two-year-old son yelled from his father's lap. Everyone laughed as her husband whispered in the small boy's ear. The child squirmed and waved until Sabrina finally motioned for him to stand beside her at the front. He toddled forward, grabbed her leg, then popped his thumb into his mouth.

"What a cutie," Gramps whispered.

Ryan nodded. Anticipation welled in him as another sister, Natalie, walked toward the altar. Next came Robin, then Amanda. Kylie had deemed them both her matrons of honor. Ryan squeezed his fists. With all her last-minute errands and hair appointments and whatever else she did, he'd only seen Kylie at the rehearsal and the dinner that followed. They'd hardly spoken two words together that someone else hadn't instructed them to say. And it was killing him.

Kylie and her father stepped into the aisle. Ryan sucked in his breath.

"She's a beauty, even with her face covered," Gramps whispered.

Ryan couldn't respond. He nodded and asked God to help him remember every detail of his bride as she and her father walked toward him.

"Who gives this woman to this man?" the minister's voice boomed through the church.

"Her mother and I do." Kylie's father lifted the veil over her face and kissed her cheek. Her gaze found Ryan's. Ready to claim his bride, Ryan puffed out his chest, longing to shout to the world that beautiful Kylie Andrews had chosen him.

He took her hand in his and led her to the altar where they made their vows. The promise, the covenant, the commitment weighed his heart with a heaviness of bliss and contentment. In sickness, in health, in good, in bad, whatever life held, he would honor his vows to the woman God had given him.

When the minister instructed, he kissed her as his wife, then took her hand in his and faced their family and friends.

"I now present to you," the minister addressed the audience, "Mr. and Mrs. Ryan Watkins."

Ryan scooped her into his arms and started down the aisle.

"You're supposed to carry me over the threshold of our home," she whispered into his ear, trying to control her giggles.

"I told you I'd never take too long again." He kissed her cheek.

She nestled into his chest. "You did say never again."

"Never again."

∞

Kylie glanced down at her watch, afraid they would miss their plane to Belize. The missions trip in January had been an experience she'd never forget. She'd fallen in love with the people in the community. They were planning another trip in two months, in July. Today, they'd go as honeymooners and visit their friends there. "Are you sure you have to have whatever it is you forgot?"

Ryan smiled and tapped the steering wheel. "I thought I could wait, but I can't."

Kylie scrunched up her nose. "What?"

He turned the corner and started toward his house. "Close your eyes, Ki."

"What is going on?" She clamped her lips in a straight line, trying not to smile at him.

His lips bowed up. He bit the bottom and frowned, in a pitiful attempt not to grin. "Just close them."

"Okay." Kylie shut her eyes, then popped one open.

"Kylie Watkins!"

She squished them shut. "I like the sound of that."

"Me, too." He stopped the car and hopped out. Everything in Kylie wanted to open her eyes and look around, but she didn't want to spoil his surprise. Her door opened, and Ryan's hand took hers.

"Can I open them?"

"Nope." He gently pushed her head down then out of the car. "Be careful." He wrapped his arm around her as he guided her steps. Her heels crunched against the gravel driveway. "Okay, open your eyes."

Kylie opened them to find Gramps standing in front of her, holding a small, golden retriever puppy. "Oh." Kylie took him in her arms. "He's so cute."

"Didn't you say you wanted a godly husband, two kids"—he gathered her in his arms and whispered in her ear—"which I'm willing to work on. . ."

Her neck and cheeks warmed under his sincere, longing gaze.

He continued, "A dog and—"

She smiled and lifted her eyebrows to tease him. "I think you're forgetting something."

"No, Ki, I'm not." He turned her around, and she gasped. A white picket fence scaled the entire front of his home. One of his handmade poles stood next to the porch with their names written on the sign and two cardinal birds perched on top.

"A white picket fence." Kylie held the puppy closer to her chest, then gazed up at the man of her dreams. The man who listened to all the things she longed for. The man who wanted her to have them all.

"Oh, Ryan." She put the puppy down in the yard then touched Ryan's cheek with her hand. "There isn't a more wonderful man for me in all the world."

She stood on tiptoes and kissed his lips. With all her heart, she had pursued what she thought God had called her to—a family, a job, stability. When she finally gave over control to her heavenly Father, He lavished her with everything she had ever pursued. She gazed at her new husband. Only more. Right down to the white picket fence.

PURSUING THE GOAL

Dedication

To my middle daughter, Hayley. How many soccer and basketball games have we attended? Too many to count! I've relished every minute. I'm so thankful for your sweet, sensitive spirit. May you always strive for the best goal—Jesus.

Thank you to my husband, Albert, who has supported and encouraged me every moment on this journey, as well as my girls, Brooke, Hayley, and Allie, who spent fall break being very patient and allowing Mom to write half of each day to meet the deadline. Rose McCauley, you are a gem. Your quick crits have been a lifesaver! Most important, thank You, my Lord and Savior, for saving me, loving me, and guiding my life, for wrapping Your arms around me when I've needed You most. May my life reflect You.

Chapter 1

Chloe Andrews watched the soccer ball fly toward her then used her hip to push an opposing teammate out of the way. With the ball about to land a few feet in front of her, she moved forward then turned and arched her back, forcing the ball to roll down her chest. She took control of the sphere with her foot then pivoted and dribbled around the fullback—the last player before the goal. Taking a split-second glance toward the coaches on the sidelines, Chloe smiled in satisfaction. *They're watching.*

She turned her attention to the goalie, one of her close friends on Ball State University's soccer team who was also playing for the opposition in this practice scrimmage. Squinting her eyes, Chloe studied the target. Renee could dive with precision to the right of the goal. Her weakness was the left. Zeroing in on the left corner, Chloe dribbled another step, twisted her hip then smashed the ball with her right foot. It zoomed toward its destination, and Renee jumped, arms extended over her head. But Chloe's kick was hard, and the ball smashed into the net. Score!

"Yes!" Chloe pumped her fist through the air. A teammate scrimmaging on her side ran up to her for a high five.

"Ten-minute break. Get some water!" Coach Collins yelled from the sidelines.

Chloe headed toward the table that held the sports drink container and plastic cups. She felt a shove from behind. Chloe turned, and Renee grinned. "I knew you had me."

"What can I say? When you got it, you got it." Teasing, she blew on her fingertips then brushed them against her shoulder.

Renee laughed. "I suppose." With the back of her gloved hand, she wiped sweat from her forehead. "It's barely ten o' clock, and I'm about to suffocate out here."

"It is super hot, even for August in Indiana." Chloe fanned the front of her soppy T-shirt. She grabbed a glass of water, took a good swig, and dumped the rest over her head. "We still have an hour left."

Renee groaned. "Don't remind me." She took a drink. "How was your visit with your family?"

"Good enough, I guess. One of my brothers, Dalton, had to make a trip to

131

Indianapolis for something. I met him and his wife and kids up there for dinner." She shrugged. "Don't get me wrong. I love to visit with my nephews and nieces and everyone, but I just don't feel I really belong."

"Why?"

"I don't know." She threw her cup into the plastic trash bag. "Probably 'cause all they ever talk about is God-this and God-that. I get tired of it."

"Humph. I would, too. Why don't you just tell them you don't want to hear about it?"

"They'd die." Chloe looked away from Renee. All the Andrews family ever wanted to do was talk about the wonderful blessings God had given them, be it another baby, a good job, safety in the coal mines, at school, going to the grocery. They praised God for every little thing they did. If they walked out the front door and didn't get hit by a truck, they were praising God about it. They really got on Chloe's nerves.

The funny thing was, the Andrews clan, as people liked to call them, all believed Chloe agreed with their sentiments on God. In truth Chloe thought God was great. She loved to hear stories about Him when she was growing up, but her true comfort had always come from her soccer ball. After a long day at school or a breakup with a boyfriend or a day when Daddy was coughing extra hard battling black lung disease, Chloe would go outside and dribble her soccer ball. It was always there for her—sure and steady.

Renee nudged Chloe's arm. "Did you see the new assistant athletic trainer?"

Chloe shook her head.

"That man is hotter than the sun beating down on our backs." Renee smiled. "Take a look at him. He's standing by Coach Collins."

Chloe glanced at the man towering several inches above her coach's short stature. Sporting a red Ball State T-shirt and black shorts, the new guy looked to be in pretty good shape, but Chloe couldn't distinguish anything about his facial features or even his hair color with the Cardinals cap planted on his head. "How can you tell?"

Renee wiggled her eyebrows. "I've seen him up close." She nudged Chloe's arm with her elbow. "And he is sizzling."

Chloe threw back her head and laughed. "Are you sure he's a mere mortal?"

"Girl, I'm telling you—I'm not sure."

"You stay here and drool." Chloe slid her left foot around a nearby soccer ball and shimmied it with ease in front of her. "I'm heading onto the field to impress Coach Jiminy Cricket—I mean Jimmy Collins."

"You'd better not let Coach hear you say that. You'll be running around this field until you're puking your guts out."

Chloe winked and motioned for Renee to follow her onto the field. "Come on.

I'm gonna score another on ya."

Renee threw her cup in the trash. "Wouldn't doubt it."

⚜

Trevor Montgomery lifted the baseball cap off his head then wiped the perspiration from his brow. Though soccer had been his passion for as long as he could remember, he couldn't deny he liked the sport much better once the weather turned a bit cooler. Placing the cap back on his head, he scanned the field for Sarah, the fullback he'd been guiding through physical therapy the last few months. Her knee had healed nicely since her surgery in May, but Trevor felt confident the girl wouldn't be back to full ability for another several weeks.

A tall girl zoomed past him. Though obviously muscular, her build was much thinner than her teammates'. She reminded him more of a model than a soccer player—until he watched the ball shuffling between her feet as if it had always belonged there. "Her control is amazing."

Coach Collins nodded, and a slight grin bowed his lips. "Yep. She's pretty awesome, all right. We've put twenty pounds on her in the four years we've had her."

"What?"

The coach smacked his gum and nodded. "You heard me right. Chloe was thin as a blade of grass when we picked her up from a small school in Otwell, Indiana, but, boy, could that gal dribble and shoot."

Trevor watched as Chloe kicked the soccer ball, nailing it into the goal. Her long, sandy-brown hair whipped around her face as she turned and high-fived one of her teammates.

"Got me again." The goalie scooped the ball from inside the net and threw it to the middle. "But I've figured you out, friend. That's the last one."

Trevor smiled when the tall beauty shrugged her shoulders and blew her friend a kiss. She moved like a gazelle with graceful motions back to the center of the field. "She's a senior, huh?"

"Yep. I'll hate to see her go. Works hard. Couldn't ask for a more coachable player." He smacked his gum again. "Does everything I ask. No questions. No complaints."

⚜

"What Coach don't know won't hurt him." Chloe bent down and untucked her shoelaces from inside the tops of her cleats.

"Chloe, you can't take those laces out. It's Coach's biggest pet peeve." Liz, Chloe's other roommate and one of the fullbacks for the team, pushed her hair behind her ear. "Where are your Sweet Spots anyway?"

Chloe visualized her candy-red, thick rubber bands sitting on top of her dresser. Sweet Spots were the best invention to the soccer world in Chloe's opinion. A player simply had to shimmy the thick rubber over the cleat and the band would hold the shoelaces in place on top of the shoe. No shoestrings poking into a player's foot beneath the lip of the cleats. "I was in a hurry and forgot them."

"If you break your leg. . ."

Chloe stood to her full height of five feet eleven inches, towering over her teammate. "I'm not going to break my leg."

"Okay." Liz lifted her hands in surrender. "Don't say I didn't warn you."

Walking back to center field, Chloe peeked at Coach Collins. He seemed deep in conversation with the trainer. She had to admit the new guy's height alone attracted her a bit. Most men were barely as tall as she. Not that she cared too much for the opposite sex anyway. Her hometown football king, Randy Reynolds, had made sure of that. She hoped he was happy with his snooty, prom-queen wife whose daddy owned a coal mine back home in Otwell. The last thing Chloe heard was that Randy had a strapping young son and another baby on the way.

A growl formed deep in her throat. Money had obviously meant more than every ounce of affection and love she had conjured for the overgrown country boy. *I'm glad he broke it off with me. I probably would have done something stupid like marry him right out of high school.* She took her position as center forward. *And I'd have missed out on this.*

The whistle blew to start the scrimmage again. Molly, the new sophomore center forward, dribbled the ball past Chloe. *I gotta keep an eye on that one.* Chloe turned and watched as Molly maneuvered the ball toward the goal. Having transferred from a small community college in Kentucky, Molly made a great second-string center forward. Chloe had every intention of making sure the gal stayed second string, at least until Chloe graduated.

Liz stole the ball from Molly and kicked it hard toward Chloe. Chloe ran forward to meet it. She tripped. Sharp, hot pain seared through her ankle. She fell forward toward the grass carpet. A piercing scream rang through her ears. In disbelief she realized it was her own.

Chapter 2

Trevor watched the color drain from Coach Collins's face. "Oh no! That girl never gets hurt!" He dropped his clipboard to the ground and sprinted onto the field.

Trevor turned and saw the tall girl the coach had called Chloe sitting on the ground with both hands wrapped around her foot. She rocked back and forth, scrunching her face in agony. Trevor ran toward her. He bent down next to Coach Collins. "What hurts?"

"My foot. My ankle." She spit the words through clenched teeth. A tear slipped from her squinted eyes.

"Your shoe's untied." Coach Collins growled. "Where're your Sweet Spots?"

"Sorry, Coach." She swiped her eyes with the back of her hand. "I'm okay. Just a little twist."

"Now wait a minute." Coach placed his hand on her shoulder. "Let's let Trevor take a look at it."

"I think I know my own body." Her eyes flashed with an anger Trevor knew was a mask for her pain. Despite Coach's warning, she tried to put pressure on her foot then let out a screeching howl.

"Here, Chloe." Trevor kept his voice calm but firm. Her gaze locked with his as he gently grabbed her cleat and began to loosen the untied shoestrings. She was obviously not one to willingly heed instruction, but heed it she must. Trevor never took his gaze from hers. A challenge flicked beneath her stubborn baby blues. Amused, he almost allowed a snicker to escape his lips. Almost. She'd started the staring war, and he'd be the one to finish it.

Without looking away, he pulled her sock off her foot. He grabbed the shin guard and slowly shimmied it down her leg. He watched as she sucked in her breath and scrunched her eyes shut when the protective piece touched her ankle. Looking down, he noted that her ankle and the top of her foot had already begun to swell. *Definitely a sprain. She may have a break. I hope it's not broken, Lord. It's obvious soccer means a lot to her.*

"That doesn't look good," Coach whispered and wiped his hand across his sweat-covered face.

"I think it would be best if I take her to the hospital to get an X-ray." Trevor tried to keep his tone optimistic, yet he could already tell from the severity of the swelling that Chloe would be out a couple of weeks in the best of scenarios.

"No, I'm fine." A sob spilled from her lips.

A short, stocky girl leaned toward another player and murmured, "I've never seen Chloe like this."

"I didn't even know she could cry," the other responded.

Chloe must have heard, as well, because she pushed away from him and tried to stand once more. "I'm fine. I know I'm—" She fell forward on her knees when she tried to put her weight on her injured foot.

"Okay. I've had enough of this." Trevor stood and swooped the woman into his arms.

"What do you think you're doing?" Her tear-splattered eyes widened in surprise.

"I'm getting you out of here. Taking you to the hospital." He turned and looked at Coach Collins. "I've got her. I'll call your cell as soon as I know something."

Coach Collins nodded and clapped his hands together. "All right. Show's over. Back to practice."

"I don't want you to carry me." A strong fist pounded into the back of his shoulder. "I'm okay." Her body shook in his arms as sobs overtook her. "I have to be."

He was surprised when she rested her face on his chest. She was obviously a strong woman, but he sensed her vulnerability. Everything in him wanted to protect her from her pain and embarrassment.

Once they were beside his car, he lowered her to her feet, making sure her weight was balanced on the uninjured foot. "Everything will be fine." He fished through the pocket of his shorts, pulled out his car keys, and unlocked the door. "I'll get you back on that field—"

"Your shirt!" She interrupted him, a look of horror on her face.

He glanced down at his red shirt and saw the enormous wet blotch across the front. He shrugged. "No big deal. Just tears."

"Yeah. Mine." She bit her bottom lip so hard Trevor feared she'd draw blood. "I don't cry."

"It'll dry in no time." He gently nudged her into the car and walked around to the driver's side. Slipping inside, he smiled at her. "I know. I've got another in the back." He jumped out of the car and grabbed a white polo from the backseat. Black running shorts and a polo shirt weren't exactly the best of matches, but he didn't want Chloe to be any more embarrassed than she already was.

⸙

Chloe knew her face had to be ten shades of red. *How could I have tripped over my own two feet? Now some guy I don't even know had to change his shirt because I cried all over it.* Chloe Andrews was a leader. People looked up to her. She was strong, not a babbling crybaby. She gazed out the front window, willing him to hurry so they could leave the field. The knowledge that her teammates sneaked peeks toward his car made her feel furious and humiliated all at the same time.

He slid back into the driver's seat. "Sorry."

"For what?" She tapped her fingers against the door handle.

"I didn't mean to embarrass you again."

Unwilling to let him think he could get the best of Chloe Andrews, she faced him. "You didn't embarrass me."

"I just didn't want you to feel uncomfortable with your tears on my shirt."

My tears on his shirt. Oh, the very notion of it made her blood boil. "What do I care if my tears got on your shirt? You didn't need to go change or anything. It was just a tiny spot."

A deep, guttural laugh filled his car. "Someone doesn't handle being vulnerable very well."

"Excuse me?" Heat enveloped her once more. How dare he try to psychoanalyze her! She hadn't asked for his opinion, hadn't even asked for him to help her off the field. She reached for the door handle. "I will not be laughed at."

The overgrown trainer touched something on the side of his door, and a click sounded throughout the car. "You're not going anywhere but to the hospital."

"I am not a child, Mr.—whatever your last name is. I believe I know how to unlock a door." She tried to flip the lock, but it wouldn't budge.

"Not in this car."

She glared at him. A smile that reminded her very much of the Cheshire cat from *Alice in Wonderland* formed on his lips.

"It's childproof. Once I lock the door on my side, you can't get out on yours. By the way, my last name is Montgomery." He extended his hand toward her. "Can we call a truce? I'd really like to help you with your ankle."

Chloe blew her long bangs away from her eyes. The sincerity in Trevor Montgomery's deep green eyes stirred something inside her. She wanted to trust him, to believe in him. She hadn't felt that way in a long time. What choice did she have anyway? Taking his hand, she shook it firmly. "Truce. . .for now."

"Good." He pushed the automatic button to roll down his window. "I didn't know how much longer I could hold my breath." Looking at her, he waved his hand in front of his nose. "You stink."

Her mouth dropped open. Without thinking, she punched his arm. "I can't believe you just said that."

"Truth hurts sometimes." He started the car then looked at her. "If it makes you feel any better, you *look* cute—a little disheveled but cute just the same."

She leaned back in the chair. Somehow that did make her feel better, but she'd never, not in a million years, admit it to him.

"There is no way I am staying off my foot for six weeks!"

Trevor watched in dismay as the young woman who represented Ball State's best hope for a winning season threw a wad of gauze at the young doctor who'd come into the room to tell Chloe the diagnosis for her foot.

"I can't wait six weeks. Our first game is in two." She picked up a roll of tape.

"Miss Andrews!" The doctor snatched the tape from her hand. "You are not a child. This is a sterile environment. One that demands your respect—"

Trevor reached for the doctor's arm as Chloe picked up a plastic bedpan. Confident she'd sail that through the air, as well, he pulled the doctor into the hall. "Tell me what you've found." He pulled out his Ball State ID. "I'll be her trainer. Let me tell her, and I'll deal with her."

The doctor exhaled and rubbed the back of his neck. "This is my first night for my emergency room residency." He glanced at his watch. "I guess I should say morning. It's almost lunchtime, and I haven't even had breakfast. No wonder my stomach's growling." He half chuckled, half sighed then looked at Trevor. "Between the child who threw up on me and the irate father who expressed his opinion in not the kindest of words, I am completely worn out."

"Don't worry. You'll develop a tough shell."

"So they tell me." He crossed his arms in front of his chest, letting the package Trevor assumed he'd prepared for Chloe dangle at his side. "I hope I don't get too hardened. My plan is to finish up and head over to Africa."

Trevor's curiosity was piqued. "For?"

"Missions work. I'd like to give medical care and witness to others at the same time." He uncrossed his arms. "Anyway. . ."

"I think that's wonderful. I'll pray for you."

"You're a Christian?"

Trevor rocked back on his heels. "Oh yes. My calling is to work from the sidelines, help ball players heal from injury, and share my faith every chance I get. My prayer is to get a job back home at the University of South Carolina, working for the Fighting Gamecocks."

"I'll pray for you, too." He let out a long breath. "This has been the highlight of my shift. Always good to get an encouraging reminder of why we need to keep going."

"Definitely. So what's the diagnosis?"

"Third-degree sprain."

"Ruptured ligaments?"

"Yes."

"She's going to need a cast?"

"Yes."

"A removable air cast will be good enough?"

"You know your stuff." The doctor chuckled and handed the package to Trevor. "I think an air cast will be enough. I'm going to prescribe some anti-inflammatory medicine for her." He pulled a pad out of his jacket pocket and scribbled a prescription on the top sheet. He handed it to Trevor. "I want her to stay completely off the ankle for two full weeks. After that you can begin her on some physical therapy."

Trevor scratched his chin and nodded. "Sounds good." He glanced at the door and took a deep breath.

"At least it wasn't broken."

"I agree." Trevor pointed to the door. "But I don't think she will."

The doctor patted Trevor's shoulder. "Have fun." He waved and walked down the hall. "I'll say a prayer for you with her, as well."

Trevor half smiled as he pushed open the door. His heart melted at the sight of Chloe sitting on the bed with her shoulders slumped and her gaze locked on the ground. Strands of once-sweaty hair had escaped her long, light brown ponytail and now stuck out around her head at odd angles. She was a complete mess, yet Trevor was drawn to her as he'd never been drawn to a woman before.

"Chloe?"

"Yeah."

She didn't look up at him, just sat still on the bed. He opened the package containing the air cast then knelt in front of her and fastened the cast to her foot.

"Come on." Trevor scooped her into his arms once more.

"What are you doing?" The fight had fled from her voice. Frustration and defeat replaced it.

"I'm taking you home." Trevor lowered her into the wheel-chair just outside the door. To his surprise she didn't argue, allowing him to push her to his car. Once she was nestled under her seat belt, he slipped into the driver's seat and drove away. Only able to get her address from her, Trevor focused on getting her home. He'd take her into the apartment and talk to her there.

After pulling into the lot, he jumped out and scurried over to her side. She opened the door and pointed toward the third apartment door. "There's a key under the mat."

"Okay. I'll open the door then come back for you."

She nodded, and he made his way to the apartment. Her quiet defeat was worse than her irrational fire. *She's probably a ticking time bomb that's going to blow the minute I tell her the prognosis.* After unlocking the door, he walked back to the car, lifted her out of it, and carried her into the apartment. He set her on the couch.

She clasped her hands in her lap and stared up at him. The fire was back. Not only could he see it; he could feel it. "How bad is it?"

"Well. . ."

"Broken?"

"No."

Though she probably hadn't meant for him to see it, Trevor watched her shoulders fall in relief. "Sprained?"

"Yes."

A smile warmed her face. Trevor couldn't help but notice how her eyes smiled with her lips. The expression was one of the sweetest he'd ever seen. "That's not so bad. I'll walk it off."

Trevor shook his head. "No, Chloe. This is a third-degree sprain. You've ruptured ligaments. You'll need to wear an air cast and rest it completely for two weeks. Then I'll begin you on some physical therapy. You should be ready to play in about six—"

"Our first game is in two weeks."

Trevor stared into her eyes. "You'll have to miss it."

"No. I won't."

Trevor spoke calmly but firmly. "Yes, Chloe. If you don't rest your ankle and stay off it for the next two weeks, you'll make the injury worse and prolong your recovery."

She shook her head. "I'll be back on that field in a week."

"No." The phone rang on the end table beside Chloe. It rang again. "Are you going to pick it up?"

"No."

"Why?"

"It's my mom, and I don't want to talk."

Trevor smiled. He'd tell her mother about the injury. Maybe she could talk some sense into Chloe. Before she realized what he was doing, Trevor swiped the receiver off the table. "Hello."

"Hello?" The woman on the other end sounded confused. "I believe I've called the wrong number."

"Are you trying to reach Chloe Andrews?"

Chloe grabbed his arm and whispered through clenched teeth. "What do you think you're doing?"

Trevor covered the phone with his hand. "Telling your mother."

"You will not." Chloe tried to grab it from his hand, but Trevor stepped out of her reach.

"Who is this?" Concern laced her mother's voice.

"It's okay, ma'am. My name is Trevor Montgomery. I'm an assistant athletic trainer for Ball State University. Chloe has had a bit of an injury. I've just brought her home from the hospital. Now I'm going to head to the drugstore to pick up her medicine and some crutches."

Her mother gasped. "Is she all right? I'm coming—"

"It's all right, Mrs. Andrews. Chloe will be fine. I'll let her tell you what happened."

Trevor smiled as he handed the phone to Chloe. The look she returned was one that spoke of her desire to cause horrendous pain to his person. He couldn't help but laugh out loud.

Chloe covered the phone with her hand. "I'll get you for this."

He winked. "You don't scare me, Chloe Andrews. In fact, the fire that blazes in your eyes and the grit that fills your spirit do nothing but intrigue me."

Chapter 3

Chloe hung up the phone after nearly an hour of conversation with her mother. Having attempted to explain to her mom that she would be okay in a few days, Chloe leaned back against the couch cushions knowing it would be a matter of days before Lorma Andrews drove up for a visit. *She'll probably bring Daddy with her.* Chloe closed her eyes. She could hardly bear the thought of seeing her father. Black lung disease had practically taken over his frail body. His coughs hurt her ears. Keeping her distance from him was the only way she had learned to cope with her father's illness.

Chloe jumped when the front door swung open and Liz and Renee bolted inside, with Coach Collins behind them.

"What did they say?" Liz fell to the carpet at Chloe's feet. Renee plopped onto the recliner beside her.

Coach walked over to her. "How are you?"

"I'll be up and at it in a couple days." Chloe tried to smile as a bolt of pain dashed through her ankle as if protesting her words.

"No. She won't."

Chloe looked up to find Trevor shutting the door. He held a bag in one hand and a pair of crutches in the other. Chloe cringed at the sight. There was no way she was using those things for the next few weeks.

"She'll be using these for the next few weeks." Trevor leaned the crutches against the wall. He pulled a container of pills from the bag. "It's been a few hours since your injection at the hospital. My guess is you're needing a couple of these pretty bad about now."

Chloe scowled at him. She would not admit to him, not even for a moment, that she needed something to ease the throbbing in her ankle. She'd rather lie in bed in a cold sweat all night than endure his know-it-all glances.

"How bad is it?" Coach Collins looked at Trevor.

"Third-degree sprain. She'll be out six weeks."

"Six weeks!" Liz, Renee, and Coach exclaimed in unison.

Chloe closed her fists. Everything in her wanted to throttle the trainer. "He's wrong." Chloe spit the words through clenched teeth.

"No. I'm not." He looked at Liz and lifted a couple of pills in the air. "I need to get her a drink of water so she can take these. Where are your glasses?"

"There are some bottles of water in the fridge." Liz didn't take her gaze off Chloe. Disbelief cloaked her and Renee's faces. Coach rubbed his forehead with his forefingers; frustration etched his features. Chloe wanted to crawl under the couch and hide. First she'd spent an hour on the phone with her mother. Now she had to witness her coach and teammates' disappointment.

"Here. Take these." Trevor held out a glass of water and two pills.

She gazed up at him. Desperate to blame him for all that had happened, the sympathy and kindness radiating from his eyes made her want to cry. . .again. She looked away. "I don't want them."

"Take them."

"You do what he tells you." Coach Collins pointed his finger at her. "We need you to do everything he says so you can get better and back out on that field."

Chloe noted the tone in his voice that seemed to say, "Don't worry. All will be fine." Many a player had dug her grave and buried her career with that tone in the past. Though he intended it to sound encouraging, Coach meant he would do whatever necessary to pick up the team and go on—without her. Unbidden tears welled in her eyes. The last thing she wanted was to cry in front of her coach and roommates.

"How about if I help you get settled into your room?"

Chloe looked up at Trevor. He winked. *He knows I'm about to come unglued, and he's getting me out of here.* She nodded and reached her arms around his neck when he bent down to pick her up. *Why is he being nice to me? I've been nasty to him since the moment he came onto the field.*

With ease he carried her into her room and set her on the bed. She combed her hand through the hair that had escaped her ponytail. "Really I need to clean up."

"I know. I just thought you needed to be alone for a minute."

Chloe studied the trainer, the man she'd probably spend a good amount of time with over the next few weeks. Dark stubble had formed on his chin, darker than his hair. It gave him a strong, masculine look and also made his green eyes brighter. There was no question he was attractive, and she definitely enjoyed sparring with him. A smile threatened to form on her lips.

He touched her chin for a moment. "I'll pray for you, Chloe."

She frowned, and her heart fell into her stomach. *Just what I need, more people praying for me.*

⬥

Trevor tucked the treasured Bible under his arm as he made his way to the church building. It was one of his most prized possessions, and he loved to feel the edges of the duct tape that made up the book's binding. His mother had passed away a little more than twelve years ago, when he was only sixteen, but the notes and written thoughts that filled her Bible made him feel closer to her.

He knew her better now than he ever had when she was alive.

He stepped into the building, and his body involuntarily shook from the change in temperature. The cool air-conditioning was a welcome relief from the heat that beat down on him outside. Fall couldn't arrive fast enough.

A vision of a disheveled and pain-filled Chloe sitting on the hospital bed swept through his mind. She had invaded his thoughts quite a bit over the last twenty-four hours. He'd itched to visit her today but decided to give her a day to come to terms with the injury. He couldn't decide whether to smile or shake his head at the unruly yet passionate behavior of the woman. Without a doubt he'd pay her a visit tomorrow. He feared she'd be up trying to walk on her ankle if he didn't keep a close eye on her.

"Hey, Trevor. How's it going?"

Trevor turned at the familiar voice. Joy filled him when one of the men's soccer players walked up to him and shook his hand. "Hello, Matt. I'm glad to see you here again."

"It's been fairly interesting." Matt shrugged his shoulders. "Besides, quite a few attractive women attend this Bible study." He winked.

Trevor grimaced, wanting Matt's reason for coming to church to be more about seeking and less about flirting. *Ah, but, Lord, You say Your word will never come back void. I need to trust You to do a work in him.* "That's true, but what do you think about the Gospel of John?"

Matt furrowed his eyebrows. "I can't decide. I don't know when he's speaking literally and when it's figurative. The book's keeping my attention, though, which is more than most college professors can do." Matt let out a laugh.

Trevor laughed, as well. "If you ever have any questions, I'd be happy to answer them if I can."

"That'd be great." Matt's gaze followed one of the women who walked past them into the room. He looked back at Trevor. "Hey, I heard there was an injury on the women's team. Chloe Andrews?"

"Yep. She has a third-degree sprain in her ankle. She'll be out six weeks."

Matt shook his head. "Man, that's too bad. She's like their starting center."

"Yep."

"She's kinda cute, too."

A knot formed in Trevor's stomach when Matt wiggled his eyebrows and winked.

"I'll agree she's cute, but as to her ankle, she and I will work on it. We'll get her back on that field as quick as possible." Trevor knew he sounded a bit more possessive than he should have, but the idea of Matt thinking of Chloe more like a package of meat and less like a gifted, spirited young woman grated on Trevor's nerves.

"You'll work wonders." Matt patted Trevor's shoulder. "I might stop at the grocery store on the way home, pick up a few flowers, and take them over to Chloe's apartment." He nudged Trevor with his elbow. "Tell her I'm thinking about her."

Trevor tried not to frown. "That would be. . .nice."

"Guess we'd better go inside."

Trevor watched as Matt walked into the room and sat beside the young woman he'd noticed entering only moments ago. Trevor willed back a scowl as he took a seat in front of Matt and turned to the scripture the Bible study leader had written on the board.

He tried to focus on the words from the leader, but the woman behind him giggled at something Matt had whispered. Everything in Trevor wanted to turn around and punch Matt in the jaw. How could the guy flirt with one woman when he had plans to go flirt with another right after class? *Why does it even bother me?* He knew the answer. It was Chloe Andrews. The woman had fascinated him in a way no one had before.

But she doesn't know You, Lord.

Trevor's heart sank at the truth of it. He'd never been one to chase after women, wasn't worried about dating in high school or college—until Chloe. Now she was all he could think about. *Lord, this isn't good. How am I going to be her trainer and keep my feelings at bay?*

"Did you hear what the scripture just said?" The leader's voice drew Trevor from his thoughts. "Let me read God's Word again. Jesus said, 'And I will do whatever you ask in my name, so that the Son may bring glory to the Father. You may ask me for anything in my name, and I will do it.'"

Trevor peered down at the text before him and reread what the leader had said.

"Now let me ask you," the leader continued, "do you think this means that if we want a Corvette, Jesus will get us one?"

"Works for me." Someone whooped from behind.

"Sorry, but that's not at all what Jesus is saying." The leader laughed. "Although I'd love a '67 Mustang. Jesus is saying that when we ask for the things He wants, when our requests match His, God will give us what we ask."

"I've been asking God to save my father for ten years," responded a tiny blond a few seats from Trevor. "Surely that is in God's will."

"Yes, it is." The leader nodded his head. "But your father has to decide to accept Christ." He smiled and pointed at her. "You keep praying."

Trevor closed his eyes. *God, I'm falling for a beautiful young woman who I have a hunch doesn't know You. Please draw her to Yourself. May she receive You as Lord of her life, and until she does, keep my heart safe.*

"I *knew* it." Chloe looked through the peephole in the front door. She opened the door. "Mama!" Chloe shifted her weight onto one crutch as she opened the door wide. She hated using the crutches, but when she had tried to put weight on her foot first thing that morning, pain shot through her ankle with such intensity she thought she'd broken it. "Where's Daddy?"

Her mother set her suitcase inside the door and hugged Chloe. "Too sick to come." She pulled away and held her daughter at arm's length. "You have to get down to Otwell and see your father. He's not doing well."

Chloe cleared her throat. Thinking of her father's illness, knowing it would claim him eventually, hurt her to the core of her being. She thought of the many nights all eight children and her mother would sit on the front porch and sing hymns while Daddy played his guitar. It would be only a matter of time before her four older sisters would start fighting over who had the best singing voice. Being the youngest and closest in age to her three older brothers, even though one—her twin—was only ten minutes older than she, Chloe was never included in the fights. *It's silly. I always wanted to fight with them, but they never even acknowledged I was there.*

"Hi, Chloe."

Chloe looked up to find one of her sisters standing in the door. "Kylie, I'm surprised you came." She gazed at her sister's blossoming midsection. "Wow! I didn't even know you were pregnant."

"Well, you don't come down to see us much, and we don't get too many phone calls. Come here, squirt." Kylie stood on tiptoes and enveloped Chloe in her arms.

"I hate that name."

"I guess it really doesn't fit anymore since I have to practically jump up and down, even with you leaning on crutches, to give you a hug."

Chloe grinned. "True."

"Bet you didn't know Ryan and I are adopting two children from Belize also."

"What?"

"Yeah. As soon as the adoption is finalized, I'm really going to be a mommy."

"I can't believe it. You're not still working, are you?"

"No. I won't be able to do that—"

"Girls," their mother interrupted. "Let's talk once we actually get in the apartment and settle Chloe down on the couch."

"Sounds like a plan. My foot is throbbing." Chloe started to make her way to the couch.

"I can't believe you just admitted that."

Chloe turned at the deep voice that spoke behind her. Trevor Montgomery, one of the few men able to do it, peered several inches down at her. She stuck out her tongue at him. "I can't very well admit it to you. You think you're right about everything."

Trevor laughed and extended his hand to her mother. "I'm Trevor Montgomery."

"Lorma Andrews. It's a pleasure to meet you."

Chloe glanced at Kylie as she eased down onto the couch. Kylie pointed toward Trevor then fanned her face and smiled as if to say that Trevor was hot. Chloe couldn't hold back her chuckle when he turned to Kylie and caught her making the gesture. Kylie's face blazed redder than Trevor's when he extended his hand to introduce himself.

"Now that you've met my family, I'm ready for you to fix my ankle." Chloe saved her sister from having to say anything to Trevor.

"I won't be able to fix it." He walked over to her, bent down, and pulled the Velcro from her air cast. After taking it off, he touched both sides of her foot. She flinched despite her attempt not to. "It's still quite swollen." He shook his head. "You're just going to have to rest it for a few weeks. You are still putting ice on it, right?"

Nodding, Chloe's heart fluttered when his fingers stayed just above her ankle. He rubbed the swollen spots, asking if any hurt. Heat filled her at the tenderness of his touch, and Chloe wondered if her face blazed as her sister's had only moments before. Glancing at Kylie and noting the smirk draping her features, Chloe knew her face glowed just as she feared. "A few weeks is too long." She pulled her foot away from him.

Trevor rolled his eyes. "Yes, but if you want to get back in the game, you have to do as I say."

Chloe's flutters flitted away at the tone of his voice. They were replaced by hot anger streaming through her veins. He was not her boss, her daddy, or her coach. He did not know everything. Her body would heal quickly, faster than he could ever imagine. She'd show him!

"So have you had any visitors?" His gaze scanned her apartment until he spotted the vase of flowers on the dining room table. "Someone sent you flowers?"

Chloe shifted in her seat. "Yes. Matt stopped by last night. You probably know him. He plays on the—"

"Matt Ellis."

The scowl that filled his expression piqued Chloe's curiosity. Why would Trevor care if Matt brought her flowers? If she didn't know better, she'd believe Trevor was jealous. *That's ridiculous. He's made it perfectly clear that I am nothing more than an aggravation to him.*

Trevor's scowl disappeared, and he looked at her mother. "How long are you staying?"

"Just a couple of days."

"That's too bad." He stared at Chloe and seemed to force a smile. "It's going to be hard to make her stay off her ankle."

"I can try to stay a bit longer," her mother answered. "It's just that—"

"No. You need to go home to Daddy." She turned to Trevor. "My father was a coal miner for years. Now he's very ill with black lung disease."

Trevor stood and touched her mother's shoulder. "I'm sorry. My mom died from breast cancer when I was sixteen. It was the hardest thing I've ever experienced."

Chloe studied Trevor. She couldn't imagine the pain he must have felt. Yet he hadn't become bitter by it. He didn't seem to have distanced himself from people. Chloe could hardly even visit her father. He was alive, yet she didn't have the courage to go visit him because it hurt *her* too much. Shame filled her heart. As soon as she could, she would make the trip to Otwell to see her daddy.

"What's his name?" Trevor's question interrupted her thoughts.

"Richard Andrews."

"If it's all right, I'll add him to my church's prayer list. I'll be sure to pray for him every day, as well."

A tear slipped down her mother's cheek. She brushed it away with the back of her hand. "That would be wonderful. Thank you."

Chloe watched as Trevor bent down and gave her mother a quick hug. The man was perfect. Except for the "praying" thing. She'd had her fill of praying growing up in the Andrews home. In her opinion, not a whole lot had come of it.

Chapter 4

Why do you keep asking me about Trevor Montgomery?" Chloe dropped her crutches against the bleachers at the soccer field and sat down. She helped coach a local soccer team of young girls. Most of the teens were already on the field dribbling their soccer balls around each other before practice started.

Kylie lowered onto the bleacher with a loud sigh. "I don't know. He's kinda cute, super attentive to you"—she leaned closer to Chloe—"and he's a Christian."

"Humph." Chloe bent over to see if her ankle had started to swell again. Yesterday it had almost looked normal, but when she tried to make her way without crutches to the bathroom in the middle of the night, the ankle swelled again. *A whole week's passed, and it's still swollen.* She growled and hit the bleacher.

"It's not going to heal unless you listen to your trainer. . .your very handsome trainer."

Chloe glared at her sister. "I don't care that he's cute. Don't care that he's attentive. And I definitely don't care that he's a Christian."

"What's that supposed to mean?"

"Nothing. I'm just not interested. Okay, Kylie?"

"Fine." Kylie stood. "I'm going to the bathroom. Could you do me a favor?"

"What?" Chloe snapped.

"By the time I get back, decide to be nice. I'm sorry about your ankle, but I'm tired of listening to your pouty, poor-me attitude." She pointed her finger at Chloe. "And you need to shape up in the way you're treating Mama. You were raised to be respectful and kind, but you've acted like a spoiled brat since we got here. We're leaving tomorrow, and there's no telling when you'll decide to grace us with your presence again. Act like you're happy your mother has come to see you." She turned and stomped toward the restroom.

Chloe rested her elbows on her knees and looked at the ground. She had acted like a jerk the last few days. But it was her ankle. If it weren't for her injury, she'd be her normal, happy self. *"No matter my circumstance, I have learned to be content."* Her father's echoing of the apostle Paul's words filled her mind. He'd spoken of contentment several times when she saw him last. He'd coughed and hacked, and his face had scrunched up in obvious pain each time he said it. She didn't understand how he could talk of peace no matter what.

Her heart felt heavy, and she closed her eyes. *What am I missing?* Her ankle started to throb, and she wished to yank out the pain and throw it away from her.

"Hey, Coach." Interrupting her thoughts, one of the teen girls plopped down beside her. "What happened to your foot?"

"Sprained my ankle."

"Is that all? I sprained my ankle once, and Mom told me to walk it off. I did, and it was fine."

Chloe frowned. "I wish mine were that easy."

The girl sighed. "I guess you won't be able to practice with us today."

"Only from the sidelines."

"That stinks."

"Believe me." Chloe tightened the Velcro on her air cast. "I totally agree."

<hr>

Trevor stayed close to Chloe as she walked on crutches toward the soccer field. Two weeks had passed since her injury, and her ankle wasn't healing well. It still swelled when she tried to walk on it. She'd been silent on the drive over. He knew watching the first game of the season, her senior season, was almost more than she could bear. The team and coaches had gone onto the field, warming up before the game. He and Chloe took their seats beside the team's bench. Glancing at her, his heart constricted at the longing that showed on her face.

What can I say to make her feel better? He peeked at her profile. Strands of long hair escaped her ponytail and kissed her cheek. Long dark lashes fanned from eyes that focused with intensity on the happenings on the field. Her straight posture exuded a confidence unlike that of many women he knew; yet he had seen the vulnerability she tried so hard to hide. She was a force to reckon with. A pillar of strength for her team. A pillar built on sand that had begun to shift.

Ah, Jesus, I'm intrigued with her. I can't deny it. I want to know her better. More. He shook the admission away. Being honest about his feelings was one thing, but succumbing to them was quite another. He could think of Chloe only as a soccer player in need of his expertise. *Unless she gives her life over to You.*

No. He couldn't think like that, couldn't entertain considering a relationship with her. Sure, he would pray for her, and one day she might receive Christ into her heart. But he'd known far too many Christians who found themselves in wrong relationships because they'd banked on the hope that one day their other half would accept Christ.

"Chloe?"

"What?"

Her response was quick, almost harsh, and Trevor nearly laughed out loud. He was thinking of relationships, and Chloe had given him every reason to believe she found him to be the most aggravating, annoying man on the planet.

Why would I want to mess with the woman anyway? She's completely difficult.

Chloe looked at him. "I'm sorry I snapped at you." The blue in her eyes shimmered with the threat of tears. "This is harder than I expected."

"I know." Desire to wrap his arm around her shoulder and fear she would be offended by the gesture warred within him. He nudged her arm with his elbow. "How was your visit with your mom and sister?"

"Good. I guess. They left a couple of days ago." She nodded her head then looked away from him. "I need to go see my dad."

"I'd be happy to take you to see him." Trevor leaned back, surprised at his offer. "I mean, if you want me to."

"Why would you do that?" Her icy blue eyes pierced him.

Why would he? Because he was attracted to her? Because he wanted to know her better? Because he wanted to share his faith with her? A good Christian would say the latter, but Trevor knew his heart. He was treading on ultra-thin ice, and if he wasn't careful, he'd have more than slipping to worry about. A dip in freezing water was more likely. "To help you out, I guess."

She nodded as the team raced from the field with only minutes before the game was to begin. "I may take you up on that."

Coach Collins flopped down beside him. He pointed to Chloe, who was talking to a teammate. "How's my girl?"

Beautiful. Wonderful. A gem that needs the mire washed away from it by the pure blood of Jesus. None of those estimations was what her coach wanted to hear. "Doing all right."

"How much longer?"

"I don't know. I hoped to begin physical therapy by now, but her ankle is still swelling." He shrugged his shoulder. "Maybe five weeks. If she listens to me."

Coach Collins frowned. "Is she not doing what she's supposed to?"

"I have a feeling she's tried to walk on it a few times, but true injury has a way of forcing us to believe it's there."

"Molly's taking her place for now. She's been doing well in practice. We'll see how the game goes. We won the coin toss."

The coach stood and huddled with the girls. After he gave a quick pep talk, the team parted, and the starters ran out on the field. The referee blew the whistle, and Molly took control of the ball, dribbled past the fullbacks, and kicked it into the goal. The fans went wild with excitement, as did the players.

"Did you see that?" Coach clapped his hands. "I've never seen a gal take control and score so quickly. Not in a college game anyway." He cupped his hand around his mouth. "Great job, Molly!"

Trevor glanced at Chloe. Though a smile bowed her lips and her hands met and separated in a clap, fear filled her eyes. Molly had taken her spot.

Molly has my spot. She glared at the air cast wrapped around her ankle. *It has to heal. Now! Yesterday!* Peeking at Coach, she watched as he jumped up and down and his fists pumped the air. Her hands grew sticky as a cold sweat covered her skin. Her senior year. Her last season to play for the Cardinals. And she sat on the bench like a second-string player. *At least a second-string player has the chance of getting in the game. I don't.*

She peered out at the partially filled stands. It would have been nice to see her mama and daddy out there. A sudden wave of memories cascaded through her mind. It was her last game of high school. The whole family had come to support her. Each with their faces painted green and yellow—the school's colors. Even her youngest nephew, only eight months at the time, had paint smudged on his cheeks. All of them had her number, lucky thirteen, painted in deepest gold on the front of their green sweatshirts. The October night had been bitter cold, even for Indiana. But they'd come. All of them. To support her. She'd not only scored every goal for her team, but also been awarded a full-ride scholarship to Ball State University.

She snapped from the memory. For the first time in four years, she didn't feel able to control a soccer field. Didn't feel capable of putting an opposing player in her place with amazing dribbling skills. She watched as Molly took control of the ball again. For once someone was better than she was. Chloe longed for her family.

She needed someone besides herself.

Chapter 5

Chloe checked her reflection in the Muncie Mall restroom mirror. She raked her fingers through her hair, still surprised at how much she liked her new haircut. The long layers the stylist had trimmed into her tresses that fell well past her shoulders gave life to her normally plain style. Opening her purse, she fished out her melon-colored lip gloss and applied it to her lips. The subtle color complemented her sleeveless sweater perfectly. It was an unusual occasion that Chloe felt pretty or even feminine. This happened to be one of those rare moments.

And she liked it.

After shoving the lip gloss back in her purse, she snapped the bag shut and lifted the long skinny strap over her head, allowing the strap to rest on her left shoulder and the purse to rest at her right hip. Though more of a sporty look, it was the only way she could carry it and use her crutches. Her moment of femininity rushed away as she leaned on the crutches.

She felt anything but pretty using them.

Remembering a friend from high school who'd had to use a walker because of cerebral palsy, a flash of shame shot through her. Chloe had always deemed Rebecca beautiful, as had everyone in her class. *It's just hard when you're not used to them,* she told herself. She stood up, putting her weight on her good foot, and lifted her arm above her head. Walking from shop to shop had left a large raw spot under both of her arms. Each step was agony, but there was no way Chloe would admit it to her friends.

"You about ready?"

Chloe dropped her arm when Liz stepped into the rest area. "Yep." She leaned into her crutches and gritted against the pain as she followed her friend.

"Renee wants to stop by her favorite department store. There's a jacket she said she's been eyeballing for weeks. With all the sales going on today. . ."

The raw spots took precedence over Liz's babbling. Chloe tried to listen. She ground her teeth with each step she took, the pain was so intense. This was their shopping trip to celebrate their first victory of the year, and she didn't know how she would make it through several more hours. She couldn't fathom enduring the pain, but she couldn't admit defeat, either.

"Chloe, I'm going to grab a pretzel. Want to go with me?"

Glancing at the owner of the voice, Chloe was surprised to see it was Molly, the gal who'd taken her position on the soccer field. Chloe had given the younger girl the cold shoulder all day, and in truth Chloe had zero desire to hang out with the sophomore. She planned to earn her spot back as soon as her ankle decided to cooperate, but the chance to sit a moment or two was too enticing to pass up. "Sure."

After making her way to the stand, Chloe ordered a pretzel with chocolate dip and a large soda. She grabbed her pretzel and realized she wouldn't be able to carry her dip and drink, as well. She scowled at her crutches. She hated them. Everything in her wanted to throw them through the glass display window before her.

"I've got it. You go sit."

Chloe looked at Molly. The girl's expression was tender, compassionate, and completely infuriating. But what choice did Chloe have? "Thanks." She forced a smile. Why had she agreed to this outing in the first place? Trevor would kill her if he found out. And her ankle throbbed nearly as much as it had the first day.

Flopping onto one of the benches in the center of the mall, she pushed a fake leaf from the potted tree beside her away from her face. She laid the crutches against the pot and leaned back on the bench, allowing a soft sigh to escape her lips.

"They're no fun, huh?" Molly sat beside her and scooped Chloe's food from the tray then handed it to her.

"What?"

"Your crutches."

Chloe shrugged. "I'll live."

"Use baby powder."

"What?"

"On your arms. It doesn't take away all the pain, but the powder keeps you from getting too raw."

Chloe stared at her pretzel. Obviously her attempt at showing no pain had failed. She took a drink, fighting the emotions welling inside her. Chloe Andrews had always been the strong one. The one who could outplay everyone, even her brothers' friends. Now she had to use baby powder for her chafed armpits. The humiliation was unbearable.

"You know I had to sit out my entire senior year in high school. Broke my foot in two places." Molly's voice was soft. She picked off a piece of pretzel and popped it into her mouth.

Chloe turned and took in the girl sitting beside her. Molly, though several inches shorter than Chloe, was a powerhouse. Even sitting casually, the muscles in her arms and legs flexed slightly with each move she made. Her short, apparently dyed blond hair was cut so she had straight bangs parted to one side and blunt spikes around the back of her head. The mere sight of Molly screamed athlete. Chloe tilted her head. Or punk rocker. But Molly's dark chocolate eyes were kind and honest. Her gaze extended help and friendship, as did her smile.

Chloe swallowed, realizing she'd never once extended an offer of help to the sophomore, never even asked how practice was going or if transferring was working out for her. Her feelings of leadership waned as she inwardly admitted she hadn't been the leader she should have been to this teammate and probably others. "How'd you break it? Driving in on a goalie?"

A twinge of pink dotted Molly's cheeks, and her lips bowed up. "Actually. . ." She pulled off another piece of pretzel and dipped it in her nacho cheese before taking the bite. "It's a bit embarrassing." Swallowing, she feigned choking and shoved her straw into her mouth.

Chloe laughed and smacked Molly's back. "Come on. You gotta tell me now."

"Okay, okay." Molly set her cup on the floor. She brushed crumbs from her legs. "My little brother's skateboard was sitting in the driveway one day. I'd seen him do flips and whatnot on the thing and wondered what it would be like to try to stand on a board on wheels." Molly stopped, shook her head, and stared at the ceiling.

Chloe felt her eyebrows lift as her mouth opened. This was the last thing she expected. "And. . ." She motioned for Molly to go on.

"And our driveway is on a bit of a hill. Which I hadn't considered when I jumped on the board." She clapped her hands. "The thing shot down the driveway so fast I hit the curb at the bottom, went flying through the air, and landed in the road."

"You're lucky you weren't hurt worse."

"My mom saw the whole thing. She laughed so hard, wishing she'd had the camcorder. She felt sure we'd have won the grand prize on *America's Funniest Home Videos*."

"But your foot."

Molly nodded. "Yeah. It was tough. I was captain of our team. Felt like I'd let them down." She shrugged her shoulders. "In a funny way it was the best thing that ever happened to me. I realized the team was made up of more people than just me. We even came in second in the state that year."

Chloe gripped her drink. Condensation cooled her fingertips. She put the cup down and wiped her hands on her capris. How could anyone believe an injury to be a good thing? Chloe surely didn't. She knew it took more than just her to make up the team, but she was still a valuable part of it, a needed component. Glancing at Molly, her heart and mind warred within her. Molly had taken Chloe's spot. Maybe this kindness and the pep talk were nothing more than a facade, a way of making Chloe want to give in to the injury and allow Molly to steal her place. *Time will tell if Molly is really just playing me.*

A contemporary Christian song suddenly blared from Molly's purse. She scooped her cell phone from it, pushed TALK, and held it to her ear. Chloe only half listened to the one-sided conversation as she watched people walk on strong, healthy legs back and forth in front of her. Her mind replayed every encounter she'd had with Molly, trying to decipher if she should trust the sophomore.

"The girls are heading this way." Molly interrupted her thoughts. She put her phone back in her purse. "They shouldn't be here for another twenty minutes. Maybe we could call someone to come pick you up."

Chloe frowned. "What are you talking about? I'm going home with you guys."

"Some of the guys from the men's soccer team are with them."

"So?"

"Trevor, too."

Chloe lifted her eyebrows as a wave of panic washed through her. "Oh no."

Molly bobbed her head and grabbed the pretzel from Chloe's hands and picked up the drinks from the floor. Standing, she shoved them into the trash and helped Chloe to her feet. "If we move quick, he'll never know you were here."

"You knew I wasn't supposed to come."

"Oh yeah."

"You didn't say anything."

"I understood."

"Now you're helping me out of here so my trainer doesn't go ballistic on me."

"Well, yeah."

Chloe let out a long breath. "You really want to help me, don't you?"

"I'd like to think we're friends." Molly turned to face her. "At the very least, we're teammates."

Chloe touched Molly's arm, realizing the sophomore was a teammate in the truest of ways. She wanted what was best for Chloe. Molly was different from most of the girls. Though it pained her to admit it, she was different from Chloe, as well. *I can change all that. I can become the person who cares about what's best for others.* "Definitely friends."

"Who can we call?" Molly pulled out her phone again.

"I don't know. Both of my roommates are here." She followed Molly's much-too-quick steps toward an exit. "How 'bout Sarah? She's not here."

"Good idea. She's back at practice after her knee surgery, so she's definitely got to be able to drive again." Molly scrolled through telephone numbers on her cell phone as Chloe made her way past another store.

"Tell her I'll sit right out front—" Chloe ran into what felt like a brick wall. She gasped and peered up at the man. "I'm so sorry. I'm..."

The man's brows met in a furrowed frown, and his gaze settled on her foot. He crossed his arms in front of his chest. "Imagine seeing you here." Trevor's voice dripped with sarcasm.

"Busted."

❦

"Well, I. . ."

Trevor watched as Chloe's gaze darted from him to the displays around him. Her lips pursed together, and he knew she was trying to conjure a good explanation for being at the mall when she should be resting. In his experience, athletes were notorious for pushing their injuries too far. In the limited time he'd known Chloe, he'd recognized she was an athlete. He'd have to keep reminding her of her need for rest. *I'll probably have to padlock her door and physically sit on her to get her to stay off that ankle.* Frustration seethed through every inch of his marrow. The woman would never heal if she didn't heed his instructions.

Molly shut her cell phone. "Guess I don't need to call Sarah."

Chloe's cheeks blazed red. "Guess not."

"Why were you calling Sarah?" Trevor lifted his eyebrows and glanced from one girl to the other. "Trying to make an escape from the big, bad Trevor?"

"Something like that." Molly looked away.

"Of course I am an adult. Capable of making my own choices," Chloe mumbled.

"Yes, but if you want back on that field—"

"Hey, you guys." Liz's voice interrupted Trevor. "I'm so glad we caught up with you." Liz put her arm around Molly. The majority of the men's and women's soccer teams huddled in a mass in the center of the mall. "Matt wants to go to Pizza King."

"Matt hungry." Matt wiggled his eyebrows and rubbed his stomach.

"Yum." Molly nodded. "I love Pizza King. We don't have any where I'm from."

"Where are you from? The moon?" Matt elbowed Trevor and snorted.

"No, Kentucky. But I love Pizza King so much I may graduate and start my own chain back home."

"I love their barbecue sauce supreme." Chloe shifted her crutches, and Trevor noted the raw spots under her arms. Not only did the woman not need to be waltzing around the mall, but he also would have thought she'd have enough sense to wear more than a sleeveless sweater to pad her arms. Even though the color did look pretty on her.

"Let's go, then." Matt moved closer to Chloe. "You look gorgeous."

Her skin turned pink, and she looked at the ground. "Thanks."

Trevor's heart raced, and his hands clammed up. Couldn't she see? Didn't she know Matt was a shameless flirt? But there she was acting flattered by such a

157

shallow comment. *Even if I was thinking the same thing. Why didn't I say it first?*

The group had already made its way out of the mall. Only Matt and Trevor had lingered with Chloe. Searching for something, anything, to say, Trevor shoved his hand in his jeans pocket, yanked out his car keys, and gripped them. His blood boiled at the very thought of Matt going after Chloe.

"You want to ride over with me?" Matt's voice dripped with sweetness, making Trevor want to punch the younger man in the nose.

Chloe giggled and nodded her head as Trevor shook his. He couldn't believe Chloe was gullible enough to fall for the infamous flirt's charms. Jealousy and disbelief filled him as his mind raced for a way to keep Chloe from Matt.

"Hurry up!" one of the men's soccer players yelled to Matt as they walked into the parking lot. "The doors are locked." Two other players gestured to Matt, as well.

Trevor's grin spread over his face, his cheeks almost pained at the fullness of it. "Looks like your car's loaded. Chloe can ride with me."

Matt glanced at him. "Unless you want to do a buddy a favor and give those guys a ride."

Trevor shrugged. "Can't do it. I haven't cleaned my physical therapy equipment out of the backseat of my car yet."

"Fine. See ya at Pizza King, Chloe." Matt walked away from them.

Trevor unlocked his car and opened the door for Chloe. He took her crutches from her and laid them in the backseat on top of all his stuff. *I should have cleaned this mess weeks ago.* He inwardly chuckled. *Sometimes procrastination pays off.* He walked around the car and settled into the driver's seat.

"Go ahead and let me have it."

He glanced at Chloe as she buckled her seat belt then stared out the windshield. To her, he was the constant naysayer, the antagonist, the enemy. How he wished they had met under different circumstances. And that she was a Christian. *Oh Lord, I should have found a way to let her ride with Matt. I can't pursue her.*

"Go ahead. I'm waiting."

Trevor started the car. "I wasn't going to say anything to you about your ankle." He pulled out of the mall parking lot and into traffic. "I did notice you have a raw spot under your arm. . . ."

"Ugh." She slapped her leg. "I wish I'd never worn this sweater. It was new, and I liked the color. . . ."

"It looks nice on you."

She looked out her window. "Thanks."

"I have some ointment that might help your arms."

Chloe listened to the chatter around the table at Pizza King. Matt kept *accidentally* bumping into her foot under the table. She was beginning to believe it was his adolescent way of flirting with her. Evidently he didn't remember she had a severely sprained ankle and each little tap hurt like crazy.

She bit into her pizza and glanced at Molly and Trevor. Whatever they were discussing must have been interesting, because they seemed completely enthralled with what the other had to say. Both had surprised her on this outing. Molly had been kind to Chloe when she had nothing to gain, when Chloe had been anything but kind to her. Trevor also didn't lay into her for not listening to his instructions. He'd pointedly, without reservation or confusion, told her to stay completely off her ankle. She didn't heed him, and he didn't get mad. *But why?*

Deep in her heart she knew the answer. Molly and Trevor were like the Andrews clan. The whole lot of them. They probably loved God. Probably had a relationship with Him. Talked to Him as if He was present and could do something in their lives.

As if He could provide money when none was there.

As if He could heal ankles that had been injured.

As if He could take black lung out of a man.

Sure, God had provided money for her family each time they needed it. Even allowed her sister Kylie to marry a wealthy husband who loved to help the family. And Chloe's ankle, given time, would heal.

But what about Daddy, God? He's not going to heal. He's going to die from black lung. A man who has been nothing but good all his life, who has followed You and cared for his family. A wonderful, wonderful man. How is that fair?

A single tear slipped down her cheek. She swiped it away, realizing she still sat at the table with her friends around her. Gazing at each face, she sighed. She didn't think anyone had seen her moment of weakness. No one except Trevor. A puzzled look overtook his features as he silently mouthed, *Are you okay?*

She smiled and nodded then grabbed her soda and took a long drink.

"I have an idea." Matt clinked his fork against the side of his red plastic cup. "Let's go putt-putt golfing."

"That sounds great." Liz motioned for the waitress.

Dread filled Chloe's heart. Her arms were throbbing, more so than her ankle. She wanted nothing more than to go back to the apartment, draw a hot bath, and soak for an hour or more.

"Sorry, you guys, but I'm beat. I have some equipment I need to give Chloe for when we start our therapy sessions." Trevor looked at Chloe and winked. "If it's all right with you, I'll take you home and give it to you now."

"That would be fine." Relief swept through her. Whether he realized it or not, Trevor had just acted like an angel sent from God. She studied him a moment, watching as he walked around the table, picked up her crutches, and helped her to her feet. Maybe he wasn't an angel but a messenger from God. With the same story she'd heard all her life. The one her whole family put their complete faith in.

Everyone except Chloe.

Chapter 6

Trevor jingled his keys as he strode up the sidewalk to Chloe's apartment. Something had changed with Chloe since their outing at the mall and Pizza King two weeks earlier. She'd begun heeding his instructions and had even started some rehabilitative exercises a week ago. So far her ankle had held up well, but he knew the fact that she'd already missed several games weighed heavily on her heart. *Which is why I have a surprise for her today.*

In truth Liz and Renee had come up with the surprise. He'd received an unexpected visit from the twosome four days ago. At first he'd been hesitant to go along with their plan, especially since both would be visiting their families and couldn't go with him. But when they'd used Liz's cell phone to call Chloe's mom, the older woman had expressed such excitement that Trevor simply couldn't deny the request.

A flash of uncertainty zipped through him. *Chloe may not be as gung ho as her mother and friends think she'll be.* He shook his head, squelching the thought. Biting the inside of his lip, he suppressed his anxiety as he knocked on the door. She opened it, and he noticed her faded jean shorts and red university shirt. He had to admit she looked nice. Sure, her attire fit the mission she thought they had—rehabilitating her ankle—but he couldn't deny her natural appearance attracted him.

"You look cute." The thought slipped from his lips.

"Yeah, right. You're lucky I showered." She snorted and punched his arm. "If my trainer wasn't such a slave driver, I wouldn't be such a sweaty mess after one of his sessions."

He glanced down at her ankle, which still sported an air cast for protection, but she carried no crutches to chafe her arms. "True, but you're healing nicely."

She nodded as she shut the front door and started down the sidewalk. "But I'm dying to get back on that field."

"I know. You'll get there."

Trevor opened the car door for her then walked around to the driver's side. Slipping in, he buckled his seat belt, started the car, and drove toward Interstate 69. He tried to pay attention to what Chloe was saying but couldn't stop wincing every time she diverted her attention to the scenery around them. *This is supposed to be a surprise, but I know she'll figure it out. At any moment I'm going to hear it. So* far she hadn't caught on that Trevor was heading in a completely different direction from the university. Turning onto I-69 South, though, he noted that Chloe's eyebrows were furrowed.

"This isn't the way to the university. Where are we going?"

"Not to the university." Trevor tried to hold back the smile that threatened to overtake his mouth.

"Look—we don't know each other that well." She played with the seat belt buckle. "You have to tell me where we're going, or I'm jumping out of this car."

Trevor threw back his head and laughed. "You've got to be kidding." He glanced at Chloe and saw nothing but determination etching her features. Growing serious, he cleared his throat. "Chloe, I wouldn't hurt you."

"I know you won't hurt me, but I don't like not knowing what's going on."

Trevor nodded his head. The vulnerability thing. He should have thought of that before he let himself be bamboozled into taking her on this trip. He'd hoped to get a good ways toward Otwell before revealing the mystery, but he should have known Chloe would never go for it. "We're heading to Otwell."

She frowned. "Otwell? Why?"

"To visit your parents."

"My parents? But we have practice tonight. I can't miss. It's over three hours one way, and—"

"I already told Coach we wouldn't be at practice. Chloe, it's Labor Day. It's an optional, workout practice. You know that. Besides, you can't practice with them yet."

"Told Coach? Told Coach! Trevor, I want to get my spot back. How am I going to do that if I miss practices? Even optional practices? What if I had a paper due Tuesday that I needed to work on tonight—or a test?"

"School just started a couple of weeks ago."

"So? I could have some really picky, crazy professor. You can't just do these things without asking me."

"We wanted to surprise you. Liz and Renee thought this trip would be good for you." Frustration welled within him. Her friends had been wrong, so very wrong.

"Liz and Renee? What do they—?"

"They came to my office a few days ago. They thought a trip to see your family would get your mind off your ankle."

Chloe crossed her arms in front of her. "What do they know? You should have asked me. Just turn around. Go back."

"I can't. Your family knows we're coming."

"Great." Chloe leaned back in the seat and let out a sigh. "Thanks for the surprise." Her tone was laced with sarcasm.

Trevor grabbed a piece of gum from his car's console. After unwrapping the paper, he popped it into his mouth. It was going to be a long drive down there and probably an even longer one on the way home. He glanced at Chloe, whose body posture reminded him of a two-year-old's. *I've got it. No more surprises.*

⌘

Chloe flinched as each one of her family members hugged her when she walked through the door. They were an overwhelming crew. Her oldest sisters, Sabrina and Natalie, had three children each. Kylie was pregnant with her first, with two more to come from Belize. Dalton had five children; Amanda had seven. Gideon, Cameron, her twin brother, and Chloe, the babies of the family, were the only ones without a passel running around their feet. Somehow the whole lot of them, spouses included, fit inside Mama and Daddy's small three-bedroom, one-bath house.

"Let me through." Chloe watched as her mother gingerly pushed her way past children and grandchildren to get to her youngest daughter. Her mother threw her arms around Chloe, squeezing with more strength than Chloe would have believed her mom could muster. "It's good to see you, dear. Your father will be so happy you've come."

Dread filled Chloe as her mother guided her toward her parents' bedroom. The room seemed to fog over when she walked into it, and Chloe felt as if she had stepped into another world. She couldn't possibly be inside her parents' bedroom to see her daddy. At any moment he would jump out through the closet door and lift her up over his shoulders and twirl her around as he had when she was little. He was still strong. Still healthy. He had to be.

She could hear her brothers and Trevor talking about football teams in the background. The sounds of children playing and her sisters chattering echoed around her. Steam gurgled from the door. The fog had been real, seeping from the oversized humidifier resting in the corner. A clear cord connected a large machine to the near lifeless figure that raised its hand from the mass of blankets and pillows covering the bed. The hand motioned her forward. Tears clouded her eyes, and she took slow, small steps toward it.

Peering down at the figure—her daddy—the dam broke, and tears streamed down her cheeks. He hadn't looked like this the last time she saw him. He'd been sitting up, eating snacks in bed and telling jokes. Sure, the same tube had stretched from his nose to the machine, but he'd been able to move around. It was obvious that was no longer possible.

A slight smile bowed his lips as he reached for her hand. "Chloe." The word cost him, and he sucked in several quick breaths.

"Oh, Daddy." Chloe allowed the pain and fear to fill her heart. Gently she enveloped her precious father in her arms and drew in the smell of him—still the same as when she was a girl, only now mingled with sickness. Memories of him strong and happy flooded her. Sitting on the front porch singing. Passing the baseball with her brothers. Kicking the soccer ball. Fishing. Helping Mama in the kitchen and stealing kisses when he thought the kids weren't looking.

Hardly any of him was left. Releasing her hug, she peered into his deep blue eyes. No. All of him was there. Just in a different form. A form she didn't like and didn't want to see. Dipping her head, she kissed his forehead then grabbed his hand in hers. "How long has it been since I've seen you, Daddy?"

"Almost nine months." Her mother's soft voice answered for him. "He's missed you. We all have."

"I'm sorry." Regret overcame her, and renewed tears filled her eyes. "So sorry."

"You're here now." Her mother's gentle hand rested on her shoulder. "Let me show you something." She picked up a photo album from the nightstand beside her father. "Your brothers and sisters and I have been keeping an album of you. Your daddy loves to look at it. Each and every night."

Chloe peered at the album then back at her father. His eyes shone with happiness. He raised his eyebrows and nodded his head. "I think he wants me to look at it."

"He probably wants to look at it with you."

Chloe took the album from her mother's grasp and watched as she walked out of the room. Chloe opened to the first page. It was a picture of her soccer team. The names of all her teammates were written in calligraphy underneath the picture. The next page was a photo of her dribbling the ball around an opposing player. As she flipped through more pages, she watched as her father's smile grew and his eyes glistened. She turned the page, and her father pointed to a picture of Chloe celebrating after scoring the winning goal.

"So proud." He whispered the words as he reached over and touched Chloe's cheek.

"I've missed you, Daddy." He smiled and nodded as she grabbed his hand in her own. "It hurts to see you sick. You've got to get well."

Compassion filled his expression as he slowly shook his head. He pointed and gazed at the ceiling. "Jesus."

"No, Daddy." Chloe's eyes widened. "We want you here. We. . .I need you."

He tightened his hold on her hand ever so slightly but still weakly. "No." He swallowed and pointed to the ceiling again. Unblinking, he stared into her eyes. A sweetness cloaked his expression. An excitement, as well. "Jesus."

Chloe nodded as an unknown peace filled her. He was ready, and she had to be. "Okay, Daddy." Placing the album back on the nightstand, Chloe pulled the chair as close to her father's bed as she could get it. "How 'bout we just spend some time together?"

The hours moved too quickly as Chloe shared one story, thought, or question after another with her father. When Mama walked into the room and said it was time for supper, Chloe never would have imagined she'd been talking for so long. She looked at her watch. "I can't believe it's this late."

Her mother's eyes looked sad. "Yes, I know you'll have to be leaving soon." She patted her husband's hand then gazed at Chloe. "We've missed you so much."

"I'll be back. I won't stay gone again." She leaned close to her father and kissed his sunken cheek. "In a week. I'll be back in a week."

Daddy nodded and whispered, "Love you." He closed his eyes and took long breaths.

"He's plumb tuckered out." Mama fluffed the pillows around him then turned and wrapped her arms around Chloe. "We'd love to see you again next week."

Chloe followed her mother out of the bedroom. Glancing around the room, she was surprised to find everyone gone. Only Trevor sat on the living room sofa flipping through one of her mother's landscaping magazines. A giggle welled in her throat. "Plant many flowers?"

Trevor looked up at her and smiled. "One day I might."

"I'd love to see you use those hands for something besides killing my ankle."

"Hmm." A playful glimmer flashed in his eyes. "My hands might not hurt that ankle if its owner followed instructions."

Chloe planted her hands on her hips, feigning insult. "I'll have you know I've been doing just as my trainer directed."

"Okay, you two." Mama swatted the air. "It's almost seven, and you have well over three hours of driving ahead of you." She crossed to the table and picked up a plastic bag. "I've packed enough food for both of you. You shouldn't have to stop for anything, except maybe gas." She turned toward Chloe. "Go ahead and use the restroom before you leave."

"Mother!" Chloe's mouth dropped as a low chuckle sounded from Trevor.

Mama winked at her. "I was going to tell Trevor the same."

Within moments the twosome had said their good-byes, settled in the car, and headed down the road. Overwhelming emotion swelled within Chloe. She felt happy and sad, thankful and hurt all at the same time. Staring out the window, she studied the passing cornfields and cow pastures. Trevor didn't offer conversation, and she appreciated his thoughtfulness. Fatigue weighed her down, and she found her eyelids begging to close. Maybe shutting them just a moment wouldn't hurt.

"We're here."

Chloe jumped at Trevor's whispered words and light touch. She blinked and wiped her eyes until they focused on her apartment door. "That was fast."

"You slept a good ways."

She felt the heat in her cheeks. "Sorry."

"Don't be sorry."

She opened the car door and fumbled with her seat belt. Glancing back at Trevor, she peered into his eyes, hoping he could see to the depths of her being. "Thanks. . .I mean, I. . ." She picked at a thread that hung from her shirt. "I'm really glad you took me. Thank you."

"You're welcome." The sweet sincerity in his gaze made her heart feel warm. "Anytime. I'll walk you to the door."

"No. You don't need to."

"I don't mind."

"No. It's not like we're on a date."

He lifted his eyebrows and seemed to hold his breath as a blank expression washed over his features. Her comment obviously surprised him. But why? Perplexed, Chloe stepped out of the car and started to shut the door.

"Chloe. Wait." He reached into the backseat. "Don't forget your purse. Your mom found it."

"I didn't take my purse."

"You didn't?" He gazed at the object in his hand.

"Let me see it." She fumbled through the contents for a wallet of some kind. A salvation tract fell out. Chloe reached down and picked it up before searching more. Finding the wallet, she opened it. "It's Natalie's. I bet she's looking for it everywhere. I'm going inside to call her. I'll have to overnight it, but what if something happened or it was lost? I'm sure all her credit cards. . .I'll have to get this back down there to her."

"I will be happy to take you if she can wait until the weekend."

"You would?"

"Sure. I loved your family. They're a lot of fun."

Chloe smiled. They were definitely a lot of things, and she had to admit fun was one of them. "I'd appreciate that. I'll see you tomorrow for my therapy session." She furrowed her brows. "I *am* having therapy tomorrow, right?"

"Yep. I'll see you tomorrow."

Chloe walked into her apartment and fell on the couch. Thankful her roommates were already in bed, she stared at the ceiling. Seeing her father had been the most emotionally exhausting thing she'd ever done. She remembered the expression on his face as she flipped through the pages of the photo album. Her whole life had been soccer for several years now. The sport completely absorbed her. And somehow it didn't seem enough.

Something was missing.

⌖

Trevor pushed his alarm clock off. Opening one eye, he peered at the red, digital numbers. *How can it be five thirty already?* Grabbing a pillow under his arm, he rolled over and closed his eyes again.

The phone rang.

Punching the pillow away, Trevor sat up. *Who would be calling at this hour?* He glanced at the clock that now read 9:00. *That can't be right.* He rubbed his eyes and looked again as another ring sounded. *Oh no. I'm sure it's the school wondering where I am.*

He cleared his throat and picked up the phone. "Hello." He cleared it again after his greeting came out a bit raspier than he'd hoped.

"Mr. Trevor Montgomery?"

Trevor frowned. He didn't recognize the voice, and the last thing he wanted right now was a telemarketing call. "Yes?"

"This is Walter Spence. I'm the head coach of the men's soccer team at the University of South Carolina. . . ."

Trevor dropped the phone on the bed. Surely he'd heard wrong. He'd dreamed of USC since before he'd started his own college career. The man's voice continued to stream from the receiver, and Trevor picked it up and held it to his ear.

"We have an opening for an assistant athletic trainer and would like for you to come in for an interview. How about next week?"

Trevor couldn't speak. What was happening? Was he dreaming?

"Mr. Montgomery, are you there?" Mr. Spence was asking.

"I'm here. That would be wonderful."

Trevor couldn't recall another thing they spoke about, though they talked for several minutes. Thankful for the pen and paper inside his nightstand drawer, he had been able to write down his interview day and time.

He hung up the phone. "The University of South Carolina." The words slipped from his lips. Excitement welled in his heart. He'd longed to be closer to his dad, yearned to work at the university he'd grown up around. How many USC games had his parents taken him to? Too many to count. When he was a boy, the only clothing colors he owned were garnet and black, in support of his Fighting Gamecocks. "This is my dream job." In a minute, in a second, he'd pack his things and head to his hometown.

Chloe's face filtered through his mind. He'd not been able to squelch the attraction he felt toward her. Through God's help he'd never acted on his feelings. He'd never told her how he thought of her almost every waking hour. *"It's not like we're on a date."* Her response to his offer of walking her to the door popped into his mind.

No, they weren't on a date. They never could be, and the reality of it sliced through his heart. *Maybe moving away is the best thing I could do.*

Chapter 7

Chloe sat on the bench in front of her locker in the women's locker room. The drip of a faucet in the shower area plopped to its own rhythm. She'd never before heard the place so quiet. Her ankle throbbed. She knew it was swelling again. Though she'd gritted her teeth and gripped the examining table while the doctor checked it, she had no doubt the doctor would deem her unfit to play.

"It's only been four and a half weeks since the injury, Chloe." Doc's voice penetrated her mind. *"In the best of circumstances, you shouldn't be able to play for another two weeks, but I'll take a look."*

She didn't understand why the man had acted so put out by her request. She wanted to get back on the field, help her team. It was her last year, and she'd already missed over two weeks of games. She and Trevor had been working on her ankle, and everything was going great. But now. . .

Why? She peered down at her foot. *Why won't you heal? For the last two weeks I've done everything Trevor told me to do.* The fact that she did nothing he'd instructed her to do the first fourteen days slipped into her mind, but she pushed the thought away. It didn't make sense that her ankle wouldn't get better. It was sprained, not even broken.

Chloe thought of the tract she'd found in her sister's purse. Curiosity at the cartoon figures made Chloe read through it. The same salvation plan she'd known since she was a child spilled from its contents. "Accepting Jesus is simple." Her Sunday school teacher's words rang through Chloe's ears.

Sure, accepting is simple, but what if you don't believe, don't trust? Chloe folded her arms in front of her. She did believe in God. Just a glimpse of nature and she couldn't deny Someone much greater than anyone she'd ever known created it. And she saw proof of changed lives in her family. But the trust thing. It always tripped her up. Like now with her ankle. Mama had promised to pray for her, and Chloe knew she had. Trevor had said he'd pray for her, and she believed he had, as well. Chloe clenched her fist and hit the bench. *Does that mean You want it to stay hurt?*

"Sometimes God allows things to happen in our lives to draw us closer to Him." Daddy's words when he first learned he had black lung echoed in her mind. She tried to believe what her father said—after all, he never lied. And she saw his

faith grow deeper and stronger as the illness worsened, but she'd never been able to understand why the pain was necessary.

What's the point in my not getting to play my senior year? Nothing good can come of it. She looked at Molly's locker a few down from hers. The girl had continued to check on Chloe, calling her on the phone, stopping by the apartment. *But I want to be the one scoring the goals.*

Maybe I have a different goal. A soft nudging touched her heart. She shook her head, unsure where the feeling came from.

The door to the coach's office opened, and Trevor stepped outside. Deep green eyes seemed to pierce her as he raked his hand through his dark hair. The mass of the man towered over her, and Chloe admitted her attraction to him. *Maybe Trevor is a goal I could have.* She shook the thought away. The last thing she needed to think about was romance. Healing, that was her focus.

"We're ready."

Chloe stood and made her way gingerly to the door. Pain shot through the side of her ankle as she walked.

"It's hurting again, isn't it?"

Chloe turned and looked into his soft, compassionate eyes. Infuriating. She didn't want his compassion. She wanted him to fix her. "No, it's not."

A slight sigh escaped his lips as he pointed toward a chair for her to sit in. Lowering herself into it, she took in the frustrated expressions of the other three men in the room—her coach, the assistant coach, and the doctor.

After clearing his throat, the doctor clasped his hands together. "I'm not going to mince words with you, Chloe. You've reinjured your ankle. You'll need another six weeks off."

Chloe jumped out of her chair. "Six weeks! There're only eight weeks left in the season."

Coach Collins stood nose to nose with her the best he could. In truth he had to look up into her eyes. He pointed at Trevor. "And this time you're going to do everything that man says."

❦

"You're going to have to rest it again." Trevor followed Chloe as she half stomped, half limped into her apartment. "It's not going to get better if you don't."

She turned toward him, her hair flipping across his face. "The stupid thing is never getting better. I might as well bundle it up and play ball."

He'd had it. The woman acted like a toddler. She was aggravating. Frustrating. Infuriating. "Do you really think you can hit a soccer ball with that ankle?" He slapped his hands on his thighs. "Maybe you can hit it, but would you be any help to your team? Who's supposed to benefit here? The team you say you love so much? Or you?"

"How dare you talk to me that way! I love my team. It's my last year, Trevor. Of course I want to play. It's my job to play." She pointed at him. "It's your job to fix me."

"I can't fix you unless you listen. We'd been working on rehabilitating it. Slowly. You've done something. Did you work out at the gym without me?" Her face turned crimson, and he knew he'd guessed right. He shut her apartment door. "And guess what, Chloe Andrews—you're back on rest and ice."

"Oh no." She shook her head then pointed to her foot. "We're going to rehabilitate this thing. Right now."

"No, Chloe." He stepped toward her and grabbed her hand. Towering over her, he peered into eyes as blue as the ocean. The storm within them radiated with fierce passion for her sport. Her strength drew him. Lowering his head ever so slightly, he realized how much he wanted to claim her lips with his own. Her head tilted backward slightly, and Trevor knew she would accept his kiss.

"What's going on in there?" Liz's voice sounded from down the hall. "What did Doc say?"

Chloe broke away from him and swallowed slowly. She'd been affected as much as he. The knowledge of it warmed his heart.

Liz walked into the living area. Renee followed and added, "Do we get our star center forward back?"

Trevor stared at Chloe. She still seemed confused by what had almost happened between them. He shook his head slowly, never taking his gaze from her. "No. She's not back."

She scowled. The moment evaporated as quickly as it had developed. "Yes, I am back."

"No. Chloe, your ankle needs rest and ice—"

"Why can't you just fix it? Rehabilitate it. Let's strengthen it."

"It has to heal first. Completely. You have to stay off your ankle. Again."

"I have to take Natalie's purse to her."

Trevor furrowed his brows. Where had that come from? "You're not driving."

Chloe rested her hand on her hip. "I can drive if I choose to drive."

She wants her independence. Trevor took a slow breath. He needed to be calm, patient with her. He'd be every bit as upset if he were in her position. "I will take you." He tried to reach for her hand, but she pulled away. "Chloe, we agreed I would take you."

"No, I'll go by myself. I'm a perfectly capable woman who gets really tired of being bossed around!"

"If you want to go to Otwell," Trevor said, trying to remain calm yet firm, "I'm going with you to make sure you stay off that ankle."

"This is your fault. I did everything you said."

He'd had it. Trying to be reasonable with Chloe was like trying to put a cast on a broken toe. It was impossible. "Everything? I doubt it." Flustered, Trevor turned toward her roommates. "She has to rest her ankle. No walking. Get her crutches—"

"No! I don't think so."

Trevor ignored her and continued to look at Liz and Renee. "If she doesn't listen to me, she won't play a single game, not even a practice, for the rest of the year."

⁂

"He's infuriating, Daddy." Chloe leaned back in the chair beside his bed. "Why can't he just fix my ankle? But no. He can't do that. I have to go back on rest. . .and ice. He wouldn't even let me drive here by myself."

Her father pointed at her. "Loves you." He covered his mouth to cough then smiled beneath his closed fist.

"Oh no. I don't think so." Chloe stood and fluffed the pillows around her father. "Are you comfortable, Daddy?"

He nodded then grasped her hand in his. "Good. . .to see you."

"It's good to be here. I wish I hadn't taken so long to visit. I guess that's one good thing about Trevor. He was the one who got me here."

Daddy smiled and nodded again.

Chloe gently rubbed his forearm. "We've visited for a long time, and you look so tired." She leaned over and kissed his forehead. "I'll let you rest awhile." She grabbed her crutches from against the wall and hobbled to the bedroom door then turned to take another look at her father. His eyes had already closed, and his chest lifted and fell in labored rest. She whispered, "I'll be back in here before I leave, Daddy."

On crutches Chloe made her way into the kitchen. Her mother stood over the sink cleaning fresh carrots and celery. Sabrina scooped spoonfuls of chocolate chip cookie dough onto a baking sheet. "Where is everyone?"

Mama turned and looked at her. "Playing ball with your fellow."

Chloe huffed and leaned against the cabinet beside her mother. "He is anything but my fellow. The man is a nuisance and obviously incompetent at his job. I've been on these things forever." She lifted the bottom of one of her crutches.

"And I'm sure you've listened to all his instructions." Sabrina pointed her spoon at Chloe.

"What is it with everyone thinking I don't listen? I always listen." Chloe hobbled over to the table and plopped down.

"Ha!" Her mother dropped the vegetables in the sink and looked at her. "This from the daughter who kicked clothes under the bed when her mother told her to clean her room and then said she'd done just as she was told. The daughter who hid her vitamins in the dog's food and promised up and down that she'd taken them."

Chloe bit her bottom lip to hold back her giggle.

"Or the sister," Sabrina began, "who didn't touch her big sister's nail polish when she'd been told to leave it alone, and yet the polish was painted all over her toes and even part of her feet."

"Come on, Sabrina." Chloe rolled her eyes. "I wasn't that bad."

"Oh yes, you were." Mama pointed a carrot at her. "And I'd be willing to bet you're still as hardheaded as ever."

"But you love me anyway." Chloe smiled at her mother and batted her eyes.

"Yes, I do." Her mother kissed the top of her head.

"If my hunch is right, so does a handsome guy out there playing basketball with my husband and siblings." Sabrina licked the tip of her spoon.

"Yeah. . .whatever." Chloe hit the air. "That man's mission in life is to exasperate me."

"Which is why he brought you all the way down here not once but twice in a week's time." Her mother started arranging celery and carrot sticks on a vegetable tray.

"That's just because it's his job to take care of the Ball State players." Chloe grabbed a carrot and popped it into her mouth.

Mama and Sabrina looked at each other and said in unison, "Yeah. . . whatever."

Chloe giggled at them. "Okay. I give. What can I do to help?"

"Now she asks." Sabrina slapped her thigh then opened the oven door and slid the cookies inside.

"All you have to do is eat." Mama stood and walked toward the door. "I'm just going to call in the troops."

Sabrina bent down and whispered in Chloe's ear, "What do you want to bet your trainer man will come running?"

"Of course he will. Everyone comes running for Mama's cooking."

Sabrina shook her head. "Nah. This time it'll be for Daddy's girl."

The notion was preposterous. She and Trevor did nothing but argue. Mama hollered that it was time to eat, and Chloe watched as the Andrews family stampeded into the house. Trevor followed, talking to her brother Gideon. He looked up, and their gazes met for a moment. He smiled and winked. *He couldn't have feelings for me. Could he?*

Chapter 8

Trevor was exhausted. His muscles ached, and the crick in his neck was a killer. Probably the drive to and from Otwell two days before and the flight to South Carolina yesterday had finally begun to take their toll on his body.

He walked into his parents' home. Though his mom had been gone for over a decade, his dad had never replaced her furniture. The paisley-printed blue-and-white curtains draping the windows and Victorian ceramic figurines adorning a corner hutch along with the overstuffed deep navy couch and loveseat made it still feel like their home. Only one item changed the room—an oversized, brown leather recliner that massaged one's back at the push of a remote control. His dad had added his "man's" chair to the otherwise feminine living room some seven years earlier.

Trevor fell into the chair, dropped his briefcase beside it then kicked off his black, tasseled dress shoes. Loosening the new deep crimson tie that had threatened to choke him for the last few hours, he leaned back and allowed the footrest to pop up.

Or maybe the exhaustion came from the interview. The last two hours had been nothing short of intense.

Four men and one woman made a horseshoe shape around a long table. He sat at the center of the horseshoe facing them. One by one the men's soccer coach, the athletics director, the women's soccer coach, the university doctor, and the man who would be his direct boss drilled him with question after question. It had been just over a half hour since he'd left, and the only question he could remember answering was his full name. The whole thing was a blur, a nervous blur. Still, the warm departure the five gave him assured him he must have done well. *Lord, I pray I did.*

The idea of being an assistant athletic trainer for the Fighting Gamecocks still sent chills of excitement through his veins. For as long as he could remember, he'd dreamed of working there.

He reminisced about many years earlier when he'd gone to a soccer game with his parents. He couldn't have been more than ten, and the mid-October weather had been much cooler than usual. Mom had bundled him into several layers of shirts and socks in addition to the long johns she'd made him wear under his pants. He'd complained about the extra load the whole way in the car as sweat beaded on his forehead. Once there, he'd been able to focus on the game, cheering his team, as many people huddled under blankets for warmth. That night his dad had surprised him with a team poster signed by the coach. Yes, he'd love to live closer to his dad again.

Sighing, he pushed the remote and let the chair massage his tense back. The mid-September weather today was anything but cool. He wiped away the perspiration that had gathered at his hairline. Closing his eyes, he leaned farther back.

"How'd your interview go?"

Opening one eye, he looked up at his dad. The years had been good to Vince Montgomery. He still carried a straight, strong stature. Only his salt-and-pepper hair and the crow's feet that fanned from his eyes revealed him to be a middle-aged man. A sprinkle of overgrown stubble dotted his jaw and chin. "I think it went well." He sat up in the chair and turned off the massager. "But I can't remember a thing they asked."

A deep chuckle filtered through his dad's lips. His eyes laughed with him. "Typical. I could never remember anything after an interview."

"They said they'd contact me. I hope it won't be too long."

"I'd say it will be fairly soon. Their guy had to quit midseason due to some kind of family circumstance."

"Yeah, but I wouldn't quit Ball State midseason. It's not fair to them."

"That's integrity talking, and I'm glad to hear it." His dad patted Trevor's shoulder. "If you're up to it, I'd like to treat you to lunch."

"Food. I'm always up for food." Trevor stood and walked toward his old bedroom. "Just let me get out of these clothes."

"I thought we'd go by and put some flowers on your mom's grave, as well."

"Okay." Trevor cringed. He hated visiting his mom's grave. He didn't understand it, either. She wasn't there. She was in heaven with Jesus. He grabbed a T-shirt and jean shorts from his suitcase. But it made Dad feel better. *I guess it's Dad's way of still being able to take care of her in some small way.* He slipped on a pair of comfortable sandals. "I'm ready."

Trevor followed his dad to his new, oversized four-by-four truck. They drove to a nearby steak house, one of his dad's favorite places to eat. Trevor loved their fried onion appetizer and prime rib dinner, as well. Once seated, he watched his dad push the menu to the side. "No need to look. I get the same thing every time."

Trevor pushed his away. "I know what I want, too."

The waitress, a woman Trevor guessed to be in her midforties, approached their table. She grabbed a pen from behind her ear and winked at his dad. "You want the same as always."

He nodded. "Yep."

She turned to Trevor. "And who's this nice-looking young man?" She rested her hand for a moment on his dad's shoulder. "Why, Vince, this must be your son. He looks just like you." She looked at his dad and smacked her chewing gum. "He's quite the looker."

His dad guffawed. "I'd say he's quite a bit better looking than I am." He nudged her arm. "You'd think the boy could find himself a date or two. You know I'm not getting any younger, and I'd like to see a few grandchildren before I die."

The woman swatted the air. "You're fit as a fiddle, Vince Montgomery. You let that boy be. He'll find him a wife when he's ready."

Trevor gazed at the woman's left hand—no wedding band. Their banter could be defined as nothing less than flirting. Given the amount of time his father obviously spent at the restaurant, Trevor wondered if the two might be interested in each other. Trevor swallowed and plastered a smile on his face. The idea felt weird, yet there was no reason his dad shouldn't consider dating again. The man was still young. Mom would want him to be happy and share his life with someone. The more he thought about it, the better the idea sounded.

He took in the woman's light blond hair, cut in a short, trendy style. Her pale blue eyes glimmered with a deep-down happiness. She seemed to be in good shape like his dad. She had to be since she was a waitress and spent hours on her feet every day.

The two continued to banter even after Trevor gave her his order. Throughout lunch he considered the idea. He watched his dad and the waitress talk every chance they had. What reason would his dad have for not pursuing a relationship? More than twelve years was a long time. Surely he wanted to have some companionship.

The thought brought a picture of Chloe to his mind. Though she aggravated him to his very core almost every time he saw her, he felt more drawn to her each moment. Her zeal and zest magnetized him. Her passion was contagious. And her beauty, well, it was uncontested. In sweats, early in the morning, or made up for an afternoon out with friends, the woman astounded him.

But she's not for me. The fact that every time we see each other we get into some type of argument. The fact that she doesn't listen to a word I say, even in the area of my expertise. The fact that she's afraid to get close to people. Though he knew the visit with her parents the week before had induced a subtle change in her demeanor, she was still off-limits.

She doesn't know You, Lord.

Shaking the thought away, he determined to focus on this time with his father. He only had today before he'd have to head back to Muncie, and he didn't want to spend it pining for a girl he'd never date.

With their meal finished, his dad paid for their lunch, and they headed to the grocery store to pick up some flowers to put in the urn in front of his mother's grave. Since Trevor hadn't been to the cemetery for quite some time, his dad wanted him to pick the flowers. With Labor Day having just passed, he selected several shades of red, blue, and white.

"She'd like these." His father took them to the cashier and started to pay.

Trevor covered his father's hand with his own. "You bought lunch, Dad. At least let me buy the flowers."

His dad nodded and put his wallet back in his pocket. In silence they left the store and headed to the cemetery. His dad drove slowly along the winding road that ran past plot after plot, tombstone after tombstone. Trevor felt sick. He wasn't sure if it was the motion of the truck or the fact that they drew closer to his mother's grave.

He wanted to remember her happy. He wanted to remember her fixing dinner at the stove, bending over the washing machine to pull out wet clothes, kneeling in front of her flower garden in the yard. He hated seeing the tombstone. Glancing at his dad, he fought his frustration. Dad loved visiting it.

His father stopped the truck beside her grave. He got out, walked over to it, and traced her name with his fingertips. Gripping the flowers in his hands, Trevor slowly opened the truck's door and stepped outside. He moved to the tombstone, lifted the wilting flowers from the urn, and replaced them with his own arrangement. Fingering the flowers apart, Trevor's gaze roamed the chiseled words. "Loving wife and mother. A blessed child of her Creator."

Trevor stood to his full height and glanced at his father. He appeared to be studying Trevor's arrangement to see if it met with his approval. Shoving his hands in his pockets, Trevor shifted his weight from one foot to the other. "Does it make you feel sad to come here?"

His dad's face lit with a smile. "Oh no. I love to visit." Trevor nodded, and a shadow fell across his father's face. "Does it make you feel sad?"

Trevor shrugged. "A little."

"We can go back to the house, son. I would never want to make you feel uncomfortable. I just assumed you felt the same peace—"

"No, Dad." Trevor lifted his hand to stop him. "I want to do this with you. It's just that I like to remember her doing. . .doing normal things, like laundry and dishes, when she was healthy."

A contented smile settled on his father's face. "Ah, me, too, son. But until I see your sweet mother in heaven, this is the only way I know of to visit her. Well, sort of visit her. I know she's not here. But this is the last place I got to see her, or her casket anyway, so. . .I guess I don't know exactly how to explain it."

Trevor watched as his father's eyes misted over. The love between his parents had been strong, true and united by their heavenly Father. It was the kind of relationship Trevor wanted. Needed.

Several minutes passed before the two stepped back into the truck. In silence his father wound around the road that led out of the cemetery. Once back on the main road, Trevor sneaked a peek at his dad. Contentment, not sorrow, etched lines into his father's face, and Trevor wondered again why he had never dated. Maybe he could never let his mother go. "You've never stopped loving her?"

His dad smiled. "Oh no. I never will."

"Is that why you don't date?"

"No. I would date."

The admission surprised Trevor, and he knew his mouth gaped open in astonishment.

His dad chuckled. "I see you're surprised."

"To say the least."

"I think your mom would be all right with me dating. I would want her to if I had passed away years ago."

"Then why don't you?"

"God hasn't shown me the right person yet."

"What about the waitress at the restaurant?"

"Betty? Oh no. We're just friends. She still struggles from a twenty-year abusive marriage. Her husband just died a few years back from liver cancer."

"But—"

"Son, I'm not looking. But if God sticks the right woman in my life, the one He's chosen, then I won't argue with Him. God knows what I need."

His father's last sentence struck Trevor's heart. *God knows what I need, too. I don't have to worry about Chloe. I'll stay close to Him, and He'll guide my heart.*

<hr>

Chloe drank in the cathedral ceilings and wide-open feel of the sanctuary. The walls were chocolate colored and trimmed with creamy white. Individual hunter green cushioned chairs sat on a lushly carpeted floor. Drums, guitars, a baby grand piano, and multiple microphones stood on an elevated stage. MAY WE KNOW YOU MORE was written in dark bold letters on a banner that hung behind the stage. "I've never seen anything like this."

Matt leaned toward her. "It's pretty cool, huh?"

"My home church is much smaller, more traditional looking. A podium. A baptistry. Piano. Pews."

"Wait 'til they start the music. You'll flip."

Chloe settled into a chair beside Matt. A kind-looking man passed by them and handed her a bulletin. She skimmed the contents and was stunned to see the multiple songs they planned to sing. They'd never get out of here. *Oh well. It's just one Sunday.* She leaned back in the chair and gazed at the people around her. "Didn't you say Trevor goes to this church?"

"Yeah, but I don't see him. He'll be sorely disappointed he missed you."

"What's that supposed to mean?"

"You figure it out."

The music started before Chloe could say anything else. The tempo was upbeat, and the drummer, guitarists, and pianist were all dressed in comfortable clothes. Glancing down at her long black skirt and button-down red jacket, she suddenly felt overdressed. She watched the lead singers, four of them. They seemed transformed by the music. They lifted their hands, and though their eyes were closed, their faces shone with awe and reverence for the One they worshipped.

Others around her started to stand, and Chloe was unsure what to do. Soon Matt was on his feet. He clapped with those around them. Chloe stood and rested her weight on her good foot. She scanned the audience, watching the faces. Several people had raised their hands and seemed to sing as loud as they could. Song after song played, the tempo flowing then ebbing on perfect cue. Something stirred in her heart. These people praised in genuineness. Chloe could feel it.

The music slowed, and Chloe broke away from watching the people. She gazed at one of the large screens behind the band. The words to the song rolled across the screen. Words of love and praise, honor and commitment. Words of longing and yearning. From God. For us.

For me?

The words pricked her spirit. She wanted to draw near to God. Wanted to know Him. Wanted to trust Him. But she was afraid. So afraid. What if He let her down? What if He allowed more sadness in her life?

The band slowed the music as a man walked onto the stage. He began to pray. By the time he'd finished, the music had faded away. The preacher laid his Bible on the adjustable metal podium. He carried it toward the center of the stage, set it down then opened his Bible. Looking at the crowd, he smiled. "Our Lord Jesus tells us in the book of John, 'I have told you these things, so that in me you may have peace. In this world you will have trouble. But take heart! I have overcome the world.'"

Chloe gripped the strap of her purse. *Oh boy. Here we go.*

Chapter 9

Two weeks had passed since Trevor had gone to his interview at USC, and he'd heard nothing. Not a word. Frustrated more than he would have imagined, he stepped out of his car and slammed the door. Walking into the Cardinals' stadium, he spied Chloe sitting on the bench. She watched the team warm up for the game. It was obvious she scrutinized each move they made as she shifted back and forth in her seat with each kick of the ball.

It pained him to look at her. She'd been able to start working her ankle again the week before, and his attraction had grown more intense the last few visits. But seeing her walk into his church a few days ago had nearly caused his heart to burst with excitement. Learning she'd attended with Matt the week he was in South Carolina had sent his mind into a gyro of emotions. Jealousy that she'd gone with another man and excitement that she'd opened her heart to attending church.

He zipped up his Ball State jacket. *Dear Lord, You're going to have to save her soul or move me away from her.* Taking a long breath, he made his way to the bench. "Hey, Chloe."

"Trevor." She looked up at him. Her face broke into the sweetest smile he'd ever seen. Her light blue eyes flickered with delight. Whether for the game or to see him, he wasn't sure. "Have a seat." She patted the bench right beside her.

"Sure." Trevor sat next to her. She whipped her head around as she watched one of her teammates dribble toward another player. A whiff of strawberries floated toward him. Shaking his head, he glanced down at her bandaged foot. "How's your ankle today?"

"Pretty good." Chloe turned and peered into his eyes. Her gloss-tinted lips bowed up, causing a small dimple in her left cheek. Trevor noticed that the dimple only appeared when she offered a slight smile. "No more swelling."

Trevor raised his eyebrows. "You're listening to your trainer?"

"I am."

"Well, that's a change."

"I know. A lot of things are changing about me. It seems I have more unanswered questions, and yet the more I voice them, the more content I feel."

"So you're getting your answers?"

Her brows furrowed. "That's the funny thing. Not really. But I *feel* the

179

answers are coming. Does that make sense?"

"Sure." *No. Not really. As time passes, I'm feeling more confused. About Chloe. About my dream job. About everything.*

Chloe looked at him. "After this past week's sermon, I've been reading Genesis."

He nodded and watched one of the girls dribble the ball to warm up. "Really?"

"Yeah. I remember studying the story about Abraham offering up Isaac when I was a small girl in our Sunday school class."

"He didn't actually sacrifice him."

"I know. God provided a ram. But Abraham was willing to. He was willing to give up his most precious possession." Chloe grabbed a bubble gum wrapper from her pocket and stuck the gum she'd been chewing inside it. "When I was a girl, I hadn't realized how precious Isaac was to Abraham. Isaac was the promised child."

Trevor nodded. "Which is why Abraham could trust God either to let the boy live or to bring him back to life."

"Yeah, but would you trust God that much? I mean, think about it. Could you listen to Him tell you to kill the thing you love most and then go out and be willing to do it? For real?"

The things he loved most flooded his mind. His dad. His dream job in South Carolina. He gazed at Chloe. The sincerity filling her face tugged at his heart. Sacrificing her would be unimaginable. "I don't know. It would be hard."

"For me it would be like having to give up soccer." Her voice came out just above a whisper.

"How do you feel about that?"

"I haven't decided."

Trevor stared at Chloe as she watched her teammates continue to warm up. Gazing at the scoreboard, he saw it would be a matter of minutes before the team members made their way over to the bench to begin the game. The urge, pure and honest, to wrap his arm around her nearly overwhelmed him. Reaching around her, he squeezed her shoulder. "I'm still praying for you, Chloe."

She turned and threw both arms around him. "Thanks, Trevor." Peering down into her mist-covered eyes, he knew she meant it.

Chloe slipped into the passenger's seat of Trevor's car. Her roommates had decided to hit Pizza King for a late-night snack, but Chloe wanted to go home. Though he hadn't acted overly excited about it, she was thankful Trevor had been willing to take her. She buckled her seat belt. Trevor had spoken hardly two words to her after the game started, and she couldn't help but wonder why. If nothing else, they usually found something to argue about.

Her cell phone rang from inside her gym bag. She unzipped the side and felt her way through socks, bandages, and whatever else she'd thrown in there. Finally retrieving the phone, she flipped it open and hit the TALK button. Her mother's tears sounded before her words spilled out. Chloe listened in horrified silence. Finally, she was able to force her lips to move. "I'll be there as soon as I can." She clicked her phone shut and stared at it.

"What is it?" Trevor's voice shook with an evident knowing.

She looked over at him. He knew. Of course he knew. They'd learned so much about each other in such a brief time. But this was something she didn't want him to know intuitively. She didn't want it to be true. She wanted to open her phone, call her mama back, and beg her to take back what she'd said.

That wouldn't happen.

"My daddy." Her bottom lip quivered as tears began to spill down her cheeks. "He's gone."

"Oh, Chloe." Trevor swerved into an open parking lot and turned off the car. He leaned across the seat and wrapped his arms around her. Needing his comfort, Chloe buried her face in his shoulder. His fingers stroked her hair, reminding her of how her mother cared for her when something made her cry. "I'll take you down there tonight."

Lifting her head from his shoulder, she wiped the tears from her eyes. "You will?"

"Of course. You call your mom back. I'll drop you off at your apartment. You pack while I run back to mine and grab a few things."

"You'll take me?"

"Yes."

Chloe sat up in her seat and wiped her eyes again with the back of her hand. "Oh, thank you."

Trevor started the car again, and memories of her family squishing into their midsize station wagon flooded her mind. He pulled into the driveway, and she remembered her daddy and mama dropping her off at this apartment four years ago. New tears poured forth, and Chloe shook her head. "I can't do it. I can't go in there by myself. Everything is reminding me of Daddy. Please go with me."

"Okay."

Trevor's gaze held such tenderness as Chloe dug through her purse for her keys. She couldn't find them. Shaking the bag, they jingled. She could hear them, but she couldn't find them.

"May I?" Trevor pointed to her purse, and Chloe handed it to him. In one sweep he pulled out her keys.

Never before had she felt so incapable, so fragile. It was as if her whole body was shutting down one part at a time. She opened the car door, and a memory of her father holding her hand as they walked to the ice cream shop after a good dentist visit danced through her mind. The remembrances wouldn't stop. They assaulted her no matter where she looked, even with her eyes shut. They were immobilizing, making her feel vulnerable.

Trevor guided her into the apartment. She sat on the bed, clutching her pillow while her trainer rummaged through her things to pack. What was happening to her? She couldn't function. *God, I needed Daddy.* Her heart filled with emotion—love for her daddy, sadness that he would go, anger that God would take him.

He was the best daddy, the best husband to her mama, the best man in the whole world. She wanted to see him again. Wanted to sit in the chair beside his bed and hold his hand. Wanted to look at her album with him. More than that, she wanted to hear his sweet baritone voice fill the porch as he picked his favorite hymns on the guitar.

Somehow she ended up back in Trevor's car. The trunk slammed, and she jumped. Trevor slid into the driver's seat beside her, mumbling something about stopping by his apartment for clothes. As she gazed out the window, memories continued to spiral through her mind.

"In this world you will have trouble." The preacher's words from two weeks ago slipped into her psyche. *"But take heart! I have overcome the world."*

"But, God," Chloe mumbled as her tears began to burn her face, "how can You overcome this pain?"

⌛

Trevor stared at his reflection in the bathroom mirror at the home of Chloe's sister. Today was the funeral. Tomorrow he'd be back at work. With her father's passing on Friday evening, Trevor only had to take one day off work in order to stay with Chloe. Though he'd offered to get a room at a hotel, the family would hear nothing of it. But since her mother's house was packed with immediate and extended family, Trevor had stayed with Kylie and her husband.

He adjusted the knot of his mint green and navy tie. "You can do this." He buttoned his navy suit jacket. The last funeral he'd attended had been his mother's. He'd promised himself then not to go to another.

Offering to take Chloe to her family had cost him. While she slept fitfully in the car, he realized he'd be forced to attend another funeral. Unsure how he would respond and unwilling to break down in front of a family he hardly knew, Trevor had fought sickness the entire stay. He'd never felt so queasy. He was afraid wounds that had not fully healed would open and fester, so he'd spent much of his time during calling hours in the lobby of the funeral home.

He flattened the comforter on the bed one last time then grabbed his car keys from the nightstand. With extra family in for the funeral, Trevor had to stop by the Andrews house and pick up Chloe and possibly a few children.

After pulling into the driveway, Chloe stepped outside and shut the door before he had a chance to get out of his car. She slid in the passenger's side. "Hey." Her voice sounded soft and tired.

"Is anyone else riding with us?"

"No."

"Okay."

Trevor focused on his driving as he headed to the funeral home. The loss of his mother pricked his heart, and he felt true empathy for Chloe and her family. Even after all these years, he still missed her. He guessed he always would.

He stopped the car and reached for the door handle. Chloe grabbed his hand, and he turned toward her. "Trevor." The pitch of her voice rose, and she squeezed his hand tighter. The storm in her eyes brewed as tears pooled within them. "I appreciate this so much."

"It's okay."

"No." She shook her head. "You've been there for me at every step from my ankle to my daddy." With her free hand she took a tissue from her lap and wiped her nose. "Most people wouldn't do that."

It's because I love you, his heart screamed within him, and he knew it was true. Chloe Andrews was the only person on the planet who could ignite him as she did.

Her voice cracked. "Will you stay with me today?"

And every day for the rest of our lives. Trevor cleared his throat. "Of course I will."

◈

Chloe watched as they lowered her father's casket into the earth. One of her nieces picked the guitar and sang his favorite hymn, "Amazing Grace." A hush fell over the family as the chains were lifted away and only the casket remained deep inside the ground. A sniffle sounded—then another.

A strong hand grasped hers, and she peered into Trevor's eyes. He enveloped her in his arms, and she savored his embrace. She needed his support, his warmth.

She thought of her father's face as he lay lifeless in the ornate mahogany box. Peace had filled his features. It radiated from his expression. Even in death. He was with Jesus. She had no doubt in her mind.

More than anything she wanted to be able to see him again. She knew Jesus was her only way to do it.

Chapter 10

Ten days had passed since Chloe's father died. The grieving process had been a strange one. The first few days she felt numb, almost sick from the numbness. Only pain and sadness could ebb their way into her heart at intermittent times. Those were the days she contacted her professors about the classes she'd missed. Then she'd spent a long weekend with her family. They'd sifted through her father's personal belongings, finding old love letters from Mama and notes and handmade gifts from each of the children, things they'd never known he'd kept.

The last night of her visit, Natalie's husband had taken Daddy's guitar to the porch and picked some of the songs her father had always played. Peace she'd never felt flooded her soul; then longing immediately followed. The feeling kept her perplexed the whole evening and into the next week. How could she feel peace and longing at the same time? When she thought of Daddy, peace. When she thought of moments with him, longing.

She bent down and adjusted the slim brace that enfolded her ankle. Healing was coming to a close. Finally, under Trevor's scrutiny, she was able to work out with her team. Opening the gym door, she inhaled the mixture of sweat, body odor, and rubber. Though most found the smell offensive, Chloe relished it, knowing it meant she was nearing her goal of getting back on the soccer field. Now she had newfound purpose in making it back in the game. She longed to score just one more goal in honor of her father.

Opening her locker, she placed her gym bag inside. She lifted her hands over her head and stretched as far as she could before bending over and touching her hands to the ground. She skimmed the facility, looking for Trevor. With only four weeks left in the season, she didn't want to do anything that would jeopardize her chance of playing.

She saw him at a weight bench spotting one of their freshmen players. *Brandy.* Chloe cringed. The gorgeous redhead was nothing but a flirt. More than one of her teammates had had words with the girl over her flirtatious actions with their boyfriends. Chloe had even caught her batting her eyes at Coach Collins, which was wrong for several reasons. The man was married, and he was twice their age. To his credit he never responded to Brandy, but her actions sickened Chloe just the same.

She watched as Brandy struggled to lift the bar, and Trevor's lips and body language showed him encouraging her to do so. Her face scrunched, and her arms shook as she finally hefted the bar onto its rest. Brandy popped up from the bench and clapped her hands in excited animation. Trevor smiled and nodded his head. He lifted his hand to give her a high five when suddenly Brandy wrapped her arms around him and landed a big kiss on his cheek.

A knot formed in Chloe's throat, and her heart sank. She watched in horror as the freshman nestled her face against Trevor's chest. Trevor patted her back twice then tried to move away, but Brandy held tight. Anger quickly replaced the nauseous feeling that had overcome her. She stomped over to them and placed both hands on her hips. "Trevor!"

Brandy released her grip, turned to face Chloe then crossed her arms in front of her. "Hi, Chloe. What's up?" She cocked her head to one side. "Trevor was spotting my bench press. Is that a problem?" Brandy's words were laced with a challenge.

Chloe felt her face grow warm. She had no claim to Trevor. As one of the assistant athletic trainers for the university, he helped several players on Ball State's teams. They weren't dating, merely working together to get her ankle healed.

Still, they'd spent so much time together over the last few weeks. Trevor had been a pillar of strength to her when she needed him most. She'd grown close to him—in a sisterly way. At least she had thought so.

Seeing him with Brandy's arms around his neck had instilled a new feeling within her. She hadn't seen the green monster in a long while, not since high school, but she had to admit she recognized it now. Jealousy, pure and full, had swept through her and taken over her senses.

She stepped back. Trevor was free to like whom he wanted. She didn't want him, or did she? The thought sent a whirl of emotions spinning through her, one on top of the other. Her focus had been her foot then her daddy. She wasn't ready to think about this. Whatever *this* was. "I. . ." Her voice came out soft and shaky. She cleared her throat. "I just needed to know where I should work out first."

Trevor stepped away from Brandy. "Why don't you start with some leg lifts?" His voice was soothing as he placed his hand at the small of her back and led her to an open bench. He adjusted the weight to the amount she needed. She sat and positioned her feet behind the padding, and Trevor kneeled beside her. "Did that bother you?" His voice came out in little more than a whisper.

"Did what bother me?" Chloe tried to sound nonchalant, but the shaking in her voice no doubt gave her away.

"Brandy hugging me."

"Why would that bother me? You're my trainer. I'm your trainee. It's not like we're dating or anything."

"That's all I am? Your trainer?" Trevor's voice didn't hold bitterness or anger. Instead, it begged the question to be answered.

Chloe stared into his eyes. He was more than the university's assistant athletic trainer, more than a friend. When had her feelings changed? She looked away and focused on her legs, moving the weight up and down. She couldn't tell him the truth. Not now. Not when she hadn't even had a chance to think about what she was feeling. "I don't know."

He stood, and she felt him watching her as she continued her repetitions. Trying to forget the whole conversation, she focused on her legs. They burned under the exercise, a good burn, the kind that let her know they were strengthening once again.

"I was wondering." Trevor leaned next to her once again. A rush of heat filled her neck and cheeks, and she knew they flamed red. "I have two tickets to the Colts game tomorrow."

"The Colts?" She turned and looked at him. She loved football. The Colts were her favorite team. Her family used to watch them every time they came on television. Once when she was a small girl and the coal mines were doing well, Daddy'd had the money to take the whole family to a game. She'd never forget that day.

A slow smile formed on his lips. "You wanna go?"

"Well. . ." Chloe pressed her lips together.

"As friends."

A chuckle welled deep within her. "Definitely." *The only problem is, I think I feel more toward you than just friendship.*

❧

What am I doing, Lord? Trevor shifted his weight from one foot to the other as he waited in the concession line behind the never-ending stream of Colts fans. It was obvious something had changed between him and Chloe since the Brandy escapade at the gym. Today she'd blushed when she opened the apartment door to greet him.

Chloe only blushed when she got caught doing something she wasn't supposed to do. Maybe falling for him was something she wasn't supposed to do.

He shoved his hands in his jeans pockets as the line moved forward half a step. He'd given in to his attraction to Chloe long ago, but he still sought God's help with his love for her. She was out of reach, unattainable, not a possibility, until he knew she'd accepted Jesus into her heart.

Though she'd softened since her father's death, she hadn't told him of any commitment to the Lord.

And what about his dream job? It had been a whole month since he'd had the interview, and Trevor still hadn't heard from them. Not a letter or even a

186

phone call. He'd pretty much given up hope on the job. *But surely they'd call me and at least tell me they'd decided on someone else.*

He moved forward again. Finally, it was his turn to order. "I'll take two souvenir drinks and two hot dogs. One with mustard and relish. The other with mustard and ketchup."

"You got it." The woman smiled and rang up his total. He handed her the money, and another woman gave him a brown paper container holding his order.

"Thanks."

The woman nodded. "Enjoy the game."

Carefully making his way past spectators who crowded at every turn, Trevor found the correct entrance and walked down toward their seats. The weather was perfect—not a cloud in sight. The sun warmed them more than usual for an autumn day in Indiana, and yet the cool breeze kept a slight "football" nip in the air. Chloe turned, and the wind blew strands of hair into her face. She smiled and pushed them away from her mouth, and for a moment Trevor wished to be a strand kissing her sweet pink lips. Her eyes danced with delight as he made his way closer. *How could a man resist her, Lord?*

"Did you have any trouble?" She reached for her hot dog and drink from the container as he sat beside her.

"None at all."

"Good. Look what I got." She laid the hot dog in her lap, held her drink with one hand, and reached down to pick up an oversized foam fist with one finger raised in the number-one sign. She giggled and raised it over her head then yelled for the team when they took the line, preparing for the snap.

He smiled and bit into his hot dog. She hadn't seemed this happy in a long time. In fact, he'd never seen her so thrilled. Between her ankle injury and her father's illness and death, he'd mainly seen Chloe having to cope with serious and hard situations. It was good, really good, to see her enjoy herself.

Leaning back in his seat, he bit into his hot dog then took a long drink. He listened and sneaked peeks at Chloe as she cheered on the team. Soon he became enthralled with the game. The score was seven to seven with only a minute left in the third quarter. The Colts had just failed to make the forty-five-yard field goal. He watched the defensive team run onto the field. The ball was snapped. The opposing quarterback launched the football like a missile through the air. The Colts defender ran toward the wide receiver. Trevor leaned forward and punched his fist through the air. "Catch it. Come on. Catch it."

The Colts player scooped the ball into his hands and ran back toward their goal.

"Yes!" Trevor flung his arms open. His hand hit something. He turned toward Chloe and gasped. Red ketchup, yellow mustard, and brown soda covered her shirt.

She squealed and jumped up, trying to brush off the ice cubes. Her hot dog flew into the air, hitting the older man in front of them. "I'm so sorry!" she cried. She leaned over and tried to pick up the hot dog, but the man threw it to the ground and waved her away.

Trevor stood stunned as she scooped up napkins from both of their seats and tried to wipe her shirt. He snapped out of his shock then and started handing her more napkins as he moved into the aisle. She stepped out, too, and hurried toward the bathroom. Still somewhat taken aback, he followed her. "I can't believe I did that."

Chloe threw a wad of napkins into the trash and turned to face him. Ketchup and mustard dotted her nose, forehead, and chin. Streaks of the condiments had even landed in her hair. "Well. . ." Chloe shook her hands as the soda dripped off her long-sleeved shirt. "This will be memorable."

"I'm sorry. I'll—"

A giggle interrupted him, and he looked at Chloe to find her wiping a drop of mustard from her cheek. She smeared the glob on his nose then broke out into full-blown laughter. "I'm a total mess." She squeezed the bottom of her shirt, and more brown liquid dripped onto the floor. She doubled over and laughed harder.

Her laughter was contagious. Trevor joined in until his cheeks and his sides hurt. "The least I can do is buy you a new shirt."

Nodding her head, she rubbed her cheeks with both hands and giggled anew when she saw ketchup and mustard covering her palms. "I think I'll let you do that."

<hr />

Chloe took the long-sleeved T-shirt Trevor had bought her and made her way into the women's restroom. She gasped when she saw the mess staring at her in the mirror. Grabbing several paper towels from the dispenser, she wet them then hustled into a stall. She removed her soiled shirt and wiped off as much as she could.

Her jeans were soiled, as well, but she'd just have to wear them stains and all. She rolled her eyes. *We need to get out of here—and fast.*

After unlocking the stall, she walked to the trash bin and threw away her shirt. *I'm not talented enough at doing laundry to get those stains out. I'm glad it's not one of my best shirts.* Staring into the mirror, she grabbed more towels and wiped the mustard and ketchup from her face. She opened her purse, grabbed her brush, and combed through her hair. *Ew. This is so gross. And I've definitely smelled better.* She smiled at her reflection. *But it was funny.*

A new giggle escaped her lips. That was the best laugh she'd had in a long time.

And she'd needed it.

"Thanks, God." The words slipped from her lips before she'd had time to think about them. She frowned into the mirror. *Where did that thought come from?* She bit the inside of her lip and shrugged her shoulders. Wherever it came from, it felt right.

Chapter 11

Sweat trickled down her temple, onto her cheek, and down her neck. Chloe fumbled through her purse for her door key. Her muscles burned, and her foot throbbed but in a good way. Trevor had given her the workout of her life at the gym.

"Howdy do, stranger lady." Renee pulled open the door, nearly scaring Chloe.

"Whew. Thanks." Chloe reached to steady her racing heart. "I must have left my keys in my room."

Renee fanned her hand in front of her nose. "How did you get home?"

"Trevor."

"He must have no sense of smell. Girlfriend, you reek."

Chloe stuck out her tongue at her friend. "Hard work is what you smell."

"You've been spending a lot of time with our trainer of late." Liz walked into the living area clad in a plush purple bathrobe with her hair rolled up in a towel. Light green goop covered her face. She held a carton of mint chocolate chip ice cream in one hand and a spoon in the other.

"Aren't you the epitome of beauty?" Chloe smiled. "Date tonight?"

"Don't you try to change the subject." Liz shook the spoon at Chloe. "What's up with you and the trainer?"

Renee walked over to Liz and crossed her arms in front of her. "Yeah."

"Guess what! Trevor said next week I'm back on the practice field."

"Really!" Renee enfolded Chloe in a bear hug. She pushed away. "You really do stink."

Liz started to hug Chloe but instead patted her arm. "I can't wait until you're back out there with us."

"I know. I'm so excited." Chloe lifted her gym bag higher onto her shoulder. "I'm hitting the tub."

Dropping her stuff in her room, she grabbed a clean set of clothes and her purse. As she made her way into the bathroom, she heard Liz's faint voice. "She still avoided my question."

Chloe smiled. She knew she had done just that.

"Oh well, we'll hit her up later," Renee's voice responded.

Maybe they'll forget. Chloe shut the bathroom door then started the water.

She added a capful of soap to the stream. It had been a long time since she'd had a bubble bath, and today Trevor made sure she'd earned one. She slipped into the tub then reached over the edge for her purse. She searched it for the stats Coach Collins had given her so she could study them while she soaked. Her purse fell to the floor, and she leaned over to pick up the contents, a cascade of bubbles hitting her in the face. Giggling, she blew the suds away.

One week. I'll be back on the field in just one week. She could hardly believe it. Time couldn't have moved any slower.

Daddy won't be able to collect my news clippings. A wave of emotion washed over her. She missed him so much. She'd have to visit her family before she hit the field again.

She scooped up the paper into her hands. Pushing more bubbles away, she opened the pamphlet. It wasn't stats from Coach Collins. It was the tract that had fallen from her sister's purse. *How did this end up in there? I thought I gave everything back to her.*

Thumbing through it, the words seemed to jump out at her in a way they hadn't before. She turned the page and looked at the picture that depicted God's love. "John 3:16..." Chloe gazed at the tile on the wall and recited from memory. "For God so loved the world that he gave his only Son that whoever believes in Him won't perish but have eternal life." She looked down at the pamphlet and smirked as she read the verse. "Well, I was close."

The meaning of the verse began to sink into her heart as she turned the page and read aloud, "For all have sinned and fall short of the glory of God." She thought of the time she'd wasted, not going to see her daddy because she couldn't bear to see him ill. He'd missed her, and she could never get that time back.

She moved to the next page. "But God demonstrates his own love for us in this: While we were still sinners, Christ died for us."

She closed the tract. Christ died for her. She'd known it since she was a small girl. He died for her. A sinner. All she had to do to receive Him was trust Him. Why was trust so hard?

The bubbles had subsided, and she gazed down at her foot in the water. No trace of injury showed on her ankle, yet she'd missed almost the entire season. *If it hadn't happened, Trevor never would have taken me to see my family. I wouldn't have seen Daddy before he died.* The realization of it weighed on her. She'd played many a soccer game. She may not play competitively after this year, but she planned to coach as long as breath remained in her body.

She'd never get time with her daddy again.

The injury caused circumstances to happen that allowed her to see him not once, but twice, before he died.

God, You have a hand in everything, don't You? And You work it all for good.

Excitement welled inside her. For the first time she realized she could trust. God was worthy of her trust. Long before she was born, He had proven himself worthy of her trust. She wanted—no, needed—to trust Him. The immediacy of it quickened her pulse. Her heart beat faster in her chest. She wanted Him to live within her. Lifting her face to the ceiling, she closed her eyes and invited the blessed Savior into her heart.

❧

Glancing at his watch, Trevor stepped into the meeting room. He still had five minutes. Letting out a long breath, he took a seat. He'd rushed home after a good, long workout with Chloe only to find that Sam Stanley, Trevor's boss, had left a message on his machine about an impromptu meeting. In barely a half hour's time, Trevor showered, shaved, dressed, and made it back to the university.

He looked around the table, noting the athletic director, Sam, Coach Collins, and the university's head women's basketball coach. A thrill crept up his spine as he wondered if they planned to give him some kind of promotion. After all, he was the only other assistant athletic trainer here, and he'd heard Sam was considering retirement. *I haven't been on long enough. I shouldn't get my hopes up. It wouldn't make sense to give me Sam's job. Besides, what about USC?*

Ten minutes passed, and Trevor wondered why someone hadn't started the meeting. He looked at his watch then at the clock on the wall. It was definitely time to start.

"He should be here any minute," Sam whispered to the athletic director.

"He'd better be good."

"He is." Sam wrung his hands. "He was top of his class, recruited by several major schools. He's perfect."

Uneasiness filled Trevor. In his heart he could sense this meeting would not be what he'd hoped. The door opened, and a light-haired man who couldn't have been more than twenty-two walked in. He nodded to each of them. "I apologize for being late. Would you believe I got a flat tire?" He wiped at his pants. They seemed wrinkle-free and clean to Trevor.

Sam stood and patted the man on the back. "You're fine, son. No one can help a flat tire. Just ten minutes past anyway." He scanned the room. "Colleagues, meet Jackson Wilcox. He's the man I'm recommending for the additional assistant athletic trainer position. I believe he has the potential to take over for me in the next few years."

Trevor's insides churned. He watched in shock as the young man shook hands with everyone around the table. When his turn came, Trevor could barely lift his hand. The man took his seat and smiled at each of them as he took résumés from his briefcase and passed them out.

Trevor scoured the contents. The man had just graduated from college at the end of the summer. As Trevor guessed, he was barely twenty-two and had zero experience. None. Except what was required for school. His grades were good enough, but the number of fast-food jobs he'd had over the last four years was a red flag in Trevor's opinion. He didn't seem to stay anywhere longer than six weeks.

Why would Sam do this? I thought I was too young to be considered, but I have six years on the new graduate. He stared at Jackson. He was definitely good-looking, and suddenly Trevor wasn't sure he wanted Jackson to be available to work with Chloe when Trevor was helping another athlete. He shook his head. *What am I thinking? I can't even ask her out on a real date because she's not a Christian. I can't keep her from seeing other men.*

The athletic director's secretary walked into the room. Though well past middle age, the woman was fit and always looked attractive. Jackson winked at her. A baffled look covered her face while pink colored her cheeks.

How unprofessional! Trevor looked around to see if anyone else had noticed Jackson's behavior. To his dismay each person was studying the younger man's résumé.

No. Trevor did not want the man working with any of the women's teams. And especially not Chloe. Sam cleared his throat. "Trevor is a wonderful asset to our university." Trevor sat up straighter. "I'd like to let him keep doing the great job he does, and I'll train Jackson." He turned to Trevor. "I called you in because I'm afraid your load may increase while we're getting Jackson situated."

Trevor could hardly believe his ears. He would have more responsibilities *and* Jackson would get preferential training. The rest of the meeting was a blur as they discussed various job descriptions, expectations, and salary. The man would even start out making more than Trevor had when he first landed his job. Jackson was too young and inexperienced to begin at such a high salary.

The whole thing was appalling.

The meeting ended, and with a mumbled good-bye, Trevor made his way to his car. He rolled down the windows and allowed the cool air to slap his face as he drove home. He needed all the help he could get to simmer down. Reaching his apartment, he jumped out of his car and made his way inside. He yanked the number to the University of South Carolina from his refrigerator and picked up the phone. Dialing, he waited as several rings ensued.

"University of South Carolina athletic office," a friendly female voice said over the line.

"I'd like to speak with the athletic director if he is available."

"I'm sorry, he's out of the office, but I can take a message."

Trevor raked his fingers through his hair. "Sure. This is Trevor Montgomery. I had an interview with him about an assistant athletic trainer position a little over a month ago. I wanted to check the status of the position."

"Oh, Mr. Montgomery." The woman's voice grew stronger with recognition. "Mr. Spence, the team's coach, had a death in the family, so we haven't made any job decisions."

"I'm sorry to hear about that for him. Thank you for your time."

"Mr. Montgomery." The woman's voice lowered to a whisper. "If it makes you feel better, I think they liked you a lot."

Trevor felt the smile growing on his lips. "Thank you." He hung up the phone. *Yes, it makes me feel a lot better.*

Chloe noted the bounce in her step as she made her way to a local Laundromat. Lugging the overflowing hamper actually felt good for the first time ever. With her ankle injured and having to hobble around on crutches, Chloe had spent the last several weeks at the mercy of her roommates when it came to getting her clothes clean. Liz had ruined two of her shirts by throwing them in the dryer when they were supposed to air dry. And if Chloe had waited for Renee to do a load or two for her, she would still be waiting. She felt confident Renee had articles of clothing in her room that could stand up and walk around.

Resting the hamper on her hip, Chloe reached to pull open the door. "Here. I'll get that for you," a female voice said from behind.

"Thanks." Chloe watched as Molly opened the door and let Chloe go inside. "I've never seen you here before."

Chloe hefted the hamper onto a table beside two washing units. "I used to come every Tuesday, but when I injured my ankle, I had to let my roommates do it for me."

"Today's Friday."

"I know. They didn't do laundry very often."

Molly laughed. "Are you saying there's more?"

"Oh yes."

"Do you want some help?"

Chloe shook her head. "No. I just have another smaller hamper. But thanks."

She walked outside to her car, grateful she needed only an ACE bandage to get there. The last several weeks had been quite humbling for her. She depended on her roommates for laundry, for dish washing, for grocery shopping. So many things had been difficult without the use of her foot.

And the truth was, neither of her roommates completed tasks as Chloe did. She chuckled. When she'd been a young girl, she and her siblings often feigned the ability to do things as well as Mama. Sometimes Mama would give up on them and do the work herself, but usually she was too smart for those games and just made them redo the work.

Chloe carried the last bit inside and separated the wash into whites and colors. After filling three loads, she dropped her quarters into the machines and started them. She added soap to each one then plopped into a chair across from Molly.

Her teammate was flipping through a magazine about home designs. Chloe tried not to stare at Molly. She couldn't help but wonder what the sophomore would think when she found out Chloe would be practicing with the team again.

Molly had been nice to her at Pizza King and had called several times to check up on her. Molly said they were friends, and Chloe wondered if the sophomore was a Christian also. They played the same position, though, and being human was still part of their lives. If a gal threatened her spot on the team, Chloe wouldn't be jumping for joy about it.

"So how's the foot?" Molly laid the magazine on the table and looked up at Chloe.

"It's good." Chloe nodded and tried to sound nonchalant.

"Has Montgomery told you when you can come back to practice?"

Well, if that's not a coincidence. She must have heard about it from someone. "Actually, I get to practice with the team next week."

Molly leaned forward in her seat. "Chloe, that's great. We still have three weeks left in the regular season. You should get to play."

"I hope so." Chloe searched Molly's face for signs of hypocrisy, but the younger woman truly seemed happy for Chloe. Her cell phone rang from inside her purse. Berating herself for her distrustful attitude, Chloe pulled it out and pushed the TALK button. "Hello."

"Hey." Trevor's deep voice spoke, sending flutters through Chloe's veins. "What's up?"

"I just wanted to make sure we're still heading to your mom's house tomorrow."

"Yep."

"Okay, I'll pick you up at eight in the morning."

"I'll be ready." Chloe pushed the OFF button and dropped her phone back in her purse. She looked at Molly again.

The younger woman pulled a packet of gum from her pocket. "Want a piece?"

"Sure." Chloe took it, opened the wrapper, and popped the gum into her mouth. Guilt pricked at her heart. Molly had reached out to her a couple of times now, and Chloe hadn't been as receptive as she should have been. *Help me, Lord. I may not be playing, but I want to be a good leader. I wouldn't mind having a new friend, either.* She glanced at Molly. "I'm heading to see my family tomorrow."

"I'm really sorry about your dad."

Chloe nodded. "Thanks." She twisted the strap of her purse. Making small talk with the girl who was playing her position proved harder than she imagined, yet Chloe felt a drawing toward her that she couldn't explain. "Trevor's going with me."

Their buzzers sounded, and they walked over to the washing machines. "You two seem pretty close."

Chloe pulled her clothes from the washer and shoved them into a dryer. "I don't know what's going on between us, to be honest."

"Yeah. I know what you mean. There's a guy I've been interested in for quite a while, but I'm not sure if he's right for me."

Chloe listened as Molly shared her heart. A bond seemed to form between them as they waited for their clothes to dry and then folded them when they finished. Chloe never would have imagined becoming friends with the girl who'd been playing her position, yet she felt a kindred spirit in Molly. Once finished, Chloe loaded her car with her clean clothes. Her heart spilled over with thanksgiving at the new friendship God had given her. *God, You can do anything in my life. Help me always to be willing to let You.*

Chapter 12

Chloe scooped up the dice and rolled them. She picked up the metal shoe and moved it eight spaces. She turned to her sister Natalie and extended her hand. "I passed Go. Give me two hundred dollars, please."

Natalie, playing the role of banker for the game, gave her four fifty-dollar bills. "You guys are going to have to go through your money and trade me five one-hundred dollar bills for one five-hundred."

Their mother, Sabrina, Amanda, Kylie, and Chloe all fished through their money and traded with the bank. Mama picked up the dice to roll. Instead, she held them in her grip and looked around the table. "How long has it been since we played Monopoly together?"

Sabrina pushed a lock of hair behind her ear. "Mama, you and Kylie and I played just last week."

Mama shook her head. "No. I mean all of us."

Chloe shrugged her shoulders. "I don't know." She peered at her sisters, all so different from her. Each one was married. Each one had or would soon have a home full of children. She glanced at Kylie—she would have a biological child and two new adopted children in a matter of months. None of them had been particularly fond of sports. They had always been like the four musketeers, and she was the kid outsider.

"Well, I've been busy having babies." Amanda lifted her fussy six-month-old daughter out of her car seat.

Mama smiled. "That's true. With seven babies, you've almost caught up with your mom."

"My boys keep me hopping with all their football and soccer practices. Soon we'll be adding basketball." Sabrina looked at Chloe. "Mike's the starting center forward for his middle school, just like his aunt."

"Really?" Chloe felt a niggle of guilt wedge inside her heart. She spent tons of time with her university team and with the girls' team she coached, but she didn't know her own nephew played.

"Yep." Sabrina beamed. "He's their leading scorer."

"I'd love to see him play."

"They're going to be in a tournament in Indianapolis in two weeks. Maybe you could come."

"I'd love to."

Mama wiped her eyes with a tissue. "You girls can't imagine how happy it makes me to see you all at this table. I wish your daddy were here."

Silence enveloped the room. Chloe shuffled her game money. "Daddy always won."

"Always," said Amanda.

"Do you think he cheated?" Kylie furrowed her brows in a straight line. "I mean, how could the man *always* win?"

Natalie huffed. "How could you think Daddy was a cheat? The man was a saint."

Mama burst into laughter. "Don't you girls go putting your daddy on a pedestal. He was a man." She leaned forward. "And if you want my opinion, I think he had to be fudging somewhere."

"Mother!" Sabrina lifted her hand to her chest. "Daddy was not a cheat."

"Come on, Sabrina." Her mother slapped her hand on the table. "The man won every time." She fanned her money then and stretched her hand across the vast property she owned on the board. "And maybe he taught me his trick."

Chloe bit the inside of her lip, holding back her laughter. Mama was definitely winning by a long shot. She folded her arms in front of her. "So how are you winning? You were always the first to go bankrupt."

Her mother leaned forward and shook her head. "I have no idea." Giggles erupted from each of the sisters.

"Hey, quiet down in there. We can't hear the game!" yelled Dalton.

"Sorry about that," Mama hollered back. She wiped away the tears of laughter that had pooled in her eyes then touched Chloe's hand. "Something's different about you."

"I bet it's that tall, dark, handsome fellow sitting in there on the couch." Sabrina popped several mixed nuts into her mouth.

"Do tell." Kylie leaned across the table closer to Chloe.

"Yeah, you can't keep secrets from your sisters," added Amanda. "It's against the rules."

Chloe grinned. "What rules?"

Amanda shrugged. "I don't know. Sister rules."

Chloe took a drink of her soda then set the glass back on the table. "I do like him."

"I knew it." Natalie clapped her hands.

"We all knew it." Amanda scoffed at her sister. "We've been waiting for her to figure it out."

"Shh." Chloe placed her finger over her lips. "Trevor doesn't know. And Amanda's right. I didn't realize it until just the other day. But that's not what's different about me."

Chloe glanced at her mother. Tears glistened in the older woman's eyes. "Am I to believe. . . Do I dare to dream that my prayers of twenty-three years have been answered with a yes?"

A smile lifted Chloe's lips. Of course her mother knew. She could always tell when things were wrong or right with each of her children. If only Daddy could have known, too. "Yes, Mama. I've asked Jesus into my heart."

"Praise God." Mama clapped her hands as squeals erupted around the table. Her sisters stood and wrapped her in a group hug.

"Hey, we can't hear the game!" Dalton yelled.

"Put a muzzle on it, little brother." Natalie, the shortest member of the family, stomped into the living area. "We can make noise if we want to."

"Now listen here. . ."

The sound of her brother and sister fussing faded as Chloe's heart filled with love for her family. *God, I understand why I didn't fit in with my sisters. It wasn't because I was the youngest or because I loved sports and they didn't. It was because they knew You and I didn't. Thank You, Jesus. Finally, I fit in.*

❧

Trevor listened as Dalton and Natalie had an arguing match over who could be loud and when. Soon Natalie walked back to the dining area. Muffled sounds floated from the women, and he heard Chloe's mother say, "You have to tell him."

Tell who? About what? Though he was an avid NFL game watcher and he enjoyed being with Chloe's brothers and brothers-in-law, his favorite team wasn't playing, so the women's noise distracted him. *Maybe just being near Chloe distracts me.*

Chloe walked into the room. Her face was flushed. "Who's playing?"

Dalton looked at her and growled. "Don't you come in here disrupting our game, too."

"I just want to know who's playing, you big meanie."

"No, you don't. You want to bother us," Dalton shot back.

Chloe swatted the back of his head. "I do not."

Trevor shifted in his seat to watch Chloe and Dalton. "Do all siblings fight like this?"

Gideon chortled. "Most grow out of it. We don't."

Trevor laughed. Chloe sat beside him on the couch then leaned close. The light scent of her perfume beckoned him, and he sat board straight so as not to grab her and plant a huge kiss on her lips. Goose bumps covered his skin when she whispered in his ear. "Who's playing?"

He coughed and cleared his throat. "The Patriots and the Bengals."

"Would you be willing to go somewhere with me right now, or do you want to wait until after the game?" She whispered again, and Trevor caught a whiff of her cinnamon gum.

"I'll go now."

"Good." Chloe stood and walked over to the coatrack. Trevor followed her. She took her jacket and put it on. "Don't forget—" She turned abruptly, slamming face first into his chest. "Oh! I didn't realize you were so close."

"It's okay." Trevor peered down at her. Pink tinted her cheeks. He cupped her chin with his hand, longing to lower his lips to hers. He'd never been so drawn to her as he was today. Maybe going with her was the worst thing he could possibly do, but he wanted to go so much.

"Where're you going?" Dalton's voice interrupted his thoughts.

"Out," Chloe snapped at her brother.

Dalton leaned forward in his chair. "Trevor, you don't have to do what she says. These women think they can rule our lives. I've got news for them—"

"Now listen here. I am not making—"

Trevor laughed. "It's okay, Dalton. I want to go."

"We'll have dinner ready when you get back," her mother called from the other room.

"Okay." Chloe moved away from him and toward the door.

"Do I need my keys?"

"Nope. We'll walk."

Trevor followed Chloe through their backyard. The wind had cooled substantially in the last few weeks. Fall had come, and Trevor relished it. He noted that most of the leaves still held their green, but some had already changed to yellow, salmon, and deep orange. The grass was plush beneath their feet from the recent rain. Soon the first frost would come and force the foliage into hibernation. "Where are we going?"

"Someplace where we can have peace and quiet. There isn't much of either at my house."

Trevor shoved his hands in his pockets. "I love coming with you to your house. You have a wonderful family."

She stopped and looked up at him. "Do you really think so?"

"Definitely."

"I'm so glad." A smile formed on her lips as she grabbed his wrist, forcing his hand from his pocket. "We're almost there."

Trevor turned his wrist until her hand fell into his. Her fingertips were cold but felt soft and perfect around his. He wondered if she would break his hold, but she didn't.

"We're here." She let go of his hand and pointed to a stream. Several large trees surrounded the water on each side of its banks. A wooden swing hung from an oversized limb of one of the trees. "I can't believe this is still here." Chloe sat on the swing and swayed slightly.

"Is this where you played as a girl?"

"One of the places."

"It's nice." Trevor shuffled his feet. Why had she brought him here? To show him a stream and a swing? Did she just want to get away from all the noise?

"I have a surprise I want to share with you." She stood and made her way closer to him. "I believe it's something you'll understand."

"Okay." Trevor studied Chloe. She stepped closer to him, and his heart raced. A glimmer shone in her eyes. Her nose and lips were brushed with color from the cool air.

Though a tall woman, she stood on tiptoes, grabbed his arm then cupped her hand around her mouth to whisper in his ear. "I've accepted Jesus into my heart." She took a step back and stared into his eyes.

Trevor gazed down at her. "You have?"

She closed her lips, her eyes glistening with tears, then nodded her head.

"Oh, Chloe." Trevor pulled her into his arms. The love he felt spilled from within him. He'd bottled it, tied it, held it back as long as he could. Releasing her only at arm's length, he caressed her cheek with the back of his hand. A lone tear streamed down her face, and he brushed it away.

Sweetness radiated from her eyes, and he could take it no more. Lowering his lips to hers, he kissed her with the strength of the emotions he'd tried so hard to hold at bay. She received his kiss, and he felt as if his body might leave the ground in flight.

He released her, and she cuddled against him. He kissed the top of her head. "You don't know how long I've waited to hear you say those words."

"Am I to think you have feelings for me?" she murmured.

"Oh yes. Since the first moment I saw you."

"Really?"

He nodded and released his hold of her. "I've prayed for you to receive Christ more often than I've prayed for anything in my life. I even begged God to take you out of my life if you wouldn't receive Him."

"I'm glad He didn't take me out of your life."

"Me, too. Nothing can keep you from me now."

Chapter 13

Chloe slipped on her black pants and buttoned the waist. She grabbed her silver necklace with the oversized blue gem and fastened it around her neck. Fidgeting with the collar of her deep blue, button-down silk shirt, she scanned her closet for her black heels. She found them, slipped them on, and stood in front of the full-length mirror. The shirt and necklace brought out the color of her eyes. The pants, long enough to span her legs, rested midway down her heels.

The extra height on her five-foot, eleven-inch frame usually made her uncomfortable—but not when she stood next to Trevor. He was one of the few men she'd met who still towered several inches above her. And she loved it.

Twisting, she stared at her reflection. She combed her fingers through her hair. She looked nice. Felt pretty. Not sporty, not tomboyish, but feminine and attractive. *I could get used to this.*

Grabbing her purse from the bed, she walked into the living area and glanced at the clock. Trevor would be there any minute.

"Wow. You look nice." Renee unfolded her legs and set her cereal bowl on the end table. She reached over and touched Chloe's shirt. "Soft."

"Where're you going?" Liz blew on the top of her coffee cup.

"Church."

"Again?" Liz furrowed her brows. "But you didn't get back from your family's house until like midnight last night."

"I know."

Liz popped a grape into her mouth. "Isn't this like the second or third time?"

"Third. You guys could go with me if you want."

"No thanks." Renee folded her legs back under her.

"Are you going by yourself?" Liz seemed interested, which encouraged Chloe.

"Trevor's coming to get me."

Liz snorted. "That's why you're going."

"No. I'd go without him." Chloe peeked out the window and saw that Trevor had pulled up. She looked back at Liz and Renee. "If you want to, we could all go together next week."

"Count me out," Renee said, grumbling.

Liz shrugged.

The doorbell rang, and Chloe walked to the door. "Okay. I'll see you guys later." *God, if You can change me, You can change anyone.*

Opening the door, she bit her bottom lip as a wave of excitement and sudden embarrassment hit her at the thought of Trevor picking her up as a date. "Hey." She fiddled with her purse strap.

"Hey." He bent down and kissed her cheek. "You look beautiful."

Contentment flooded her heart. She wished so much that Daddy could see how happy she was now, even without playing soccer. One day, in heaven, she'd tell him all about it.

⬥

Trevor settled into a seat beside Chloe. Scanning the church sanctuary, he saw Matt approaching them. A wave of jealousy washed over him at the thought of Matt flirting with Chloe. He pushed the feeling aside. God had been working on Matt's heart, and Trevor needed only to encourage him.

"Hey, Matt." Trevor waved and patted the seat beside him. "Why don't you join us?"

"Sure." Matt shook Trevor's hand then pushed his way to the open seat beside Chloe.

Great. Now I have to listen to him flirting with Chloe. Lord, I won't be able to handle it.

"So did you two finally decide to make yourselves an official couple?" Matt's voice interrupted his thoughts.

"Yep." Chloe's smile lit up the room. She gingerly took Trevor's hand in hers.

"It's about time. Watching you two was giving me a headache."

"What was giving you a headache?"

Trevor turned at the female voice beside him. He peered at one of Chloe's teammates. What was her name?

"Molly." Surprise sounded in Chloe's voice.

That's her name. I haven't seen her at church before.

"I'm glad you came." Matt's voice sounded more hesitant than Trevor had ever heard it. He turned and noted that the man's face burned crimson.

"How could I resist an invitation to church? I've been looking for a church home since I transferred to Ball State." The tiny blond ran her fingers through her short hair.

Matt stood and motioned for her to sit beside him. "I'm glad you couldn't resist. Maybe I can convince you to have lunch with me afterward."

"How about just church? Maybe I could meet you at a Bible study sometime."

Matt frowned, and Trevor wondered how many times the guy had been turned down. Still, Trevor was glad the girl hadn't fallen for Matt's charms. He knew Matt could be a wonderful person, but Trevor hoped he would focus on getting to know the Lord before he found himself a girlfriend.

Molly turned to Chloe and Trevor. "I didn't think I'd make it. It's been quite a morning."

"I'm glad you're here." Chloe patted her leg.

Molly studied Chloe. "You know, you look different."

Chloe smiled. "I can't wait to tell you all about it."

Trevor's heart soared. Chloe did look different. She was the most unique person he'd ever met before she accepted Jesus; now she had the sweet, Christ-filled spirit to match. The music started, and Trevor stood with the congregation, lifting his voice in praise for God's blessings.

An off-key noise sounded from somewhere. Soon a slight squeak followed. He frowned and shook his head. Where was that noise coming from? He looked at the stage. Maybe some of the equipment or one of the microphones wasn't working right.

He heard the noise again and peeked over toward Chloe. She was lifting her hands toward the heavens. Her eyes were closed, and her mouth moved with the words of the music.

Turning away from her, Trevor closed his eyes and focused on the words. *Okay, Lord, You tell us to make a joyful noise to You. And that doesn't mean it has to be perfect.*

He sneaked another peek at Chloe. He could see the sweet expression of worship on her face, and he couldn't help but adore her openness of praise.

The music ended, and Chloe leaned close to him. "I don't usually sing in church."

He nodded. This was probably true. He'd seen her at only one other church service, and he'd noticed she didn't sing then.

"I don't sing very well. My brothers used to torture me about it, but my parents insisted we sing when we were supposed to." She looked toward the cross that hung at the front of the sanctuary. "Now I find I love singing. I feel so close to God, so much in reverence and awe of Him."

"That's all that matters." He grabbed her hand and squeezed it tight. "Our praise is always pleasing to the Lord."

She peered up at him and smiled. Her eyes shone like the sky on a clear day. "Thanks, Trevor."

No. Trevor inwardly shook his head. *Thank you for reminding me what true praise is all about.*

❧

Chloe stepped to the side as Trevor opened the door to the restaurant that was known for its breakfast. He placed his hand at the small of her back and guided her in. His gentle touch sent tingles through her. She'd never felt cared for as a woman. Sure, she'd thought Randy had cared for her as a man did for a woman, but they had been so young, still in high school, and she had been foolish. Now she could honestly pray that he and his wife were happy.

The waitress led them to their booth. Chloe slipped into one side and picked up the menu. Gazing at the many breakfast dishes, she had a sudden longing for one of her daddy's cheese, tomato, and green pepper omelets. As a small girl she'd scoffed at the idea of putting those nasty vegetables in her mouth. Daddy had pulled the food away. "I'll be more than happy to eat your share." He'd licked his lips and cut off a piece. Shoving the piece in his mouth, he'd rubbed his belly, declaring it the best food in the world.

His antics were too much for a small girl, and Chloe ended up taking the omelet back. She was surprised when she bit into a small piece. The spicy taste had been yummy, and she actually liked the feel of the cooked tomatoes on her tongue.

"I'd like you to meet my dad." Trevor's voice broke her reverie.

"I'd love to."

"He's flying in from South Carolina when soccer season is over."

"That'd be great."

The waitress returned and took their orders and the menus. Chloe folded her hands on top of the table and looked at Trevor. He furrowed his eyebrows and rubbed his jaw. Chloe frowned. "What's wrong?"

Trevor twisted the cloth napkin in his hand. "What are we, Chloe?"

"What do you mean?"

"I mean, I'm your trainer. I work at the university you attend."

"Is there a problem with your working for Ball State and my being a student? After all, I'm twenty-three years old. It's not as if I'm a minor or something."

"No. I don't think there's a problem with that. I just mean. . ." He picked up the fork and knife and placed them back in the napkin, folding them one way and then another. "My feelings for you are strong."

Chloe rested her hand on his. "I told Matt we're a couple." She swallowed. "I think we're definitely more than friends."

"Definitely. So what do we say?"

"We're dating?" She shrugged her shoulders, and heat suddenly warmed her cheeks. She felt more like a teenager than a grown woman. And yet the innocence and newness of their relationship felt wonderful and refreshing. "I want to be your girlfriend."

Trevor intertwined his hands with hers, lifted them to his lips, and kissed the tips of her fingers. "I think I'll like saying Chloe Andrews is my girlfriend."

Chapter 14

Chloe joined her teammates on the practice field. Elation filled her when Renee kicked the ball to her and Chloe felt no pain in kicking it back. The stiff bandage around her ankle was a bit aggravating but an easy compromise to be able to return to the field. She glanced at Trevor and Coach Collins on the sidelines. They were deep in conversation, and she hoped Trevor was telling him she was okay to play. *This is my chance to prove I can do it.*

She lined up with her teammates in three rows inside the penalty box. Their objective was to dribble the ball around a maze of cones. The first row of players to finish without knocking over any cones won. She got in the middle line, noting Molly stood to her right and Liz to her left. No question she'd beat Liz, but Molly—she wasn't sure.

Controlling the ball with her feet, Chloe dribbled around the first cone then the second. Molly and Liz kept pace beside her. They went around the third then the fourth. Liz knocked over a cone. Now she had only Molly to contend with. Knowing Coach Collins watched, Chloe made her way around the fifth cone. A sharp pain bolted through her ankle. She grimaced but continued. The sixth cone. Molly pushed ahead of her when they dribbled to the out-of-bounds line and back to the cones in reverse order.

Trying to pick up lost ground, Chloe dug in her heels and cut the ball sharp against each cone. She still trailed Molly by only a fraction of a step. Kick. Slice. Kick. Slice. Only one cone to pass. She kicked the ball harder than she'd intended to pass the last cone. To compensate, she extended her leg and caught the ball with her injured ankle instead of her foot. Fire whipped through and brought sudden tears to her eyes. She dribbled back to the starting line just behind Molly.

"You okay?" Molly turned to Chloe then took a long, deep breath and blew it out.

"Sure." Chloe wiped the tears from her eyes and sniffed. The wind brushed her face. She tried to chuckle. "Makes me tear up."

Molly lifted her hand for a high five. "That was pretty good footwork for a gal who hasn't practiced in weeks."

Chloe grabbed her side and squeezed the cramp. "Thanks."

Practice continued, and Chloe had never felt so exhausted. *I've been out of regular practice for nine weeks. It feels like nine years.* Sucking in a long breath,

206

Chloe determined to keep up with the other girls. She would not quit, even if it killed her. Finally, Coach Collins blew his whistle then yelled, "That's it! Good practice, ladies."

Exhilaration kept her feet moving. She'd made it through the whole practice. She'd probably spend the evening soaking in the tub and the next morning moving at a snail's pace wishing someone would take away the misery of her muscles, but she'd stuck it out the full three hours of practice.

"Andrews, come here." Coach Collins motioned for her. Trevor stood beside him. She couldn't decide if concern or pride marked his face. She knew he didn't think she'd make it the whole practice. He'd told her to sit out if her ankle hurt. Well, of course it was going to hurt a little. She hadn't *really* worked it out in weeks.

"What's up, Coach?" Chloe took a long drink of water then plopped onto the bench. The muscles in her legs and back immediately tightened. *Oh boy, I'm in for some pain. Note to self: Take some naproxen immediately when I get home.*

"Trevor wants to check your ankle."

Chloe's heart thudded against her chest when Trevor bent down in front of her. He unlaced her shoe and slipped it off. Reaching for the top of her sock, she giggled. "I'd say it's not going to smell so hot. You want me to do that?"

Trevor grinned and whispered, "You're incapable of smelling any way but wonderful."

"Ha-ha. Very funny." Heat rushed to her cheeks, and she looked up at her coach. He was talking with Molly, and Chloe sent up a silent prayer of thanks that he hadn't heard Trevor. She cocked her head and shrugged her shoulders. "Suit yourself."

Trevor pulled off her sock and shin guard. Wrinkling his nose, he fanned the air. "I take it back."

"Hey!" Chloe punched his shoulder, and Trevor laughed. He unwrapped her brace and checked out both sides of her ankle.

"Does this hurt?" He twisted her foot slightly to the right.

"Nope." She shook her head.

"How about this?" He twisted to the left.

A shot of pain raced down her foot. "Not. . ." Everything in her wanted to tell him it didn't hurt, but she couldn't lie. "Not too bad."

A slow smile spread over Trevor's lips. "Thanks for being honest." He moved closer to her and patted her knee. "Guess what. It's going to hurt a little bit. It's stiff from not being used as much."

Relief flooded her. "So when—?"

"You can play in the next game."

Her heart pounded in her chest. "You mean it? Three days?"

He nodded and turned toward Coach Collins. "She can play in the next game."

"Wonderful." Coach shook Trevor's hand then turned to Chloe and shook hers, as well. "I'm glad you're back." He looked at Trevor. "Can I talk with you a moment?"

"Sure." Trevor stood and squeezed Chloe's shoulder then followed her coach.

Molly sat on the bench and wrapped her arms around Chloe. "I'm so happy you can play again."

"Me, too." Chloe leaned over and put her brace and sock back on. She glanced at Molly. "Are you really happy I'm healed?"

Molly frowned. "Of course I am."

Chloe sat up, searching Molly's expression. The Holy Spirit had changed Chloe. She realized how selfish she had been. If she were in Molly's shoes, she would want the injury to last the whole season. "It's just that. . ." Chloe bit the inside of her lip. "Well, we play the same position and. . ."

"You think I'd want you to stay injured, right?"

Chloe shrugged.

"Remember when I told you about having to sit out my whole senior year of high school? That was really hard for me." Molly rubbed her hands together. "If it hadn't been for my relationship with God, I wouldn't have made it."

"We haven't actually talked about it, but I thought you might be a Christian."

"Oh yes."

"I figured." Chloe picked at a piece of lint on her shirt. "I mean, you were at church on Sunday, and you've always been—well, different from other people. Like Trevor and my family."

Molly hugged Chloe again. "That's the best compliment you could ever give me."

Chloe felt the smile growing on her face. "I'm a new Christian, too."

Molly clapped her hands. "That's wonderful. The best decision of your life."

"Yeah." She pointed to her chest. "I feel a peace I've never known before." Chloe listened as Molly shared about different things God had done in her life. Molly suggested several Bible studies Chloe could think about doing. She felt their friendship blossom even more as Molly talked, a friendship based on more than what Chloe wanted or could get out of it. A friendship based on faith.

Chloe understood why Molly was truly happy her ankle had healed. She wanted what was best for Chloe. In an instant she felt the same for Molly.

∽∾

Trevor walked into his apartment and dropped his keys on the table. After kicking off his shoes, he opened the refrigerator and grabbed a bottle of water and a container of leftover soup. He set the container in the microwave and turned it on. Gazing at his answering machine, he noted two messages. He pushed the button. The first message—a hang-up call—he deleted. The microwave beeped. He took out his soup and stirred it with a spoon.

"Mr. Montgomery, this is Walter Spence from the University of South Carolina," the man's voice said over the machine.

Trevor dropped the spoon into the bowl. So much had happened over the past week, he hadn't even thought about the job at USC.

"I'm sorry it took so long for me to get in touch with you. I had a death in my family. . . ."

Yes. The receptionist told me. His dream job may be a possibility. The idea seemed surreal, unattainable.

"We'd like to offer you the position. I know you've been working primarily with the women's soccer team at Ball State, but if at all possible, I need to meet with you. . ."

The rest of the message faded away. The University of South Carolina was offering him the position.

He pumped his fist in the air. "Yes!" he yelled through the apartment. No one could hear him, and he didn't care. His dream job. He had his dream job. An additional perk—he'd live near his father. *It's too good to be true.*

A beep sounded, notifying him the message had ended. He'd have to listen to the whole thing again.

Chloe's face popped into his mind. He fell into his oversized recliner. "Chloe." What would he do about her? She had another semester of school left at Ball State, some ten and a half hours away from USC. *That's okay. We can have a long-distance relationship until she graduates. Then. . .*

Then what? Was he ready to ask her to move all the way to South Carolina with him? That sounded a lot like a marriage proposal. Were they ready for that? He leaned back in his chair and stared at the ceiling. She'd also been excited about spending more time with her family. Moving to South Carolina would put a lot of distance between her and them.

His cell phone vibrated in his pocket. Shifting in his chair, he grabbed the phone and pushed TALK. "Hello."

"Hey, Trevor," Chloe's sweet voice said.

"Hey. You had a good practice."

A sigh sounded over the phone. "Thanks, Trevor." Her voice caught, and she paused. "It's been a good day."

A good day? Yes, it had been a good day for him, as well. The job he'd wanted for years had been offered to him, but it would take him away from the woman he'd fallen in love with.

"It sure has." He continued to stare at the ceiling, wondering if or when he should tell her his "good news."

"I'd like to do something to celebrate."

"Well, let's see." He scratched the stubble on his chin. "Have you ever been to that state park in New Castle?"

"Summit Lake?"

"Yeah. That's the name of it."

"Oh yes. That was one of our vacation spots when I was growing up. It was a park, which meant free." She laughed. "I have a lot of good memories from there."

"We could go for a picnic."

"That's a great idea."

"You don't have practice tomorrow, right?"

"Nope. Coach has some family thing he has to go to or his wife is going to kill him."

"No classes, either?"

"Nope. My classes are on Mondays, Wednesdays, and Fridays."

"Let's go tomorrow then."

"Sounds good."

"It's a date."

He heard her gentle sigh over the phone. "Definitely a date."

Trevor pushed the OFF button on his phone with a growl. He wanted to spend time with Chloe. Wanted to get to know her more. To date her. To love her. To marry her. But he'd known her only a few months, and commitments took time to develop.

And his job offer. He'd wanted this job since he was a boy. For years.

He stood and walked into the kitchen. As he took a swig of his water, his kiss with Chloe filtered through his mind. He slammed the bottle onto the counter. No doubt about it. He loved her. He'd prayed either God would move him away from her or she would accept Jesus into her heart. She'd accepted Christ, and he had the chance to move. The decision rested in his hands.

He leaned his elbows on the counter and combed his fingers through his hair. "Oh, Lord, what do You want me to do?"

Chapter 15

Trevor tapped the top of his steering wheel, waiting for the light to turn green. *I'm just going to take her with me. Have a long-distance relationship until she graduates in May, then ask her to move to South Carolina, too.*

He pushed on the gas when the light changed. Looking at his reflection in the rearview mirror, he nodded. *It'll work. Maybe she can get a job with the Gamecocks, as well. We could travel to see her family as often as she likes.*

Turning into her apartment parking lot, he shifted the gear into PARK. *By then we'll feel ready for marriage.* He nodded again. *Yes, it makes sense. And if our relationship doesn't work, we'll part ways, and I'll still be working at the job I've always wanted.*

He growled. Sure, his idea made sense, except that it was selfish and completely unfair to Chloe.

He looked up as Chloe opened her front door. *She must have seen me pull up.* A breathtaking smile slid across her face. She gave him a little wave then reached back inside and hefted a cooler into her arms. Trevor sucked in his breath. He had no intention of parting ways. She'd intrigued him before she'd accepted Christ. Since then the obvious change in her demeanor and spirit had only heightened his feelings for her.

He threw open the car door, bounded up the walk, and grabbed the cooler from her hands. She stood on tiptoe and kissed his cheek. "Hey, good-lookin'."

Noticing her red shirt, khaki jacket, and dark jeans, Trevor let out a whistle. "I'd say you're the good-looking one."

Her giggles warmed him as she headed for the car. Opening the driver's side door, she pushed the button to open the trunk. "I've been looking forward to this all day." She walked to the back of the car and watched as he set the cooler inside. "I hope you like what I fixed."

He shut the trunk then turned toward her. "If you fixed it, I'll like it."

A Cheshire-cat smile formed on her lips, and she cocked her head and raised one eyebrow. "You have no idea if I have any culinary abilities, Mr. Montgomery. I may send you reeling, wishing you'd never asked me"—she placed her hands on her hips and batted her eyes—"to be your girlfriend."

Her teasing worked on him like ice on a sprain, and he grabbed her in his arms and kissed the tip of her nose. A growl formed from deep inside him. "I'm not after your cooking abilities—just your kisses."

Crimson colored her cheeks as she lifted her lips to his for the briefest of kisses. He reached to pull her close, but she escaped his grasp, winked, and hopped into the passenger seat.

Pulling his keys from his pocket, he slipped into the driver's seat and started the car. Soft perfume filled his senses. "You always smell so good."

"It's Beautiful."

He laughed. "You're in a good mood and fishing for compliments? You're quite flirty, too."

Chloe wrinkled her nose and hit his arm. "Beautiful is the name of the perfume." She crossed her arms in front of her. "And if my flirting is bothering you, I can definitely stop."

Staring at her pouty expression, he caressed her cheek with the back of his hand. "Never stop."

"I won't." She looked back into his eyes. The promise held within her gaze was that of commitment. He knew in his heart that she was meant for him, the one God had intended. There was no "if our relationship doesn't work out." This one would stand the test of time.

After turning onto the straight stretch that led to New Castle, Indiana, and their park destination, Trevor gently took Chloe's hand in his. Her fingers felt perfect within his grasp. He glanced down at her hand, noting her short fingernails. She no doubt kept them clipped because of the abuse they took from her sport of choice. He liked that they weren't manicured. To him, they proved her willingness to work hard, to give up a luxury many women enjoyed, for the love of something she held dear.

He peeked at her as she brushed strands of light brown hair away from her face. He wanted her love, yearned for it. Deep within him he sensed she was falling in love with him. Pleasure filled his heart. *She'll be willing to go with me, Lord. There'll be no problem at all.*

<hr>

Chloe's heart drummed faster as they neared Summit Lake Park. Her parents couldn't afford to take them on vacations to Disney World, the Grand Canyon, and other famous places, but they always managed to conjure up the means to visit one of Indiana's state parks. Summit Lake had been a family favorite.

"I have a little surprise for you." Trevor parked the car near a camping area. Picnic tables and a playground sat shaded beneath large trees adorned with red, orange, and yellow leaves.

Her eyes widened. "You do?"

He twisted his mouth in contemplation. "But you have to tell me. Do you want to eat now or later?"

She bit the inside of her lip, considering the several hours it had been since she'd eaten her cream-cheese-covered strawberry bagel. But she had nibbled bits of tuna fish salad and fresh fruit pieces as she prepared their lunch. "I can wait."

"Good." Trevor jumped out of the car, raced over to her side, and opened the door for her. Taking her hand in his, he helped her out of her seat. "Follow me."

He held tight to her hand as he made his way down a beaten trail. A cool wind breezed through her hair, kissing her cheeks and nose. The sun shone high, heating her some, but the touch of Trevor's strong hand warmed her in a comforting, belonging way that she relished to the tips of her toes.

Breathing in the fresh scent of nature, Chloe took in the trees towering around her on each side. God's arrangement of color—the shades of green and brown with splashes of autumn yellows, burnt oranges, and almost pink reds—was better than anything she'd seen a florist put together.

A tiny salamander scurried across the path in front of them. The urge to chase the little fellow into the wooded area stirred within her. She and her siblings used to collect as many as they could to scare Mama. She always pretended fear and would holler for their father to do something with his children. They would double over with laughter, the whole time knowing the little things didn't scare Mama one bit.

Shaking her head, she focused on the path ahead of them. Soon the trees cleared, and the lake appeared. She drew in her breath at the majesty of the deep blue water. Visions of paddleboating with her siblings danced through her mind. She always ended up with her twin brother, Cameron. They paddled with all their might to catch up with their big brothers and sisters. By middle school they were finally strong enough to keep up. *Never could beat Dalton and Gideon, though.*

Trevor led her onto a dock then pointed down at a small boat. "Well, climb aboard."

"You rented a boat?"

"Yep. Called yesterday and reserved it. A friend of mine owns the rental boats. I picked up the key from him."

She clasped her hands as adrenaline rushed through her. They'd never rented a motorboat. Never been to the middle of the lake. Trevor stepped into the boat then took her hand in his. Her leg shook as she stepped gingerly into the swaying vehicle. Sitting in the seat beside Trevor, she watched as he bent down, picked up a life jacket, and handed it to her. "Thanks."

After pushing her arms through both sides, she snapped the locks in front of her and tightened them as much as she could. She pulled her hair out from beneath the jacket and released it, letting it flow over the top. Trevor unlatched the rope that attached the boat to the dock and let the boat drift out into the lake. The hum of the engine started with the twist of the key, and Trevor drove toward the center. "What do you think?"

"I think I can't believe it took me this long to accept the Lord." Chloe drank in the beauty of the lake. The deep blue beneath her. The greens and autumn splashes around her. The clear sky above cradling a smattering of cottony clouds. The smell, clean and pure, drew her, and she closed her eyes and inhaled deep breaths of God's fragrant gifts to the earth.

"It is amazing, isn't it?"

"He is amazing, Trevor." She leaned forward against the edge of the boat, watching the slight waves that formed from their boat's slow movement through the water. "How could it have taken me this long to believe in Him?"

"It doesn't matter. You believe in Him now."

"But I could have known Him years ago. Think of the people who've come into my life that I could have been a witness to."

"You know Him now." Trevor's voice took on a strong air, and he moved closer to her. "God tells us in Ecclesiastes there's a time for everything. He knows the right time, which leads me to something I wanted to tell you—"

"But my daddy died without knowing of my decision." Her mouth suddenly parched, she stood up to grab a drink from the small cooler at the back of the boat. "I was the only one—"

The boat bounced slightly in the water, and Chloe's leg hit the right side, knocking her off balance. Swinging her arms around, she tried to steady herself. She watched Trevor, almost in slow motion, reach for her.

But he was too late.

Her head and shoulders hit the water first.

<hr />

Trevor sat at the picnic table, waiting for Chloe to come out of the bathroom. He was thankful he had a pair of jogging pants and a sweatshirt in the car. At least she'd have something dry to wear. He arranged the paper plates Chloe had packed in the cooler. The tuna salad sandwiches looked delicious, and with it being well past time for lunch, he admitted he was glad she wanted to go ahead and continue the picnic despite her dip in the lake.

He grinned, remembering the stunned look in her eyes when the life jacket bobbed her straight up in the water. She'd laughed and snorted so hard when he lifted her back into the boat that he nearly lost hold of her several times from trying not to laugh.

And I almost got to tell her about the job. He snapped his fingers. Leaning his elbows on the table, he lifted a quick prayer for another good opportunity to tell her about South Carolina.

"Not exactly how I planned to look for our picnic."

Trevor turned at the sound of her voice. His heart quickened its pace on seeing her. His clothes hung on her frame, which was much smaller than his. Clean of all makeup, her nose and cheeks were pink from the cool air. Her hair, full and disheveled, looked as pretty to him as when she fixed it. "Your hair's dry?"

"Automatic hand dryer." She made a turning gesture with her hand. "I just turned the nozzle around." She lifted her hair on one side. " 'Course the only comb I had was my fingers. So what you see is what you get."

Trevor stood and grabbed both of her hands in his. "I think you look good." He wiggled his eyebrows. "Real good."

She patted her stomach. "Well, I'm *real* hungry. I'm glad you have the food ready."

They walked to the table and fixed their plates. Trevor asked a blessing on their food then took a bite of his sandwich. Within moments they'd finished the food, and he threw away their trash while Chloe packed what was left in the cooler. He carried the cooler back to the car and put it in the trunk. Chloe peered up at him. "Was there something you were going to tell me in the boat before I decided to take a little dip?"

My chance. Thanks, Lord. "Yeah. . ."

"Oh." Chloe pointed to one of the swings in the playground area. "Can we go sit on the swings while you tell me?"

"Sure."

Chloe grabbed his hand and practically skipped to her destination. Flopping onto the flat rubber-covered board, she gripped the chains extending from the top board with both hands. As she began to swing lightly, tears gathered in her eyes.

"Are you okay?" Trevor reached over and wiped her cheek with his thumb.

"I'm sorry, Trevor. So many memories have invaded my thoughts today. They've been wonderful, just. . .overwhelming."

"Do you want to share what you're thinking right now?"

She pushed her swing higher as a slight smile formed above her quivering chin. "You know I'm the youngest out of the eight children. There're five girls, but the first four were close together, then two boys, then Cameron and me. By the time I was old enough to play, my sisters all cared more about boys and makeup than they did about spending time with a kid sister. Which meant I had to play with—"

"The boys."

"Yeah."

Trevor watched as she wrapped her arm around the chain and brushed more tears from her cheeks. He wanted to stop her, to enfold her in his arms and let her cry, but he could feel she needed to share this with him.

"One year," she continued, "we came here, and my sisters settled into four swings. I ran up beside them and jumped on a fifth one. They went higher and higher until I thought they would flip over the top. I tried to do it with them. I pushed my legs forward then backward, forward then backward, but I just couldn't get my swing to move."

"How old were you?"

"I don't know, maybe five. Cameron could do it by himself, but for some reason I just couldn't get the hang of swinging."

Chloe slowed her swing, and Trevor followed beside her. "The girls started teasing me. I wanted to cry, but instead I just yelled at them, calling them every mean name I could think of. The girls hollered for Daddy. He came running toward us. He listened while the girls told him the things I'd said."

Chloe stopped her swing and twisted back and forth. "Daddy sat there and looked at me for several minutes. I clutched the chains as tight as I could, expecting him to let me have it for the things I'd said. Finally, he smiled and walked behind me. Pushing from behind, he said, 'Girls, I think Chloe just wants to play with you.'"

"And he was right." Chloe stood and stepped away from the swing. Trevor watched her inhale slowly. "I never fit in with the girls." She looked at Trevor. "Until the last visit."

She smiled and walked toward him. "I guess it's because I'm older." She shook her head. "No. It's because of the Lord. Or maybe it's both, but you know my sisters and I bonded. Truly bonded. I can't wait to get to know them better. When I graduate next spring, I'll be able to move close to them all again and make up for lost time. Did you know Kylie even called me the other day just to tell me about her baby checkup? It was wonderful, Trevor. Truly wonderful."

Trevor stood and wrapped his arm around her. "I'm happy for you, Chloe." Uncertainty warred within him as they walked together toward his car. He couldn't ask her to leave her family. If she said yes, she'd be miserable. If she said no, he'd be crushed. *Lord, I thought the plan made sense. I thought it was all worked out.*

Chloe lifted her hands to her lips. "Trevor, you were going to tell me something?"

"Not a big deal." He bent down and kissed her lips gently. *It was just my dream that has come to fruition, but if I take it, I lose you.*

Chapter 16

Chloe tightened the brace around her foot. After slipping on her shin guards and socks, she put on her cleats and laced them tight. She shimmied her Sweet Spots over the laces to ensure they didn't have the chance to come untied and trip her again. Standing, she looked at her reflection in the mirror. Locks of hair had already fallen out of her ponytail, so she pulled it out and fixed her hair again. She shoved her hands on her hips and let out a sigh. A slow smile formed across her lips as she nodded at her reflection. "Chloe Andrews is back."

She scooped her bag off the floor and headed onto the field with her teammates. Inhaling the sweet aroma of fresh-cut grass mixed with popcorn, Chloe felt the adrenaline pulsing through her veins. She skimmed the bleachers as fans filtered inside the stadium. Blinking, she noted a large group holding red signs with the number thirteen painted in black. *That's my number.*

Looking closer, she saw her mother waving her hand at Chloe. Her heart beat faster. Her family had come to cheer her on for her first game back. She lifted her hand and waved to the troop of them. It seemed half of the right side of the bleachers stood and whistled and cheered when she did.

"You have quite a fan base." Molly snickered and nudged her shoulder.

"An advantage of being one of eight."

"I'd say so."

Coach Collins motioned the girls around him. "We won the toss. We get the ball first." They huddled around him as he went over the starting lineup and the plays he wanted to execute. Once finished, the team circled around, each member placing her hand in the center, and yelled, "Go, Cardinals!" The starters took the field.

Chloe sat on the bench. *It's okay. Wouldn't have expected to start. It's my first game back, and Molly has done well in my place.* She rubbed her hands together then blew into them. The temperature had dropped dramatically as evening approached.

She scanned the sidelines for Trevor. *I wonder where he is.* She squinted at the bleachers where her family sat, thinking he may have gone over to tell them hello. He wasn't there, either. *He'll come. He's probably here somewhere.* She unscrewed her water bottle and took a quick drink.

The game started, and Molly took control of the ball. Chloe cheered as her new friend made her way toward the opposing team's fullbacks. One of Xavier's players swiped the ball from Molly and dribbled it up the field. She kicked it to one of her team's forwards. The girl dribbled past Ball State's fullbacks and toward the goal. *Come on, Renee. You can do this.*

The player smashed the ball hard to the left. Renee's weak side. *Come on, Renee.* Chloe watched in what seemed slow motion as her roommate leaped into the air, arms extended over her head. She made impact and smacked the ball out of the goal.

"Yes!" Chloe jumped up and pumped her fist through the air. "I knew you could do it!"

The Cardinals took control of the ball again. Within no time the first half was over. Chloe patted a puffing Molly on the back. "You're having an awesome game."

Molly sucked down a drink of water. "Number forty-four's kicking my back."

"She likes to steal from the right. Keep her on the other side of you."

Molly nodded then rested her head between her knees. "'Kay."

Chloe listened as Coach went over strategies for the second half. With the game tied, zero to zero, and Molly obviously exhausted, Chloe felt sure Coach would put her in the game. But as the clock wound down, Molly hit the field, and Chloe hit the bench.

Again.

Frustration welled inside her, and she skimmed the crowd and sidelines for Trevor. He still hadn't shown up. She couldn't imagine his missing this game. Looking toward her family, she smiled and waved. Once again they broke out into cheers for number thirteen.

The second half started and ended, and Chloe spent the duration on the bench. Ball State won, two to one. Molly scored both goals. Chloe congratulated her friend as she made her way off the field. Though she'd wanted to have a chance to play, Chloe felt truly happy for her friend.

She sat in the locker room and half listened to Coach's final comments about the game. Trevor had never shown up. But why? When Coach finished, she gathered her things and met her family at the entrance. She hugged her mom. "I didn't know you were coming."

"Mike's tournament in Indianapolis starts tomorrow, so we figured we might as well head over to Muncie and watch our favorite Cardinal."

"All right." Chloe tousled her nephew's hair. "When's his first game?"

"Nine o'clock in the morning." Sabrina hugged her sister. "We're so glad to see you."

Chloe looked at her family. "Aren't we missing a few people?"

Amanda waved her hand in the air. "Do you mean husbands and small children?"

Chloe nodded.

Gideon crossed his arms in front of his chest. "These sisters of yours decided to leave their little ones with their husbands. Their husbands decided Cameron and I had to keep an eye on the women."

Chloe burst out laughing. "So, Mike, you're the only grandchild here?"

"Yeah, but I'm hanging out with my buddies as soon as we get to the hotel," her nephew told her.

Natalie hooked her arm with Chloe's. "We thought we'd kidnap you and take you to the hotel with us."

Amanda took her bag from her hand as Kylie hooked her other arm and said, "Yep. Then we'll stay up late into the night playing board games."

Mike pointed to his chest and said again, "I'm staying in a buddy's room."

Chloe looked around at her four sisters—Kylie, Amanda, Natalie, and Sabrina—and her mom. This probably would be the only time they'd ever be able to hang out with no little ones running around. Not that she didn't love her nieces and nephews, but they did require a lot of attention.

"What about the guys?" Chloe cocked her head toward her brothers, Cameron and Gideon. "And where's Dalton?"

"Dalton had to work," said her mother.

"Really—we're not babysitting you guys." Gideon grinned. "Cameron and I are going to Danville to check out an apple orchard I'm thinking of purchasing."

"Really? That's a huge endeavor." Chloe gaped at her brother.

"That's why I'm *checking* into it. No commitments. Yet."

Chloe wrapped her arms around her mama. "I think this kidnapping sounds like a lot of fun."

⟡

Trevor twisted his fork through his chicken-flavored soup noodles. Long strands clung to the fork and each other until the entire bowl was twirled around his utensil. He lifted the glob to his lips and bit off a piece. It was stringy. No taste.

Dropping his fork into the bowl, he propped his elbows on the table and stared at the juice that had spilled on the floor in front of his stove. He leaned his head forward and raked his hand through his hair.

No peace. He hadn't felt peace in days.

Pulling at the collar of one of his favorite Fighting Gamecocks T-shirts from high school, the garment now felt stiff, too tight. As if it were telling him something. He huffed and pushed away from the table. Standing, he pulled off the shirt. *It's not as if I haven't gained a few pounds in the last ten years. Of course the shirt is tight.*

He walked to the washing machine and threw the shirt inside. Slamming the lid, he turned and glanced at the clock. The game had ended three hours ago. He wondered how Chloe had done. Since he hadn't had any calls from Coach Collins, he assumed her ankle held up nicely for the game. *But what did she think about me not being there?*

He knew she had to be upset with him, but he couldn't go. He'd tried. Got ready and everything. But when it came time to pick up his keys and head out the door, he couldn't do it.

He threw his hands in the air. "Lord, it's my dream job. The one I've prayed for all this time. What am I supposed to do?"

Nothing.

He slapped his hand on his thigh and walked into the living area. Flopping down in his favorite chair, he picked up his Bible and skimmed the concordance for topics he could look up to guide him, to encourage him. Something. Anything.

Nothing leaped out at him. Frustrated, he flipped through the pages, randomly opening and closing the book at different places. Finally, two words caught his attention: "Good teacher. . ." He looked at the top of the page and saw he was in the Gospel of Mark, chapter 10.

He glanced down at the passage again and read aloud. " 'Good teacher,' he asked, 'what must I do to inherit eternal life?' " Trevor continued with the words in red, the ones spoken by Christ. " 'Why do you call me good?' Jesus answered. 'No one is good—except God. You know the commandments: Do not murder. . .' "

Trevor skimmed the rest of Jesus' words as the man's next question stood out to him. " 'Teacher,' he declared, 'all these I have kept since I was a boy.' "

Trevor pushed his fingers against the words of the next verse. "Jesus looked at him and loved him." Trevor scratched his chin. Of course Jesus loved the man. He was incapable of anything less. He read on to what Jesus said. " 'One thing you lack,' he said. 'Go, sell everything you have and give to the poor, and you will have treasure in heaven. Then come, follow me.' At this the man's face fell. He went away sad, because he had great wealth."

Trevor shut his Bible and looked at the ceiling. "Lord, what does that have to do with me? I'm not a man of great wealth. I just want to know what to do about my job offer and the woman I've fallen in love with."

The phone rang. Trevor picked it up and read the caller ID. *Chloe.* He closed his eyes and held his finger away from the TALK button. What could he say to her? She'd want to know why he wasn't at the game, and he still didn't have a real answer. The answering machine picked up then beeped. Chloe's voice spilled through it. "Hey, Trevor. I don't know what happened to you tonight. I. . ." Her voice faded for a moment. "I didn't play, but Molly had a great game. We won two to one. She scored both goals. Listen. I'm going to Indianapolis with my mom and sisters." A giggle sounded. "They're kidnapping me and taking me to my nephew's soccer tournament. You can call my cell—" The answering machine clicked off, and Trevor laid the cordless phone back in its receiver.

She hadn't played, and he hadn't been there to encourage her. He was a louse. He glanced at the Fighting Gamecocks mug sitting on his coffee table. A louse still torn between the woman he loved and the job he'd always wanted.

Chapter 17

His mind was made up. He'd spent the last two weeks fighting with himself about what decision would be the right one. He'd finally made up his mind. Two games had passed since he'd given Chloe's ankle the necessary approval to play, but Coach had yet to put her in. He'd stood by her and encouraged her after he missed the first game she could play in, but he'd kept his distance, too. Chloe had asked him multiple times what was wrong, but he'd put her off. He had to, until he knew what he was going to do.

And now he did.

He knocked on Chloe's apartment door, hoping she was home. She answered in a sweat suit with her hair knotted on top of her head. "Trevor!" Her eyebrows lifted in surprise, and she pushed hair that had fallen from her ponytail behind her ear. "What are you doing here?"

"Two days before the last game, and I want to take you to lunch."

"Now?"

"Yep."

She bit her lip. "Can I change real quick first?"

"If you want."

She opened the door, and Trevor sat on the couch. "Where're Liz and Renee?"

"Liz is taking a nap." She placed her finger over her lips then whispered, "Renee—I don't know. Be right back."

Chloe walked down the hall, and Trevor heard a door shut. Within moments she returned with her hair brushed straight and wearing jeans and a deep purple sweater. "You look cute."

She smiled and kissed his cheek. "Thanks."

"I thought I'd take you to Ivanhoe's." They walked to his car. Trevor opened her door then moved to his side, slipped in, and started the car.

"I've never heard of Ivanhoe's."

"You've lived in Muncie for almost four years and have never been to Ivanhoe's?"

She shrugged. "Never even heard of it."

"It's a little restaurant on the outskirts of town. It'll take us about twenty minutes to get there." He tapped the steering wheel and thought a minute. "It

222

may not even be in Muncie, but anyway, they have the best lunch menu—and homemade ice cream, too."

"Sounds good."

"You should try the chicken salad over fruit. They add grapes and nuts to the chicken salad, giving it a great taste. And the fruit is delicious. I haven't yet tasted a sour or unripe piece."

"I'm glad I haven't eaten yet."

"For dessert I'm buying you a clown ice cream."

"A clown ice cream? What—?"

"They put a scoop of ice cream in a cup then cut a cone down the center, laying one half at the top of the ice cream like a hat. Then they put whipped cream, candies, and whatever goodies you choose on the scoop to make the clown's face. Your nephews and nieces would love it."

"Sounds fun."

He peeked at her, and she smiled. He was talking her head off. What had gotten into him? Nervousness. That's what it was. He was anxious about telling her his decision.

After pulling into the parking lot, he shut off the car, and they got out. She grabbed his hand. Her skin was soft and warm beneath his fingers. She peered up at him, and her lashes brushed her cheek when she blinked. "I'm glad you brought me."

They stood behind several couples in line. Finally, their turn came. They placed their orders, and Trevor paid for their lunch. He carried their drinks and their ticket to a booth along the wall closest to the street. She laid her purse beside her. "I can't wait to try the chicken salad."

Suddenly Trevor couldn't find words to speak. Being at Ivanhoe's made him realize the time to tell her was upon him. The cashier called their number, and Trevor picked up their tray of food and took it back to their table. He slid into his seat, and Chloe stretched her hands across to him. "Will you say grace?"

"Sure." He took her hands, his thumbs of their own volition caressing them. His prayer came out jumbled. By the time he'd said "amen," he wasn't sure if he'd even asked a blessing on their food. He wiped the back of his hand across his forehead. Tiny beads of sweat had formed. *Get a grip, Montgomery.*

Taking a deep breath, he gazed into Chloe's eyes. He opened his mouth to speak, but nothing would come. Instead, he stabbed his chicken salad with his fork and took an oversized bite. Beginning to choke, he grabbed his napkin and coughed into it.

"Are you okay?" Chloe tried to stand and leaned over the table to pat his back.

He lifted his hand and coughed once more. "I'm okay." Wiping the napkin across his mouth, he added, "I'm fine."

Chloe ate a piece of cantaloupe. "This is good."

Trevor could only respond with a nod of his head. He felt a trickle of perspiration slip down his forehead. Brushing it away with his napkin, he exhaled through his nose. He had to get a handle on himself. He was falling apart. *This is ridiculous. You've made the decision. Just tell her.*

He opened his mouth again then looked up at her. The sweet expression on her face made his stomach flip. She laid down her fork and covered his hand with hers. "I can tell you want to say something."

"Yes, Chloe. . ." But the words wouldn't come. He frowned and swallowed the knot in his throat.

"You can tell me anything."

He tried again, but no sound left his lips.

"I'll go first." Chloe touched his cheek with her fingertip. "Trevor, I love you. I've never felt this way about anyone before." She covered her mouth with her hand then laughed. "I've said it. Trevor Montgomery, I am over-the-top in love with you."

❧

His expression fell, and Chloe realized Trevor's thoughts did not mirror hers. He shook his head. "That wasn't what I was going to say."

"Oh." She pulled her hand away from her face. Resting it on the table, she drummed her fingers on the cool, laminate-covered wood. She peered out the window and watched a lone car pass by. A knife wedged in her heart would have hurt less than his words.

She knew he had been distant the last few weeks, but she'd chalked it up to his being busy with work or whatnot. *What a fool I am.* She closed her eyes. *Why, oh why, did I blurt that out?*

Trevor's voice interrupted her thoughts. "I care about you, Chloe." His hand touched hers, and she recoiled from him.

Opening her eyes, she watched as he flattened his napkin against the table then picked up one edge and rolled it between his fingers. His gaze seemed trained on his menial task, and he opened his mouth again to speak then clamped it shut.

She would not interrupt him this time. She'd sit still, straight, and silent, waiting for him to tell her whatever big news he had to share. Maybe that he'd found someone else. The thought crushed her, but she purposely kept her chin up.

"I've taken a job in South Carolina." He glanced up at her. "It's one I've always wanted. I'll have the same position, but it's a good increase in pay, in my hometown, close to my dad."

She folded her hands in her lap. She couldn't fault him for that. Maybe she could go with him after she graduated. The wonderful time she'd had with her mom and sisters in the hotel flooded her mind. She'd finally bonded with them. *But, Lord, I'd go if You wanted me to.*

A stirring filled her spirit. No. She was to stay. Finish school. Spend as much time with her family as she could. Besides, he wasn't asking her to go. She could hear it in his voice, see it in his eyes. He was saying good-bye. Unbidden tears pooled in her eyes. She swiped them away. "I understand."

He rubbed his forehead with his fingers. His eyes held a sadness.

She lifted her fork and scooped up a bite of chicken salad. "I really do." Putting it in her mouth, she fought back a gag. Her appetite was gone. "But I think I'd like to go home."

Trevor nodded. "Okay."

The ride home was silent. And so long. Emotion, painful and raw, constricted her lungs and scraped at her throat. Finally at her apartment, she waved good-bye and walked to her door. Unlocking it, she stepped inside, thankful no one was home.

She slipped out of her clothes and into the softest pair of pajamas she could find. Dropping onto her bed, she picked up her remote control and turned on the television. Every station she flipped to had a couple kissing or fighting or walking or talking. She turned it off, grabbed one of her pillows, and cradled it to her.

Tears filled her eyes, and sadness filled her heart. She loved him. She really did. She'd told him, and he'd rejected her. Allowing the bitter flow of emotion, she fell face-first onto her covers. "Lord, why? Why, Lord Jesus? Why?"

She cried and called out to God until her whole body was spent. As she lay faceup on her bed, her eyelids drooped with exhaustion. Her chin quivered, and she pleaded once more. "Why, God?"

"In this world you will have trouble." The preacher's voice as he read Jesus' words that first Sunday morning she'd attended church floated through her mind. *"But take heart. I have overcome the world."*

"Dear Jesus," she whispered as she drifted off to sleep, "overcome the hurt in my heart."

Chapter 18

Trevor looked at his watch: 2:00 a.m. He pulled off the road and into the gas station lot. He filled up his tank then walked inside and bought an extra large cup of coffee. After dousing the liquid with several hazelnut creamers and packs of sugar, he stirred the coffee from a dark brown to a pale mud color. He lifted the cup to his lips and blew on the top. After taking a sip, he frowned then shrugged. The hot, syrupy drink would keep him awake, even if it did taste like flavored sugar.

Trudging back to his car, he wiped his eyes with the back of his hand. He'd tried to stay busy after dropping Chloe at her apartment. Went to the grocery. Washed some laundry. Flipped through television stations. Her admission of love for him assaulted him at every turn. Finally, though early in the evening, he tried to go to bed. Closing his eyes proved impossible.

After an hour of tossing and turning in his bed, Trevor had jumped up and packed his clothes. Convinced that seeing the school and his dad would cure his ailing heart and mind, he'd decided to head to South Carolina.

Noting the green road sign approaching, he tallied the hours in his mind. *I should be at Dad's by around seven o'clock. I'll slip into bed for a quick hour of shut-eye then head to church with him.* He blew on the top of his coffee then took a slow drink. *Yep, after spending a day with Dad then touring the university on Monday, I'll know my decision was the right one.*

❧

Tucking the new Bible her mother had bought her under her arm, Chloe walked into the singles' Sunday school classroom. She spied Molly and Matt sitting beside each other in the front row. They appeared deep in discussion over something Molly was pointing out in her Bible. She'd seen them discussing spiritual issues a lot lately. She hoped Matt was coming to realize his need of Jesus, and she wondered if anything more was developing, as well.

Molly looked up and motioned for Chloe to join them. She sat down beside her friend. "Hey, you two. What are we discussing today?"

"Why Jesus calls Himself a vine," Matt mumbled.

"What?"

Molly pointed to the scripture. "John 15."

"And why God says He's a gardener," added Matt.

God as a gardener was no stretch of the imagination in Chloe's opinion. Her trip with Trevor to Summit Lake had reminded her what a wonderful artist of nature He was. *Trevor.* Pain filled her heart as she opened her Bible to John 15. All night she'd contemplated telling Trevor she'd go with him to South Carolina. She felt that maybe he hadn't offered because he didn't want to put her in a position of moving farther from her family. After all, she was convinced her love for him had blossomed through God's leading, but she still couldn't find peace in telling him she'd leave. Did the feeling come from God or her own selfishness?

"Pretty much what Jesus is saying"—Molly's explanation captured Chloe's attention—"is that those who believe in Him must remain in Him, in the vine. See in verse 5 where He calls us the branches? If we, the branches, stay grafted in Him, the vine, if we stay in His Word, stay in fellowship with Him, we can do the good things He wants us to do."

Chloe shook her head gently. Following Trevor wasn't an option. She knew it to the core of her spirit. Maybe this would be a pruning time for her. She closed her eyes, thinking of her father's death, her ankle injury. Pruning was hard. It hurt.

Still, each time her mother pruned her rosebushes, the branches always grew back bigger, stronger, and with more beautiful blossoms. She had to trust God to do the same with her life.

Trevor had awakened and prepared for his visit early Monday morning. The day before spent with his father had been a good one, despite the fact that his dad kept asking him what was wrong. Trevor had brushed him off with each question. Even more disconcerting was the distance he felt from God. Reading his Bible didn't help. Prayer didn't help. Even the sermon from his hometown preacher left him feeling empty.

Shaking his head, he made his way down the university walkway leading to the athletics office. Small trees dotted the campus. Some still held several fiery leaves, but much of the foliage had found its new home on the ground, dead, beneath its one-time source of life.

The lack of fullness on the branches brought an unexplained sorrow to his spirit. His heart slowed, and his legs grew heavy moving his weight across the path. A slight drizzle began to dampen his head and shoulders. Lifting his briefcase over his head, Trevor walked the last bit to the office.

He stepped inside the building and shook the water from his briefcase. Brushing the droplets from his shoulders and arms, he combed his fingers through his hair. He grabbed a mint from his pocket and slipped it in his mouth.

Finding the correct office, he stepped through the door and greeted the secretary. "Hello. I'd like to see Mr. Walter Spence."

"Do you have an appointment, Mr.—?"

"Trevor. Trevor Montgomery. I'm the new assistant athletic trainer." When the words slipped from his mouth, his stomach churned and cramped worse than any indigestion he'd ever felt.

The young woman smiled. "Mr. Spence will be thrilled. He just got to the office. Let me tell him you're here."

She disappeared into the next office. Within moments Walter Spence bounded out in front of her. "Trevor." He grabbed Trevor's hand and shook it. "What a wonderful surprise. Did you come to check out your office? Some of the people you'll be working with?"

"Actually, I've come to tell you I can't take the position."

"What?"

What? What did I just say? The knots in his stomach seemed to untie, and the heaviness in his chest began to lift. Peace flooded his heart, and he knew he'd said the right thing. A smile tugged at his lips. He covered his mouth and coughed it away. "It seems, Mr. Spence, that I'm going to have to stay at Ball State a little longer."

"Did they offer you more money?"

"No." Trevor shook his head. "Nothing like that. It's just the right place for me to be at this time." And it was. He knew it from the top of his head to the tips of his toes.

Mr. Spence crossed his arms. "This may not be the wisest of choices."

In the world's eyes, probably not. After all, he'd make more money at South Carolina, and working for his alma mater had been his goal; but it wasn't the world he was trying to impress. He wanted to stay in the will of his Lord. "Maybe not, but it's the one I have to make."

Mr. Spence's eyebrows met in a straight line. "Okay, then. I wish you the best of luck." He shook Trevor's hand again then turned and walked back into his office.

Trevor nodded to the young secretary whose mouth hung open. "Have a great day, ma'am."

He practically floated out of the office and back to his father's house. Bursting through the front door, he yelled, "Dad!" He hurried through the living room and into the kitchen. "Dad!"

"What is it?" His father stepped out of the pantry, a frown shadowing his face.

Trevor grinned. "I'm not taking the job."

"What?"

"I'm not moving to South Carolina. I'm staying at Ball State."

"Is that a good thing?"

"It's a wonderful thing." Trevor patted his dad's back. "I have so much I want to tell you. Are you able to go back to Muncie with me? Just for a few days. I'll fly you back."

His dad leaned against the cabinet and scratched his jaw. "You show up on my doorstep yesterday just before church. Now you want me to drive to Indiana with you?"

Trevor lifted his eyebrows and nodded. "Yep."

"This must be something pretty important."

Trevor laughed. "It is."

"Then what are we waiting for? I gotta pack." His father walked out of the kitchen and toward his room.

Trevor glanced at his watch. "Hurry, Dad. If we get out of here quickly, we might just make it to the second half of the game."

"Does this have anything to do with that woman you keep telling me about? The one who hurt her foot?"

"It was her ankle." Trevor rubbed his hands together with excitement. "And yes. She definitely has something to do with it."

Chapter 19

The last game of the season. The last game of her college career. Chloe stepped onto the field. She gazed across the long stretch of deep green grass. She looked at the goals, the white painted lines mapping penalties and boundaries. Taking in the concession stand, the bleachers, the spectators, the referees, she wanted to relish every facet of her surroundings. Relish and remember. She closed her eyes, painting the picture in her mind.

"Hustle out there!" Coach's command tore her from her memory making. She opened her eyes and rushed to the field to begin warming up with the team. Looking down at her jersey, her eyes misted. She'd been lucky thirteen since she was five years old, playing in her hometown recreational league. This was probably the last time she'd wear the number.

Not only was it the last game, but it was also senior night. She scanned the stadium for any sign of her mama. *Still not here.* A wave of sadness washed over her. Mama and Gideon would be recognized with her at halftime, but not Daddy. *I know he's dancing on streets of gold with You, though, Lord. That makes me feel better.*

Dribbling the ball, she peeked at the sidelines. Trevor wasn't there. He hadn't been at church, either. *He's probably moving to South Carolina.* She'd thought he felt something for her. After all, he even asked if she'd be his girlfriend, but it hadn't been enough.

"Chin up." Molly nudged her as she dribbled beside her.

Chloe tried to smile, but the muscles around her mouth didn't want to cooperate.

"This is your night." Molly wrapped her arm around her shoulder and squeezed.

Chloe snorted. "Yeah, but I probably won't play." She looked at Molly. "Not that I don't want you to play. I mean. . ."

"I know exactly what you mean. I bet Coach will put you in tonight."

"Don't bet on it."

"I'll ask him to."

"Don't you dare." Chloe grabbed her friend's arm. "I want to go in because Coach feels I'm needed for the team, not because you or I asked."

"We can ask God."

Chloe stared at Molly. For Chloe to go in, it almost certainly meant Molly would hit the bench, and yet her friend was willing to sacrifice, even pray that Coach would allow Chloe some time on the field.

"Hustle in, ladies!" Coach hollered from the sidelines.

"Come on." Molly extended her hands to Chloe.

Chloe hugged her friend then took hold of her hands.

"Lord," Molly began, "it's Chloe's last night of college ball. I know You have a wonderful plan for her, and You may even bless her to work with her favorite sport for years and years to come." She squeezed Chloe's hands. "It's been a rough season with her ankle injury. I remember all too well how hard it is to sit out. Tonight, precious Jesus, we ask You to allow Chloe some time in the game. Have Coach put her in then bless her on the field. We know You've heard our prayer, and we trust You with the answer, be it yes or no. We love You, Lord. Amen."

Tears slipped from Chloe's eyes as she opened them. She noticed that tears pooled in Molly's eyes, as well. "Molly, I'm so thankful God put you in my life."

Molly hugged her. "Me, too."

Chloe scanned the field, noting the entire team had taken the bench. Coach Collins stood with his hands on his hips watching them. He popped his gum, and Chloe couldn't decipher what he thought of their quick prayer. *Maybe it will be a little nugget to lead him to You one day.*

He motioned them to the side. They hurried over and listened as he reviewed their starting play. Every senior was starting, except Chloe. Her heart sank. Molly must have felt it, because she elbowed Chloe and whispered, "We have a whole game ahead of us."

Chloe nodded and took her well-worn seat on the bench. She peered into the stands and saw an entourage of fans dressed in red and black, waving flags painted with the number thirteen. This time it appeared her entire family had made it. She smiled and waved at them. They whooped back at her. If she didn't play a single moment today, the knowledge that her whole family had come to support her filled her to the depths of her being. For the first time her family meant more than her sport, and she had never before felt so content.

If only Trevor were here. She inhaled then blew out a long breath. *I love him, Lord, but I'm going to trust him to You.*

⚬∞⚬

"It must be almost halftime." Trevor ran a comb through his hair then tried to press out some of the wrinkles in his pants.

"I think I hear the announcer." Vince Montgomery zipped up his jacket.

"Oh no!" Trevor started for the entrance and turned to his father. "Hurry, Dad. I want to see her be recognized." They made it to the bleachers as one of the seniors was being called. Trevor skimmed the row still waiting.

"Is she out there?"

Trevor nodded and pointed toward her. "She'll be called after one more girl. She's number thirteen." He looked up at the scoreboard's clock. "I wanted to talk to her before the second half."

"Well, get on over there."

"Let me introduce you to her family first." His words came out a bit snappier than he'd intended. His nerves were getting the best of him.

"Son." His dad touched his arm then pointed to the stands. "Her family will be easy enough to find."

"Let's go." Trevor started toward them.

His dad grabbed his arm. "No. I'll go meet the family on my own."

"But—"

"No buts. I'm fifty-one years old. I know how to make friends." He winked. "Go to your girl."

"Thanks, Dad." Trevor raced around the field to the bench where the Cardinals' team sat. He watched as Chloe's name was called and she and her mom and brother walked to the center of the field.

"She looks beautiful, huh?" Molly said beside him.

"Yeah." Trevor stared down at her. "I'm sure she's told you what I said. I was a fool. Wasn't listening to—"

Molly nodded toward the field. "Save it for her. She's coming."

Trevor looked onto the field. He and Chloe made eye contact as she walked alone toward the team. Her mom and brother had already returned to the stands. A moment of happiness flicked through her eyes, followed by hesitation and uncertainty.

"Just remember flowers and chocolate can go a long way to win a lady's heart," Molly whispered to him. "I mean, a woman could enjoy them practically every single day of her life."

Trevor chuckled. "I'll remember that."

"Hello, Trevor." Chloe's voice was guarded. "Have you already begun your move?" She bent down, grabbed her water bottle, and took a quick drink.

"I need to talk to you." He reached for her hand. "Will you come with me for just a moment?"

She avoided his gaze. "I don't know. Coach needs—"

"It'll just take a second."

"Fine." She tossed her water bottle toward the edge of the bench.

He guided her a few yards away from the team. His mind searched for the words to say. Ten hours of driving and he hadn't figured out what to say first. He'd hurt her, and somehow he had to tell her, had to show her. . . *Guide me, Lord.*

"Trevor, I really have to get with my team." She started to turn away.

"Wait." She faced him, and he tried to swallow the knot in his throat. Confusion filled her expression, and he prayed his eyes showed the love he felt for her. "Chloe, I'm not moving."

She furrowed her brows. "What? Why?"

He peered out at the horizon, gazing at the deep red and pink of the beginning sunset. "I'm not supposed to move to South Carolina. I've always dreamed of the job. Always wanted to work there. When the offer came, I just figured God had given it to me. But—"

"I don't understand. You'll be closer to your dad—"

"I don't think it's what God wants. I didn't feel right about it." He took her hands and caressed their softness with his thumbs. "Don't you see? God brought you into my life."

Tears filled her eyes. One slipped down her cheek. Trevor brushed it away with the back of his hand. Her chin quivered as she looked at the ground and whispered, "I would have prayed about going with you."

"I know, sweetheart." He cupped her chin, lifting her face to allow her gaze to meet his. "But I knew God wanted you to stay here. Finish school. See your family."

"You're right. I asked Him."

Trevor rubbed his thumb against her cheek. "I love you, Chloe Andrews. I'm not leaving you."

She smiled. "I love you, too, Trevor Montgomery."

"I still want you to be my girlfriend."

"On one condition." Chloe lifted her finger in the air.

"What's that?"

"You're not allowed to dump me again."

He glanced at her coach, who seemed to be waiting not too patiently for her return. "Never."

⌘

"Molly, head out to center forward." Chloe's heart fell at Coach's words. "Chloe," he continued, "I want you at right forward."

"What?" She leaned forward, unsure she'd heard him correctly.

"Are you not able to play right forward?" he said with a growl. The tie game obviously had him feeling anxious.

"No. I'll play." Excitement coursed through her, and she looked up at Molly, who was quietly clapping her hands. Biting her lip, she jumped up and high-fived her friend.

"Let's go."

Chloe followed Molly onto the field. Peeking at the stands, she gave a short wave to her family. Trevor sat beside her mother and a man she'd never seen before. Her family's hollering drowned out the rest of the crowd.

Within moments the referee blew the whistle, and the game began again. The other team quickly dribbled the ball past Chloe. She turned and watched in trepidation as their forward made her way past Liz, as well. The girl shot hard at the goal. Relief filled Chloe when Renee caught it and kicked it back to the right side of the field.

Chloe used her chest to roll the ball to the ground so she could get control. The same girl swiped it away from Chloe and dribbled again toward Liz. Glancing to the sideline, she saw Coach pointing at her and then at his temple. He wanted her to get her head in the game.

Help me, Lord. Chloe watched as Liz stole the ball and kicked it up the center. Molly got control of the ball and dribbled a couple of steps toward the goal.

"Man on!" Chloe yelled as an opposing player ran toward Molly.

In a quick motion Molly smashed the ball with her right foot. It sailed through the air and slammed into the left side of the net. One to zero. Chloe ran over to her friend and gave her a high five before they ran back to the centerline for the opposing team to kick off.

Minutes passed as both teams fought for a goal but to no avail. Molly took control of the ball again. She dribbled toward the middle. "Man on!" Chloe yelled as the same player tried to steal the ball from Molly.

"Your turn!" Molly screamed as she kicked the ball hard to the right toward Chloe. The field was wide open except for one fullback charging from the left toward her. Chloe dribbled toward the goal. The goalie leaned left then right, preparing for Chloe's shot. Inching her way closer, Chloe twisted her hip and with all the strength she could muster kicked with her right foot.

The ball seemed to move in slow motion toward its hoped-for destination. The goalie dove toward it, and Chloe watched as she nipped it with the tip of her fingers. But the kick had been too strong, and it sailed into the net.

Score!

Chloe pumped her fist through the air as cheers erupted from the fans. Molly raced to her and wrapped her in a hug. *Thank You, God, for allowing me one more goal. Daddy, that was for you.*

Minutes later the game ended. The Cardinals had won two to zero. Chloe lined up with her team to shake hands with the opposing players. Reaching the last player, Chloe looked at the goal where she'd made the last score of her college career.

She'd spent her life striving for that goal. Her whole existence had been wrapped up in making as many soccer goals as she could tally, and she had many to her name. Looking up at the night sky, she noted that the moon's face seemed to smile down at her. The smattering of stars that brightened the sky sent her into awestruck wonder. God had given so much beauty to His creations.

She felt afresh that she was one of His precious creations. He'd formed her with a goal. One that had included a soccer field—but, more important, one that included a relationship with her Lord and Savior, Jesus. He was her ultimate goal. Her ultimate score.

Chapter 20

May

The whistle blew, signaling the end of the recreational game. Chloe congratulated her team of young girls for their win. She waved to the opposing team's coach and her friend Liz. "Good game!" she hollered and pointed to her watch. "But I gotta hurry."

"Get going." Liz waved her away before the two teams were able to shake hands.

"Thanks." Chloe grabbed her bag and ran to her mother's car. Her mom was to rush her to the apartment to get ready for the wedding then drive Chloe back to the field in only two hours' time.

"You took long enough." Her mother cupped her cheeks and kissed her forehead. "Five minutes to and from the apartment gives us about an hour and a half to bring you back here. You don't want to be late to your own wedding."

"You're right about that. Where is everyone?"

"Some of the girls are at the apartment, though I'd say they're just about ready to head over here. The others are already at the pavilion." Mama laughed when Chloe looked back at the field. "They'll make sure everything is perfect. Now buckle your seat belt so I can get you ready."

Chloe obeyed. Within no time Chloe had showered and was sitting in a chair while her mom curled, twisted, and sprayed her hair. Her sisters had all left, and Chloe soaked in the light chatter of her mother as she worked. Growing up, Chloe rarely had time alone with her mom. She wanted to relish every moment.

"This veil is beautiful." Her mother placed it on Chloe's head. The material felt soft on her shoulders as her mom bobby-pinned it into her hair. Chloe's heart fluttered, as she knew the time drew nearer. She longed to see her soon-to-be husband, to become Mrs. Trevor Montgomery.

Her mother opened the makeup kit and started applying blush to Chloe's cheeks. Many women spent their wedding day getting ready in some beauty parlor. Chloe had spent hers coaching a soccer game. It didn't matter to Chloe. No one fixed her up as well as her mama. Dotting her lips with gloss, Mama stood away from her. "Gorgeous. Now stand up and let's get you into that dress."

Chloe stepped into her dress and lifted it up over her. She turned, and her mother zipped up the dress then buttoned the multiple pearls that covered the zipper. Gently bending down, she slipped on her low-heeled shoes.

She stood to her full height and faced her mother. "Well?"

Mama covered her mouth with her hands. Tears glistened in her eyes, and she shook her head. "You're so beautiful." She embraced Chloe. "Daddy would have been so proud of you."

Closing her eyes, Chloe thought of her daddy's reaction when he'd seen each of her sisters for the first time in their wedding dresses. She envisioned him responding the same with her. "I wish Daddy could be here, too."

"We won't be sad." Mama pushed one of Chloe's curls behind her shoulder. "God has blessed you with a wonderful man, and I believe his father will treat you as if you were his own daughter." She touched Chloe's cheek. "You always needed your daddy. God's blessed you with a second one."

No one could ever replace her daddy, but Mama was right. God had blessed her with Vince, and he loved her as if she were his own child. He'd even agreed to walk her down the aisle. "I know, Mama."

Chloe looked in the mirror for the first time. She did look beautiful. Her blue eyes glowed beneath the soft browns and pinks Mama had dusted on her eyelids. The light pink lipstick was just enough to add a bit of color to her lips. Her long brown hair was swept up into a high clip with tendrils of curls rolling down her shoulders and back. "Mama, I'm going to have you fix me up every day."

"We need to go." Mama looked at her watch and grabbed Chloe's hand. "My baby's getting married in thirty minutes."

They drove back to the soccer field. Chloe walked carefully toward the pavilion, trying hard to hide from Trevor's sight until the wedding. She looked around the corner of the cinder-block restrooms and saw Trevor, her brothers, Matt, and their preacher standing on the soccer field beneath one of the goals.

Her sisters had decorated the goal with wildflowers of every color—yellow, pink, purple, white, blue, and even splashes of red. Chairs were lined up in rows on the field. An aisle had been made between them to allow her bridal march. She'd wanted a wedding that showed God's wonderful, natural creations—trees, green grass, blue sky, flowers that grew on their own in nature. She'd also wanted to wed at the place where she'd spent most of her life, the place God had used to lead her to Trevor—a soccer field.

Her sisters and Molly rushed to her. The soft red dresses looked lovely on them. She hadn't wanted to choose between her married sisters, so she'd asked them all to be matrons of honor and Molly her maid of honor.

"You look beautiful." Molly fluffed the bottom of her veil.

"I'd say." Trevor's dad walked up behind her. "It's just about time." He offered his arm. "Ready?"

"Oh yes."

❧

Trevor knew at any moment his heart would burst from his chest. He'd never been so excited and nervous at the same time. He watched as Sabrina, then Natalie, made her way down the aisle. Kylie followed, then Amanda. "I can't take it. There're too many of them," Trevor whispered to Matt.

"Hey, I heard that," Dalton said beside Matt. "I agree."

Trevor bit back a chuckle as Molly made her way down the aisle. He glanced at Matt. His friend's eyes glowed at the sight of his fiancé. Matt had accepted Christ a short time after the season ended. He and Molly had been an item ever since. In fact, Trevor and Chloe would be in their wedding in just a few months.

The "Wedding March" played from the sound system they'd set up behind him. Finally. It was time for his bride. His dad and Chloe stepped out from behind the pavilion.

She took his breath away. Her long, straight white dress hugged her curves to perfection. A thin diamond necklace sparkled in the sun, drawing his attention to her slender neck and collarbone. Beautiful. He longed to see her face beneath her veil. His dad needed to hurry up, needed to get his bride down that aisle and into Trevor's arms.

They stopped a few feet in front of him. The preacher's words sounded like gibberish as he waited for his father to lift her veil. He had to see her. Had to look into her eyes. Had to see the slight curve of her lips. He clasped his hands, trying to fight the urge to throw her over his shoulder and declare her his own.

His dad touched the veil. Slowly, so achingly slowly, he lifted the tulle away from her face. Trevor took her hand in his, gazing into her eyes. The storm simmering in them was one of passion and promise, electrifying and stirring. "Wow! You're beautiful," he whispered before they faced the preacher.

Within moments they recited their vows of love, today and forever, no matter the circumstances. Trevor focused on his words of promise. He drank in the sincere inflection in her voice, the way her gaze never parted from his, the slow nodding of her head as she recited her vows. For as long as he lived, he would stay committed to her.

At one time he had believed his dream was in South Carolina. God showed him a new dream, a better one, one that would fill his days with happiness and his nights with warmth. One that came from the Lord Himself.

"I now pronounce you man and wife," the preacher's voice boomed into the air. "You may kiss your bride."

Trevor lowered his lips to hers. Their sweetness beckoned him to kiss her a second time. *Thank You, Lord, that the dreams You give are so much better than the ones I think up.*

⌘

Chloe stood beside the table of finger foods under the pavilion. She picked up a piece of cheese and slipped it into her mouth. Having not eaten since well before lunch, she was famished. She gazed at her new husband, standing with her brothers.

He smiled at her, and her heart beat faster. She watched as he excused himself from them and made his way to her. "You look happy, Mrs. Montgomery." He lifted her chin and gently kissed her lips.

She closed her eyes. "I think I could hear that said every day for the rest of my life."

"You will." His longing to be alone was evident in his voice.

She reached up and touched his cheek. "This has been the most perfect wedding."

He chuckled. "That's because it included you." He bent down and kissed the tip of her nose.

"And you." She tilted her head up and kissed his lips. Looking past him, she saw the soccer goal covered in flowers of various shades. She'd sought after that goal all her life. Worked for it. Sweated for it. Yearned for it.

She'd given her life to God. He was in control now. In His amazing grace, when she wasn't even looking, He'd given her a man who exceeded her dreams. God had even given her the position of coaching the girls' soccer team at Muncie Central High School in the fall.

"You're thinking awfully hard." Trevor reached for her hand and kissed her knuckles. "What thoughts are running through that beautiful mind of yours?"

"That I'm finally pursuing the right goal."

"Oh?" Trevor's eyebrows furrowed into a straight line, and he looked at the goal where they'd wed.

"I'm after God's goals for my life." She turned his face until their gazes met. Reaching up to him, she caressed his cheek with her hand. "I praise Him that His goal includes you."

IN PURSUIT OF PEACE

Dedication

This book is dedicated to my youngest daughter, Allie. Allie, I love your zest for life, your ability to make us smile, and that you are your own unique self. There is no one like Allie, and I praise God for you. Seek Him always!

Thank you Albert, Brooke, Hayley, and Allie, who have always been a tremendous support to me. Thank you Rose McCauley for being such a wonderful crit partner and JoAnne Simmons for being such a great editor. Most importantly, I praise You, Jesus. You give us dreams and then You fulfill them in the way that is best for Your glory. May I always live for You.

Chapter 1

Peering from a second-story window, Lydia Hammond watched as the little critter's nose dug into the loosened soil of the newly planted bed of impatiens. Pink and white petals flew through the air like a fireworks explosion. The damage did not deter the critter as it plowed into the neighboring daylily whose bright yellow flowers had only just begun to open.

"That little rascal!" Using all the strength she could muster between her thumb and index finger, Lydia tried to pry open the window's lock. "Ugh." She pounded the glass when the lock wouldn't budge.

Her new puppy—the part lab, part beagle, part whatever that she'd felt sorry for because the most adorable boy Lydia had ever seen was giving puppies away at the local supermarket, and it happened to be the last one in the box, so she'd melted and taken the little ball of fur despite her better judgment—looked up at her. The puppy seemed to smile mischievously before plowing his face and front paws back into the broken leaves and mutilated petals.

She pounded again, but the animal simply dug with more tenacity, as if he knew his time was limited. And still his little bottom and tail, lifted high in the air, wagged with excitement, as if he'd found the greatest creation of God—dirt.

"George!" Lydia yelled as she raced down the stairs of her grandmother's Victorian home. Without taking the care it deserved, she flung open the heavy front door, one of the few original items her grandparents had been able to nurture back to life after they purchased the century-old house. Of course, her grandfather had passed away before Lydia was born, so she'd always considered the home her grandmother's. She pushed open the beveled-glass storm door designed specifically to complement the original door.

"George!" she yelled again, thinking for some odd reason how the name she'd given the critter really didn't fit him. He should be called "Scamp," or "Rascal," or "Nuisance." George really didn't even sound like a dog's name.

"Listen here, you little ragamuffin." She bent down to pick up the puppy. Instead, George lifted his dirt-covered nose from the soil and jumped toward her. Filthy paws painted her light khaki capris in various places. His tail wagged in utter delight as she twisted and turned, trying to grab the puppy without adding additional splotches to her clothing.

243

Finally getting hold of him around the belly, she scooped him into the crook of her arm but still tried to hold him away from her chest. "Look what you did." She pointed with her free hand toward the mess he'd created. She'd spent several hours that morning planting flowers the way she'd seen Grandma do it the four years Lydia lived with her during her parents' bitter divorce.

A shot of pain arrowed through her heart as Lydia thought of her earthly champion's death. Grandma had only been gone four months. Though Lydia hadn't lived with the older woman for five years, she still envisioned Grandma rocking on the front porch, standing in the kitchen pondering which dessert to bake, or hanging clothes on the clothesline as she did every summer because "windblown garments smelled better than dryer-dried clothes."

Lydia was thankful her mother and aunt were allowing her to stay in Grandma's house. She had been here three weeks. She needed a fresh start, and being near Grandma's memories seemed right. *Of course Mom would say I've had plenty of fresh starts.* And in truth, her mom was right. Lydia'd had more jobs in her twenty-four years than most people had in a lifetime.

Through high school, she'd worked at various fast-food restaurants, a grocery store, and even a video store. In college, she'd worked at an elementary school as a custodian, which meant she cleaned vomit-ridden floors, missed urinals, and worse. If she had her way, she'd never clean again. Yet because she loved getting to know the kids and their families, she decided to take a few education classes. That lasted a little over a semester.

A year later, Lydia landed a job at an art gallery. She loved meeting the interesting people who painted and sculpted. She found their passion contagious and decided to take a few art classes in college. That didn't even last a full semester.

She met a girl who got her hooked on aerobics, and she studied to be an aerobics instructor. Lasted a year.

She tried her hand at a bank job. She worked at a movie theater. And a dentist's office. She tried working with infants at a day care—definitely not her kind of job. After the first nasty diaper, Lydia hightailed it out of there.

Then she met a girl named Samantha Lily. Sam had a contentedness Lydia had never before witnessed, except in Grandma. When the job got hard, Sam stuck it out. When money became tight, Sam kept on going. When Lydia's grandma died, Sam proved to be a constant friend. When Lydia had questions about why Sam proved different, Sam told her about Jesus.

Lydia's life completely changed when she met Him.

She closed her eyes and muttered a quick prayer for Sam's protection. Lydia hadn't spoken with Sam since she began her position as a teacher in China. "May she lead many to You, Jesus."

A beep sounded from inside the house. She opened her eyes and gasped. "The pie! I'm glad I set the timer." Lydia looked down at her little varmint. "You're coming with me." George wagged his tail and licked her hand. A smile tugged at her lips. She couldn't deny she liked the little guy's never-ending enthusiasm.

Racing into the bathroom, she grabbed the hand towel from its hook. She held George over the tub with one hand and scrubbed his head and paws with the other.

Beeps continued to echo through the house, and Lydia's heart sped to match them. "I don't want that pie to ruin, but I don't want you to ruin any of Grandma's furniture either." The pup squirmed in her hand, and she released him when she felt confident he wouldn't make a bigger mess in the house.

She quickly washed her hands before rushing into the kitchen. After grabbing two pot holders off the countertop, she pulled open the oven door. The sweet aroma of cinnamon and apple filled the air. The lightly browned piecrust looked perfect as Lydia pulled her homemade dessert from the oven. "I think she'll like this. As soon as it's cool, I'll cut two generous pieces out of it."

Lydia glanced down at George, who'd joined her in the kitchen. His eyes seemed to beg for a taste as his wet nose sniffed the air. She bent down and scratched his head. "Pie is not for puppies, but hopefully Mrs. Andrews will like it."

Lydia thought of the older lady she had met at church on Sunday. Mrs. Lorma Andrews had been the first one to greet Lydia. She'd even sat with her. The woman reminded Lydia so much of her grandmother that when she learned Mrs. Andrews lived only a mile away, Lydia knew she had to visit her.

"We're just going to walk right over there. The exercise will be good for both of us." She looked at George. "Maybe you'll want to take a nap when we get home."

Wishing she'd been able to use fresh apples to make the pie, Lydia'd had to settle for store-bought ones. Her grandma had an apple tree in the backyard, but it was still too early in the summer. Apples wouldn't be ready for picking until closer to fall. *Hopefully, it will still be good. Even Mom can't help but approve of my apple pies.*

She headed toward the stairs so she could run up to her room and change clothes. Her mother's approval had always been so important to her. For some reason, she wanted Mrs. Andrews to be pleased with her, as well.

≈

Gideon Andrews gripped the last two buckets of peaches in his hands. Having decided to try something new, he'd sectioned out a few rows of orchard land to the west of his home and planted several Eldorado Miniature peach trees. The fifteen-acre apple orchard had been a lucrative purchase for him two years before. The previous owner, Gideon's agricultural mentor during his college years, decided to retire with his new wife and move to Florida, leaving an already established, well-known children's activity area filled with several pieces of playground equipment, an apple art activity area, and even a petting zoo. The transfer of ownership had been as smooth as a full-grown, fresh-picked apple.

Gideon gave the credit to God. His entire life had God's fingerprints all over it. He knew God, and God alone, had blessed him with the chance to purchase the orchard just four years out of college.

Old Amos, their local supermarket manager, had predicted the worst. *He won't make it six months.* The man had pounded his fist against a counter when Gideon's mentor had introduced him to Amos.

A smile lifted Gideon's lips. Now, Amos bought from Gideon before any of the other orchard owners. In fact, it was Amos who'd encouraged Gideon to try growing another fruit. "How 'bout some peaches?" The old man raised his eyebrows and winked. "I believe you could make you a good piece of money off peaches, as well."

And peach trees Gideon had planted. He figured it would be worth it to try his hand at an additional fruit. Having decided to start small at first, Gideon would plant more trees if the peaches sold well locally.

The weight of his load lightened as Gideon thought of the six filled buckets already sitting next to his back door. It was still early, the middle of June, and he'd been able to pick eight bucketfuls. He wouldn't sell these. Mama would enjoy canning some, and they could eat some fresh, as well. She could make a few pies, maybe some tarts. His mouth watered at the thought of Mama's homemade peach cobbler covered with vanilla ice cream.

Mama's moving in with him about a year ago, more than a year after his father's death, had been quite an adjustment. He wasn't used to having someone tell him to tuck in his shirt, wipe his shoes, and shave his stubble. In the past, he'd let his beard grow out the full week, waiting to shave before church on Sunday. Mama'd have none of that. "God gave you a nice face," she'd fuss, "and I want to see it." He shook his head. He wouldn't argue with clean clothes on his back, crisp sheets on his bed, and home-cooked meals filling his belly. No, the good definitely outweighed the bad.

His house came into view, and he noticed again that several of the roof's shingles seemed loose in the back. They'd had some good rain through May, and he'd neglected to check it out when he first noticed it. *This afternoon I'm going to take a look.*

He took another step and found his foot slipping. He flapped his arms to keep from falling backward. Peaches spilled from his buckets. "What in the world?"

Gaining his footing, he looked down and noted the partially smashed peach wearing his shoe print. "It must have fallen. . . ." He surveyed the yard splattered with peaches. "What happened—"

Before he could finish, a black-and-brown-speckled ball of fur tore around the corner of the house. Juice spilled from the peach the creature had clutched between its jaws. Upon seeing Gideon, the critter dropped the fruit and raced toward him. It yelped and wagged its tail while scratching at the bottom of his jeans.

"Where did you come from?" Gideon scooped up the animal and strode toward the house. The pup tried to lick his hand, and Gideon repositioned him. He was cute, but they did not need a dog. Gideon's ire rose as he walked past a dozen or more smashed peaches. *I'm glad Mama is here, but she cannot just decide to get a dog without at least talking with me about it.*

He passed more damaged fruit. *How am I supposed to tell if I want to plant more next year if I can't see if I like the fruit? I'm not selling something that isn't of good quality.* He passed the buckets; each lay toppled over.

"Look what you've done," he growled at the pup as he neared the back door. "Mama, we do not need a dog! You need to talk to me about these things!" He burst through the door. "Come out here and see what it's done. It's ruined—"

A young woman jumped up out of a chair. Her eyes, lighter than the sky above him, widened in surprise. She pushed long locks of reddish-blond curls behind her ear. "I'm sorry." She grabbed the pup from his hands. "George, what have you done now?" she whispered through gritted teeth.

Gideon glanced at his mom. Her lips lifted in a tight smile, but he knew she masked a scowl. Her hand firmly planted on her hip gave away her frustration. "Gideon, this is Lydia Hammond." Mama motioned toward the beauty, whose face had reddened to the point that her freckles had disappeared. "She's living in her grandmother's home. You remember Marian Smith?"

"Uh, sure." He glanced down at his feet and realized he'd tracked a bunch of dirt onto the floor. "I'm. . ."

"I'm sorry. I don't know how he got off the leash. I'll pick up the mess right now." Lydia opened the door.

"No. It's no big deal." His all-of-a-sudden parched mouth burned, and his throat closed, making it hard for him to swallow or speak. Clearing his throat, he willed his mouth to obey his need to speak. "I didn't mean to sound so abrupt."

"It's my fault." She raced out the door and started gathering peaches before he could say another word.

He turned to Mama, whose anger proved evident now. "We better go help." She started out the door.

Dumbfounded, he watched the two for a few seconds. He was a heel. A big, overgrown heel. He always barked before he knew the facts. Now he'd embarrassed his mother and a woman—a rather attractive woman. He stepped out the door. "It's really not necessary."

"I think that's most of them." Lydia turned toward him, made eye contact for a moment, and then looked away. Red spread across her cheeks. "I'm sorry to meet you under these circumstances. I was really excited to see you." She sucked in her breath. "I mean. . .because Mrs. Andrews spoke so much of you. Not your looks per se." She flailed her free hand in front of her face. "I mean. . .she said you were nice looking." Her blush deepened. "Not that I care. I mean. . .I *care* because I like your mother. But looks don't matter. I mean. . .I guess they matter some." She smacked her thigh then waved slightly. "I'll just go now. Bye."

"What?" Gideon scratched the top of his head. Was the woman saying he was cute or ugly? Why would they talk about that anyway? He'd had enough matchmaking in his life. If Mama was considering setting him up, he'd have to let her know better. He turned toward Mama. Pinched lips, squinted eyes, and a snarl lifting one side of her nose told him that now was not the best time to discuss matchmaking. Feeling very much like a little boy again, he shrugged his shoulders. "Mama, I didn't know you had a guest."

"You embarrassed that poor child to death," Mama reprimanded. "She's new here and lonely. She's taken Marian's death hard, and her good, Christian neighbors should be there to lend her a helping hand."

Gideon smacked his hands to his sides. He'd never meant to hurt the woman. He would never intentionally hurt anyone, not even the little pup that ruined six buckets of peaches. "I'm sorry."

"I think you'll have to tell Lydia that."

Gideon blew out a long breath. He glanced toward Lydia. She'd already made it a good distance from his house.

"What's wrong, Gideon?" His mother's tone had changed to concern. "You're not usually that quick to anger."

"Nothing really." The day started to press down on his heart at his mother's innocent question. If she pried, he feared more emotion than he cared to display would spill from within him.

"Is it Jim?"

A jab of realization spiked his gut. He couldn't keep anything from Mama. She knew him too well. Jim, his faithful worker and friend, had hinted several times about his daughter and grandsons. "Maybe."

"Take that to the Lord, son."

Gideon looked up at the heavens. "I'm trying, Mama. But Jim's right. Maria does need some help."

"God provides in His ways. We don't need to fix things that aren't ours to fix." Mama patted his arm before she walked into the house.

Gideon stared at the clouds that lay serenely in the sky. Maria was a wonderful Christian woman, and Gideon adored her two sons. Widowed, she took care of the boys and worked hard at her job. But she struggled, and it was hard for Jim to watch.

Jim had worked the orchard for years—the last two with Gideon, and two decades before that with Gideon's mentor. Jim had his own ideas of how to help Maria. They involved Gideon and a lifetime commitment. Jim liked the idea. Maria seemed okay with it. The boys would probably be fine with it.

But Gideon just wasn't so sure.

Chapter 2

L ydia couldn't remember the last time she'd been so embarrassed. Well, in truth, it hadn't been *that* long ago. The first remembrance that came to mind was when she went to the hospital to help her friend who'd just had a baby load up her things to go home. Lydia had found a bowl of sorts and filled it with several toiletries. When an unbelievably handsome male nurse came in and chuckled, Lydia couldn't figure out what was wrong.

"It's a bedpan." The nurse laughed, pointing at the container. Lydia dumped out the contents as the guy continued to chuckle. "At least it was new."

Lydia shook the memory from her mind. At least she hadn't told the nurse that she and his mother had been talking about how cute he was! Warmth spread up her cheeks, and she quickened her pace as she remembered how Gideon's expression had changed from anger to embarrassment to humor as she fumbled over her words.

She scaled the steps to the front door and walked inside. She sat George down on the floor and stared down at him. "Are you going to cause this kind of trouble every day?" He winked, a reflex surely, and wagged his tail. "Great. Even my puppy thinks I'm funny."

After flopping on the couch, Lydia slipped off her shoes. She turned and lay back, resting her head on the arm cushion. Gideon looked like an adorable, scruffy farmer. His worn jeans had dirt patches at his hips where he'd obviously wiped his hands. His somewhat-white T-shirt couldn't hide his broad shoulders. His sandy brown hair and facial stubble were actually a shade lighter than the kiss the sun had given his face and arms. The mixture caused his eyes, a swirling of green, hazel, and brown, to pop. A chill raced through her. *He has amazing eyes.*

"Knock it off." She smacked her hands against the cushion beside her hips. George barked and jumped on the couch beside her. He tried to lick her hand, but she swatted him away. "No more kisses. I'm mad at you, remember?"

He ignored her words and nestled his nose beneath her hand. She couldn't help but giggle when his wet nose reached her palm. "All right, little guy." She picked him up and wiggled him back and forth. "Down you go." She set him on the floor then leaned back again.

She had no business thinking of Lorma's son in such a way. He may have looked scruffy, but he was obviously meticulous when it came to his fruits. Lydia

Hammond and meticulous did not get along well, as Lydia's perfect mother would have no problem pointing out. Lydia always messed things up, and thinking about Gideon's eyes was a mess-up waiting to happen.

She started to count the pointy parts in the spackle on the ceiling. By the time she got to ten she laughed out loud at the ridiculous activity. *Hmm.* She rested her hands behind her head. This spot would be much more comfortable than the floor to do crunches. *I'm sure it's not as effective, but if I do an extra ten or twenty, maybe I'll get the same results without killing my back.*

She maneuvered herself until her head and her feet lay flat on the couch. Placing her palms behind her head, she intertwined her fingers. *Definitely not a firm foundation, but hopefully it will still be effective.*

Slowly, she lifted her head and chest. "One." She lay back and inhaled. Up and exhale. "Two." Back and inhale. Up and exhale. "Three." She continued several more times. "This hurts my back worse." She flopped against the couch.

"That's because you're supposed to do it on a hard surface."

Lydia jumped up and screamed. A man had broken into the house! She grabbed the first thing in her reach and threw it at him. The tall figure ducked as a sofa pillow flew past his head.

Lydia gasped when she recognized Lorma's son. "What are you doing here?" She frowned as she noted he held her dog's leash in one hand and her puppy in the other. "And how did you get in?"

"Well, I came to return this." He handed George's leash to her. "And your pup was digging in your flowers, so I picked him up, as well." He raised his eyebrows and cocked his head. "Am I to assume this little guy got out of the house without you knowing it?"

Lydia blew a wisp of hair from her eyes. "Yes. I don't know how he managed to get the door open." She sighed. "I must not have closed it all the way."

"I know a really good obedience trainer."

Hurt welled inside of Lydia. Her dog messed up his peaches. She can't close a door. She's the only goof who does crunches on a couch. Now she can't train a pup. Flighty, her mother called her. Irresponsible. Lydia liked to think of descriptions like spontaneous and adventurous. On the other hand, when her mother asked her when she would ever be content to settle down, Lydia started evaluating her life. Contentment was what she wanted, more than anything. She wanted to find something and be happy. Jesus had given her a contentment she'd never known, and yet she still grew restless as she searched for God's purpose for her life.

"You don't have to take him to a trainer. You could train him yourself." Gideon put George on the floor.

"I doubt it," Lydia muttered.

"Sure you could. There're lots of dog obedience books on the Internet and at the library."

Lydia studied Gideon's face. He had a scar, probably an inch long, above his right eye at his hairline. Its whiteness stood in contrast to his sun-darkened skin. But it was his eyes and the sincerity shining from them that held her captive. They didn't seem to swirl together as they had before. The green framed his pupil while the hazel wrapped around the green and the deep brown circled the hazel. Like a bull's-eye. "Do your eyes change with your mood?"

Gideon's eyebrows met in a line as a smile curled his lips.

Lydia bit her bottom lip and scrunched her nose. She'd said that out loud. Yep, she'd asked him *out loud* if his eyes change. Foolish mouth. Foolish, nonstop-getting-me-into-trouble mouth. How many scriptures were there that focused on that nemesis—the tongue—and how many times had she read them? And yet, she still said whatever happened to be on her mind the moment she thought it!

"Yeah. People do tell me my eyes change. Mama can look at my eyes and instantly know what kind of mood I'm in, almost what I'm thinking even."

Lydia giggled and blinked slowly. "What does a bull's-eye mean?" *Oh my. I just flirted with him. I just blatantly flirted with him. Please, God, help me here. I'm digging myself deeper and deeper.*

The phone rang, and Lydia jumped. "Oh. I better get the phone. Thanks for bringing the leash back."

She started to turn away, but Gideon touched her arm. She peered up at him. The green around his pupils deepened. "It means I've seen something that put a smile on my face, something I like." He winked, then turned and walked out the door.

Lydia watched him. What had he seen today—her dog mutilate his peaches and her flowers? He'd witnessed her fumble every word she spoke. Oh, yes, and he had seen her doing crunches on the living room sofa. She'd given him plenty to smile about all right. He'd probably be laughing the whole way home. And yet his eyes didn't quite express teasing. It was something. . .

The phone rang again. Lydia shook her head and ran into the kitchen toward the phone. She picked it up. "Hello."

"Hi, Lydia. It's Mom."

"Mom!" Lydia smiled and swallowed at the same time. She loved her mother. With all her heart she loved her, but her mom rarely saw the good in Lydia. At least that's how Lydia felt. Her mom was a successful lawyer in Indianapolis with plans to run for state office the next term. And what was Lydia? Right now, unemployed and trying to learn more about the God she'd given her life to and what He wanted for her.

"I just got back from visiting Allison and the girls."

Lydia cringed. Her older sister had two beautiful school-age daughters and her own dental practice in a small town in Kentucky. "How are they doing?"

"They're terrific. You should think about visiting them. Maybe Allison can give you some ideas."

Lydia chose not to ask what kinds of ideas. She already knew her mother meant business ideas. Something that would make Lydia stable and success-ful. The problem remained that Lydia just wasn't sure what God wanted. "I've enjoyed Grandma's house. I painted the downstairs bath—"

"Oh, good. That's what I wanted to talk with you about. I'm planning to stop by for a visit on Friday."

"Friday?"

"I can only stay until Sunday afternoon, but I wanted to see you about Grandma's house. You know how your Aunt Grace is. She wanted me to make sure you weren't changing anything in Grandma's house."

"I haven't, Mom. The house belongs to you and Aunt Grace. I know that, and I would never do anything to hurt Gran—"

"I know, but I need to make sure. My beeper is going off. I'll see you Friday."

The phone went dead. Lydia pulled it away from her ear and stared at the numbers. No "How are you doing?" No "I love you." Just "I need to make sure you're not hurting Grandma's house." Lydia sighed. She longed for a better rela-tionship with her mother.

And her Aunt Grace. Lydia huffed. So much for a name fitting a person. Her aunt had anything but grace. Well, that wasn't exactly true. Her aunt was an exquisite entertainer. She knew all the "right" people and all the "right" things to say and do in front of them, but she remained clueless when it came to exhibiting grace. Her aunt had never been one to put up with the recklessness or misbehav-ior of others. Including Lydia.

God, how did I get into this family? I know if I settled into a job, Mom would be happy. Aunt Grace, too, I suppose. I understand Mom's frustrations with me. I've been a little bit of everything over the years. Even now, I'm living on money Grandma left me in her will. Really, it's not very practical. I've changed since I met You, but I'm still not. . .

Lydia sighed and hung up the phone. She walked to the kitchen, opened the refrigerator, and grabbed a bottle of water. After taking a quick drink, she shut the door and peered at one of her grandmother's magnets. Grandma didn't really fit into the family either. In fact, Lydia was a lot like her grandmother. She read the verse on the magnet quietly at first. Allowing the meaning to sink in, she read it again, aloud. "'For I know the plans I have for you,' declares the Lord, 'plans to prosper you and not to harm you, plans to give you hope and a future.'"

God, You have a plan for me. One that is especially designed for me. I trust You to show me in Your time.

◈

Gideon chuckled as he made his way back to his house. He hadn't intended to scare Lydia when he went into her home. His hands were full with a pup and a leash, and since the door was open and he couldn't knock, he thought he'd just step inside. He hadn't expected to see her doing crunches on her couch. Crunches, for crying out loud. He laughed again.

That woman was interesting. He'd have to give her that. He couldn't deny she was quite attractive, as well. Usually freckles were not one of his favorite physical traits, but something about hers enhanced her appearance. Maybe it wasn't the freckles. Maybe it was the ice blue eyes or that cute, slightly upturned nose.

But she was flighty, too. He scratched the stubble on his chin. No, not really flighty, but spontaneous. Yes, he liked that description much better. He'd met her only an hour ago, and already he had no idea what to expect her to say or do. He liked that. She lightened his mood and brightened his afternoon. If only her phone hadn't rung, he would have loved to spend a bit more time getting to know her. *Or getting to know what she thinks about the way I look.* Gideon laughed again. She couldn't keep her honesty to herself if she tried. He liked that, too. She was genuine. Already he could tell she was the real deal.

"Hey, Gideon, where'd you run off to?" Jim's scratchy voice sounded from up ahead. "Something funny happen?"

Gideon cleared his throat. "No. I just had to run something back to our neighbor for Mama."

"I see." Jim looked back at Lydia's house. "Marian's granddaughter's awful pretty, wouldn't you say?"

Gideon shrugged. He had no reason to feel uneasy. Jim was his employee, but lately Jim had been too consumed with Gideon and Maria and matrimony. "She's attractive, I suppose."

Jim shoved his hands in his pockets. " 'Course, she has plenty of means to provide for herself. Her mom, her grandma, God rest her soul. . . . She even has a good home to live in."

Gideon closed his eyes. *Here we go.*

"My Maria has to rent a tiny one-bedroom apartment for her and the boys. She does all she can, but. . ."

"I'll be happy to help her out with groceries or clothes."

Jim balked. "She won't take no charity. She's a good Christian woman who'd work hard alongside a good Christian man."

Gideon stopped and turned toward his employee. "What are you trying to say, Jim? Why don't you just—"

Jim turned away and swiped a leaf off a tree. "I'm just saying the Bible tells us to care for widows and such. My Maria is a widow—a kind, caring, attractive lady."

"I agree, and I would love to help her out. But if you're talking about commit—"

Jim laughed and swatted the air. "I'm not talking about anything particularly. Just mentioning the facts." He rubbed his hands together. "Having to move those boys away from their home in Wisconsin after their daddy's death has been hard on all of them. But they've had time enough to grieve."

"Jim, it's only been eight months. I've spent my life letting God lead my love life, and I don't feel comfortable rushing into—"

"Oh, come on now." Jim patted Gideon's shoulder. "Let's not think of that. How'd we get on that to begin with? A man couldn't work for anyone better." Jim let go of Gideon's shoulder and walked on ahead.

Gideon watched him for several seconds. *God, what do I do about this? Do You want me to think of Maria in the way Jim wants? Show me.*

He moved ahead. Within moments, the bushes rustled beside him. Gideon looked over, expecting to find a squirrel. Instead, Kelbe, Maria's five-year-old son, jumped out and wrapped his arms around Gideon's waist. Giggling, Jeremy, the three-year-old, scurried around the bush and wrapped himself around Gideon's leg. Gideon laughed as he tried to move forward. "Oh no, I've been attacked, but I am stronger than these little creatures."

Kelbe slid down to wrap himself around Gideon's free leg. Gideon walked like Frankenstein's monster toward the house. "You may think you can beat me," Gideon wailed, "but I am stronger than the both of you together."

"Let's get him, Jer," Kelbe hollered as he rose up and started to tickle Gideon's waist.

"You can't win, I say." Gideon bent down and tickled Kelbe's stomach. Jeremy tried to jump on Gideon's back, but Gideon turned and tickled him, as well.

The game went on for several minutes until Jeremy and Kelbe fell over from exhaustion. Gideon took several deep breaths, as well. No amount of work or exercise could top a five-minute tickle match with Maria's boys. "How 'bout you two run up to the house and ask Mrs. Andrews for a drink of lemonade?"

"Yeah!" Jeremy rolled his chubby legs to a standing position then raced for the house. "Miz Adrew. Wemoade!"

"What?" His mother's voice filled the air. He could see her confused expression even from a distance.

Kelbe hopped up and ran for the porch. "Gideon said we could have some lemonade."

Gideon watched his mom smile. "Well, sure. Get in here." She opened the back door and disappeared inside with the boys.

After one long breath, Gideon wiped most of the dirt from his shirt and jeans.

"They're a handful, huh?"

Gideon turned toward the voice. He smiled at Maria. "Yes, they are, but in a good way."

"Hmm. Try getting them in bed at night. It's an hour-long process." She grinned, exposing deep dimples on both sides of her cheeks.

Gideon took in her shoulder-length dark hair. By all accounts, it appeared very soft. She had a lovely smile, straight white teeth. Her eyes were a bit of a dull green; however, their shape was quite attractive.

But there was no spark—no gut desire to get to know her better.

She was a wonderful person. A great friend. Had adorable kids. But that was all. He didn't feel anything else. Didn't know if he could ever feel anything else.

Gideon scratched his stubble. "I'm sure you're a very patient person."

Maria gazed at the ground. Gideon noted that her eyelashes were so long they seemed to touch her cheek with the motion. *That's a really attractive thing— long eyelashes. Most of my buddies love it when ladies bat their lashes.* And yet, Gideon felt nothing.

"Your mom invited us for dinner." She traced a line in the dirt with her sandal. "For all I know, Daddy invited us." She looked up, and Gideon couldn't decipher the meaning of her words. Did she feel frustrated with her dad or did she agree with him? "Anyway, I hope you don't mind."

Gideon clapped his hands then rubbed them together. "Of course I don't mind. You and the boys are always welcome, but I'm starving. I hope dinner's ready."

"It is." Maria grinned. "It's your favorite." She winked. "I helped."

Gideon's stomach plummeted. She was the second woman to flirt with him today. This time, however, he didn't feel hungry for more. Instead, he'd lost his appetite.

Chapter 3

Before George's barks had time to reach their full tirade, Lydia heard gravel popping in the driveway, no doubt signaling the arrival of a new, sleek Mercedes. After scooping the pup into her hand, Lydia peeked past the ivory lace curtain.

A force, often stronger than the winds of a thunderstorm, stepped out of the polished silver vehicle. Rita Louise Hammond wore a fitted navy suit, white button-down blouse with an oversized collar, and shiny red heels. A red strap that connected perfectly into a small navy purse rested obediently on her shoulder.

Lydia could hear her mother's confident voice in the back of her mind. "A bit of red to a woman's attire does the same as a red tie for a man." She'd raise one eyebrow and smirk. "Expresses power."

Lydia glanced down at her gray, cutoff sweatpants and Indiana University T-shirt. Why hadn't she dressed in a nice pair of capris and a summer sweater, or a pair of decent shorts at least? She knew her mom would come dressed to the nines. *It's no wonder she thinks I'm irresponsible. I'd think I'd have more sense than to dress like this knowing she was coming.*

She blew a stray curl from the front of her face. *Oh, well. This is who I am.* She peeked back through the window and watched as her mother studied the chewed-on daylily. Lydia had tried to conjure life and uprightness from the poor foliage George had demolished, but remnants of the pup's presence remained. Her mom frowned and rubbed her lips with her index finger. A proven sign of her aggravation.

Deciding she might as well get their greeting over with, Lydia opened the front door and walked outside. "Hi, Mom. I'm glad you came."

Her mom screamed and swatted at her right thigh. She jumped from one foot to the other, smacking her leg, her chest, then her face. Lydia felt her mouth drop open as she stood in shocked silence while her mother blew air from her lips and blinked several times. Finally, still running in place, she shook her head, messing her hair with her fingertips.

"Mom. . ."

"What was that?" Her mom's eyes glazed with fear. She rested her palm against her chest. Her gaze sought the ground around her. "There it is."

Lydia watched as her mother stomped on a beetle and ground it into the earth. She'd never seen the woman so erratic and upset. She knew her mouth still gaped open, but she couldn't seem to shut it.

"There." Her mother breathed out and swiped her hand through her hair then pressed her crisp pants. She looked up. Surprise filled her mother's eyes when Lydia made eye contact with her. One side of her mom's mouth lifted slightly.

Lydia couldn't stop the gurgling that formed in her stomach and made its way up her chest and into her throat. It started as a slight giggle, but when her mother's soft laugh filled the air, Lydia lost her composure and burst into deep, gut-wrenching laughter.

It took several moments, but Lydia got herself together and gave her mom a hug. "I am glad to see you."

"I see you have a friend." Rita petted George's head.

Lydia marveled at her mom's tenderness. Reveling in the moment, she pointed toward the disheveled flowers. "Yes, George is the little scamp who decided to chew on my garden."

Her mom's mood darkened, and she headed toward the door. "Well, I hope he hasn't damaged any of Mother's furniture."

"Oh, he hasn't." Lydia followed behind. Why had she brought her mother's attention back toward those flowers? She shook her head.

"You said you painted Mother's bathroom?"

Lydia hadn't realized her mother had paid any attention to her saying it over the phone. "Yes. I painted it a—"

"Upstairs or downstairs?"

"Downstairs." Lydia released a slow sigh as Rita's heels clicked against hard-wood toward the bathroom. Her mother was back to her usual self. Critical. Formal. Nothing at all like Lydia. *God, will we ever be able to see eye-to-eye, or agree on anything for that matter?*

"Purple!"

Her mother's exclamation echoed through the house. Lydia rolled her eyes. "It's not purple, Mom."

Rita stuck her head out the door. She lifted her eyebrows and pierced Lydia with a scowl. "Surely you know your colors, Lydia Anne."

"I know my colors!" Anger welled within her, and it took all her strength not to stomp toward the small room. "It's a light plum, and if you look beside the vanity, you'll notice I hung one of Grandma's favorite pictures. I matched the walls with the color of the girl's dress."

Mom snarled. "I don't know why Mother always liked this cheap, old picture, but I suppose it looks all right in here." She walked out of the bathroom.

Lydia held tight to George as she followed her mother around the house.

Rita had a comment for every speck of dust, every rumpled pillow, every scratch on the floors, and on and on.

Lydia felt she would scream before her mother finally made it into the kitchen. Trying to add something positive to the visit, Lydia pointed toward the counter. "I made a pie for you."

"Yes. I thought I smelled something."

Lydia knew the mixture of apples and cinnamon was tantalizing, but, as usual, her mother couldn't seem to bring herself to say anything nice. "I'll just put George in the backyard. . ."

"Honestly, Lydia, I don't know why you didn't do that to begin with."

Lydia put the pup in the backyard before heading to the sink to wash her hands. "Have a seat, Mom." She nodded toward the table she'd arranged in front of the oversized bay window.

The view of some of Indiana's best land spilled through those panes. She loved living in Danville. Lydia could gaze at Grandma's flower gardens and farther past them to the grass, trees, and wildflowers that seemed to go on forever.

"Make sure you use plenty of soap. I don't want that creature's germs on the food."

"Of course." Lydia had to bite her lip to keep from saying anything disrespectful. God instructed her to honor her mother, but sometimes it was just plain hard.

She took a knife from the drawer and sliced through the pie. Perfect, it was still just a tad warm when she laid the pieces on the plates she'd already set out. After grabbing the ice cream from the refrigerator, she dropped a scoop to the right of each slice. Lydia took the desserts and utensils and sat across from her mom. She forced a slight smile at her mom then focused on her pie. *Mmm, this is good.* She had added just a touch more sugar this time, and Lydia felt surprised at what a difference such a small amount made.

"Lydia Anne. . ."

Lydia exhaled. What could her mother possibly want to berate her about now?

"This is the best pie I've ever tasted."

"What?"

"Lydia, this is wonderful. I knew you were good, but this. . .it's better than Mother's."

"Better than Grandma's? Oh no, no. . ."

"Yes, it is." Her mother leaned over and grabbed Lydia's hand. "You should consider selling these. You'd make a fortune." She fell back against her chair and laughed. "I've been so worried about you wasting your life. One job after another, and here you have a domestic talent. I mean I knew you liked to bake, but who'd have thought a daughter of mine could do it this well?" She snorted. "Hammond

women are meant to be powerhouses, pillars of their community, and here I've
raised a Betty Crocker."

Lydia was afraid to let her mind believe what her heart felt. Sure, her mother
almost meant the compliment as an insult. Not a new concept in Lydia's life, but
still her mother thought she had talent, that she was good at something. For
the first time in her memory, Lydia had pleased her mother. Lydia relished the
moment. She liked it. She liked it a lot.

⁂

Gideon tucked the dog obedience books he'd purchased under his arm. He'd
intentionally picked the cheapest ones he could find on the Internet, not because
of the price but because they were the most used. He didn't want Lydia to think
she'd filled his thoughts the last few days and that he was desperate to do anything to see her again. If she happened to believe he'd had the books around the
house for a while, that would work for him. Of course, if she came right out and
asked, he'd never lie. *It's not really even a lie of omission, because why would she care
where I got the books?*

No, it's more about motive.

He shook his head against the unwanted thought. He'd just give her the
books, not overanalyze why, how, when, or what he got them for. He'd just
give them to her. Just see her again. Just hear her fumble over her words. He
grinned.

Her house came into sight. The mile walk proved not only good exercise,
but since he didn't need to take his truck anywhere, he didn't have to tell anyone
where he was going. They assumed he was hard at work in the orchard. No one,
Jim especially, would ask him any questions. Man, how he'd become tired of
questions and suggestions.

A ball of fur bounced through the grass a ways in front of him. "What in
the world?" Soon he heard the half yelp, half bark of Lydia's puppy. "Hello there,
George." Gideon bent down and picked the little guy up. As before, the pup tried
to lick his hand, his arm, any surface of body the pup could find. "You're friendly,
I'll give you that."

Gideon walked the rest of the distance to her house. Now he had two reasons to see her. He headed to her porch, but before he could knock, the door
opened and Lydia stepped outside. "Hi, Gideon."

An unexpected thrill raced through him at the sound of his name from her
lips. He blinked. *I've lost my mind. Some weird sickness has overtaken my thoughts
and made me a sap.*

Lydia put her hands on her hips. "George, I've been looking everywhere
for you."

Even her reprimand to the little fur ball proved the cutest thing he'd seen in a while. Gideon didn't know what it was about Lydia, but he couldn't quite reach his fill of seeing her. The pup barked. Gideon forced himself back to reality and handed the pup to Lydia. "He must have gotten out again."

Brilliant line, Andrews. Way to impress the girl.

Lydia shook her head. Gideon couldn't help but notice the sun dance across the red and blond strands of her hair. *Wow! What a gorgeous color!* Her cheeks blazed pink, setting off the blue in her eyes. Either she felt embarrassed the dog had gotten out again or she was furious with the little critter. No matter what, he needed to get his head straight and form sentences that were at the very least conversational.

Her face fell into the most adorable pout he'd ever witnessed. The woman would be able to get him to purchase the moon simply with the expressions of her face. "There's got to be a hole in the fence in the backyard. I don't know how he's doing it."

A job, yes. If he had a purpose, a reason to help her, then maybe his mind wouldn't race off so much. "I don't mind taking a look for you."

"No, no. You've helped enough. Thanks for bringing George back." Her eyes widened and her skin turned white. "Don't tell me he'd run all the way to your house."

Gideon shook his head. "No." He looked down at the books. "I was heading over here to bring you some books on obedience."

She frowned.

He cleared his throat. "Remember we'd talked about. . ."

Her eyebrows lifted and her lips bowed into the prettiest shape he'd ever seen. "That's right. Thank you." She took them from his hand. "Did you get these on the Internet for me?"

Gideon puckered his lips. *Now who asks that? Who even thinks to ask if something was purchased on the Internet? They're used. Most people would believe them to be the giver's property.* Gideon sighed. Not Lydia. She was too open, too honest with her thoughts. He'd have a hard time tricking her with anything. Her innocence would pick up on it.

I'll tell her if she asks. It's not a lie of omission. His own thoughts smacked him in the face. *Okay, God. I was trying to be sneaky. She called me out on it. Forgive me, Lord.*

"Yes, I did buy them for you."

"Why?"

"To apologize for the way I'd behaved." *Sorry again, God. Not exactly true, but now that I think about it, I'm glad I bought them as a means to say I'm sorry.*

"Oh." The questioning look on her face just about had him unglued. He had to think of a way to change the subject. He noticed the Mercedes. "Very nice car.

Didn't know you had a Mercedes."

She blew a strand of hair from her eyes. A beautiful gesture, like blades of wheat blowing with the wind, only much prettier. Gideon lost the beginning of her response. Somewhere he thought he heard her say "mother." He asked, "So, it's your mom's car?"

She frowned again. "That's what I said." She placed her hand back on her hip. "Are you all right?"

"I'm fine." Gideon noticed she had five freckles on her nose. Well, several little ones, as well, but five that he could really count. Three kind of clumped together on one side while the other two spread out a bit on the other side. Very cute.

"I asked if you wanted a piece of pie."

Gideon scratched the stubble at his jaw. He had to stop staring at the woman. He'd scare her to death if he didn't act more like a gentleman. "I'd love a piece of your pie."

He followed her through the living room and into the kitchen. She turned around and almost ran into him. Almost, but not quite. He would have loved a reason to wrap his arms around her for a second.

She motioned toward the table. "My mom's asleep in the spare bedroom upstairs. She's spending the weekend with me."

"That's nice." By the pained expression that wrapped her face, Gideon wondered if it wasn't such a nice thing.

Lydia laid the plate of pie on the table. It smelled good, and he wondered where she'd bought it. He took a bite. "This is terrific." He jammed his fork back into the piece and shoveled pie into his mouth. "Where did you get this?"

"I told you I made it."

"When?"

"Out on the porch."

When I started daydreaming about freckles, no doubt. "Well, this is really good."

A slight blush tinted her cheeks, and her eyes smiled contentedly with her lips. "You're the second person to say that today. Thank you."

In all his twenty-eight years, Gideon had never felt such an urge to kiss a woman. He didn't know it was possible for a man to go "cuckoo," as he and his brothers used to tease their sisters. Somehow, this lady who couldn't keep track of her dog, whom he'd only met one time before, this woman, who'd captured his mother's heart, had also captured his.

He loved the idea of it.

❦

It was almost eleven when Lydia crawled into her bed. She couldn't seem to shake the pleasure that filled her heart with her mother's and Gideon's approvals over her pie. Her mother's commendation remained especially sweet.

She picked up her Bible. Before Sam left, Lydia had promised her friend that she'd read through the New Testament. Lydia had made it all the way to First Thessalonians. She wondered at all she'd learned about God. Some things still confused her. Sam had told her that would be true until they reached heaven. Even with questions, God had strengthened her faith in Him. Already, she couldn't imagine living life, even living a day, without Him.

After grabbing her pen and pad on the nightstand, Lydia opened her Bible. She began reading about the book of Thessalonians, that it had been Paul's letter to the city of Thessalonica. She started reading the verses, making notes on her pad. She read through chapter one and on to chapter two. She stopped at verse four and frowned. She read it again. *What are You telling me here, Lord?*

She read the verse one more time aloud. " 'On the contrary, we speak as men approved by God to be entrusted with the gospel. We are not trying to please men but God, who tests our hearts.' " She shut the book and closed her eyes.

Not trying to please men. Not trying to please men. A lone tear spilled down her cheek. She swiped at it, causing more to fall. "Oh God, I've been so consumed with pleasing men. Well, Mom, more than anyone, but I'm consumed with it. I always have been. I've felt like a failure in her eyes."

Lydia reached for a tissue on the nightstand. She wiped her nose and her eyes. "I am to please You. Oh Jesus, forgive me. Mom doesn't know You. I need to be a witness to her. I thought pleasing her would make me a good witness, but that's wrong." She had to stop to blow her nose. "Pleasing You is what will make me a good witness. Forgive me, Lord. Help me to seek Your pleasure above everything. I love You, Lord."

Lydia jotted the scripture down in her notepad. She flipped through the pages before, noting all the verses she wanted to commit to memory. Her gaze found one from Galatians that mimicked the Thessalonians verse. Without a doubt, God wanted her to please Him, and Him alone. She closed her Bible and turned off the light. She wanted to chew on the verse while she slept. She wanted to evaluate where her talents were, where her pleasures were. She wanted to sit still and listen to what God had to say.

She no longer wanted to live to please men.

She wanted to please God.

Chapter 4

A m I now trying to win the approval of men, or of God? Or am I trying to please men? If I were still trying to please men, I would not be a servant of Christ."

Gideon stopped and listened to the animated voice playing from his mother's Bible CD. The narrator continued on. Gideon could tell by the flavor of the words that the writer was Paul, but he didn't know which book was being read. He searched through the kitchen and into the living area until he finally found his mother cleaning pictures in the hall. "What book of the Bible are you listening to, Mama?"

"Look at this picture." She held up one that displayed his entire family before Pa died. "Remember this?"

"Yes. It was Kylie's wedding. But which book of the Bible are you listening to?"

His mama shook her head, swatting her hand in front of her face. He knew she lamented his father, probably missed her other children, as well. "I can't remember. I'll go look."

She shoved the picture in his hand and walked back into the kitchen. A twinge of sadness, maybe even loneliness, tugged at his heart. His pa's death had been hard, but at the same time, Pa had been so miserably sick. It felt almost crueler to pray for Pa to have more time on this earth. Pa rejoiced with angels and saints in heaven now. Of that, Gideon remained sure.

And yet, as time passed, over two years now, Gideon found himself missing Pa more, not less. It seemed odd to him. Wrong, in some way. Maybe it was because seeing Pa so sick proved harder than seeing him die. Maybe as time drifted by, Gideon remembered the times Pa had been healthy more often than the times he had been ill.

Gideon looked at the picture in his hand. With his thumb, he caressed the brass frame. Pa had been sick in this picture, yet he was smiling. He felt so happy, so proud that Kylie had found a wonderful Christian man. The whole family loved Ryan. Ryan had been Gideon's greatest encourager while he went to college to major in agriculture. Not only had he encouraged, he'd financially aided, as well.

Gideon looked back at the expressions on his parents' faces. Mama's smile was apparent, even though her face was turned as she looked at her husband of so many years. Pure pleasure wrapped her expression. His pa smiled at the camera, content and happy as could be. No one who looked at this picture would have known black lung already tore away at his insides, leaving him sick and unstable, especially at night.

But that wasn't how Gideon remembered Pa. He didn't think of him in terms of this picture or the all-too-short years that followed. He thought of him on the front porch of their old house, strong and healthy, playing the guitar and singing hymns as loud as his deep voice could muster. Gideon remembered him playing basketball with them when they were teenagers and playing the card game of war with them when they were young.

A memory of Pa standing behind Mama as she washed the dishes flooded his mind. Pa had leaned down and kissed Mama's cheek, and the lot of them, probably five of the eight kids, saw the show of affection and squealed in protest. Pa only chuckled while Mama shooed him away.

He wanted a love like that.

"It's Galatians," Mama's voice sounded from down the hall. "I'm listening to Galatians."

Gideon blinked back to reality and hung the picture back on its nail. "Thanks, Mama." He headed toward the stairs. He had a few minutes before he needed to get back to the orchard. A quick peek at Galatians wouldn't take much time.

"Lorma! Gideon! Someone!" A scream sounded from the yard. Gideon raced out the front door to find Maria sitting on the ground, holding three-year-old Jeremy in her arms. Blood patched his shirt and pants as well as the front of her shirt. Crying, Kelbe stood beside them holding a three-foot pipe with blood covering one end.

"What happened?" Gideon scooped the boy out of her arms and raced to the bathroom. "Where is he bleeding?"

Maria ran behind him. "His thumb."

"It was a accident," Kelbe mumbled through tears. Maria must have been holding him now, as well.

"What's wrong?" Mama yelled.

"Get some towels, Mama." Gideon placed the child's bloody hand under the faucet. Turning on the cold, he hoped it was just a small wound, maybe needing a few stitches. A large chunk of Jeremy's thumb flapped over, and Gideon thought he would vomit. Pushing the flesh back, Gideon grabbed one of the towels Mama had gotten and wrapped it around Jeremy's thumb. "Start the truck. We're going to the emergency room."

"No, my car has his car seat. I just don't think I can—" Maria looked down at her shirt and tears welled in her eyes. "I don't think I can drive."

"Give me your keys." Gideon held the towel around Jeremy's thumb while Maria searched her purse. The blood seemed to have stopped quickly. Gideon hoped that was a good thing.

Once he had the keys, only a matter of moments passed until the two boys, Maria, and Gideon were buckled into seats and Gideon was driving to the nearest hospital.

"How did this happen?" Gideon asked Kelbe. The vision of the five-year-old holding the pipe sent cold chills up his spine. If Gideon's guess proved right, it was the device his mother purchased, which was meant to go under the doorknob to help keep perpetrators out. But it was missing the rubber parts that went on each end. When Pa died, Mama had bought one for each of the doors. What was Kelbe doing with it?

"We were playing with Mrs. Andrews's door thingy."

Yep, just as Gideon suspected.

Kelbe went on. "I pulled the bendy parts off, and we were jumping over it, trying to see who could jump the highest." Kelbe's voice cracked, and Gideon looked in the rearview mirror to see his lower lip shake. "I didn't mean for Jer to get hurt. I didn't. . ."

"It was an accident." Maria's voice remained calm and reassuring as she patted her oldest son's leg with her free hand. She held the towel around Jeremy's thumb with the other.

"Yes, Kelbe. It was an accident." Gideon added, "I should've had Mama get rid of those things when she moved here. The rubber pieces are constantly coming off."

Maria looked at Gideon. Her eyes shone with her appreciation for supporting her son. The expression felt intimate, more so than Gideon really felt comfortable with. He cared about the boys, and Maria for that matter. Of course he wouldn't say anything to hurt them, but he wasn't sure he wanted expressions like that.

They made it to the hospital, and Gideon carried Jeremy into the emergency room. Maria and Kelbe followed behind. Once inside, Gideon handed Jeremy to Maria and allowed her to take care of all the registration forms. He grabbed Kelbe's hand and led him to a vending machine. After the little guy purchased a snack and drink, they sat together in front of the lobby television.

"I'm glad you helped us." Kelbe kicked his legs, which couldn't quite reach the floor, beneath the chair. "Mommy was real scared."

"I think she was doing all right." Gideon tried to reassure him.

"No. Mommy don't like blood. Makes her sick."

"Your mom's a tough lady."

"No." Kelbe shook his head. "One time I got bit by a dog when I was four." Kelbe lifted his face and pointed to a scar beneath his eye. "Mommy fell down and fell asleep. Daddy had to take me to see the doctor." Kelbe lowered his face and dug his hand back into his bag of pretzels. "Daddy's not here no more though."

Gideon's heart broke for the little guy, for both little guys. They needed a dad. Gideon knew how important a good father was in a boy's life. He'd had one of the best ever.

Lord, are You trying to tell me something?

Lydia looked at her watch. "Ugh. It's almost eleven and I still haven't made it to the grocery." Her stomach gurgled from a lack of breakfast, and her head had a small drummer inside it, beating ever so softly yet consistently against her brain. She hadn't had her morning coffee and bowl of oatmeal, and she could feel Mr. Grouch shaking his fist up at her from the trash can inside her gut.

She'd spent the week since Mother left going through Grandma's attic. As a pleasant surprise, she'd found the sweetest painting of a small boy sitting on a garden stool holding a bug of some kind. A faithful pup sat beside him. The lavender flowers in the background of the painting perfectly matched the bathroom she'd painted, so she'd taken the treasure to a framer to select a mat and frame.

That had been two hours ago!

She pulled into a parking space at the grocery and turned off the engine. "Who'd have thought it would take so long to pick out a picture frame," she growled as she pulled her ponytail holder out of her hair, ran her fingers through her wayward curls, and fixed the ponytail again. Believing she'd be in and out of town in one hour at the most, she hadn't fixed her makeup or put on decent clothing. She was covered in a wrinkled T-shirt, neon pink slippers adorning her feet, and her long, flannel pajama pants—multicolored polka dots over stripes. What had beguiled her to buy such an atrocious pair of pants? She nodded her head, remembering. They were a gag gift from a college friend. She lifted one eyebrow. . .she'd bought the neon shoes herself.

Oh well, what does it matter what a gal looks like? Isn't beauty about what's inside? She giggled. Most people would at least allow others to see the beauty of being dressed in daytime clothes when coming to town. She held back a snort. The clothes were the least of her worries. She'd die if anyone spoke to her; she hadn't even brushed her teeth. She thought she could drop the picture off and that was that, but no, she had to select various shades, sizes, and whatnot. It's a wonder the framer didn't keel over from her foulness.

"Mother would be appalled." She spoke to her reflection in the visor mirror. After rubbing the front of her teeth with her finger, she pinched her cheeks for some color. "We're not trying to impress men," she announced with confident flair. Looking to the heavens, she added, "But I guess that doesn't count when it comes to brushing my teeth. I could have at least done that."

She *would* just head right back to her house, shower, and come back, but she didn't have any coffee at home, and the little drummer guy would not leave her poor brain alone until she did something to feed him.

With a shrug of her shoulders, Lydia flung her purse on her arm and hopped out of her car. The chances of seeing anyone she would know were slim to none. She'd only been to church twice. Outside of the Andrews, she really hadn't met anyone. *Really, it's highly unlikely I'll see. . .*

"Lydia, is that you?" A sweet voice sounded from behind her.

No way. It is not possible. Lydia turned ever so slowly. *Please let her be alone. Please let her be alone.* It wasn't like Lydia had spent *all* her waking hours thinking of Gideon Andrews and his sandy hair and scruffy face that made him appear so manly. No, she'd spent a whole lot of her sleeping hours thinking about him, as well. "Hello, Mrs. Andrews." She spied her friend. Alone. *Thank You, Jesus.*

"I told you to call me Lorma." The older lady clucked and her salt-and-pepper beehive hairdo wiggled. "I haven't seen you in a week."

"Well, my mom came to visit."

"That's wonderful."

"And I've been cleaning out the attic."

"Settling in. Good for you." Lorma patted her arm. "I want you to come for dinner tonight."

"Oh, I don't know."

"Yes, I insist. And bring your pup."

Lydia envisioned Gideon storming through the door, ready to pummel her sweet, quickly growing ball of fur. The same sweet thing that had chewed a hole in the carpet in the bedroom. The carpet, of all things. Thankfully, it had been in a perfect spot for an end table.

"I won't take no for an answer." Lorma lifted her eyebrows.

"Okay. What should I bring?"

"How 'bout one of your pies? I've had a hankering for another taste all week. You really should think of selling them."

Lydia's heart swelled to the point she thought it might burst. *The third person to say that this week.* Maybe God had a plan with her pies. She'd keep her eyes and ears open to what He showed her. Excitement welled inside her, not just at the thought of selling pies but also at the thought of totally surrendering every aspect of her life to God.

"I better get to the car before my ice cream melts." Lorma walked away with a wave. "I'll see you tonight. Five o'clock."

"Okay. Thanks, Lorma."

Lydia headed into the store. The drummer's rat-a-tat grew stronger. Oh, how she missed the coffeehouse she used to go to in Indianapolis. The quaint shop sold the best scones and muffins and the most delicious coffee. A sigh escaped her lips as she thought about it.

"Not feeling too well today?" the woman behind the deli asked.

Lydia forced a smile. "I'm fine. I just haven't had my morning coffee, and my head is throbbing."

"I understand that. My husband's job was relocated, but when we lived in Muncie, I used to visit the neatest coffee shop at least three times per week. This place was really unique; it was actually in a lady's home. A really nice old Victorian-type house..."

The woman continued to chatter for several minutes longer. The pounding in Lydia's brain grew louder, and she could focus on nothing except coming up with a polite way to end the conversation.

"...and the woman who owned the place made the most amazing pies."

Lydia perked up, forcing the drummer to take a moment's reprieve. "Really?"

"Oh, yes."

"I really miss that coffee shop." The woman wiped her gloved hands against her apron front. "Oh well. Is there anything I can get for you?"

Lydia got some chicken and tuna fish salads then continued on her way through the store. The woman's words replayed in Lydia's mind. *God, could this be something I could do? Show me, Lord.*

After grabbing her final item, a gallon of milk, Lydia headed for the check-out aisle.

"Ouch."

Lydia gasped as she pulled her cart away from a pair of well-worn jeans. "I'm so sorry." She looked up.

It was Gideon.

Of course.

❧

"Hello, Lydia." Gideon couldn't help but take in the oversized polka-dot-and-striped pants and not-so-matching T-shirt. To anyone else, she must have appeared worse than what the cat dragged in, as Mama always said when his sisters tried to wear the grunge look to school. To him, she looked adorable.

"Oh, hey." She pushed a curl behind her ear. Another endearing motion he'd noticed she did quite often.

"Getting some groceries, I see."

"A few." Lydia picked up a scandal magazine, opened it, gasped, and put it back on the rack.

He could tell she tried to avoid talking to him. No doubt because she probably *had* just rolled out of bed. He had to bite back a chuckle. He never knew what to expect from Lydia. She was totally different from any woman he'd ever met. She was completely Lydia, and no one else.

"Did you have a good visit with your mom?"

She looked at her nails. "It was fine."

"Good. I take it for granted that I get to see my mom every day."

She nodded. She still wouldn't look at him. He found her enchanting, over-the-top endearing. He just wanted to scoop her up and tickle a hearty laugh out of her. Why tickle her, he wasn't sure, but that's exactly what he wanted to do.

"Did you find them okay?" Maria's voice interrupted his thoughts.

Gideon looked toward the entrance to the store and nodded. With his peripheral vision, he noticed Lydia saw Maria, as well.

"You've been in here a while." Maria's eyes still flitted with anxiousness from the last few hours they'd spent at the hospital. Despite the need of twenty stitches in his thumb, the doctor assured them Jeremy had *luckily* missed the nerves and wouldn't need surgery. Gideon called *luck* by the name of God. Maria glanced back out the door. "I just wasn't sure if you knew where to look."

"I got 'em." Gideon held up the package of Spiderman Band-Aids.

"Okay, I'm going back to the car with the boys." Maria waved and walked out of the store.

Gideon looked back at Lydia. A stunned expression wrapped her face. She almost appeared hurt. "Her dad works for me. Her son was hurt. I had to take him to the hospital."

She nodded, but her demeanor had changed.

Once again, Gideon felt like a heel. He knew Lydia thought there was something between him and Maria. Really, there wasn't, but he just couldn't decide if there should be. It was Lydia who made his heart beat faster, Lydia who put a smile on his face. But Maria needed him. Kelbe and Jeremy needed a dad. Jim had always been good to Gideon, and the older man remained convinced that God had Gideon picked out as Maria's next husband. In truth, if Lydia hadn't moved to Danville, Gideon probably would have started dating Maria. She was a really nice Christian lady with great kids. But was she what Gideon wanted?

Maybe I'm just a selfish man. Scripture tells us to take care of widows and those less fortunate.

A slight tightness formed in his heart. *Remember Mama's CD. Look at Galatians.*

Show me, God.

A peace settled in his spirit as a scripture floated through his mind. God was talking to Moses when he feared going back to Egypt. Moses didn't know what to say as to who sent him. "I am who I am," God answered. Without a doubt in his heart, Gideon knew "I am" would guide him to a right decision.

270

Chapter 5

Lydia rolled the dough Lorma had made from scratch for the dumplings. Lorma stood over the sink picking chunks of meat off the cooked chicken. Rolling the pin over the dough one last time, Lydia knew it was smooth enough to cut noodles, but she wasn't sure of the necessary consistency for dumpling dough. "My grandma used to make chicken and noodles, but I've never had chicken and dumplings."

Lorma looked at the dough on the table. "Fold it up and roll it back out a couple more times, if you don't mind."

"Okay." Lydia began to do as she was told.

"Dumplings are what we always made back in Pike County. You can make them from canned biscuits or Bisquick, but I always like to make them myself." She turned and winked. "Gideon likes them that way."

Warmth flooded Lydia's face, and she brushed the back of her hand against one cheek in an attempt to hide the blush she knew had formed. "I don't know where Pike County is."

"Eastern Kentucky."

"My sister and her family live in Kentucky."

"Really. Where about?"

"Lawrenceburg. She has her own dental practice."

"Well, Pike County's a good ways southeast of your sister." Lorma stopped picking at the chicken and looked outside the kitchen window. "I'd love for you to meet our family."

"I would, too. You have seven kids. . ."

"Eight. My oldest, Sabrina, has three boys. All almost grown. My next girl, Natalie, has three girls. Kylie's after that with an adopted boy and girl and a biological daughter. Amanda's taken over the group with a set of twin boys and five girls. My first son, Dalton, has four sons and a daughter. Gideon's next. Of course you know he doesn't have any children. Then there are my twins, Cameron and Chloe. Chloe's been married a little over a year; no children yet. Cameron, like Gideon, still hasn't found his bride."

"Wow." Lydia held both hands in the air trying to count her fingers. "I lost count of your grandchildren."

"Twenty-one grandchildren all together—ten boys and eleven girls. And I still have three children who don't have any." Lorma clicked her tongue. "The Lord sure has blessed us."

"Can you imagine all those people on this farm?" Lydia envisioned Gideon the first time she met him, when he was mad at George for making a mess. She couldn't even wrap her mind around the chaos of twenty-one children, and she hadn't done the math to figure out how many adults were in that combination Lorma spoke of.

"It's pure heaven. They're coming for the Fourth of July. You'll have to come eat with us and watch the fireworks. My boys put on quite a display."

"I'd love to." Lydia giggled, as heaven was not the scenario her mind had created. Remembering Gideon's response to her puppy ruining his peaches, Lydia wondered what Gideon acted like when his family came to visit. "So, do they all live in Pike County?"

"Oh, no, we moved from there years and years ago. Five of my kids live in southern Indiana. Chloe and Cameron live in Muncie, and of course, Gideon lives here in Danville. Enough about my brood." Lorma washed her hands then wiped them on a dish towel. She sat beside Lydia at the table, pulled off a piece of the dough, and rolled it between her palms. "Like this." She placed the ball on flour-covered wax paper. "Tell me about this coffee and pie shop idea."

Lydia's heart beat faster with excitement. "It's still a rough idea. Maybe you can help me with some of the kinks. I thought of sectioning off part of Grandma's house and making it a coffee room of sorts. I could sell different coffees and make homemade pies."

"Hmm. Who would want to come? Who are you really gearing your place to suit?"

Lydia hadn't thought of that. Who was she targeting? Well, people her age loved to go to coffee shops to socialize with friends and work on assignments for college. But she also wanted to open her shop up to senior ladies who wanted to spend time together. Maybe mothers who needed a few hours without the kids. Hmm. It proved a lot to think about.

"Do you want to focus mainly on women, or men, too? How will you fund opening it? What long-range plans do you have?"

Lorma's questions swirled inside Lydia's head. So much to think about. She needed a pad and pen to jot down some ideas. Needed to find out where to go for financial numbers. How would she plan?

"Lorma, will you help me?"

The older woman's eyes twinkled, and the crow's-feet on their outer side seemed to dance when she smiled. "I'd love to help you." She leaned over the table. "I took some business classes at a tech school right after Richard passed away. My kids didn't know about it." She giggled like a schoolgirl. "I'd love the opportunity to put some of that knowledge to work."

"Perfect, I—"

"And your pies. You've got to make those scrumptious apple pies as the shop's specialty."

Lydia sat back, relishing Lorma's excitement. God was already confirming what He had in mind for her life.

⌘

God's not showing me anything. Gideon kicked a small branch across one of the orchard's paths. His trees were doing beautifully. The weather had been exceptional for apple growing; even his peach trees had produced better than he'd anticipated. The treatments had taken well; no signs of disease or insect infestation. This year would probably be the best ever in terms of his crops.

So far it had been the worst in terms of his personal life.

He was sick to death of listening to Jim hint about Maria's need for a husband. He'd become equally disgusted that no matter how much time he spent with the woman, no matter how many times he witnessed her kindness toward her children, him, and his mother, he still had no feelings for her whatsoever.

Several times he'd reconciled himself to forging ahead and talking with Maria, dismissing the way he felt completely. After all, didn't the Bible say the heart is deceitful above all things? Then Lydia's face would pop into his mind, and he'd be flustered like an old mother hen all over again.

If only that woman had stayed in Indianapolis.

Maybe that was the answer to his qualms. He just needed to keep himself good and aggravated with her. Then he wouldn't think about her sky blue eyes and never-ending, ripened-peach-colored curls.

Stop it, man. He pulled a partially broken twig off a nearby tree and tossed it to the ground. That kind of thinking was not going to help him.

Walking toward the house, he spotted George. The scamp was digging a hole the size of the Grand Canyon beside the shed. A perfect hole for Gideon to step into and break his leg when he tried to get out the weed trimmer. Great, Lydia was visiting.

Well, it appears she hasn't looked at the books I bought her. Gideon snapped his fingers, and the pup looked up at him. George's tail wagged rapidly as he raced toward Gideon. *That's a good idea. If I stay aggravated with her, maybe I'll get her off my mind.* He scooped the dog into his hand and bounded toward the house. After hooking George's collar back on the leash, he stomped the dirt off his boots. Determined to see Lydia as just a pretty woman who'd become a friend to his mom, he pushed open the front door.

Lydia was rolling dumplings beside his mother. The light from the kitchen window shone around her, making her look like an angel delivered from heaven to grace his kitchen.

He growled. *Yeah, she's just a pretty woman. Nothing more.*

❧

Lydia sucked in her breath when Gideon walked into the kitchen. She hadn't meant to. In truth, she didn't know why the man had such an effect on her. His hair lay in a mess on top of his head. His stubble, definitely more than a day old, practically covered his cheeks and chin, even his throat. He'd look like a burly mountain man if it weren't for the fact he was actually quite lean in his build, except for his broad shoulders. She squinted, trying to decipher how his eyes looked today.

Realizing he knew exactly what she was doing, Lydia averted her gaze back to the dumplings and puckered her lips. With terrific effort, she managed not to rebuke herself out loud, but she had no idea if pink covered her cheeks. It probably did.

"George got off his leash again."

Lydia glanced back at Gideon. He'd turned away from them. His voice sounded gruff, more like it had the first day she'd met him. Obviously, he didn't like her dog. Either that or he found her totally inept at taking care of George. "Sorry." Her voice cracked, and she inwardly berated herself for being so wimpy and so stinking attracted to the grouch.

Gideon opened the refrigerator, grabbed a pop, and then shut the door. "He dug a huge hole in front of my shed."

Lydia stood. "I'll go fix—"

"You just sit right down." Lorma grabbed her hand. "Dogs are supposed to dig holes."

"Still, I'll—"

"Sit."

Lorma pointed to the chair, and Lydia couldn't help but obey. She loved the maternal ways of the older woman. She'd missed them since Grandma died.

"Listen here, my grumpy son." Lorma pointed toward the open chair beside her.

"I'm not grumpy."

"Oh yes, you are," Lorma said. "But that's beside the point. I want to tell you about Lydia's business. We've been planning it all afternoon."

Lydia watched Gideon's eyebrows raise just a hair. He seemed interested in what she planned to do. For some reason, that really pleased her. She listened while Lorma shared the plans they'd made. As discreetly as possible, she watched Gideon's expressions. She wondered what an orchard owner—a man who worked with his hands day in and day out—would think about a quaint little coffee shop.

"I've already told her she can have all the apples she needs free of charge this year." Lorma patted Gideon's hand. "She'll come pick them, of course, but you'll need to haul them over to her house."

Lydia watched as Gideon's eyebrows formed a slight frown. Her heart raced as she imagined his thoughts. She hadn't expected Lorma to offer free apples, and in truth, Lydia had never agreed to take them. She figured she'd pay Gideon when it came time to purchase fruit.

"And she needs the rooms fixed up a bit." Lorma went on. "I told her that I knew you wouldn't mind helping."

Gideon's frown deepened, and he looked down at his hands.

She hadn't requested his help either. That was Lorma's idea. She would never presume upon someone else to do her manual labor for her. If Gideon did help, she intended to pay him. Of course, she wouldn't be able to tell Lorma that.

Gideon cleared his throat. "You shouldn't go offering someone's help when you haven't asked. . ."

Lydia sat up straight in the chair. Hackles raised on the back of her neck. "I think I'll be all right on my own, Lorma." She was not a beggar. She would not force anyone to help her do anything. "And I insist I pay for any apples I need. I can always go to another orchard. . ."

"I'll not hear of it." Lorma placed her hand on her chest. "You are our friend, and we'll do whatever needs to be done to help a friend. Right, Gideon?"

Lydia looked at Gideon. He still stared at his hands. "It's a bad idea."

"You see. . ." Lorma smiled at Lydia then snapped back at Gideon. "What?"

Gideon stood and walked toward the door. "She can have all the apples you want her to have, but it's a bad idea."

"It's not a bad idea." Lorma shook her head, looked at Lydia, and pulled off another piece of dough. "And we'll be glad to help."

Lydia had to force herself not to glare at Gideon. It obviously wasn't settled in his mind. A bad idea, huh? *He thinks I'm incapable.* A silly, flighty girl who doesn't have what it takes to be a business owner. He had no faith in her. He proved no better than her mother. The thought of it weighed down on her chest. Inhaling deeply, she lifted her chin and pulled off another chunk of dough. Well, he didn't need his help. She didn't even need his apples. If it weren't for Lorma, she'd grab her purse and her pup and head out of there.

Why had she ever thought Gideon Andrews attractive to begin with? He was nothing more than an overgrown grump!

Chapter 6

Pulling off the plastic wrap covering the fireworks his brother-in-law had just given him, Gideon walked into the house. He put the evening's display in a container and snapped the lid. They would stay locked in his room and out of the way of the children until dusk.

Making his way downstairs, he listened to his sisters, Kylie and Sabrina oohing and aahing over Lydia's apple pie. He peeked around the corner and saw Mama standing beside Lydia, every bit as proud of the young woman as if she were her own daughter.

Why does Lydia have to be so cute? Maybe he wouldn't be so enamored with her if her curls didn't flow past her shoulders like a waterfall and if her eyes didn't battle the sky on a clear day for beauty.

Sabrina pinched off a piece of Lydia's piecrust and popped it into her mouth. Her eyes widened. "Lydia, you'll make a fortune selling these."

He watched as Lydia's cheeks darkened. Her blushes were almost irresistible to him. Every time pink spread across her face, he itched to kiss its warmth. *And the woman blushes at least once every time I see her.*

"Lorma's planning the shop with me." Lydia pushed a strand of hair behind her ear. "Your mom has a lot of business sense."

Gideon bit back a snort. The shop idea was simply ludicrous. Danville didn't have a large enough population to support such a shop. How many people would want or have the time to sit in someone's actual house and pay for coffee and pie? It made no sense to him.

But Mama remained all for it. Now, she'd not only invited Lydia to their family Fourth of July supper, but Jim, Maria, and Maria's boys, as well. If he didn't enjoy spending this limited time with his nieces and nephews so much he'd be upstairs in his room with some kind of stomach bug.

Glancing out the kitchen window, he saw Natalie and her husband and three girls pull into the driveway. An escape. Gideon darted out the back door and ran to his sister's car. He hugged his sister and each of her girls then shook hands with Natalie's husband.

"Are we going to play football?" Natalie's ten-year-old, Tabby, asked.

Gideon leaned down and pinched her chin. "You think you're big enough to take on your Uncle Gideon this year?"

276

She giggled, stuck out her chin, and nodded her head. "Oh yeah. You're going down this year."

"You and what army's going to get me down?"

"We're the army, Uncle Gideon."

Gideon turned and saw two of Amanda's older girls and Kylie's daughters all racing toward him.

"Get him!" they screamed in unison.

Before Gideon could prepare a defense, the four girls and Tabby jumped on his legs and back. Hands covered his stomach, his shoulders, and his legs in an effort to tackle him. Staying upright appeared the best way to ensure no one was smashed when he fell, but the girls had gotten bigger and stronger over the last year.

"I think they're actually going to get him down!" Natalie's thirteen-year-old, Terri, exclaimed. "I'm in this time."

Gideon took a deep breath and gritted his teeth. Now it was a matter of pride. He couldn't allow his girly nieces to force him to the ground. He'd stand strong no matter how many of them. . .

His foot slid a bit in the dirt.

No problem. With the strength of a determined mule, he slid it back in place. "Aha, charge!"

This came from one of the nieces who was not currently attached to his body. Another girl who had grown quite considerably in the last year, Gideon noted. One of Amanda's, if he heard the voice correctly.

Before he could analyze further, he felt the impact of the stringy, yet unbelievably strong body hanging from his shoulders on his back. If it was the last thing he did, he would not budge.

A quick peek at the house exposed six women—four sisters, his mother, and Lydia—watching the show. Five of the six were doubled over in laughter. Lydia stood still, gripping the porch post with one hand, the other placed over her heart as if she were saying the pledge of allegiance. The utter shock and wide-eyed expression suggested she had never seen anything like this in her life.

How many girls did he have hanging onto his body? He started to count. *Let's see, two clung to one leg. . .*

His knee started to give. With more strength than Superman, he popped it back into its straightened position.

One on his other leg. One dangled from his back. Two had wrapped themselves around his waist. Surely, they were uncomfortable. Probably doing more damage to each other than to him.

But Gideon Andrews would not budge.

"This year, Uncle Gideon, you're going down."

Gideon turned and looked eye-to-eye with his oldest niece, fifteen-year-old Tilly. She held his youngest niece, Amanda's poor, innocent two-year-old, on her hip. He glanced beside her. The last three of his nieces—the ones who weren't already attached to his legs—smiled with the most ornery, mischievous smiles he'd ever seen in his life.

"Charge!" Tilly yelled.

This can't be good.

The remaining five joined the six. Girlish squeals sounded all around him. Hands and feet picked and kicked from every angle. Before he had a chance to take another breath, his right foot slipped in the dirt and his left knee buckled.

He hit the ground.

Twenty-two hands, twenty-two feet, and eleven girls jumped off him and into the air in triumph. They had grounded their up-to-now undefeated uncle.

He looked at Lydia and sheepishly shrugged his shoulders. "First year they got me."

Lydia had never seen so many people climb on one person in her life. The grin that never left Gideon's face was proof of his love for those girls. The women around her burst into cheers when Gideon hit the ground. A bit hard, she feared, but no one seemed distressed, so she didn't say anything.

"That was worth the drive." The last sister to arrive handed a casserole dish to Kylie and kissed Lorma on the cheek.

Lorma turned to Lydia. "Lydia, this is Natalie. Natalie, Lydia."

Lydia shook hands with the woman. All of Gideon's sisters were exceptionally attractive. Lydia, with her face splattered with an innumerable number of freckles, felt yet another moment of self-consciousness.

"It's so good to finally meet you." Natalie wrapped her arms around Lydia. "Mama's talked nonstop about you every time I call. It's about time I can put a face to the name."

Lydia forced her mouth to grin. This family proved amazingly kind, but just as amazingly overwhelming. Never in her life had she been around so many people, especially so many children. Mother's incessant manners kicked in, and Lydia found her tongue. "I'm happy to meet you, as well."

Natalie studied her for a moment. Lydia pushed a stray hair away from her face and noted an ant crawling up the porch post.

"Overwhelming, huh?" Natalie's voice stayed low enough that only Lydia heard her.

Lydia looked back up at the woman she knew had to be more than a decade older than herself, and still Natalie looked as if she'd just finished college. "In a good way."

Natalie wrapped her arm around Lydia's shoulder and squeezed. "Definitely in a good way. You'll miss us before you know it."

Warmth washed through Lydia as she realized this family exuded everything she'd wanted growing up. She'd experienced a good deal of love and acceptance with Grandma, but her mom and sister. . . Well, Lydia was just never as "good" at things as they were.

When Allison tried out for cheerleading, she'd not only made the team, she'd become captain. When she joined the Students Against Drunk Driving club, she'd become the president. When she'd gone to college, she'd made a 4.0, even tested out of her first biology class.

Mom was even more distinguished. Top lawyer in her firm. Running for state office. There was no doubt in Lydia's mind she'd win. On top of her career, she'd been PTA Treasurer, an author of a self-help book, and more.

Lydia could not keep up. Deep down, she'd never really even wanted to.

Looking at all Gideon had been blessed with in his life and having discovered Christ as a personal Savior and intimate friend, she wanted contentment and peace—the kind only He could give—and quietness and assurance that could only be found when she spent time with her Father.

The world looked so different. She watched as a good bunch of the children played football. One of the older girls held the youngest boy, handing him an animal cracker with a free hand. Two of the smaller boys chased a bug of some kind in the grass. Most of the men stood beside the shed talking. She looked in the door at most of the women bustling over the food.

This family seemed different, too, and she was excited to get to know them.

She looked back into the yard. Gideon held a small boy in his arms. The dark-haired child couldn't have been more than three. An older version of the boy stood beside Gideon, holding onto Gideon's pant loop. The gorgeous woman from the store stood just a few feet in front of him.

Embarrassed to be staring but unable to look away, Lydia watched as the smaller boy held up his thumb in front of Gideon's face. Gideon grimaced as he kissed the boy's bandaged finger. The older boy said something, and Gideon looked down at him and smiled.

Something flew near the woman's face. She swatted it away. Even when she scrunched her face at the insect, she still looked beautiful. The bug flew toward Gideon and the smaller boy. The boy squirmed in Gideon's hand, but Gideon held him tight. The woman swatted the bug away from Gideon's hair above his ear.

She swatted again, and Lydia felt her heart collapse into her stomach.

"She's quite a beautiful woman."

Lydia gasped and placed her hand on her chest. She smiled at Gideon's youngest sister, Chloe. "You scared me."

Chloe nodded toward the woman. "Her name is Maria. She's a widow."

Lydia tried to look around at the other people playing and talking in the yard. They seemed to blur together, and Lydia willed herself not to shed a single tear at this happy gathering.

Chloe continued. "I think her mother was a catalog model when she was young." Chloe pointed to the men in front of the shed. "Jim, Maria's dad, he's one of Gideon's workers. He and his wife sure did have some really beautiful kids. I've seen pictures of Maria's sister. . .before she passed away in a car accident."

Lydia frowned and looked Chloe in the eye. "That must have been terrible for them."

"Yeah. Maria was pretty young, if I'm remembering right." Chloe looked up at the sky. "It's going to be a beautiful night. Perfect for fireworks."

Lydia gazed at the heavens. The sky was gorgeous—shades of blue and purple hung toward the ground while veins of pink and white adorned the middle. As Lydia lifted her eyes all the way above her head, she noted the mild blue above her. A single star dotted the sky as well as the white tracks of an aircraft of some kind. "You're right."

"You wouldn't know this, but I know my brothers better than any of my sisters do."

Lydia tore her gaze from God's natural beauty and looked back at the woman she'd met only hours before. "What?"

"You see, my parents had my four sisters, two of my brothers, then me and Cameron. Well, the girls never wanted to play with the little baby, so I always ended up with the boys."

"I see." Lydia nodded her head, but she had no idea why Chloe was telling her this.

"Since I always had to tag along with the boys, I became quite a tomboy. Got to the point where none of them could beat me at soccer, and I was a great opponent to practice with at any of their other sports." She leaned closer. "Even though they did usually beat me."

Lydia furrowed her brows. She had no idea where any of this was going. She could tell the women were doing a lot of moving in the kitchen, and Lydia hated not to help out the very first day she met them. The last thing she wanted was for Lorma and her daughters to think Lydia wasn't willing to help.

"He doesn't care about her."

"What?" Lydia stared at Chloe. "Who doesn't care about who?"

Chloe pointed at Gideon. "He may want to care about her. Gideon is about the kindest, sweetest guy on the planet, but Maria is not the woman he's after."

"It makes no difference to me." Lydia shifted her weight and crossed her arms in front of her chest. "I'm here because your mom is my friend. It's got nothing to do with Gideon."

"That's too bad." Chloe kicked a rock off the porch. "'Cause you're the one he cares about." She leaned close and whispered. "He's just not ready to admit it yet."

Lydia looked back at Gideon, Maria, and the boys. The scene was endearing, a perfect Norman Rockwell picture. They looked like the cutest family ever. It made Lydia sick to her stomach, but how could Chloe get "he likes you" out of the scene that Lydia was seeing.

"Hey, can you keep a secret?" Chloe stepped closer. "After the fireworks, I'm going to tell the family I'm expecting. You'll get to see Mama flip."

Lydia hugged her new friend and watched as she escaped into the house. For the briefest of moments, Lydia glanced back at Gideon. He looked up at her and smiled. Her heart sped as she turned and moved back into the kitchen. If only Chloe knew him as well now as she did when they were kids. Lydia had a feeling a lot had changed since Chloe had the inside scoop.

Chapter 7

Gideon hefted the box containing the metal utility shelves and placed it in the shopping cart. He rubbed his aching forearms. The load had been heavier than he'd anticipated.

"Let's see." Maria bent over the cart and read the side of the box. "It says we need a Phillips screwdriver. I'm not sure if I have one."

"I do. We'll run by my house and get it before heading over to your apartment."

Maria blinked, causing long lashes to swipe her cheek. Her smile remained sincere, yet purposeful in a way he didn't like. "I really appreciate your help." She touched the top of his hand, and he politely pulled away, shoving it in his front pocket. "I know Dad can be. . ."

Gideon couldn't help but inhale a long breath at the mention of Maria's dad. Jim had practically insisted Gideon help Maria pick up utility shelves for her apartment. Supposedly, his worker had come down with some kind of illness, even though he was as healthy as a fresh-picked apple the day before.

In truth, Gideon didn't mind helping Maria. But now she was putting pressure on him. Her stance had changed, and Gideon knew Jim was no longer the only one who wanted a ring on Gideon's finger.

"Gideon."

Gideon snapped from his thoughts and looked at Maria. Both hands were planted firmly on her hips. *I have got to start paying better attention.* "Sorry, did you say something?"

"I said we'll need to get a move on because Dad needs me to pick up the boys by five."

That was another thing that grated on Gideon's nerves. Jim felt too sick to help his daughter but well enough to care for two rambunctious boys. It was one thing to help Maria; it was another to be made to feel guilty for having not married her yet. And Gideon had just about had enough.

He might even be able to form feelings for her if he felt he could do it on his own. Widows should be cared for, the Bible said so specifically, but Gideon was still a man, and he still wanted to be the one pursuing a relationship.

"Gideon!"

A familiar voice sounded from the back of the store. He turned and saw his mother pushing a cart toward them. Her high bun shifted left to right with each step. A smile lit her face as she peered over the rim of her glasses at him.

Wearing a pair of athletic capris and matching T-shirt, Lydia walked beside her. She gave a quick wave then looked back at the slips of paper in her hands. Curls framed her face as she had her hair in two long pigtails. He hadn't seen anyone's hair fixed like that since he was a young teen. Lydia looked every bit like a young, bubbly girl.

He chewed on the inside of his mouth. *She's the reason I'm having trouble forming feelings for Maria.* "What are you doing here?" Gideon asked. Out of the corner of his eye, he noticed Maria's demeanor and expression had changed in a way he'd never seen before. The woman looked like a mountain lion ready to attack at a moment's provocation.

"We're picking out colors for the coffee room." Mama pointed to the color swatches Lydia held. "She's pretty sure she wants to go with a warm—"

"You're still thinking about that?" Gideon looked from his mother to Lydia.

"Yes." Lydia seemed to have stood up a bit more, and she focused fully on him.

"Have you talked to anyone about cost, about interest, anything? You know starting a business is not as easy—"

"Thank you for your concern." Lydia looked at his mother. "But Lorma and I have done a lot of research and—"

"Gideon is right." Maria's voice sounded more like a purr. Gideon glanced toward her and realized she'd nudged her way closer to him. "He knows a lot more about these—"

"Hogwash." Mama swatted the air. "Gideon doesn't know the research we've done." She grabbed Gideon's arm and pulled him toward her. "Now, we're down to these two colors. Which do you like?"

"Mama, I'm not picking out paint for a coffeehouse that I think you're rushing into." He sneaked a peek at Lydia. Her lips pinched so tight he worried they'd get stuck that way. The glare in her eyes exposed the anger brewing behind them.

He bit back a sigh. He wasn't trying to be discouraging. If they'd give him half a chance, he just wanted to be sure she knew what she was getting into. Opening a business took a lot of work and determination. It took a lot of long-range planning and a willingness to stick with it through the hard times. He studied Lydia for a moment. *I'm just not sure she's thought through the long haul.*

Mama clicked her tongue, forcing him from his thoughts. "Don't be ridiculous. Just choose a color."

Gideon grabbed the color swatches from her hands. "Mama, you two are moving too fast."

"Excuse me." Lydia took the palettes from him. "It's my coffee shop. If you don't want to share a preference, that's fine."

"Have you spoken with anyone besides my mom? What about start-up costs and building permits and—"

"You don't think I'm smart enough to have thought of that?" Mama's expression fell. "You don't know that I took a few business classes after your father passed away."

Now he'd hurt his mother's feelings, and he didn't know she'd attended classes, but they still needed more advice, more guidance. "Mama, I never said you weren't smart. You're one of the most intelligent women I know." The expressions on Mama's and Lydia's faces proved they were done listening. He was making a mess of this.

Mama fidgeted with the front of her sweater. Practically dismissing him, she turned toward Lydia. "Well, he'll still help you paint, Lydia."

"You're helping her paint?" Maria's voice sounded strained, and Gideon turned toward her. A moment of fury flashed across her face and was quickly shaded with a sweet smile. "I love to paint. I'll be glad to help."

Gideon looked back at Lydia, whose face had shifted through various shades of red. He noted the mutilated color swatches in her hands.

"Thank you, but I don't mind doing it myself," Lydia spit through gritted teeth.

Guilt weighed fresh on his heart. He wasn't trying to be an ogre about opening the business; he just knew how hard it was. He'd never had a chance to sit with Lydia and tell her why he was afraid for her to start it. Whether he agreed with it or not, he was willing to help her. "I said I'd help paint, Lydia." He touched her arm and ignored the slight gasp that escaped from Maria. "I will help you."

"Then it's settled." Maria clapped her hands and smiled. "We're having a paint party at Lydia's."

Gideon sighed, wishing he'd be the only one in attendance. He and Lydia needed to talk.

✑

Who did Gideon Andrews think he was? For that matter, who did he think she was? Obviously, he viewed her as incompetent. He proved no better than her mother. At least her mother had known Lydia all her life. She smacked her hand against her kitchen cabinets. This. . .this man was making judgments about her, and he barely knew her.

She grabbed a pop from the refrigerator. Sure, she tended to be a bit on the flighty side. Sitting at the table, she took a drink of the caffeinated beverage. Okay, so she'd had more jobs than she could count on both hands. So she'd taken more classes than the average person with a degree. In truth, she'd taken so many she could have a master's degree if she'd stuck with a single program. She couldn't deny she had no experience running a business and that she relied heavily on the advice of a woman she'd met only weeks before. And if she chose to be honest, she had to acknowledge that she'd spent every penny of the money she'd received from her grandmother's will and still taken out a chunk of the money she'd worked so hard to save over the years.

"Who am I kidding?" She pulled the rubber bands from her hair and raked her fingers through her tangled locks. "This is just another one of Lydia's crazy ideas. Another ridiculous notion at trying to find my niche."

She rested her elbows on the table and peered at the expansive land behind Grandma's house. "Why can't I just be stable? Content?"

Miles of lush green land swayed with the wind beyond her grandmother's expansive flower garden. Wildflowers and various weeds laced the green with purple, yellow, and red. Trees, lush and enormous, stood proudly reaching for the heavens. Some were in clusters, while others made their statements by standing alone. A row of electric poles trailed down the land, and she could see a few homes dotting the distance.

Gideon's orchard, full and healthy, lined the far right. She could see only a small part of it. To her left were rows and rows of corn. Grandma's land fell between the orchard and the corn rows. Beyond the yard, the land hadn't been cultivated. It exhibited the beauty God had originally given it.

Emotion overwhelmed her as scripture she'd read not too long ago flooded her spirit. Jesus had said something about if God could dress the lilies to be as pretty as they were, how much more would He take care of her.

A strong compulsion to be in the very presence of the majesty her God had created spurred Lydia to leave the table and walk out the back door. She strolled past the beauty Grandma had arranged and into the bounty of God's craftsmanship. Inhaling the fresh scent and welcoming the soft kisses of the wind, Lydia lifted her face to the heavens. White clouds spread across the blue as if God were making taffy of them. The day would be exceptionally warm if not for the breeze.

Closing her eyes, she allowed the picture she enjoyed to repaint itself in her mind. "Oh, Jesus." His name slipped from her lips, just above a whisper. Chirping birds and talking insects paid her no mind and continued their communications with one another. "I have no doubt of Your love for me. I have no doubt You will provide for my needs. It's me I doubt."

Tears slipped from her eyes, and she swiped them away with the back of her hand. Opening her eyes again, she noted two birds dancing with one another in the air. They made their way toward a cluster of trees and were soon out of sight.

"But I dwell within You."

The Spirit's soft pricking warmed her heart. "'I can do everything through him who gives me strength.'" The scripture spilled from her lips.

"But is this what I'm supposed to do, Lord? What if I get tired of it?" She gazed back at the heavens. "You know I don't have the best track record when it comes to sticking with what I start."

"But I do."

"'He who began a good work in you will bring it to completion.'" The verse, though not verbatim, slipped through her lips and she smiled. God hadn't spoken to her audibly, but He'd spoken to her heart, and she couldn't deny Him.

Bending down, she snipped several wildflowers from the earth's carpet. Studying the various petals and intricate combinations of colors, she could never doubt that her all-knowing Father took great pride in the intricacies of His works.

And that included her.

He cared about the ins and outs of her life. He cared about her flightiness, about her doubts. He'd formed her just the way He wanted, and He would see her through any task. Day to day. Moment to moment.

Even this.

⌘

"We're here."

Lydia barely had time to check her mascara in the mirror before Maria's voice called from the front door. Lydia peeked around the corner, and Maria lifted the paintbrush and pan higher in the air. Maria acted cheerful and anxious to get started, but Lydia couldn't help but wonder if that had more to do with the man standing beside her and less to do with a desire to assist Lydia.

Lydia opened the door for Gideon and Maria. She noted Gideon's stoic silence in direct contrast to Maria's exaggerated praises over the house. Lydia lifted her chin. She didn't need Gideon's approval. It was God she sought to please.

"Which room?" Gideon's noncommittal tone grated even more on Lydia's nerves. No one forced him to help her.

Gazing up at him, she noted the determined gleam in his eye. He wanted to complete the job quickly. Her irritation grew, and she decided not to argue with him about staying. *I won't worry about his attitude. I'll just thank You, God, for the help.*

"The parlor." Lydia pointed toward the kitchen. "It's just to the left of the kitchen."

Before Lydia could shut the door, Maria marched ahead, and Gideon and Lydia followed. Maria stopped just inside the door, and Lydia bumped into Gideon's back.

"Sorry." Lydia looked up at him. His expression softened, and Lydia found herself drowning in the depths of his eyes once again. The contrast of his sun-darkened skin with the lighter, sandy color of his stubble intrigued her. The mystery of their texture made her long to touch them.

"It's a bit small for a coffee shop." Maria snorted. "What do you think, Gideon?"

An icy glare crossed his gaze before he looked away from Lydia and into the parlor. "I have no opinion." He walked past Maria and placed the paint cans on the floor that Lydia had already covered with plastic. "I'm just here to paint."

Fury welled within Lydia. First of all, the room was not small. Second, if it weren't for the fact that she adored his mother, she'd kick him out of her house that very moment. Her attraction to him only made her more furious. She didn't want to touch his stubble; she wanted to yank the hairs off his face. *Okay, that's a bit dramatic, Lydia. Chill out a bit.*

He turned toward her and crossed his arms in front of his chest. "Where do I start?"

Lydia bit her lip. *Chill out a whole big bit.* She willed herself to stay calm and forced a smile to her lips. "Any wall would be fine." She knew her tone betrayed her feelings, but she didn't care. The man had no right to treat her this way.

The colors in Gideon's eyes seemed to swirl together as they had the first day she'd met him—the day he was angry with George. *Good. He can be just as huffy as he wants. Maybe he'll get mad enough he'll go home.*

"Gideon," Maria's sultry voice purred in such an obviously flirtatious way Lydia thought she'd lose her breakfast. "I can't pour the paint without making a mess. Will you help me?"

"Sure." Gideon's stance stiffened as he helped Maria with the paint.

Maria touched his arm possessively and glanced back at Lydia. A sly smile bowed her lips. Embarrassed that she'd been watching, Lydia looked away. What did she care if Maria flirted with Gideon? The man was more aggravating than a plantar wart.

She grabbed the other paint can and poured its contents into a second pan without the aid of the overgrown grump. Lydia had trouble believing Gideon was truly related to her sweet friend, Lorma. The quicker they could get this done, the quicker he and Maria could go home.

◈◈

The faster we can get this place painted, the faster we can leave. Gideon showed Maria how to use the roller for the third time. For a woman who said she knew how to paint, he sure had to do a lot of assisting. And it was getting on his last nerve.

What had happened to Maria? She used to be sweet and kind. He would have considered her a friend. Since Lydia moved to Danville, Maria had become a madwoman. She showed up at the orchards every day, to dinner almost every other night, and she needed more help fixing little things around her apartment than the place could hold.

Guilt nudged at his heart. Of course Maria needed help. She was a single mom with two active boys. In the past, he'd never once minded helping her. But she had changed. She didn't seem to just want his help. Her intentions had become evident in the last few weeks. What she didn't understand was that Gideon wanted to be the pursuer. He wanted to be able to get his head clear and figure out why Lydia just wouldn't leave his mind. He needed some answers from God, who had become overtly silent.

Gideon dipped his paintbrush back into the pan. Jim had become more insistent, as well. It had gotten to the point that he avoided his employee at all costs. Sometimes Gideon even neglected getting all his work completed.

Maria looked at him and pouted. "I think I need your help again."

Enough was enough. Gideon nodded toward a chair. "Why don't you take a rest? I really need to finish this."

By the soft gasp from Lydia and the ashen expression that wrapped Maria's face, he knew he had been too curt. Maria blinked several times and placed the roller in the tray. "I'm sor—"

"No, I'm sorry I snapped at you." *A heel. You're an overgrown heel.*

Lydia clapped her hands together. "You know what. I think it's time for a break. I've got some sliced meat in the fridge. Let's eat some lunch." She wrapped her arm around Maria's slouching frame and sneered back at him.

Gideon watched as the two made their way into the kitchen. *God, when did things get so complicated? Why aren't You answering me?*

He watched as Lydia pulled plates out of the dishwasher. She grabbed a loaf of bread off the counter. *It was when she moved here that everything went nuts. One small, pretty woman had turned his world upside down.*

Wiping his hands on his pants, he walked out of the kitchen. Both women looked at him. One in anguish. The other in frustration.

And it's not going to get better any time soon.

Chapter 8

Lydia wiped beads of perspiration from her forehead. With the beginning of August in sight, the weather had turned exceptionally hot. Even at midmorning, watering the flower gardens had become a sweaty experience. George, though still every bit the rascal he'd always been, was smart enough to find a lounging spot in the shade.

"I found it." Lorma burst through the back door waving a paper in her hand. George jumped up and raced over to her. "Stay down." She swatted him away. "I knew if I looked long enough I'd find the recipe." Having come over early that morning, Lorma had brought her box of recipes and scoured through the collection for one she wanted Lydia to try baking.

Lydia wiped her hands on the front of her pants. "Let's see it."

"Not with those filthy hands." Lorma held the sheet away from Lydia's grasp. Lydia laughed at how much she felt like one of Lorma's own children. God had given the relationship to Lydia after mourning the death of her grandma, and Lydia relished it. "It's my great-aunt's recipe for apple tarts. Since she passed away, I've never tasted any so good."

Lydia looked at the ingredients and directions, praying she could make them well enough to please her friend. "I'll give it a try."

"I can't wait to taste them." Lorma held the paper to her chest. "Are you almost finished out here? I thought we were going to talk about furniture, too."

Lydia couldn't hold back her chuckle. Her older friend proved every bit as excited about opening the coffee shop as Lydia, and in truth, Lorma had some wonderful ideas. "I am. Let me turn off the water hose."

Once the water stopped, Lydia and George followed Lorma into the parlor of the house. The fresh, spice-colored paint on the walls almost matched the color of the hardwood floors. "I hadn't thought about the floors when I picked out the color," Lydia admitted.

"I think it will look wonderful. You just need to get some darker furniture and pictures with darker frames." Lorma snapped her fingers. "Have you ever thought about putting up chair railing and painting the bottom half a darker color? You know, something the color of rich coffee?"

Lydia nodded her head. "That's a great idea. I think I'll buy some furniture first and see how it looks before I do anything else to the walls."

Lorma winked. "Smart girl. Gilley's Antique Mall has some really nice tables. Some are very original looking. You might be able to find a reasonably priced sofa, as well. I'll call Gideon and see if he can take an early lunch and run you over there."

Panic welled in her heart. The last person she wanted to see was Gideon. She shook her head. "No, no. Don't interrupt him. I can drive myself."

Lorma pulled out her cell phone. "Don't be silly. If you find something you want to buy, you'll need a truck to haul it back in." She lifted her hand. "Gideon, do you have time to take..."

Lydia grimaced and motioned toward the bathroom. After making her way to the "purple" room, she shut the door. Peering at her reflection in the mirror, she gripped the sides of the white pedestal sink. She loved Lorma, really, she did, but this whole let's-make-Gideon-and-Lydia-friends thing just wasn't working.

Never in her life had she felt so much aggravation with a man. He didn't support the coffee shop idea at all, yet Lorma continued to push it on him. And Maria? Well, that remained a whole different thing all together. The woman obviously had an attraction to Gideon. Lydia couldn't figure out Gideon's feelings, but she could still tell Maria felt a compulsion of some kind to prove Gideon belonged with her. *Well, she can have him.*

Even as the thought escaped her mind, Lydia sighed at the unmistakable attraction she felt for the man. He treated his mother like a treasure. His willingness to work hard was evident by just a glimpse at his home and orchard. She didn't doubt for a moment that he loved the Lord. *But I get on his nerves, that's for sure.*

A knock sounded at the door. The noise sent George into a chorus of barks. "You okay in there?" Lorma's voice held a hint of concern.

Lydia almost giggled. Lorma definitely treated her as if she were one of her own children. "I'm fine."

"Well, good. Hurry up. Gideon's going to be here in ten minutes."

Lydia gasped as she peered at her reflection. Ten minutes? She hadn't even run a brush through her hair let alone put on any makeup. *I've got to remember to be ready at all times when I'm with Lorma.*

She grabbed an oversized comb from the medicine cabinet and swept it through her curls. She pulled up her sides and bangs and clipped them on top of her head. Remembering the morning at the grocery store, she shrugged. "He's seen me look worse."

<hr />

Anxious to see Lydia, Gideon looked forward to taking her to Gilley's. Finally, he'd have the chance to talk to her about this business idea. He needed to let her know how hard it would be and how much commitment it would take. *I can't deny I'll enjoy spending a little time with her, as well.*

Mama, though her intentions were good, had never started a business. The two women were excited, but they needed some guidance. They needed to understand that their expectations might take years to come to fruition.

For that matter, Gideon wasn't convinced they ever would. Danville was a small community, and a coffee shop a few miles away from town would have a hard time thriving. People would never just "happen" upon Lydia's shop. They'd have to know about it and drive to her house to frequent it. *She's got to at least listen to me before she takes out any loans.*

Gideon pulled up to Lydia's house. Though he really didn't expect her to find a lot of stuff, he'd hitched the trailer to his truck just in case.

Mama and Lydia were already waiting outside. Lydia's long hair flowed down her back, but a clip held the front away from her face. Her blue eyes seemed to glow in the sunlight, and Gideon, once again, could not deny his attraction to her. No matter how many times he saw her, he never tired of it. At the orchards, at home, at night, he always yearned to see her again.

He jumped out of the cab and walked over to the passenger's side. After opening the door, he motioned inside. "Hop in, ladies."

Mama pointed to Lydia. "You're going to have to get in first. I can't sit on that hump in the middle."

Gideon watched as Lydia's face paled. He could see she hadn't anticipated sitting so close to him.

Mama shooed Lydia toward the door. "And you'll have to take me home before you head into town."

"What?" Gideon and Lydia asked in unison.

Lydia looked up, and her eyes met his for the briefest amount of time before she exhaled and looked away.

"Well, sure. I have to get lunch ready for you and Jim." She nudged Lydia. "Of course, you're invited, too."

Gideon noted Lydia's stance of discomfort and turned toward his mom. "Why don't we all eat at the Mayberry Café?"

Mama's eyebrows met in a frown. "Then who will feed Jim?"

"We can bring something back for him."

"That's silly. I already have leftover soup in the refrigerator. No sense in letting it go to waste. Just take me home."

"But, Lorma, I want you to help me pick out the furniture." Lydia's voice almost sounded like a whine as she hopped into the cab, her hesitance apparent as she scooted to the middle.

"Don't be silly. You've got a great eye." Mama jumped in beside her, knocking Lydia even closer to Gideon's side.

Gideon wanted to groan as he made his way to the driver's side and tried to get in without touching Lydia. An impossible feat. The poor woman sat sandwiched between his mother and him, and if Gideon didn't know any better, he'd believe Mama took up more room than necessary.

The engine growled to a start, and Mama started talking again. Gideon couldn't focus on anything she said. All he could think about was the softness of Lydia's arm rubbing against his. The floral scent of her hair tantalized his nostrils, and not for the first time, he wished he had the right to lean over and inhale his fill of her locks.

He pulled up to his house. Mama jumped out, and Lydia scooted over, all in one motion. "See you two in an hour or so."

Alone in the truck, Gideon contemplated how to approach the coffee shop subject without getting her riled. He didn't want to insult her again. A woman with her feathers ruffled never listened to reason. *Just spit it out.*

He sneaked at peek at her in the passenger's seat. She stared straight ahead. Her nose had the slightest upturn to it. He found it adorable. "Mind if we talk about your coffee shop?"

"Yes."

Gideon furrowed his brows. "Is that 'yes, we can talk about it' or 'yes, I mind.'"

"Yes, I mind."

Gideon gripped the steering wheel. Sneaking another peek, he noticed she still stared straight ahead. *Difficult woman.* "Well, I'd like to have my say just the same."

"Then, by all means."

"Are you being smart?"

Lydia's head snapped toward him. "Am I being smart?" She pointed to her chest. "You did not just say that to me. No one is asking you to help in my endeavor, so why does it matter to you?"

Because I care about you. . .too much. "Not true. Mama's asked me to help several times. Even now I'm helping."

Lydia lifted her finger to make a point then lowered it. "Your mom keeps doing that, and I. . .I don't know how to stop her."

Gideon laughed. "Mama is hard to handle, isn't she?" He pulled into Gilley's parking lot. "I bet this coffee shop is more her idea than yours."

"No, it's mine."

Gideon shut off the engine and turned toward her. "I'm not trying to be a pessimist. I just want to be sure you've checked into if enough people would be interested in a coffee shop. I'd hate for you to take out a loan and get permits if there's not a market. I don't want you to—"

Before he could finish, Lydia opened the door, hopped out, and shut it firmly behind her.

So much for trying to be diplomatic. Gideon grabbed his keys from the ignition and hopped out. She never looked back as he followed her into the antique mall.

They passed row after row of sofas, wingback chairs, and tables. Lydia never said a word.

Hardheaded woman. I wouldn't give her advice now if she paid me. Try to be a friend and she slams the door in a guy's face.

They passed a deep brown love seat that would look nice in the room.

I'm not even going to point that out to her. And I'm not going to help her discuss any prices either. Let her pay too much for all I care.

"I'm ready." Lydia headed toward the checkout desk.

"Didn't find anything you like?"

Lydia glared up at him. "No, I found some things." She smiled at the clerk. "I'd like to purchase the brown sofa, the two red wingback chairs, and both of the black breakfast tables and chairs. I'm fine with the total ticket price"—Lydia pointed toward another section—"if it also includes the throw pillows and the matching three-piece lighting set."

The clerk studied the total, chewing on her bottom lip. "You've added an awful lot of stuff to that."

"True. But the price shows I've purchased a substantial amount of furnishings."

The clerk thought another moment. "All right. Go get what you want."

As he and the clerk's teenage son packed one item after another out of the antique mall, Gideon still couldn't believe how well Lydia had negotiated. The clerk even threw in a few knickknacks for decorations.

Maybe there was more to Lydia than he realized.

Before he could ponder the notion, his cell phone rang. It was Mama.

⌘

Lydia still fumed. How much audacity did the man contain? She told him she didn't want to discuss her business with him, yet he wouldn't listen. He acted as if she were a child—an incompetent child. Quite frankly, she got enough of that from her mother.

And who told him she was taking out a loan? No one. Which is why he didn't know that she wasn't borrowing any money.

"That was Mama." Gideon clicked his cell phone shut. "Apparently, she spilled our lunch."

"What? Is she hurt?"

Gideon shook his head. "Apparently, she tripped on the mat and spilled soup all over the floor."

"What a mess. I hate it when I do stuff like that."

Gideon lifted one eyebrow, and Lydia inwardly reprimanded herself. He

293

already thought her incapable. She didn't want to give him more ammunition.

"She said for me to take you to the Mayberry Café."

"Oh, no." Lydia shook her head. "Just take me on home."

Gideon didn't say anything for several moments. Finally, Lydia peeked at him and found him staring at her. "You did really good back there."

Heat rushed to her cheeks. Though he didn't say it, she knew he meant her dealings at Gilley's. Swallowing hard, she willed her face not to darken. "Thanks."

"Let me take you to the café."

"No. It's fine. I have a lot to do at home."

"Okay, the truth is Mama said if I came home and hadn't treated you she wouldn't feed me for a week."

Lydia giggled, knowing Lorma had said just that. If she didn't know any better, she would believe the older woman was trying to fix them up. Lydia shook her head. Lorma remained just a sweet woman with a heart of gold. She didn't see Lydia as daughter-in-law material. The woman had simply adopted Lydia.

"Okay, but let it be known that I had mercy on you even though all you've wanted to do is lecture me." Lydia scrunched her nose. She didn't have to say the last part. Now he'd start in on her all over again.

"I really wasn't trying to stop you from opening the business. I just don't want to see you get hurt."

"Why?"

"I guess. . .I guess I care about you."

If Gideon cared about her, he had a funny way of showing it. Maybe it was a brotherly care. *Or maybe. . .* She shook her head. There could be no possible way the man cared for her in the manner her heart wanted. Besides, she'd spent the last several weeks trying to beat some sense into the obstinate organ.

Chapter 9

B one tired, physically and mentally, Gideon grabbed his Bible and headed for the orchard. He'd been wrestling with God for weeks over Maria and Lydia. It proved silly really, because Lydia had made it apparent she was most definitely not interested.

He trudged toward his favorite tree. Looking down at its trunk, he noted his body seemed to have imprinted itself in the worn base. Gideon found himself more comfortable leaning against that tree than sitting in most chairs.

He touched one of the small apples hanging from a branch. In just over a month, the tree would be filled with lush fruit. By its size and appearance, Gideon expected to have a good year. Economically, this year, it appeared, would be his best.

Yet he felt so disconnected from God.

He lowered himself to his favorite spot and rested the Bible against his chest. Allowing the summer's warm breeze to sweep over him, he watched a bee buzz from one clover to the next. He allowed the serenity of God's creation to wrap him in its soft embrace. It had been too long since he'd sat silently and listened for God.

Maybe that explained His silence.

Closing his eyes, Gideon tried to clear his mind of all his questions. Memories from long ago washed over him. Sitting beside Pa at church when he'd gotten caught talking. The smell of Mama's coffee long before the sun rose. Chasing his sisters with worms in each hand.

His thoughts shifted to the day he'd asked Jesus into his heart. The day he asked God to keep Pa alive through Thanksgiving. The day he asked God to take care of Mama now that she was alone on Earth.

How he wanted what Pa and Mama had. A year ago, he would have never even considered marriage. He wasn't opposed to it; he just wasn't all that interested either. Now all he could think about was Maria and Lydia.

To be honest, he only thought of Lydia.

But duty called him to Maria. Maria made more sense. She was a widowed Christian with two children. She wanted a husband, and she'd make a terrific, loting wife. There was no reason for Gideon not to ask Maria to marry him today.

Except one—Lydia.

Gideon growled. The whole thing was useless. He needed to quit overanalyzing everything and simply refer to God's Word. He opened his Bible.

"Well, there you are."

Gideon looked up. "Cameron, is that you?"

"Yep. I've been looking all over for you."

Gideon stood and hugged his little brother, who now stood every bit as tall and broad as him. "What's going on?"

"I just stopped by to see my mom and big brother."

Gideon studied the younger man. "You drove over an hour just to stop by?"

"Okay, I may have had a bit of a reason, but you have to come to the house so I can show you."

Gideon's curiosity piqued. "Show me?"

"Yep."

Gideon followed Cameron back. Long before they reached the house Gideon noticed Mama and another woman on the porch. The woman didn't look familiar, young with long dark hair, and Gideon couldn't make out who she was. Realization dawned. "Is she your reason?"

Cameron smiled and gestured Gideon to hurry. He reached the porch and grabbed the woman's hand, helping her to her feet. "Gideon, allow me to introduce you to my fiancée, Caitlyn."

"Cameron and Caitlyn. . ." Mama chuckled. "Isn't that the cutest thing you've ever heard?"

The young woman's cheeks flamed red at his mother's words, but Gideon noted Caitlyn's gaze never left his brother's face. She looked as tiny as one of those teacups he'd watched Lydia buy for her coffee shop.

A mixture of happiness and envy enveloped Gideon as he extended his hand. A slightly nervous giggle escaped when she touched it. Gideon remained speechless as he shook his soon-to-be sister-in-law's hand. Though he tried to push away the jealous feelings that warred to overtake his happiness for his brother, all Gideon could think about was being the last in his family without a mate.

<hr/>

Lydia pulled the apple tarts out of the oven. The inspector would arrive first thing the next morning for final approval of her business license. She'd been a bundle of nerves the whole day, so she'd decided to try her hand at Lorma's great-aunt's tarts. The first two times she'd tried baking them, they hadn't turned out as Lydia hoped. She made a couple of minor adjustments to the recipe before trying it again. *Third time's a charm, I hope.*

The warm, sweet aroma filled the kitchen, and Lydia's stomach growled

Her nerves had kept her from eating much. Now her stomach protested. She touched the top of a tart to check for flakiness. A bit of the apple filling burned her finger. Pulling her hand away quickly, she popped the injured finger in her mouth and raced to the sink. She placed the appendage under cold water for several seconds. The burn was small but stung miserably.

She turned off the cold water and reached for a clean cloth so she could wrap up her hand. The water dripped. She was pretty sure she had some aloe vera gel somewhere in the house; she'd just have to think of where. The water dripped again.

She grabbed the faucet knob and turned it all the way off. A steady stream poured. "What in the world?" She tried turning it the other way; the water simply poured harder.

"Oh no." She twisted the knob left and right, right and left. No matter where she tried to stop, the water still dripped.

"Why today?" She tried twisting it one more time with all the strength she could muster. The stream quickened again, and this time she'd tightened it so well she couldn't move it left or right.

"It's Sunday. No plumber's open on Sunday." Panic welled in her heart as she opened the bottom cabinet. The pipes looked fine. Of course, she didn't really know what "fine" was when it came to pipes. The stream continued to flow steadily. "God, what will I do? I'll never pass inspection." She placed her finger under the flow. "I'll never be able to pay the water bill."

Gideon drifted into her mind, and she knew she had no choice but to call him. She'd no sooner hung up the phone with Lorma than her mother called.

"How are things going?" Her mother's voice simpered through the line.

"My final inspection is tomorrow, and the kitchen sink is leaking." As soon as the words left Lydia's mouth, she knew she'd made a mistake.

"Why are Mother's pipes leaking?"

"Mom, I didn't do it on purpose." Lydia was tired of being on the defensive with her mother. She wanted once, just once, for her mother to be proud of her and excited about what she was doing.

"Who'd you call to fix it?" Rita's voice was curt.

"My friend. . .Gideon." Lydia wasn't sure she considered Gideon her friend, but what else would she consider him?

"You've mentioned him a lot. Are you two an item?"

"No!" Lydia tried to keep from screaming into the phone. "Look, Gideon's here. I've gotta go. Bye."

Before her mother could respond, Lydia hung up the phone and opened the door for Gideon. "It's the one in the kitchen."

"Are you okay?"

"Yes. Yes." Her words came out choppy. Anxiety swirled in her empty stomach, making her nauseated. Emotion pounded her head, and she feared at any moment she'd break down into tears.

"Are you sure?"

"Please." Her voice cracked, and Lydia cleared her throat. "Please fix the sink."

Gideon turned off the water to the house and within a matter of moments had changed a gasket of some kind, turned the water back on, and stopped the leak.

"See, nothing to it." Gideon walked toward her. He brushed her cheek with the back of his hand. "You look pale. Do you feel sick?"

The gentle caress and the strength and warmth of his hand broke the wall within her that she tried so hard to keep intact. Tears, one after the other, raced each other down both cheeks.

"Lydia." Gideon's voice, soft and kind, erupted another wave of emotion. Her chest heaved, and he wrapped his strong, protective arms around her.

She couldn't move. Didn't want to move. She'd never been so out of control, so in need of someone to hold her.

"It's okay." He brushed her hair with his hand and tightened his hold. "It's okay."

The fear of not passing the inspection, the hurt of her mother's continued lack of approval, the confusion of her feelings for the man who held her close weighed so heavy she wrapped her arms around him. Relishing his smell, his tenderness, his strength, she closed her eyes and allowed this moment of comfort.

Her breathing slowed, and she looked up at the man she'd been trying so hard not to love. "Thank you, Gid—"

His lips crashed down on hers with an intensity she'd never known. Every nerve awakened as she accepted his kiss. After what seemed an eternity of bliss, he pulled away, whispering something about care and forever.

All Lydia could think about was the feel of his lips—strong and masculine yet soft and tender—against hers.

⚭

If Gideon lived to be one hundred, he'd never forget the softness of her lips. He'd never felt so needed and never had such a desire to provide for the need. He'd told her he would care for her forever. And he'd spoken the truth.

Few things in his life had been clearer to him. Just as John said in the Bible, the truth had set him free. Without a doubt, the truth was he'd fallen in love with Lydia.

Chapter 10

Gideon sipped his coffee, remembering the sweetness of Lydia's touch and how she fit perfectly in his arms. It hurt him to see her crying, but it felt right to be the one to comfort her pain. He wanted to protect her, to make her happy. For the first time in his life, he longed to love a woman in the manner God spoke of in scripture—more than his own life.

The reality of the depth of his feelings struck him, and he took another sip. Did every man feel as though he could take on the world when the woman he loved was in pain? As she cried in his arms, Gideon would have done anything to make her happy and content. *I've never felt this way, Lord.*

"You're awfully quiet this morning." Mama traced the top of her coffee mug with her finger.

"Just thinking."

"Penny for your thoughts."

Gideon looked at Mama and smiled at her grin. He couldn't even begin to count the many times he'd heard Mama say that. Usually to one of his sisters. They always seemed to be the ones to do the extra thinking. Gideon and his brothers were doers. They rarely worried about anything. "I'm not sure if you can help me."

"Son, I've lived a long time. My guess is I can help you, but if I can't, I know someone who can."

Gideon loved his mother. She drove him to insanity at times, but she truly was a woman of strength and faith. He should have talked to her long ago. "What happens when what you want conflicts with what someone else needs?"

Mama tapped her fingers on the table. "Well, that depends. If you're talking about buying an expensive car just because you think you look good in it and you take on more debt than you can afford. . .well, you better not be buying that car." Mama clicked her tongue. "Or if you're talking about going to an Indianapolis Colts game because you were given free tickets but it's at the same time as your family's annual reunion. . .you better give up those tickets." Mama leaned forward and rested her elbows on the table. "But I don't think those scenarios are what we're talking about."

Gideon shook his head.

"Well, I think a person has to evaluate if he understands need from want."

"Of course I understand need from want." Gideon sat back in his chair. Mama's intense look made him uncomfortable.

"You sure?"

A car door slammed. Footsteps sounded on the porch. Before Gideon had time to respond, the back door flung open. Maria's eyes were as big as a deer's caught in headlights. "Dad is sick."

"What's wrong?" Mama guided a distraught Maria to a chair. Gideon grabbed a mug and poured some coffee.

Maria shook her head and popped up out of the seat. "He's so pale and tired. He says he can't get up. Not even to come to work."

Gideon's concern heightened. Jim never missed work. "Where is he?"

"At his apartment. He told me to go on to work, that he'd be okay." Maria's voice cracked. "I'm scared."

"It's okay, honey." Mama wrapped her arms around her. "Gideon will go get Jim. Where are the boys?"

"At the sitter's. I...I didn't want them to see their grandpa..." She cried into Mama's embrace. Gideon grabbed his keys and headed out the door.

"Call as soon as you get there," Mama said.

Gideon drove as fast as the law allowed, growing more anxious by the minute. "Lord, Maria needs Jim." Guilt nudged at his heart. If something happened to Jim, Maria wouldn't have anyone. "Please, Lord, help Jim be all right."

He parked the car in Jim's driveway and raced up to the apartment. After pushing the unlocked door open, Gideon saw his employee lying on the couch, pale as bug powder. Jim didn't even respond when Gideon checked his much-too-weak pulse. Gideon lifted him as gently as possible and took him to the truck. "Don't worry, Jim. I'll have you at the hospital in no time."

⁂

Lydia opened the door for the inspector. The tall, unbelievably thin, brown-haired man nodded his head. "Morning, ma'am."

"Good morning." Lydia tried not to destroy the hand towel she twisted in her hands. Remembering her manners, she motioned him inside. "I hope you find everything in order."

"For your sake, I hope so, too."

Lydia swallowed the knot in her throat. She didn't want to have to do this again, but from what she understood, if he found anything out of order he'd make her do the whole inspection over. "He's a stickler for the rules," a woman at his office had told her.

"Mind if I look in the kitchen? I've already checked around outside."

"You have?" Lydia placed her hand on her chest. She'd been stewing and praying intermittently for the last two hours, and he'd been out there part of the time.

He nodded. "Already made friends with your pup."

Lydia chuckled nervously. "He's quite a rascal."

"That he is. Smart, though. You ought to think about training him." He pointed toward the kitchen.

"Oh, go ahead. Do I walk around with you or wait or. . ."

"You just hang tight. I'll let you know if I find anything that needs attention."

Lydia sat on the couch. Had George welcomed the man when he walked in the backyard? Actually, Lydia was a little miffed that the dog hadn't barked a stranger warning. But then, George would have to believe he'd met a stranger in order to issue a warning, and George thought he knew everyone.

Sighing, Lydia leaned back on the couch. She grabbed the remote control. Would it be rude to turn on the television while an inspector was in the house? It might seem unprofessional for a future business owner.

She put the controller down and picked up a magazine her mom had accidentally left. Just by skimming the pages, Lydia could tell it was an I-want-the-power magazine. She put it down. She had no need for "the power." God remained her source of power. He proved much better at it than she. Left to herself, Lydia crumbled like a burned piece of toast.

Looking down at her watch, she wondered how long he would take. She knew Lorma was on the edge of her seat, waiting for Lydia to call with the news. Lydia crossed and uncrossed her legs. She twiddled her thumbs and played with her hair. She examined her nails then looked back at her watch. He'd been at it for a good hour. Surely, the man was almost done.

I know, I'll give him a slice of pie for his trouble. She jumped up and headed into the kitchen. *Would that seem like I was trying to bribe him?* She chewed the inside of her lip. When she was in school, the children always teased her about being a teacher's pet because she tried to help out. But really she was just trying to be nice. . .or maybe it was the need to please everyone coming out in her.

She tapped her foot. Opening the cabinet door, she decided being nice was a good Christian quality. She placed two plates on the counter. *If I offer him a piece after he's passed or failed me then I'm not bribing or trying to please. I'm simply being kind.*

She shook her head as she cut two pieces of pie. No one would worry so much about giving someone a dessert. *I've gotta quit overthinking everything.*

"Well, Ms. Hammond, I think I've finished."

Lydia turned around, startled by his abrupt appearance. She searched his face for positive feedback. The man had no expression.

"I need you to sign here." He handed her a paper. She looked at it and tried to see if it said anything about pass or fail. She wasn't sure what it was supposed to say.

"You can open whenever you're ready. You passed."

"Really!" Lydia looked up at him. "Nothing to fix?"

The left side of his mouth lifted slightly upward. The best smile she figured she'd get from the man. "Nothing to fix. You're ready to go."

"Thanks so much." Lydia shook his hand.

The man started to turn toward the door.

"Oh, wait. Would you like a sample of what I'll be serving?"

He raised his eyebrows. "Well, I always have had a weakness for pie."

Lydia pointed toward a chair. "I hope you like it." She watched as the inspector nodded his approval at his first bite of the pie. Excitement filled her heart. She couldn't wait to tell Lorma and Gideon that she'd passed inspection.

Without thinking, she lifted her fingers to her lips, remembering Gideon's touch. Yes, she even wanted to call Gideon.

⁂

"He's had a heart attack." The doctor rubbed his temple. "He has three blockages. We're going to perform an angioplasty procedure, but I have to warn you, his blockages are quite severe."

Maria gasped, and Gideon held her hand tighter. He knew Mama's arm wrapped around her on the other side.

"Has he had any heart attacks before?" The doctor seemed perplexed, or maybe tired. Gideon wondered how long it had been since the man had slept.

"Not that I know of, but he has been acting different lately."

"How so?"

Maria took a deep breath. "He gets tired easily. Takes a lot of breaks. He's been more irritable."

Yes, Gideon had noticed a change in Jim over the last several weeks, as well. He assumed the older man was worried about Maria. Gideon had been so frustrated with Jim's constant suggestions at matrimony that he hadn't paid attention to the possibility of something else being wrong.

Renewed guilt gnawed at his heart. As the man's employer and as a Christian, he should have been paying better attention. Gideon had been so wrapped up in his own selfishness that he hadn't noticed his own employee—his friend—had grown tired and sick.

"Not all of his tests have come back yet, but considering the degree of blockage, my guess is this is not your father's first heart attack. Has he had any numbness in his arms?"

Worry etched Maria's face. "I guess he has complained a few times, but he'd take an aspirin and sit down awhile." Maria's voice broke, and she tightened her grasp on Gideon's hand. He knew all too well how frightening it was to receive bad news about your father. He looked over at Mama. Unlike Maria, Gideon still had his mother.

"We're getting ready to prep him for surgery. Why don't you come talk to him before he goes? He's awake and stable, just tired."

"Can my friends go, too?"

"Usually we allow only family. . ." The doctor tapped his pen against the clipboard in his hand. His gaze took in Gideon and Mama.

"They are like family to my father. Please." Maria's pleading nearly broke Gideon's heart. She desperately needed comfort.

The doctor tucked his clipboard under his arm. "All right. You'll need to be quick."

Gideon followed Maria, his mother, and the doctor. The last time he'd been in a hospital was when his pa was sick. He hated the smell, hated the pristine cleanness. Everything in him wanted to turn around and walk back outside, but he knew he couldn't. He needed to be there for Jim and Maria.

They turned a corner. He saw Jim. Still pale and listless, but now his eyes were opened slightly.

"Dad?" Maria bent over beside him. Jim tried to lift his hand but could only keep it up a second. The frailty of the man who'd worked so diligently beside him these past two years made Gideon ill. Images of Pa exploded in his mind into so many remembrances that he couldn't sort them out.

Gideon watched as Jim whispered in Maria's ear.

She leaned up and kissed his cheek. "I'll be fine, Dad. I love you. You focus on getting better." She brushed back his hair. "My boys need their grandpa."

A pained expression wrapped Jim's face, and Gideon didn't know if it was physical or emotional. Jim's gaze traveled to Gideon, back to Maria, then to Gideon again. Tightness gripped Gideon's heart. It was Jim's silent message for Gideon to take care of Maria.

Well, I think a person has to evaluate if he understands need from want. Mama's response to Gideon's confusion floated to his mind. She'd spoken the words only moments before Maria burst through the door. Did Gideon understand the difference between need and want? Could he make his heart give up what it desired more than anything? *I must trust You, God, not my heart.*

"Things aren't always what they seem, son."

Gideon flinched as a nurse nudged past him. "All right. It's time to go." The woman lifted the side rails of Jim's bed and walked to the back. She looked at Maria and smiled. "He's in good hands."

Gideon could take no more. He walked out of the room, back down the hall, and out the emergency room doors. Inhaling fresh air as deeply as possible, Gideon closed his eyes. "God, I've made a mistake."

A knot swelled in his throat, and he swallowed hard. "I may have feelings for Lydia, but Maria needs me. There's a difference between need and want, and I can't be selfish. I won't be. Help me, Lord. Help me not love Lydia."

Silence swept through the air. No cars. No sirens. No people. Silence. And God was the quietest of all.

Chapter 11

Lorma, I passed." Lydia practically squealed as she opened the back door of Gideon's house.

Lorma shouted and jumped, causing her beehive hairdo to wiggle. She wrapped her arms around Lydia. "I'm so proud of you." Lydia enjoyed the older woman's light floral scent mixed with the coffee she'd had that morning.

"And"—Lydia thought her cheeks would bruise if she smiled any fuller as she shifted the plateful of treats from behind her back—"I made the tarts."

"Great-Aunt Mary's tarts!" Lorma's eyes widened and she clapped her hands like a schoolgirl. "I can't wait to taste them."

Lydia giggled. "Okay. You sit down, and I'll get you a cup of milk." Nervousness mixed with her excitement. She wanted Lorma to love these tarts. The woman had been so good to her, and this was the only way Lydia could think of to thank her. She grabbed a cup from the cabinet and opened the refrigerator door. Lydia had spent so much time here that she felt as comfortable in Lorma's kitchen as she did her own.

She poured the milk and set the drink in front of Lorma. Tearing a paper towel off the roll to use as a napkin, she watched as Lorma took a bite. Lorma raised her eyebrows as she chewed. Lydia thought she would die if her friend didn't hurry up and swallow.

Lorma took a drink of milk. "Lydia, they're perfect." Lorma's eyes welled with tears, causing Lydia's to do the same. Lorma stood and hugged Lydia again. "I haven't tasted these in more than forty years."

Lydia squeezed her friend tighter before letting go. "I'm so glad they're right. I wanted to be able to give you something to thank you for. . ." What could she say? *Thank you for being a friend when I had none. Thank you for being like a mother to me. Thank you for approving of and believing in me. Thank you for welcoming me into the church and community.* Lorma had been and done all those things and more. In Lydia's opinion, God had sent Lorma specifically to be in her life at this time. "I just wanted to thank you for everything."

Lorma patted Lydia's hand. "Lydia Hammond, you are an amazing girl with wonderful love for people. And what a talent He's given you. . .to sweeten the lives of others with sweets. Just knowing you is a gift."

"I can't wait to tell Gideon. You know he had to come over and fix my sink

305

the day before inspection." Lydia touched her lips. Just the thought of their swee kiss spread goose bumps across her skin.

Lorma's expression fell and tears pooled in her eyes. "I'd say he'll be home for lunch, but he probably won't stay long."

Concern pushed the goose bumps aside. When Lorma let out a long sig and turned toward the refrigerator, Lydia's brain whirled with possibilities. *H couldn't be sick or he would be home. Lorma was all right, or she appeared to be.* Lydi pinched the paper towel between her fingers. "What happened?"

"Jim's had a heart attack."

Sorrow filled Lydia's heart though she had only met Jim one time. She knew he worked the orchards with Gideon and that Maria was his daughter. The ma always seemed to scowl at Lydia when she came near, so she stayed away from him. Still, she didn't want him to be sick. "Is he okay?"

"He's in the hospital, recovering from surgery."

"I'm sorry. I'll pray for him."

"Yes. Why don't we do that now?" Lorma grabbed her hands.

"Okay." Lydia's palms began to sweat. She loved talking to God and foun herself chatting with Him about every little area of her life, but she still got ner vous when it came to praying aloud with others.

Lorma's hands shook just a bit, and Lydia peeked up to see she was cry ing. "Would you mind praying?" Lorma's voice cracked, and Lydia squeezed he hands tighter.

God, help me. I know I'm just talking out loud to You, but I'm nervous. And I don know Jim. And I don't think he likes me. She shook her head. *Forgive me, Lord. He sick, and this isn't about me at all.*

Taking a quick breath, Lydia began. "Dear God, we pray for Jim. He's ha a heart attack. . .well, you already know that. But we ask You to be with him. . of course You're with him. . .but to take care of him. He has family who wan to see him better."

God, I'm fumbling this up. I don't know how to pray out loud. I know I'm ju talking to You, but just me and You is so different.

She continued, "Take care of Maria and her children, too. Help them. . .b strong. Hold them close. You say we can ask for things, and we ask that Jim g better. Of course, You know what is best, and we do trust You, but we still as In the name of Jesus, I pray. Amen."

Lorma squeezed Lydia's hands. "Thank you, dear. Now, let's you and m start some lunch."

"Oh no." Gideon saw a brown fur ball that had grown several inches over the la month tied up to his front porch as he drove up the drive. George wagged his ta

306

nd barked as Gideon hopped out of the cab and shut the door. The last thing he eeded right now was to see Lydia.

Maybe this is Your way of telling me I need to apologize straight up for that kiss ince there can't be anything between us. Again, Gideon's prayer seemed to fall flat. t wasn't like he normally heard God's voice booming from the sky, but it had een a long time since Gideon had felt any peace in his relationship with his avior.

He made his way over to the pup and sat on the porch. George jumped nto Gideon's lap. The dog tried to lick every crevice of Gideon's hand. "You're a reat protector." Gideon scratched the canine between the ears. "You'd just lick n intruder to death."

For several minutes, Gideon petted Lydia's dog. He looked over the expanse f his property. He wasn't ready to face her. The attraction remained too great, nd he knew it was more than just the physical. She oozed spontaneity in her vords and actions. She kept him guessing about what she'd say or do next, and he ound it refreshing. She'd proved how much she loved people by her treatment of is mom and family, even her little dog. He scratched George's head again.

He even noted her love for God. How many times had he heard her mumling to herself when he realized she was carrying on complete conversations vith God? The simplicity and authenticity of that relationship intrigued him.

She even responded with kindness to Maria when the woman was throwing her-lf at me in Lydia's own house.

Ugh. He smacked the porch railing. Any man in his right mind would fall n love with Lydia Hammond.

But Gideon couldn't. He had an obligation. A real man cared for the needs f others before his own desires. What was it his teacher had said in school about eople of integrity? He snapped his fingers. *They do what's right when no one is ooking.* Whether people were looking or not, Gideon loved the Lord, and he vould do what was right—care for Maria and her boys.

"Gideon, you're here." Lydia stepped out onto the porch. Her gorgeous hair ung in perfect curls about her shoulders. She must have been wearing some ind of makeup that made the blue in her eyes stand out, because they practially glistened. The pink in her cheeks deepened as she stood looking at him. As lways, her beauty shone like a ripened peach.

"Yep." He forced himself to look away from her. At some point, he'd apoloize to her. He'd had no right to initiate that kiss. *Though she kissed back, and for moment I thought all the wrongs in the world had been made right.*

"I'm really sorry about Jim."

The mention of his friend's name brought sense back into Gideon's thick ead. He would not think about that kiss again. He was a man, a strong man,

and he would control his mind. "Yes, he doesn't appear to be doing well at th
moment. He's out of surgery, but he looks awful."

"I'm so sorry."

He heard the door close and thought she'd gone inside until a soft flor:
scent wafted around him. He felt a light touch on his arm and knew she'd s:
beside him. Gritting his teeth, he was determined not to look at her.

"Is there anything I can do?" The concern in her voice sounded sincere, an
it nagged at Gideon's heart. Lydia was a sweet, kind woman who deserved a ma
who would honor, cherish, and protect her. Gideon would have loved to be tha
man, but it simply wasn't meant to be.

"No."

She touched the top of his hand. Her gentle warmth stirred him. "I do hav
some good news. It's nowhere near as important as Jim's health, but it might.
I don't know."

She removed her hand, and Gideon knew he'd gone from trying to prote
himself to being rude. Lydia didn't deserve that. He turned toward her. Agai:
he couldn't help but notice the adorable freckles sprinkling her nose and the so:
curve of her lips. He'd always prided himself on being a man of self-control, bt
meeting Lydia had proved he wasn't as good at the virtue as he once believe(
"Tell me your good news."

Her eyes smiled before her lips had the chance to join them. Her exciteme:
was muted by Jim's illness, but he knew her enough to know it brewed dee
within her. "My house passed inspection."

"That's great." Gideon tried to sound happy for her. In truth, he still wasr
convinced the business would succeed, but he wanted to be supportive.

"I was so worried when the faucet started leaking." She ducked her head :
her face flamed red. He knew she thought of their kiss. He wondered if it ha
consumed her mind as much as it had his. Now would be a good time to apolo
gize to her. The sooner, the better. "Lydia, I. . ."

"There you are." Mama opened the door. "I didn't know what had happene
to you, but now I see Gideon's home. Wonderful! The sandwiches are ready
Mama lifted her finger to the side of her mouth. "You two look absolutely ador
able sitting on that porch together."

"Mama"—Gideon frowned and stood to his feet—"we are not teenagers
He noted a pained expression wrapped Lydia's face. She probably felt they woul
be a couple now. She'd probably even talked to Mama about it.

He was a heel. A big, overgrown heel. How could he have kissed her lik
that? He knew before he ever went over there that Maria was the woman h
should pursue. It was the right thing to do.

God, why does it feel so wrong?

It had been a long time since Lydia had felt so embarrassed. A memory of falling forward down the church steps after a service flashed through her mind. She would have landed flat on her face had the pastor not been there to stop her fall. Even more horrifying was that night at the service the pastor's wife had asked for a prayer for him, as she'd said he'd pinched a nerve in his back earlier that morning. Lydia had taken a pie to the bedridden man, but that didn't lessen her mortification at her clumsiness.

Okay, so embarrassment might as well have been her middle name. Maybe one could look up the word in the dictionary and find Lydia's face pasted to the side, but she still didn't like it. And she especially didn't like that Gideon was being so standoffish just days after he'd kissed her.

She stood and followed Lorma into the house. She'd been convinced the kiss meant something to him. In her mind, it had special significance. It meant they were a couple. Never had she been the kind of girl to kiss a boy on a whim or just because they had gone on a date. Who was she kidding? She'd never really gone on dates, and Gideon's kiss was the first she'd had.

That's why his treatment hurts, Lord.

Straightening her shoulders, she grabbed some bread and meat for her sandwich. She would not show Gideon that his behavior hurt her feelings. Maybe he was being too sensitive. Another trait she'd acquired from somewhere but definitely not from her mother. After all, Jim had just had a heart attack, and Gideon had arrived straight from the hospital less than an hour ago.

That's probably it, God. I'm just being selfish.

She sat at the table and ate a couple of chips. Lorma and Gideon joined her.

Lorma wiped her mouth with her napkin. "We need to do something to celebrate passing inspection."

Lydia covered her mouth and swallowed. "Okay."

"Hmm." Lorma squinted her eyes and tapped the top of her fork against her lips. "I know. Let's go to the Royal Theater. A movie made from one of Jane Austen's books is playing this weekend."

Lydia nodded. "That sounds like a lot of fun. I read one of her books in high school."

Lorma looked at her son. "What do you think, Gideon? We could go to the evening show."

"Well, I. . ."

It was obvious Gideon had no desire to go with them. The realization infuriated Lydia. In no way did she want to force him to do anything. "Why don't just you and I go, Lorma?"

"No, no. Don't be silly. Gideon wants to celebrate, too."

The phone rang, and Lorma jumped up. She read the caller ID and looked at Lydia and Gideon. "It's Chloe. She's probably just gotten back from the obstetrician's office." Lorma's eyes twinkled. "I can't wait for another grandbaby. I'll take it in the other room."

Lorma raced down the hall, leaving Lydia alone with Gideon. If she had been closer to being finished with her lunch, she'd have left, but with most of her sandwich still uneaten, she didn't want to be wasteful. She focused on her plate, determined not to talk to the man who wanted nothing to do with her.

"Lydia, we need to talk." Gideon's voice sounded low and had a pained edge to it.

"Sure." She traced a chip around her plate but didn't look up at him.

"It's about the kiss the other night."

Lydia shrugged her shoulders, trying to act nonchalant. She knew this wasn't going to be a now-we're-a-couple speech. His actions expressed nothing more than a desire to get as far away from her as he could. Her appetite fled. No way could she finish the rest of her sandwich. She inwardly contemplated how she was going to finish the rest of this conversation without crying. "What about it?"

"I shouldn't have. . ."

She lifted her hand to silence him. Hurt, pure and powerful, welled inside her. She didn't want to hear anything else he had to say. "Look, we can forget about it."

"But I'm sorry."

Anger laced through her pain. "I said just forget about it. It didn't—" She knew the words about to spill from her mouth were a lie. A stronger person would have just told the truth and accepted the rejection head on. She wasn't a stronger person. "It didn't mean anything."

"I see."

Lydia sneaked at peek at him, noting the pain that wrapped his face. Why would he look stricken? He was the one rejecting her. She didn't want to think about it. She just wanted to leave, to get as far away from him as she could. "I've got to go. . .feed George." Another lie. The dog ate when he wanted. "Tell Lorma I said bye."

She picked up her plate and stood. The chair fell backward behind her and smashed to the floor. "Oh." Without looking up, Lydia turned and picked it up.

Her nerves started to get the best of her, and her hands started to shake. *Just make it to the trash and leave. It's not that hard. Please, Lord, it's not that hard.*

After throwing away what she couldn't give George, she placed her plate in the sink. Still avoiding eye contact, she ducked her head and made a beeline out the door.

"Come on, George." She reached for George's leash, slipped, and stepped on his paw. He yelped, and the emotion Lydia had bottled filled her eyes. "I'm sorry, buddy."

"Are you okay?" Gideon's voice sounded behind her, just inside the door.

She would not let him see her cry. Not again. She'd never allow herself to be vulnerable in front of him again. "We're fine."

She unhooked George and jumped off the porch in one motion. Gideon Andrews and his kiss meant nothing to her. She stomped toward the well-worn path that led to her house.

Maybe if I keep saying that to myself, it will come true.

Chapter 12

Lydia grabbed a wad of paper towels off the roll. She scrunched them in her hand then smashed the black ants that had made a trail up her cabinet and across the counter. "Ugh. I hate bugs." She'd sprayed around the house twice, but she couldn't seem to get rid of the pests.

Glancing in her sink, she sighed. *It might have something to do with the fact that I haven't washed dishes in days.* Stacks of grimy dishes and even a moldy cup of milk stared up at her. She just hadn't been in the mood to do anything.

Forcing herself to turn on the faucet, she grabbed the bottle of dish soap and poured a generous amount into the streaming water. *If I let them soak a few minutes before I put them in the dishwasher, the gunk will come off easier.*

Once the sink filled, she turned the faucet off and padded in her oversized kitty slippers into the living area. A myriad of wrappers and open soft drink cans, a pizza box, and a half-eaten, melted tub of ice cream greeted her. *I'm going to have to put cockroach traps out if I don't get a handle on this.*

She wrapped her robe tighter around her waist. After grabbing a handful of trash, she wrinkled her nose when her finger slipped into the goopy ice-cream container. *This is ridiculous. I've been pouting like a jilted teenager. And it's about time I stop.* She sucked in a long breath and crammed the stuff into the garbage can. But she felt like a jilted teenager.

Gideon's kiss was her first ever. She knew she was a bit old to have never been kissed, but she'd always been so silly and clumsy. In school she was everyone's friend but no one's date. Which suited her just fine. She never knew when she might step on a guy's foot dancing, claw him if they held hands, or something worse.

The intense feelings she bore for Gideon were foreign to her. She didn't know how to handle them. And she certainly hadn't expected a simple kiss to pain her so deeply.

I'm just going to take a little nap, and then I'll clean this house. She made her way into her bedroom and took in the disheveled bed covers, the dirty clothes lying on the floor, and the additional mess of leftover junk food. After slipping into her bed, George jumped up beside her. The pup wagged his tail then rested his chin on the bed covers.

Feeling sorry for the little guy, she scratched his head. "You've been my faithful little friend, haven't you?"

312

George sat up on the bed and barked. He nestled his way closer to her, trying to get her to play. She petted his head and forced a smile to spread her lips. "After a nap, okay?"

Seeming to understand what she said, George circled a spot on the bed several times, trying to make himself comfortable. He finally settled in, and Lydia lay back on her pillow and closed her eyes. No matter how many different images she tried to conjure, her mind always returned to Gideon.

"Please, God, take him out of my thoughts." She grabbed a pillow and covered her head with it.

The doorbell rang, and George leaped from the bed, barking wildly. Lydia didn't move. *Maybe they'll think I'm not home and leave.* A few seconds passed, and the doorbell rang again. George's barks echoed through the otherwise silent house.

"Please go away," Lydia mumbled into the pillow. The only people she could think would visit her would be Lorma or Gideon, and she wasn't up to seeing either one of them.

A chorus of knocks sounded from the door. George's wild barks filled the air. The poor pup was going to collapse if he didn't find out who was behind that door. Frustrated, Lydia pulled herself out of bed. She glanced into a mirror and rolled her eyes. Raking her fingers through her nappy hair, she scowled. *I can always say I'm desperately sick.*

Another lie. It seemed the fibs stepped one on top of the other ever since the kiss. *This is why being single is much better.* Now, if she could just convince her heart of that.

The adamant visitor knocked several times more. "I'm coming," Lydia yelled. *If I open the door and it's a solicitor, I'm liable to give them a piece of my mind.*

Finally making her way to the front door, she opened it. Her mother, dressed in a bright red summer dress, stood with her back to Lydia. Her hand swept the expanse of the front yard as she mumbled, "That girl's not even keeping Mother's place properly mowed. What was I thinking. . ."

Lydia swallowed hard. The yard appeared in desperate need of mowing, and she hadn't weeded the flower gardens in over a week. The house looked far worse than the yard. Embarrassment flooded her. She had no business letting Grandma's house go as she had. It wasn't the property's fault Lydia's heart had been stomped on by its neighbor. "Hello, Mom."

The older woman turned gracefully around. Large, dark sunglasses covered a flawless makeup-painted face. Her mother's lips set in a deep frown. "Are you sick, Lydia?"

Lydia bit her bottom lip. She tightened the knot in her robe. "I guess I haven't felt well."

Rita took her sunglasses off her face and peered past the door. Lydia gripped the robe belt tighter as she imagined what her mother thought of the obvious mess behind her daughter. For the first time, Lydia noted the red and blue pin below her mother's shoulder that read "Vote for Hammond." Two yard signs dangled from her mother's grasp. "Are you going to let me in?"

Lydia nodded and opened the door wide. She stood silent when her mother walked in and gasped. Scanning the room, Lydia realized it was even worse than she'd first noticed. Books, magazines, blankets, shoes, clothes, wrappers, and other unidentifiable things dotted the room. She closed her eyes, praying the kitchen wasn't sporting additional ants.

The scowl deepened on her mother's face when she turned to Lydia. "Do you feel well enough to help me clean this up?"

"Yes."

"Well enough to get out of your pajamas?"

"Yes."

Her mother opened her arms wide as if showcasing the room. "May we get started?"

Nodding, Lydia made her way to her bedroom to change clothes. She could have been bedridden with the flu and double pneumonia, and her mother would still have been furious. With everything in her, Lydia wished she could share her heartache with her mother, but she knew that wasn't possible.

Rita Louise Hammond was a goal-oriented, strong woman. Things ran smoothly in her life. There was no time for emotional tirades or fits of self-pity. Her mother would have never allowed her heart to become so consumed by a man in the first place.

Lydia was so different from her mother. At this moment, a bit of her mom's coarse temperament would have been nice. It might take away some of the sting of Gideon's rejection.

No. Deep in the core of her heart, Lydia knew she didn't want to be like her mother. God wanted her to have a tender heart, and tender hearts would inevitably experience times of pain.

But, God, I've tried to be a witness to Mom. She's such a strong woman. She needs to see strong women who adore You. All she sees from me is weakness. Lydia shook her head. God was the master of taking weakness and making it strong. He could take this time of hurt and make her stronger, as well.

Inhaling the hope that God remained in control, Lydia quickly made her bed and gathered the dirty clothes off the floor. After throwing them in the hamper, she collected the trash off the end table and threw it away.

With her chin up, she walked into the kitchen. Disgust wrapped her mother's features as she scrubbed the dishes in the sink. Lydia noted a black ant scurrying down the side of the cabinet. She grabbed another paper towel, swiped him up, and threw him away. "I'll get it, Mom."

"How many days have you been sick?" Her mother's eyes lit with anger instead of compassion.

"I haven't been myself for just a few days." Lydia longed to be able to confide in her mother the true reason for her sickness, but she could tell it would only infuriate her more. "Here, let me do that. Go get your things. How long are you staying?"

Her mother handed Lydia the dishrag. "I planned to stay one night, but if you're this sick"—she swiped her hand around the destroyed kitchen—"then I'm not sure I want to risk getting what you have."

Lydia blew a strand of hair away from her eyes. She'd have no choice but to fess up. "I'm not *that* sick. I've been upset."

"You let Mother's house go like this because you've been upset?" Rita rested her hands on her hips. "Honestly, Lydia. Maybe Grace is right about you needing to make your own way."

"What?" Lydia lifted her shoulders. "Aunt Grace wants me to leave?"

Rita shook her head. "No. No. That's taken care of." She pointed at Lydia. "I'm going to town to see about putting a few signs in front of businesses. When I get back, I want this place cleaned up."

"Okay, Mom." Lydia watched as her mother stomped out the front door. Within moments, Lydia heard tires spitting gravel from the driveway. Her mother hadn't even bothered to ask about Lydia's concerns. As always, her own mother really didn't care.

<hr />

Gideon moved the love seat to the only empty place in the living area. "How's this, Mama?" He watched as she scratched the side of her head, making the whole wrapping of salt-and-pepper hair move. How many years had Mama worn her hair in that knot on the top of her head? Too many to count.

"I'm just not sure. Maybe if we move the couch over here and the love seat over there." She pointed to the other side of the room. "Maybe it would balance more."

"Mama, I just moved them out of those spots." Gideon kneaded the middle of his back with his hand. "All this moving is killing me."

"Hogwash." Mama swatted the air with her hand. "You're young and fit as a fiddle."

"Hmm." Gideon wiped his brow with the back of his hand. "Maybe if you feed me a bit of that strawberry cheesecake in the kitchen, it will recharge my battery, and I'll be able to move all this stuff again."

"You think so?" Mama crossed her arms in front of her chest and smiled.

"Yep."

"All right then." She patted his shoulder then headed into the kitchen. "A break it is."

Gideon poured cups of coffee for both of them while Mama cut good-sized slices of the dessert. They sat at the table, and Gideon cut a piece of the cheesecake and slipped it into his mouth. "Mmm. This is good."

"I can't make apple tarts as good as Lydia, but I do make a mean strawberry cheesecake."

Gideon's heart sank at the mention of Lydia. He'd been unable to keep her from his thoughts. His heart still hurt from her admission that their kiss didn't mean anything to her. He'd kissed less than a handful of girls in his life, and hers had meant more to him than he had expected.

"Speaking of Lydia"—Mama wiped her mouth with a napkin—"have you heard from her lately?"

"Not since she was here last." Gideon glanced down at his watch. *Seven days and a little over two hours ago.* He huffed at the realization that he had actually counted the hours since he'd seen her last. A man who intended to take care of another woman as a life commitment should not think in such ways.

"I haven't heard from her either." Mama scrunched her face in concern. "That's odd. She usually calls several times a week, at least every two or three days."

"Does she?" Of course he knew she called so often. Just hearing Mama's light chuckles when she talked on the phone with Lydia made Gideon feel closer to her. He knew she hadn't called. It had taken every ounce of strength he had not to race over to her house to make sure she was okay. A good neighbor would do it just out of concern, but Gideon knew his heart. He would do it because of his love. A love that he had to squelch.

Lord, help me overcome these feelings for Lydia—

"Have you heard from Maria?" Mama's question interrupted Gideon's plea.

"No. The last time I talked to her, Jim was resting fine at home. Weak but stable."

"I'm going to make some soup to take over to them later. You can go with me." Mama got up and put her plate in the sink.

Yes, visiting Maria and Jim would be good. The more time Gideon spent with Maria, the more God would allow his feelings for her to grow.

"Let's finish moving the furniture."

Gideon smiled at the commanding tone in Mama's voice. The fact that she'd kept him busy was a blessing, as well. A tired body didn't have much time to think about silly things like curly, reddish-blond hair, light blue eyes, and sprinklings of freckles.

He growled. *There's not enough work in the world to keep my mind off that woman.*

❧

Lydia pulled the tarts from the oven. Her mom had been gone for a little over two hours. Though she hadn't had time to mow the lawn, Lydia was able to get the house cleaned, weed the flower gardens, and whip up some apple tarts. Most importantly, she'd been able to spend some time in God's Word and in prayer. Something she hadn't done much of the last several days. Wallowing in pity had a way of taking one's focus off the blessings God had given. Lydia was thankful her mom had given her the opportunity to reevaluate.

The sweet, fruity scent filled the air, and Lydia breathed it in. "Mmm. I hope Mom likes these as much as Lorma."

As if on cue, Lydia heard the slamming of a car door outside. She made her way to the front door and opened it before her mom had crossed the sidewalk. "Hi, Mom."

"Well, don't you look different." Her mother's smile was one Lydia recognized all too well. It was the simpering, eat-you-up one that she used on clients and now potential voters. In truth, Lydia believed her mother to be a good candidate for office. She wasn't a Christian, but she had high morals, good ethics, and an intelligent, analytical mind. Lydia also knew her mom had a disconnect when it came to feeling, and she sometimes wondered if her mom even had emotions.

"Were you able to put up all your signs?"

"Yes, I was." Her mother pulled her sunglasses off her face as she walked onto the porch.

"I made some tarts for you." Lydia stepped back when her mother walked through the door. A wave of perfume fought the fruity smell for dominance.

"Great. I'm famished. It'll be just the snack I need before I change and we go out for dinner." She peered at Lydia. "You'll need to put on something a bit nicer, as well."

Lydia looked down at her capris and blouse. This was one of her favorite outfits. In her opinion, it was totally appropriate for any restaurant in Danville. It pained her that she never felt good enough for her mom. Never. Closing her eyes, she remembered the scriptures she'd read about pleasing God over men. *I won't let Mom's insensitivity hurt me. I have a couple dresses she approves of. I'll just change for her and go to dinner. No big deal.*

She followed her mom into the kitchen, wishing her heart believed what her mind told her. *God, You'll have to keep helping me not to be hurt because I'm not good enough for her.*

A wave of self-pity washed over her being. *I wasn't good enough for Gideon, either.* Fighting back the tears that threatened to flood her face, Lydia glanced

317

at the ceiling, allowing her inner groans of unworthiness to beseech her God's assistance. Her head knew her worth came from God; she'd have to trust her heart to Him as well. A moment of authentic forgiveness for Gideon and her mother filled her. Lydia watched as her mother grabbed a plate and napkin. She scooped an apple tart off the cooling rack and bit into it. Rita's eyes widened in surprise. "This is wonderful."

Lydia's heart swelled, not only at her mom's praise but at the awareness that God would always give her what she needed from Him. "Thanks."

Her mother shook her head. "No, I mean this may be the best tart I've ever tasted."

Lydia bit her lip, willing her eyes not to tear up. Finally, her mom showed a moment of approval.

Rita popped the last of the tart into her mouth. She wiped her hands on the napkin. "You should do quite well with the coffee shop."

Lydia felt she could soar through the air. Pleasure filled her body and straightened her shoulders. "Thanks, Mom."

Rita threw the napkin in the trash. She opened the dishwasher and stuck the plate inside. Looking up at Lydia, she grimaced. "That is if you can handle the business aspect of it." With a sigh and a fling of her wrist, she walked out of the room. "I suppose we'll find out soon enough."

Lydia's joy plummeted for a brief moment. *Oh, Jesus, this is why my focus must always be on You. Your pleasure and approval alone are all I should strive for.* A vision of Gideon's rejection filled her mind and mingled with her mother's dismissal. *God, You may be the only one who will approve of me anyway.*

Chapter 13

"Mama, what do you mean you can't go to the movie?" Gideon gripped the back of the chair so hard he thought the wood might split in two. "This was your idea."

"I know. I know." Mama nodded her head as she shoved a casserole dish of some kind into the oven. "But Maria's babysitter is sick, Jim isn't feeling well either, and Maria has to work."

Gideon released the chair and kneaded the back of his neck. He'd had double the load of work on the orchard with Jim being sidelined. He wanted Jim to take all the time he needed to get better, and Gideon wouldn't consider not paying Jim while he was down. Jim had been too faithful of an employee for too many years. However, because he still paid Jim, that left him no extra income with which to hire additional help. He didn't begrudge a penny of it, but Gideon sure felt tired. This trip to the Royal Theater had actually been an excursion he'd looked forward to for most of the week. Of course, he wasn't thrilled they'd be watching a chick flick of some kind and he'd have to deal with his conflicted feelings while sitting near Lydia.

"Mama, you have to go." He smacked his hand against the counter. "We'll take the boys with us."

"To see *Sense and Sensibility*?" She chuckled. "They'd last about two minutes."

"Well, I don't want to see some silly girl movie either. You go, and I'll watch the boys."

"No. You need a break."

"Mama."

"And it's a wonderful, silly girl movie." She laughed out loud. "My overgrown son needs to get in touch with his soft side. He's been overly bristly of late."

"Mama."

"Don't 'Mama' me." She pointed her finger at him. "You're going. You will rest. You will be nice." Though he knew she tried to sound firm, a smile lifted her lips. "And you will have fun."

"Fine, Mama." Gideon grabbed his keys off the rack and walked out the door. Arguing with his mother always proved useless. It had for Pa, and it did for Gideon, as well.

"I told her we'd take her to dinner, too," she yelled from the kitchen. "Be sure you feed her."

"Sure, Mama, whatever you say." *Should I take her shopping for a new dress, maybe take her to get a haircut, too?* He knew if Mama wanted it, he'd end up doing what she asked. Trying to ignore the spark of excitement at having the chance to spend time with Lydia alone, Gideon hopped into his truck. If he allowed honesty to take precedence, he would admit taking Lydia anywhere would be complete pleasure.

He blew out a long breath. He couldn't allow those feelings. The last thing he needed was to spend time alone with Lydia. Every time he thought of her, which was too many times to count, he saw the pained expression on her face when they spoke of the kiss. Her it-didn't-mean-anything answer still pricked his heart, but he couldn't seem to stop caring for her.

But I can control my actions. Maria and I have gotten along well for some time now. I enjoy being around her and the boys.

With Jim being so sick, they needed him now. He peered at his reflection in the rearview mirror. "And you'd do good to remember that."

<hr/>

Lydia fell back onto the couch and flopped her feet on the coffee table while she waited for Lorma and Gideon to pick her up. Overall, she'd had a good visit with her mom. Rita hadn't liked the dress Lydia picked for dinner, but she'd bragged to the waiter about Lydia opening a coffee shop. Rita hadn't like the paint color or the furniture Lydia had bought for the shop, but she'd commented that maybe once the customers tried the desserts they'd be fine. Rita had also been critical about the drive the customers would have to make, the lack of signs, the yard that needed attention, and so many other things that Lydia couldn't keep them all straight in her mind.

Gideon, too, had expressed concern about the drive. Lydia and Lorma had only talked about that aspect of the business a few times. Lorma remained convinced that once customers tried the shop, they'd keep coming and bring friends, but after listening to her mother, Lydia was a bit concerned. The fact remained that no one would just happen to drive by her coffee shop without reason. She lived only a few miles away from town, not too far by any means, but still far enough that no one would just "happen by."

Queasiness filled her stomach. What if Gideon was right? He hadn't said much lately, but she knew he felt the shop was a foolhardy idea. He hadn't wanted her to borrow money for something that would flop, which really infuriated her. He'd made several assumptions without realizing she wasn't borrowing any money to start her business. *I am using the largest chunk of my savings and inheritance though.*

She swept the thought away. She was just getting nervous because she was so close to being ready to open the coffee shop. Thinking about Gideon only brought a mixture of fury and pain anyway. Rejection and condemnation seemed to accompany Gideon when she saw him. Quite frankly, she'd had enough of both in her life with her mother. She would not tolerate any from some over-grown grouch of a man.

A vision of Gideon being attacked by his nieces came to her mind. She remembered him helping his mother in the kitchen. She thought of how much George loved him and how many people in their community seemed to have a great deal of respect for Gideon.

Okay, okay. So Gideon's not an ogre. It's just me he has a problem with.

She huffed. George's ears perked up, and he jumped on the couch beside her. She petted her fast-growing pup. "What have I ever done to rile his feathers?" George turned his head, trying to lick her hand. She grinned. "Besides saying things I shouldn't, allowing you to ruin his peaches, knocking over a chair, and a number of other catastrophes."

She laughed out loud. "God, it's a good thing I'm trying to please You and not men."

Gravel popped in her driveway, alerting her that Lorma and Gideon had arrived. She stood and grabbed her purse off the coffee table. "I'll see you later." She bent down and petted George's head one last time. After making her way out the door, she locked it and turned toward the sidewalk. Her heart sped up when she looked at her ride.

Gideon sat in the truck—alone.

❧

Gideon crunched a handful of popcorn. He thought of the surprised look on Lydia's face when she first walked out her door. The drop in her expression said it all when he'd told her that Mama couldn't go with them to the movie. He shoved another handful of popcorn into his mouth. *Well, I didn't want to come alone either. Mama and her bright ideas.* "We'll take Lydia to a movie and dinner to celebrate," Mama's words echoed through his mind. The "we'll" had changed too quickly in Gideon's opinion.

Maybe it was her sweet perfume that kept distracting him, or the fact that she'd swept the sides of her hair up into some kind of clip at the back of her head. Seeing the line of her jaw and the length of her neck, he'd immediately remembered the softness of her skin. He shifted in his chair. He did not need to think about such things. *If this movie would just start, I could concentrate on it and not on her.*

As if on cue, the lights dimmed and the screen sprang to life. Attempting to focus on the commercials, he tried to ignore the light crunch of popcorn as she took small bites. *Even her snacking is distracting me.*

He had to get out of there. If only for a moment. He leaned over. He must have surprised her because she jerked and faced him. Their eyes met. She sucked in her breath and pursed her lips. His lips were mere inches from hers. Immediate need to claim them again surged through him. He broke eye contact. "I'll be right back."

Racing to the back of the theater, Gideon made his way to the restroom. Once there, he turned on the faucet and splashed cool water on his face. This was torture. Complete and utter torture. He loved this woman for her sweetness, her tenderness, her genuine care for others. He loved her spontaneity and the fact that she carried no secrets. And yes, he had to admit his attraction for her. She had captivated him the moment he'd met her.

But the way he felt when he was with her completely took him by surprise. He wanted to protect her from anything that would ever hurt her. He wanted to wrap his arms around her and claim her as his one and only. He longed to love her openly and without reservation. With Lydia, he'd feel what he watched his parents share.

But it's not to be. God, help me. My Christian duty is to care for those who need care. Lydia doesn't need me.

She doesn't?

Gideon closed his eyes to the question that formed in his mind. Lydia was a strong, capable woman full of life and energy. She loved the Lord and sought His guidance. Maria was the one who needed his help. She needed him to take care of her.

Are you the great Provider?

The thought that pricked Gideon's heart humbled him. Was he taking matters into his own hands? Was Gideon not showing God the faith He required and deserved?

Gideon dried his hands and face with a paper towel. He stared at his reflection in the mirror. Dark bags hung under his eyes, proof that sleep had evaded him several nights in a row and that he'd put in extra hours of labor in the orchard. Weariness, in body and spirit, had become his best friend.

God alone knew what Lydia and Maria needed, but Gideon also knew God placed people in his and others' lives to help them along the way. Maria needed someone to care for her. No one denied that. It was obvious to Jim, to Maria, and to Gideon. These questions pounding his mind were simply Gideon's own selfish desires to find a way to pursue a relationship with Lydia. And Gideon refused to be selfish.

⌾

"I should be ready to open for business in a month." Lydia cut off a piece of her sirloin and dipped it in steak sauce. She'd started every possible conversation she could think of with Gideon. Anything to keep her from thinking about his amazing eyes or the perfect tone of his tanned skin.

"That's great."

She watched as Gideon stabbed his fork into his baked potato. The man must have had a vendetta against the vegetable. *Or maybe it's me.* She shoved the piece of meat into her mouth. It wasn't her fault that Lorma hadn't been able to go to the movie with them. No one forced Gideon to take her. *Well, that's probably not true. I'm sure Lorma didn't give him any other options.*

Lydia pierced her fork through the green beans. Still, she had tried to keep a positive outlook. She'd enjoyed the movie. *Sense and Sensibility* was one of her favorites. But she'd also been aware that Gideon felt less than comfortable. The fact that he'd gone to the restroom at least three times proved it.

She sneaked a peek at the man across the table from her. A frown etched his jaw while his gaze stayed focused on his plate. Fury erupted within her. She'd given him no reason to behave in such an unfriendly manner. "Gideon, is something wrong?" She knew the words snapped from her mouth, but she'd had it with him.

"Nope." He didn't look up, just jabbed his meat.

"Are you sure?"

"Yep."

Lydia chewed on the inside of her lip, watching as Gideon shoved part of his roll into his mouth. He still hadn't looked up at her. "I'm thinking I must have offended you in some way. I know we didn't part on the best of terms. . ." The memory of his rejection swelled within her heart and threatened to spill from her lips. She fought it back. "But I thought we were going to try to be. . . friends."

Oh, how she didn't want to be friends. Being Gideon's friend was like denying her heart the right to beat. Even as he sat across from her, unwilling to make eye contact, she still longed for a relationship with him—one that entailed love and commitment.

Gideon blew out a long breath and leaned back in his seat. He looked up at her for the first time. "You're right. I'm just very preoccupied." He twisted the fork. "I'm sorry."

True repentance wrapped his features. Forgiveness replaced her anger. She knew he'd had a hard few weeks. "I know you've been busy. If it was too much for you to get away this evening, I would have understood."

He shook his head. "No, I needed some time away."

She'd spent several days wrapped up in self-pity over this man's rejection. But now, she felt an overwhelming compassion for him. Her attraction to him still existed. She couldn't deny that. If she were completely honest, she knew she cared for him as she'd never cared for another man. But at this moment, she knew he needed friendship, and she could offer that. She reached across the table and touched the top of his hand.

He jerked but didn't move away.

"I'll be praying for you."

"Thanks." His features seemed to carry a burden greater than he confessed as he pulled his hand away from hers.

She noted a longing in his eyes that she couldn't quite decipher, but she didn't try to either.

An overwhelming peace invaded Lydia's soul. From the depths of her heart, she wanted Gideon's best. His best didn't have to include her, and unbelievably, she felt at peace about that. God's will was the most important thing in both their lives, and if friendship was what God designed for them, then who was she to argue with her heavenly Father.

Tears filled her eyes and she wiped them away. *God, I truly am learning that Your pleasure is more important than mine. Thank You, Jesus.*

Chapter 14

Gideon dropped Lydia off at her house and drove home. The evening had been a complete wreck. All he could think about was how much he cared for Lydia. In the midst of being consumed with his feelings, he'd been a jerk all evening.

After pulling the key from the ignition, he slipped outside and gently closed the door. He needed some time alone. Just him and God. He needed to get down to the nitty-gritty of his battle between love for Lydia and duty to Maria. He'd had all a man could take.

He took determined steps toward the orchard. With fall quickly approaching, his trees had grown to their peaks. The apples blossomed more scrumptious looking every day. Shoving his hands deep into his pockets, he peered up at the heavens that shone between the trees. "God, I can't do this anymore. I'm not hearing from You, and I can't turn off the feelings I have for Lydia."

The wind whispered back to him as it drifted past branches and leaves. He noted the dotting of stars in the vast expanse above him. If God could create the heavens and the earth, He could tell Gideon what to do about Lydia and Maria.

"Maria needs me, God. She has no husband and two boys to care for. But I love Lydia. To the depth of my core, I know I love her. I love her smile, her sweet expressions. I love her clumsiness and spontaneity. I love her love for people." He lifted his hands to his chest, never taking his gaze off the heavens above him. "But isn't it selfish for me to want Lydia when it is Maria who has the need?"

Please God, not men. The gist of the Galatians verse he'd heard on Mama's CD filled his heart. But what pleased God? Both women were Christians. This wasn't a matter of following scripture; it was a matter of the heart. If there were no circumstances involved, he wouldn't even consider Maria as a mate.

The admission tore at him. Would it be fair to spend his life with a woman whom he would have never considered if it weren't for her circumstances?

Shaking his head, he knelt in the middle of the path. "God, I need Your will. Whatever it is, show me."

His phone vibrated in his pocket. He pulled it out and pushed TALK. "Hello."

"Gideon, it's Maria. I need you to come to the hospital right now."

"Mom, where are we going?" Lydia had to raise her voice over the mufflers, whistles, and horns—a typical Indianapolis symphony. She tried to keep up with her mother's quick pace across the street. The woman walked at record speed despite the fact that she had on three-inch heels.

"My office. We have some business to settle."

Apprehension welled in Lydia's gut. She had no more than walked into the house after going to the movies and dinner with Gideon when her mother called and said she'd be at Lydia's first thing in the morning. She wouldn't tell Lydia what happened, just that Lydia had no choice but to join her for legal matters.

Lydia scaled the steps outside the high-rise building her mother worked at in the city. The air felt thick and heavy and seemed to weigh down on Lydia. The chatter of people and ringing cell phones, and a myriad of other sounds, caused her head to pound. They walked into some semblance of quiet and order once inside the building, but Lydia could barely keep up with her mom's staccato steps across the polished floors and into the nearest elevator.

Silence wrapped the crowded area when several people joined them on their quest for a floor above the first. The lighted number four and accompanying *beep* notified them they had reached her mother's floor. Before the doors had opened fully, her mom grabbed her hand and led her out. Lydia breathed a sigh of relief and took a moment to catch her breath when she finally read her mother's name, along with several others, on a plate beside an ornate door.

"Come on." Her mom grabbed her hand again and led her through the office. She didn't stop to say hello to anyone.

Lydia tried to nod and smile, but their breakneck speed did little to invite proper greetings.

Rita abruptly stopped outside a solid black door, but Lydia wasn't prepared and ran smack into the back of her mother. Rita pushed her off. "Really, Lydia." She smoothed the front of her skirt. "Straighten yourself up."

"What's going on, Mom?"

A determined expression crossed Rita's face as she grabbed the doorknob. "You'll find out soon enough." She opened the door, and Lydia peered inside.

"Hello, Lydia."

Panic wrapped around Lydia's chest when the older woman, dressed in a long black dress, stood to her feet. Lydia swallowed the golf-ball-sized knot that had instantaneously formed in her throat. "Hello, Aunt Grace."

Gideon watched as his mother wrapped Maria in an embrace. Sobs poured from the younger woman, and Gideon could do nothing but watch as her back heaved with the immense emotion. Mama crooned at her, patting her back and hair.

Gideon's body seemed to have rooted itself to the floor. He shifted his gaze to the hospital bed. The sheets were rumpled. Only minutes ago it had held his friend and employee.

But now it was empty, and Jim was dead.

This scene proved too familiar to him. It brought back too many memories of his pa's death. His sisters crying. His mother crying. Pats on the back. Too many hugs. He hated the smell of a hospital.

Gideon scanned the room. "Where are the boys?" Concern for the two guys filled his heart. They loved their grandpa so much.

"Oh." Maria released herself from Mama and wiped her eyes. "They're with a nurse out front." She wiped her nose on a tissue. "I've got to get hold of myself and go see them. They'll be terrified if they see me like this."

"I'll go." The words slipped through Gideon's mouth before he'd had a chance to think. The boys would have questions that he didn't want to answer, wasn't sure it was his place to answer. "What should I tell them. . .if they ask?"

"You don't need to do that, Gideon." She sucked in a deep breath. "I'm okay. I'll go get the boys."

Mama touched her arm. "You're not okay, dear. Let Gideon see to the boys for a moment."

Maria's bottom lip quivered as she nodded. "You don't have to tell them anything. If they ask. . ." She flailed her arm through the air. "I don't know. Bring them to me."

Gideon forced his feet to lift off the floor and moved toward the entrance of the hospital. Just as Maria had said, the boys sat in an office with a young woman. She looked up at Gideon as he approached. An expression of pity covered her features. "Hey guys, what are you doing?" Gideon kneeled to the boys' level.

Jeremy shoved a piece of scribbled paper in his face. "Color."

"That's great, Jer." Gideon tousled his hair and turned toward Kelbe. The young boy's face drew into a deep frown.

"Where's grandpa?"

"Well. . ."

"Is he still sick?" Kelbe laid his paper on the chair. "I want to go see him."

"Well, Kelbe. . ."

Before Gideon could answer, Maria swept into the room. Tears still filled her eyes as she bent down and scooped her boys into an embrace. "I couldn't let you tell the boys. I have to do it."

Gideon nodded and stood to his feet. He watched as Maria explained that Grandpa wouldn't be going home with them, that he'd gone home to Jesus. The boys' incessant questions and Maria's patient dealing with their loss tore at his heart. He felt like an intruder and yet knew he needed to be there.

God, I guess this is my answer.

∽∾

Lydia's mom motioned for her to have a seat beside her aunt. Lydia feared they could hear her knees knocking together as she tried to obey her mother's gesture. She had a feeling she knew what this was about. Dread stirred inside her. Taking her seat, she turned to her aunt. "Do you need me for something?"

"I want my share of the house."

Lydia's heart raced at the words she'd heard. She didn't have any money to give her aunt. She'd have to move. After all the work and planning, after all the sweat and excitement, she'd have to pack her things and move. But where? *God, what am I to do?*

"Now, wait a minute, Grace." Her mother's voice penetrated Lydia's thoughts. Rita leaned forward in the plush leather chair behind the desk. Lydia hadn't even realized her mother had walked away from the door, let alone taken a seat. "Surely we can work something out."

Aunt Grace nodded her head, causing the perfect dark brown curls around her face to bounce. "Yes, we can sell the house, and I will collect my portion of the money."

Lydia gasped.

"But Grace"—her mother curled her fingers together and laid them on top of the desk—"Lydia has put a lot of work into the house. A lot of her own money. I told you she was opening a coffee shop."

"I never said she could open a shop." Her aunt's stare bore into Lydia. "And no one asked me either."

"I'm sorry." Lydia wrapped her fingers around the strap on her purse. "I just assumed. . ."

"Never assume, young lady. You could have had the common courtesy to ask my opinion before you decided to try to make money off my mother's property."

Guilt filled Lydia's heart. She hadn't asked Aunt Grace's opinion. She'd talked to her mother, but Aunt Grace owned half the house. It was her right to know what Lydia decided to do with the home. Obviously, the oversight had meant a lot to her aunt. She turned to face her aunt more fully. "You're right. I'm sorry. I didn't think. . ."

"That's right, you didn't think. You never think. You just go and do and never think about what it will cost others."

Lydia sucked in her breath.

"That's enough, Grace."

Lydia looked at her mother. The protective tone in her voice was one that

328

Lydia had never known. Rita stood to her feet and walked around the desk. She leaned against it and clasped her hands. "What if I buy your half from you?"

"What?" Lydia and Aunt Grace said at the same time.

"I'll buy your half. I think Lydia has a good thing going on over there. I think her business will do well." She shrugged her shoulders. "And if it doesn't, it won't be because she hasn't put a lot of planning into it."

Lydia couldn't speak. Her mother had obviously stunned her aunt as well, because Grace didn't say anything for several minutes.

"If it's the money you want, you have no choice legally but to be willing to let me purchase your half."

"I know." The fury behind Aunt Grace's words was palpable, and Lydia shivered.

"Then I guess it's settled." Her mom slipped behind the desk again. "I'll have the papers written up."

Lydia watched in stunned silence as her aunt and mother discussed various legalities. Her mother believed in what she was doing. For the first time in her life, Rita Louise Hammond thought Lydia was doing something worthwhile. The magnitude of it rocked Lydia's core, and she didn't know what to think, what to feel, what to say.

After some time, Grace stood and peered down at Lydia. "Don't mess this up for your mother."

Her words were harsh, and they hurt, but the fact that her mother had faith in her overshadowed anything her aunt could do or say.

"I'll do my very best." Lydia smiled and looked back at her mother. She remembered the day her mother had tasted the apple tarts, the day Lydia had given her desire to please over to the Lord. She had truly set her need to please her mother at the feet of Jesus, and He blessed her with a moment of maternal acceptance. *Oh, Jesus, You are too good to me.*

Chapter 15

Lydia jumped at the sound of knocking on her front door. George practically soared off the bed, barking and growling at the noise. Lydia rubbed her eyes, trying to force them open. She strained to see the alarm clock. "Five thirty?"

She pushed the covers off as the knocks, followed by George's intertwining of barks and growls, ensued again. Grabbing her robe, she mumbled, "Who in the world would be beating down my door at this time in the morning?"

Finally making it to the door, Lydia peered through the peephole. Lorma stood fully dressed but with her hair flowing down her back in a disheveled mess. It was the first time Lydia had seen the woman's hair down, and she would have never guessed it to be so long as to flow past her shoulders. Well, it didn't exactly flow; it kind of gathered past her shoulders.

When Lorma knocked on the door again, Lydia jumped back, clearing her mind of thoughts of Lorma's hair. She opened the door, noting the distraught expression on Lorma's face. Lydia frowned. "Lorma, what's wrong?"

The older woman pushed her way through the door and started pacing in Lydia's living room. "I don't know what to do."

Fear filled Lydia's heart. Had something happened to Gideon? Starting to fully wake up, Lydia realized something terrible must have happened for Lorma to come over this early in the morning. "Lorma, did something happen to Gideon?" Lydia touched Lorma's arm, realizing something might be wrong with her. "Are you okay?"

Lorma sat on the couch then jumped up again. "I'm fine. Fine. You've got to go talk to Gideon."

Lydia let out a sigh of relief. Gideon must not be hurt if Lorma wanted her to talk to him. "Here now." She grabbed her friend's arm. "Let's go to the kitchen, and I'll make us some coffee. You can tell me what's going on."

Lorma shook her head but allowed Lydia to lead her. "He just can't do this. It's not what he wants." Lorma looked at Lydia. "I know my son better than he knows himself. And he hasn't really given this to God. I know." She pointed to her chest. "I can tell."

Lydia's concern and curiosity piqued. It was evident Lorma spoke of Gideon. But what decision had he made that upset his mother so much? Lydia had no idea. Gideon seemed as steady as his orchard. He was good to his family. He cared about his employee and his family. He and Lydia seemed to have some difficulty coming to terms on things, but Lydia believed that was because she cared about him in a way that wasn't reciprocated. Though she had moments of wanting to lash out at him for not caring for her, she couldn't force him to do so.

Lorma sat in a chair. She plopped her elbows on top of the table and rested her chin in her hand. "He loves you."

"What?" Lydia spun around to gawk at her older friend.

Lorma's gaze stayed trained on the table's centerpiece. She seemed to have forgotten Lydia was in the room. "Why he can't admit it to himself, I just don't know."

"What?"

"He's always been worried about doing the right thing. A good trait. A mother can't complain about a son who wants to do what's right, but sometimes he thinks about what he thinks is the right thing instead of what God thinks is the right thing." She looked at Lydia. "Does that make sense?"

"I have no idea what you're talking about."

"Okay, one time when he was a boy he found a small kitten along the side of the road. Something or someone had abused the animal. Gideon brought the kitty home and hid her in his room to nurse her back to health." Lorma flailed her hand through the air. "Sounds like a sweet thing to do. Except Dalton is desperately allergic to cats. The poor boy blew up like a balloon. We had to rush him to the hospital, but I had no idea what had caused Dalton's reaction. I worried over foods and laundry detergents. Later that day, Sabrina found the kitten beneath Gideon's bed. Of course, we had to give the kitty to a family who could nurse her back to health. Do you see what I mean?"

Lydia furrowed her brows as she scooped coffee grounds into the coffee filter. "I still have no idea what you're talking about, Lorma."

Lorma sighed and crossed her arms in front of her chest. "Gideon actually hurt his brother by trying to help the kitten. Helping the kitten was a noble thing, but not in the way Gideon went about it. He should have helped the kitten by taking her to another house. She was adopted by our friends and led a great kitty life."

Lydia rubbed her temples. Maybe she wasn't fully awake yet, but she still had no idea what her friend was getting at. She turned on the coffeepot. *Maybe once I get a little caffeine in me, Lorma will make more sense.*

Lorma stood and walked over to the cabinets. She pulled out two coffee mugs and set them on the counter. Touching Lydia's hand, she let out a long breath. "He loves you."

Lydia pulled her hand away and rubbed her eyes again. "Lorma, what are you talking about?"

"Gideon." The older woman smacked her hand against the counter. "What do you think I've been talking about?"

Lydia bit the inside of her lip. She tried to recall all the things Lorma had said since she walked through the door. Her friend needed to give Lydia a break. It wasn't even six yet; it was still dark outside. What did kittens and Gideon and Dalton have to do with loving her? And why would Lorma feel the need to traipse to her house in the wee hours of the morning all upset about it? "Okay. Maybe it's because I just woke up." She didn't mention that Lorma's incessant knocks had been the cause of the rude awakening. "But I have no idea what you're talking about."

"Gideon loves you."

Lydia stepped back. She swallowed the hope, excitement, denial, and disbelief that swirled within her. The softness of his kiss sprang to her mind, and she touched her lips. "No, he doesn't."

Lorma nodded. "Yes, he does."

"But he's even said—"

"He said he didn't love you?"

"In so many words, he said—"

"That's because he thinks he's supposed to marry Maria."

"What?"

Lorma poured herself a cup of coffee and made her way back over to the table. She slowly sat down. "Jim had been putting pressure on Gideon about Maria ever since her husband died, leaving her to raise the boys alone. Lately, Maria's added to that pressure, and with Jim dying. . ."

Lydia gasped. "Jim died?"

A tear slipped down Lorma's cheek. "Yes. Four days ago. The funeral was yesterday. It was so hard. Those boys. . . Maria was beside herself." She peered at Lydia. "I tried to call. I couldn't get in touch with you."

"I was at my mom's house. She had some business for me."

Lorma nodded. "I feel so bad for Maria." She placed her hand on her chest, and her voice caught. "I know how hard it is to lose someone, but that poor girl has lost her husband and now her father in just over a year."

Lydia sat across from Lorma. She placed her hand over her friend's. "Is there anything I can do to help?"

"That's sweet of you, dear, but right now everything is fine. I'll be watching the boys since Jim helped pay her childcare expenses. I kept them yesterday so that Maria could take care of some things. I'll be feeding them, but Gideon. . ." She swiped the tear from her eye. "He's planning to ask Maria to marry him."

"He is?" Sadness wrapped around Lydia's heart so tight she feared she would suffocate.

"He thinks it's the right thing to do." She shook her head. "But you don't marry someone because you feel sorry for her or just because you want to help her. God is the ultimate Provider."

Lydia searched her mind for something to say. She hurt to the depths of her core, but maybe Gideon knew best. "Well, maybe—"

"And you definitely don't marry someone when you love someone else." Lorma's intense gaze sent shivers down Lydia's spine.

"I don't believe he loves me."

"He does. He just won't admit it."

Lydia was baffled. What could she say to Lorma? She stood and walked to the coffeepot. Warm steam tickled her nose as she poured herself a cup. She believed the older woman knew Gideon better than most mothers knew their sons, but Lydia couldn't help but feel Lorma was wrong on this. Outside of their kiss, Gideon had never openly encouraged her to believe he had feelings for her. *And even that he dismissed.*

"You have to tell him you love him, too."

Lydia almost spilled the hot coffee down her shirt. She set the pot down and gawked at Lorma. "What?"

"Tell him you love him, Lydia. Force him to see he's making a mistake."

"I will not tell him—"

"You don't love him?"

The intensity in Lorma's eyes made Lydia's knees shake. She'd been trying to suppress her growing affection for Gideon for several weeks now. Yes, she'd had a bout of overwhelming sadness at his rejection. And maybe she had believed she might love him. But he didn't return the feelings, so she'd put her full effort into the coffee shop. "Well, I—"

"You love him." Lorma laid her cup on the table with a thud. "It's okay to admit it. I know you feel vulnerable, but I promise he does love you."

"Now, Lorma—"

"Lydia, you have to stop him from doing this. Maria is in the midst of sadness. She thinks Gideon will solve her problems, but God is the only one who can do that. And Gideon doesn't love her in that way. This isn't right for either one of them."

Lydia placed both hands on her hips and faced her older friend. "I will not tell Gideon I love him, like him, or can't stand the sight of him. He's a grown man, and if he chooses to marry Maria, that is his business."

Lydia coughed back the welling of emotion that filled her throat after the outburst. *God, You have to take away these feelings I have for Gideon. I can't feel this way about a man who is marrying someone else.*

❦

Gideon scratched the several days' worth of growth on his chin. Mama had been on him several times to shave his face, but he just hadn't felt like it. His heart hurt at the loss of his employee. He knew Jim was in heaven, but that didn't stop the sadness at losing his friend. It had brought back memories of his pa, as well. Good memories and sad ones.

Having the boys around the house the day before had placed additional strain on him. He enjoyed that they kept him busy—less time to think—but it felt uncomfortable for them to be there. More pressure. *It won't feel that way once I marry Maria.*

At the moment, everything was quiet. Even Mama hadn't awoken. He glanced at his watch. It was almost seven. Mama usually arose well before this time, but Gideon figured she was overly tired from all that had happened. He leaned over in his chair and scooped up the weekly newspaper. Normally he read it right away, but with all the happenings of late, he hadn't looked at in two days. He skimmed the first few pages. An advertisement caught his eye. Lydia's coffee shop opened in less than a week.

He rested his head back against the chair and closed his eyes, allowing a vision of her to filter into his mind. Her curly, reddish hair fell around her shoulders and framed her face. Joyous twinkles filled her eyes. And those cute freckles splattered along her nose. How would he ever erase them from his thoughts?

"Hey, Gideon."

Gideon opened his eyes and leaned forward at the sound of Kelbe's voice. Heat warmed Gideon's face. He felt guilty thinking of Lydia when he should be focused on Maria and the boys. "Hey, buddy. When did you get here?"

"Just a minute ago."

"Where's your mom?"

"Looking for Lorma. Will you fix me some cereal?"

"Of course." Gideon stood and walked the little guy into the kitchen. *I hope Mama feels all right. She never sleeps this late.* He helped Kelbe onto the chair then grabbed several boxes from the cabinet. "Which one do you want?"

Kelbe pointed to the one Gideon felt sure contained enough sugar to supply a candy factory. Gideon shrugged. Either his mother or Maria had bought the cereal, so it must not have been too bad for the boy. Although, that might explain why the boys ran around with more energy than he could ever conjure for the greatest part of each day.

Gideon poured the cereal into the bowl. He opened the refrigerator, scooping out the gallon of milk. Even their fridge had blossomed with character-covered treats that he'd had no idea existed. *I'm going to have to learn about these things quick if I'm going to marry Maria.*

He frowned. Every time he thought of marrying Maria, an overwhelming sadness sank into his gut. He didn't want to dread what was right to do. Surely

God would take away these feelings. He'd been praying for God to show him whom to choose—Lydia or Maria—when he received word of Jim's death. If that wasn't a sign from God, Gideon didn't know what one was.

Uneasiness wrapped itself around him. *When was the last time I spent time in God's Word?* He shook his head. Where had that come from? He'd been to church just last week. He'd been praying and seeking. God had been quiet, but it wasn't because Gideon didn't want to be in God's will.

Dread weighed him again. Something wasn't right. He still didn't have any peace about anything.

"Thanks, Gideon."

Gideon turned at the sound of Maria's voice. He wished he would feel some attraction to her, but nothing came. "No problem."

Maria smoothed the front of her pants. "Do you know where your mom went?"

"She's not here?"

Maria shook her head.

Gideon peered outside the window. "Her car's gone." He'd never even considered that she would have gone somewhere this early in the morning.

That wasn't like her. It especially wasn't like her not to leave a note or call him to let him know where she'd gone. He grabbed his keys off the rack. "I'll be back in a little bit."

I'll start with Lydia's. After turning on the ignition, Gideon shifted into drive. Within moments, he spotted Mama's car in Lydia's driveway. Relief washed over him as he pulled his vehicle in beside hers.

After jumping out of the cab, he walked up the sidewalk to Lydia's front door. He noticed she'd weeded her flowers again and that all signs of George's early-in-the-season diggings were long gone. Knocking on the door, he bit his lip. He hadn't planned to see Lydia again for a while. He figured the more distance he put between them, the quicker his heart could get over

Lydia opened the door. Concern and something else crossed her features before she lifted her lips in a tentative smile. "Hi, Gideon."

He pointed to his mother's car. "Mama's here?"

"Yes." She hesitated then opened the door more. "Come on in."

He heard shuffling in the kitchen and walked toward the noise. Spying his mother at the sink, he scratched his unshaven jaw. "Mama, what are you doing?"

"Cleaning up these breakfast dishes. What does it look like?"

"No, I mean, why are you here so early in the morning?"

"What does it matter? You won't listen to me. She won't listen to me either." She pointed to Lydia, and Lydia shrugged, lifting her hands in surrender.

"What are you talking about?" He walked over to her and touched her arm. "You're probably tired from keeping up with those boys yesterday. How long have you been up?"

"I'm fine." She shook his hand off. "Lydia is every bit as thickheaded as you. You talking about marrying people you don't—"

Gideon sucked in his breath as if she'd punched him in the gut. Surely she had not told Lydia of his plan to ask Maria to marry him. No, his mother would never do that to him. He watched as she fussed with the towel and the bowl in her hand. *Oh yes, she would.* He leaned close to her and whispered, "Mama, you did not tell Lydia about me and Maria."

"Yes, I did." She wiped her hands on a dishrag. After grabbing her purse, she stomped toward the front door. "You're both ridiculous."

Shocked, Gideon could do nothing more than watch his mother slam the door behind her. What had she said? What did Lydia think? His gaze found Lydia standing in the door leading to her soon-to-be coffee shop. She seemed as unable to move as Gideon.

Embarrassed, Gideon cleared his throat. He shoved his hands deep into his pockets. "Well, I guess I'd better go."

He moved toward the door. Lydia must still have been shocked, because she hadn't uttered a word and he hadn't heard any movement behind him. He walked out, making his way toward his truck. Things Mama may have said to her shot at him from every angle. The woman was often too opinionated and entirely too forward with her thoughts, which only surmounted his fear.

"Gideon."

Gideon turned around to find Lydia standing in the doorway. She sported a mess of disheveled hair framing her face, sleepy eyes, and an oversized robe. Lydia drew him in with intensity. "Yeah?"

"You're. . .a good man."

Gideon nodded, hopped into his truck, and drove off. What had she meant by that? Was she giving her permission for him to marry Maria? Maybe she was telling him it was the right thing to do. Whatever she meant, he felt anything but good right now.

Chapter 16

L ydia straightened the hem of her skirt. She hadn't bitten her nails since she was thirteen, but she found herself fighting off the urge every few seconds. The OPEN sign turned toward the public in the front door signified the beginning of her business.

She scanned the coffee shop again. A sofa, two wingback chairs, and several tables rested graciously in various places in the room. The rich color on the walls beckoned serenity. The robust scent of coffee muted the many flavors of tea she had ready for customers to choose from. Today, she'd serve both of her specialties—apple tarts and apple pies.

Looking down at her watch, she let out a slow breath to calm her anxious heart. She'd been open for two minutes. She frowned. "I wonder where Lorma is." Her friend had been just as excited, if not more so, about opening the shop. She'd promised to be here before the first customer. Lydia shrugged. "Well, there aren't any customers yet."

An immediate queasiness forced her to the nearest chair. What if no one showed up? She'd spent a good chunk of her savings and inheritance to open the place. Her mother had bought out her aunt's share of the house. For the first time in Lydia's life, her mom believed in something Lydia had chosen. What if she flopped. . .again?

Nausea overwhelmed her and she dashed into the kitchen for a lemon-lime soda, a ginger ale, anything that would keep her from hurling on her opening day. *Please God, not man.* The meaning of the Galatians and Thessalonians scriptures she'd read over and over the past few months flew into her mind.

She popped open her soda and took a slow sip. Scrutinizing the can, she said, "Please God, not man." She stood again. "Please God, not man." Lifting her face to the ceiling, she closed her eyes. "Oh, Jesus, I need only to please You. If this flops, then I will know You have something better for me."

Walking back into her coffee shop, contentment washed over her. The last few months had been some of the most trying of her life, and still her future appeared as uncertain as ever. She didn't know if this business would make it, and she'd invested so much into it. She still had deep affection for a man who didn't share her feelings. *Oh, who am I kidding? I know I love Gideon.* Her dog still chewed up things he shouldn't. Her mom would probably be livid if the business didn't thrive. And yet Lydia felt an inner peace. One that went deeper than the jitters she felt at her opening day.

A smile twitched her lips as she poured herself a large mug of coffee. *With God leading my life, nothing can shake me.*

◄━━◊◊━━►

Gideon picked up a broken twig off the ground. He snapped it between his fingers. He'd grown tired of playing games. He knew what he should do, what was right. Gideon just hadn't been able to do it. Well, enough was enough.

He stomped toward the house. Maria had spent the whole day with his mother. *Just go in there and spit it out. Once I've said it, I'll feel better.* After pushing the door open, he barreled down the hall, practically running over Maria as she stepped out of the restroom. "I'm sorry." He grabbed her elbow. "Are you okay?"

She gathered her footing and looked up at him. A shy smile split her lips.

Gideon frowned. The woman appeared almost timid. He hadn't seen that side of her in a while. When she first moved here after her husband's death, she'd been sad and shy, like a wounded puppy. Once Lydia moved to town, her demeanor had changed to aggressive and flirtatious. Since her father died, Maria had been determined but sad all over again. Gideon wasn't sure who Maria really was as a person. He figured she probably wasn't sure herself after all the loss she'd had in such a short time.

"I need to talk to you." Gideon spit the words out with more force than he'd intended.

"Good. I need to talk to you, too. You first." She pushed a strand of dark hair behind her ear, and Gideon wished the motion stirred him as it did when he saw Lydia do it. But he felt nothing, and the admission of it weighed his heart.

"Well. . ." He cleared his throat, willing his mouth to utter the words his heart denied. It seemed wrong, so very wrong to issue the words he sought for this woman. But feelings could be deceiving, and he needed to focus on what was right. "I wanted. . ."

Maria's brows furrowed, and she nodded. "Go ahead."

A cold sweat washed over his body. He leaned against the wall as dizziness swept through him with such force he feared landing prone on the carpet at any moment. *Just spit it out.* "I think we should get married."

Maria's eyes widened, and her jaw dropped.

Gideon closed his eyes, allowing his head to thump against the wall. *Very romantic, Andrews. Way to draw the woman in, make her feel wanted.* He gathered his courage and looked at her again. "What I meant to say—"

Maria lifted her hand to stop him. She pursed her lips then let out a sigh. Her gaze drifted to her fingertips as she mumbled, "I thought you'd never ask."

Horror gripped Gideon's heart as his question forced him into realization that he could never love Maria as he did Lydia. *What am I doing? Oh, God, You have to see me through this.*

A vision of his wedding day passed through his mind. His bride waltzed down the aisle toward him. Lydia looked beautiful. . .

He shook his head. *Maria. I must focus on Maria.*

Maria blew out a long breath, rubbed her hands together, then intertwined her fingers. "I've been waiting to hear you say that for several months now."

He forced a smile to his lips. "Good. I haven't bought you a ring. I'll let you pick one out. When shall we set the date?"

"Do you love me?"

"Well, I. . .I mean, I. . ."

"You don't." Maria touched his arm. "And it's okay." She raked her fingers through her hair. "I thought I loved you. Thought you'd be the best thing for me and the boys. But when I saw you with Lydia. . .well, I don't want to be second place."

Shame washed over him. Mama had said the same thing on multiple occasions, but he had ignored her. "Maria, I. . ."

"The boys and I are moving to California."

"What?"

"I have two aunts who live there. My mother's sisters. They've agreed to let the boys and me move in with them until I can find a job and settle in."

"But, but. . ." Gideon shifted his weight from one foot to the other. "You don't have to leave. You. . .you and the boys love it here. I could help—"

"You're a good man, Gideon, and I appreciate all you've done for my dad, my boys, and me. I know you would help." Maria rubbed the front of her forehead. "But we've gone from Wisconsin to Indiana. We can learn to love California, too."

Determination welled within Gideon. He thought of the pain her boys would feel at having to be uprooted once again. They were too young to have to deal with such instability. It wasn't right. He stuck out his chin. "My offer stands."

Maria let out a soft laugh. "You big oaf. A month ago, maybe even a week ago, I'd have taken you up on that."

"Well, then what's the problem?"

She gazed into his eyes. "You love someone else."

"Now, I never said—"

"You never said it, but"—she placed one hand on her hip and squinted her eyes at him—"it's true just the same." She smacked her hand on her thigh. "I've already told you once. I don't want to be second place. I won't do it. I know you love my boys, and I know you like me all right, but I need a man who longs for me while he's at work or when he's away. Do you long for me like that, Gideon?"

"Well, I could—"

She flailed her hand in the air. "Listen. You need to spend some time with your Maker. I know He's been doing a work on my stubborn head for several days now. Going to California is the right thing for me and my boys." She blew out a breath. "Look, I know you're a good man who wants to do what's right. Let God show you what's right." She pointed to his chest. "For you—Gideon Andrews."

Gideon watched as she turned back, headed toward the bathroom, and shut the door. She was the second woman in the last week to tell him he was a good man. Yet, both times he'd felt anything but good.

He walked into his bedroom and grabbed his Bible off the nightstand. "You and I are going to have a good talk." He looked out his window and toward his favorite spot just inside the orchard. "And this time I'm going to do a lot of listening."

⟡

Lydia smacked her alarm clock to stop its incessant buzzing. With extreme effort, she pulled back her covers and lifted herself from the bed. Her coffee shop had been open a week, and she'd had four customers. Four.

She rubbed her eyes and rolled her head around to stretch her neck. It proved hard to wake up so early, knowing that probably no one would show. She padded into the bathroom and started the shower. *God, is there anything else I should be doing to get the word out about the shop? What should I change?*

Maybe it just wasn't meant to be. Gideon had warned her about the location. He had been concerned if there was a market for such a place in their small community. She and Lorma had shrugged him off, believing Lydia's place would be unique. Even though he'd been more than hesitant about her business, Lydia couldn't deny he'd been a constant help in getting it running.

Stepping into the shower, she closed her eyes under the warm splattering of water. Oh, how she missed that man. By now, he'd probably already proposed to Maria. She really needed to stop thinking about him. But it seemed the less she saw of him the more she longed to see him again. She let out a sarcastic breath. "I guess it's true what they say, absence does make the heart grow fonder."

She shook her head. *Think about getting the shop ready today.* "Okay. I need to make another batch of apple tarts." She snarled. She and Lorma had eaten most of the first batch. She grimaced when she thought of her friend. Lorma had been just as disappointed as Lydia at the lack of customers. The four people who'd come had been friends of Lorma's from the church. One of the ladies didn't even purchase anything, just stopped by to say hello.

After finishing her shower, she blow-dried her hair, allowing the curls to lie naturally around her shoulders. She scooped her devotional and Bible into her hands and made her way to the kitchen table. Over the last few months, she'd grown accustomed to spending her quiet time gazing out at Grandma's beautiful backyard.

God, I need to know You're still in control and that I am living surrendered to You. She opened her devotional and read a scripture from the book of Philippians. Allowing the words to seep thoroughly into her heart, she gazed at the seemingly never-ending sea of foliage. "God, I choose not to worry. I will pray and petition You that I may know Your will and have perfect peace."

Feeling refreshed, she walked over to the kitchen counter. She gathered the ingredients she'd need for the tarts. George trotted beside her, wagging his tail. She looked down at him. "You know what, George, I have no idea what God has planned." George barked and lifted his nose high in the air. "I'll just keep doing what I'm doing, fully surrendered to Him. He'll show me."

The doorbell rang, and George lit into a chorus of yelps. *I really should have trained that dog in a few things more than just to where to use the bathroom.* Lydia glanced at her watch. It was way too early for a customer. Even Lorma wouldn't come over this early. She huffed. *Unless she's trying to get me to profess all my feelings to Gideon.* The doorbell rang again. "I'm coming."

Gideon almost turned around and headed home when he heard Lydia's voice from inside the house. He could hear the tapping of her feet as she approached. Part of him wanted to run. What would she say when he told her how he felt? After all, they'd only known each other for two months. But the other part of him wanted to scoop her into his arms the moment she opened that door.

The door opened and the latter desire took over. Before he had time to even think about it, Gideon bent over and grabbed Lydia into his arms. She gasped, and he realized he hadn't given her time to even know who he was. "It's okay, Lydia. It's me." He held her tight, relishing her lithe form and how well she fit in his arms.

"Gideon, put me down." Her tone did not belie the excitement he felt, and though he complied with her request, he took his own time in placing her back on her feet. "What are you doing?" She smacked at his arms. She could haul off and duke him in the face. He deserved it. He'd been a fool, and he could hardly contain himself with the freedom and the joy he felt. If Lydia didn't return his feelings—and he prayed, oh, how he prayed she did—he'd have to spend every waking moment he could sitting at her house, drinking her coffee or tea or whatever she made, and wooing her until she decided she'd couldn't resist marrying him.

"Lydia, I've spent a lot of time with God the last few days."

She crossed her arms and rubbed her triceps with her hands. "Okay, so?"

"So I came upon this scripture in Galatians." He scratched his weeklong beard. *Ugh. I could have cleaned up a little bit for her.* He put his hand down. He didn't need to worry about things like that at this moment. This moment was meant for convincing Lydia. "I believe God's been trying to speak this truth to me all summer, but I didn't listen."

She furrowed her eyebrows and took a step back.

He grabbed her hand and pulled her onto the porch with him. "There's a verse that says, 'Am I now trying to win the approval of men, or of God? Or am I trying to please men? If I were still trying to please men, I would not be a servant of Christ.'"

She gasped. Pulling her hand away, she lifted her eyebrows and nodded her head, but her expression displayed something. Maybe it was only that she thought he'd lost his mind. And in truth, he had. He'd lost *his* mind and gained God's. Somehow, he had to tell Lydia all the amazing things God had been showing him over the last week.

"Galatians 1, verse 10?"

"Yes! That's the verse." Elation filled his lungs. "You know it, too." *God, have You already prepared her heart? Oh, how I pray You have.*

Her gaze lifted past him and up to the heavens. "Yes, I know the verse. I memorized it and one from Thessalonians, too."

"Then you already know what I've struggled with. I spent the whole summer trying to convince myself that I could fall in love with Maria because she needed stability, and she and Jim were convinced I was that stability. I even told her we should get married. . ."

Lydia's gaze flew back to his. Emotion flicked through her eyes before she squinted at him. "You knocked on my door at"—Lydia looked at her watch—"six in the morning to tell me you're marrying Maria?"

"No." Gideon had to hold back the laughter that wanted to burst from within. "I'm not marrying Maria. I want to marry you."

She gasped and lifted her hand to her mouth.

The love he felt poured through his veins as he watched the pure and innocent surprise that filled her eyes. "I love you, Lydia. I've loved you all summer, probably since the first moment I met you when George ruined my first batch of peaches." Gideon glanced through the glass door and noticed the overgrown pup wag his tail, anxious to join them.

"But?"

Gideon looked back at Lydia. Her eyes brimmed with tears as she shook her head. Fearing she would reject him, Gideon grabbed her hands again. "I've spent this whole summer running from my feelings for you. I thought I was supposed to marry Maria because it was the right, the noble thing to do." With one hand, he brushed a strand of her hair, softer than he'd imagined, behind her ear. "I tried to fight off my love for you, but God wouldn't let it go. You're the one He's chosen for me."

Pulling her hands away, she swiped her eyes. "Well, I don't know what to say."

"Say you love me."

She bit her bottom lip, and Gideon thought the heavens would burst from the silence. Even the insects seemed to await her answer. A slow smile bowed her lips. "I do love you, Gideon."

Happiness welled within him as he took the antique ring he'd purchased the day before from his pants pocket. He got down on one knee and held out the elegant white-gold band with a circular diamond wrapped in a square setting and joined on each side by two smaller diamonds. "Say you'll marry me."

"I will."

Chapter 17

"Why are you getting married so fast?"

Gideon stopped adjusting his tie and looked at his older brother, Dalton. "I love her, and after all we've been through this past summer, I'm positive she's the one God designed for me."

"But we've only had a chance to meet her a couple times," Cameron joined in. "Caitlyn and I have dated twice as long as you, and we aren't getting married until spring."

Gideon laughed. "Well, I couldn't let my little brother tie the knot before me." Glancing out his bedroom window, he noted the fullness of his apple orchard. The tall trees bragged of lush green, orange, yellow, and pink leaves and full, ripened apples. Already, he'd had several school and church groups enjoy his land. He had never been so excited or thankful when Lydia insisted they marry in front of the land God had given him. "Besides, Indiana is beautiful in October."

Dalton raised his eyebrows and nodded. "Can't argue with that."

Gideon straightened the front of his black tuxedo jacket. "I'm going to find the girls."

"They'll never let you see Lydia," Cameron resounded.

"They have to at least let me talk to her."

Before his brothers could protest, Gideon walked out of the room. Making his way down the hall, he knew his slew of sisters had Lydia in one of the many rooms jam-packed with giggling women. Figuring out which one would be the test. He knocked on the closest door. "Lydia?"

"Gideon, she's not in here." Natalie's voice sounded through the door. "And if she were, I wouldn't let her see you anyway. Grooms can't see the bride before the wedding."

"I just want to talk to her," Gideon growled. He didn't care about that silly tradition. Between a rehearsal and bridal parties, or whatever they called them, Gideon had hardly had the chance to see Lydia alone over the last few weeks. He missed her something terrible and simply wanted to hear her voice before they stood before all those people. *If I get a peek at her and maybe a little kiss, that would be all right, too.*

Gideon knocked on the next door. "Lydia?"

"Gideon Andrews," Lydia's mother's voice boomed from inside the room

344

"what are you doing? It's bad luck to see the bride before the wedding."

"It's okay, Mom," Lydia's soft voice echoed. "I don't believe in luck." She sounded nervous.

Does she think we've moved too fast, Lord? We could have waited. It's just that I know she's the right one, and I've wanted so much to make her mine in name as well as in my heart.

The door opened just a crack. All he could see were mounds and mounds of white material and Lydia's exquisite face. She smiled when their eyes met, and a slight blush reddened her cheeks.

Her voice came out just louder than a whisper. "Hey."

"Are you nervous?"

"A little. What about you?"

"I can hardly wait to make you my wife." He caressed her cheek, and she closed her eyes at his touch. "You seem nervous. Did we move too fast?"

"Oh no." She nestled her cheek into his hand. "I'm just ready to say our vows and see you again. Just you and me."

Anticipation filled his heart. He longed for time with her. Just her. As much as he couldn't wait to see his bride adorned in a beautiful dress and walking down the aisle toward him, he yearned even more for time alone with her.

"Lydia," Rita's voice boomed, "shut that door."

"My mom's making me nervous." Her eyes twinkled. "I guess that's her job today."

Gideon looked at his watch. "Half an hour and you'll be Mrs. Gideon Andrews."

"I can hardly wait."

❧

Lydia placed her hand in the crook of her mother's arm. A moment of wishing she'd been closer to her father washed over her, but he had died from cancer a few years after he and her mom divorced. He'd never really had much to do with his family before that, either.

She peeked at her mother, whose eyes brimmed with tears. Her mom had done the best job she knew how. Allison had always been more like Mom, making Lydia feel like a misfit, but Lydia knew deep down her mother loved her. Over the last few months, since she and Gideon became engaged, she'd even noted hints that her mother had grown interested in learning more about God. The thought sent shivers of excitement through her.

"You ready?" Lydia whispered.

"To give away my baby?" Rita's voice caught. "Not really."

Lydia squeezed her mother's arm. "I love you, Mom."

"I. . .love you, too," her mother said as "The Wedding March" started.

Lydia allowed her mother's words to sink into her heart. Her mother loved her. It may have been the first time in her life Lydia had ever heard those words from her lips.

Amazingly, it didn't matter.

Sure, she thanked God for the relationship that was just beginning to blossom with her mom. One in which Lydia honored her mother's thoughts and suggestions. One in which Rita cared about and loved Lydia. She wanted to share fears, frustrations, disappointments, and joys with her mom. But Lydia's confidence, her confirmation of who she was as a person, came solely from God. Lydia inhaled at the truth of it. Her greatest desire remained to please her Abba, her Daddy God.

Partially hidden behind a tree, the twosome stepped out and Lydia gazed down the nature's rug that served as her white carpet. Looking beyond Gideon, the preacher, and their various attendants, she took in the mixture of deep green, pink, yellow, orange, and red colors of the leaves. She couldn't have put a more beautiful arrangement together if she'd spent thousands of dollars.

Her gaze skimmed the audience filled with friends and family. Pride, pure and innocent, swelled within her heart as she took in Gideon's family. *I can't wait to become a member of the Andrews clan.*

Saving the best for last, she took in her soon-to-be husband. The sweet, anticipatory smile that lit his face drew her to him. Her gaze connected with his, and she couldn't let go. How she longed to be in his arms, to be his wife until death parted them.

After what seemed an eternity, she found herself face-to-face with Gideon. The words of the minister and then her mother seemed to drift into the wind. All she could think about was the strong yet soft touch of Gideon's hand around hers; the mixture of hazel, green, and brown swimming in his eyes; and the slight stubble that was already shading his jaw. How she loved him!

Words of promise uttered from her lips. She saw Gideon's lips move and knew he repeated the vows, as well. All she could think of was the overwhelming peace she felt at becoming Gideon's wife.

For most of her life, Lydia had felt unstable and insecure. God had changed all that. Everything in her life had changed when she met Him. She still had a lot of growing to do, but she'd grown a lot over the last few months, as well.

"By the power vested in me"—the preacher's words penetrated her thoughts and she lifted her eyebrows to see Gideon's smile deepen and a mischievous gleam fill his eyes—"I now pronounce you man and wife. You may kiss your bride."

Gideon wrapped his arms around her. The warmth and strength of his embrace nearly took her breath. His lips met hers, and she allowed herself the bliss that swept through her. She'd never felt such happiness. But it was the peace—the amazing, everlasting peace—that filled, and would always sustain, her heart.

Epilogue

Twenty-one months later

Lydia closed the door to the house that once belonged to her grandmother. It belonged to Lorma now. Soon, it would be home to Cameron and his new bride, Caitlyn, as well. Gideon had never replaced Jim as an employee after his death. The upkeep of the orchard had become more than Gideon could bear alone, and when his brother offered to help, Gideon had jumped at the chance. Lydia could hardly wait to get to know her sister-in-law better.

After setting the basket of baked goodies and coffee on the ground, Lydia opened the back door of the car. She wiped the sweat from her brow. *Whew, it's hot.* Gideon's—no *their*—family would be arriving any minute for the annual Independence Day celebration. Lorma had most of the food prepared at Lydia and Gideon's house. Lydia had simply run over to what was once her coffee shop for a few after-dinner-and-fireworks treats.

The coffee shop, as a business, had closed a little over a year before. Though he'd been supportive to the end, Gideon had been right that people simply didn't travel out of their way to visit the place. At first, Lydia hurt at the admission of defeat, feeling she'd misheard God's direction. But when different churches, school clubs, and other groups requested gatherings at her shop for various Bible studies, meetings, and other activities, Lydia realized the shop had been formed for a reason, not for business but for ministry.

Now that Lorma, with the aid of her daughter, Kylie, and son-in-law, Ryan, had purchased the house from Lydia's mother, Lorma had taken over the bulk of the ministry. She thrived among the company that frequented her house. Lydia had never seen her mother-in-law so happy.

Lydia placed one hand in the small of her back and stretched out the slight ache she'd had most of the day. Rubbing her protruding belly with the other, Lydia smiled. With their babies due in just under a month, she was thankful Lorma had taken over the ministry. Lydia would have her hands full for a while.

Lydia jumped when her cell phone vibrated in her front pocket. She pulled out and read Gideon's name on the screen. Actually, she read the nickname

347

he'd typed into her phone for himself—My Hero. She giggled as she pushed the TALK button. "Yes, my hero?"

"That's right, and I always will be." His voice sounded husky and possessive. "Are you okay? I was starting to get worried."

She loved how protective he'd become of her since they'd discovered they'd b parents. "I've only been gone thirty minutes, but I'm coming home right now."

"You've got five minutes."

"Yes, sir." She couldn't stop the salute of her free hand.

"I love you, Private."

"I love you, too, Drill Sergeant."

Lydia laughed as she closed her cell phone. Gideon's protectiveness grew when they discovered she carried twins, so she'd taken to calling him the military name. Fine with the nickname, he'd given her one, as well. Though at time he smothered her with his concern, she knew it was out of love. She relished tha he cared for her and their babies so much.

After placing the basket in the backseat, she made her way around the ca and got in. A slight tightening surrounded her stomach, and she let out a lon breath. She'd had Braxton Hicks contractions for well over a month. The docto had told her they were common and nothing to worry about, but as the babie got bigger, the contractions had grown stronger.

She started the car and within moments arrived at her home. She notice Sabrina's and Kylie's vans in the driveway. The two were usually the first to arriv at their family gatherings, and Lydia could hardly wait to see them.

Gideon met her outside and opened the door. His smile turned to a frown. "Are you okay? You look flushed."

She laughed. "I'm fine. I just get tired quickly these days. Why don't yo carry the basket inside for me?"

"Of course." Gideon opened the back door and hefted the basket withou problem.

Before they could make it into the house, Chloe and Trevor pulled into th drive. Lydia clapped her hands. They hadn't seen their newest niece for a coupl weeks. Lydia could hardly wait to get her hands on the toddler. "I'm going t see Faith. I'll be just a minute."

Gideon chuckled. "I believe you'll have your hands full with squirming littl ones soon enough."

At his words, another dull ache draped around her midsection. She touche her belly.

Gideon touched her, as well. "Are you sure you're all right?"

She swatted her hand through the air. "Of course. I'm fine. Go help you mom."

Lydia waddled away from him and toward their newest visitors. Already Chloe had unbuckled the toddler and lifted her onto her hip. Lydia took in Faith's full head of light brown hair. If Lydia guessed right, the girl would look just like her mom. "Faith-girl, come here and let Aunt Lydia hold you." Faith giggled and reached for Lydia, who took the toddler from her mother.

Chloe smiled. "You'll get tired of this soon enough." She rubbed Lydia's belly then furrowed her eyebrows. "You're awfully tight."

"I've been having a lot of Braxton Hicks."

Chloe studied her a moment. "Is your back hurting?"

Lydia kissed Faith's chubby cheeks. "Just a bit." She looked up at Chloe. "But look at me. I'm huge."

The fifty pounds she'd gained in eight months had done a number on her confidence at times. The stretch marks and aches that went with the quick weight gain had only been tolerable because Gideon remained reassuring of his continued attraction to her.

Chloe took Faith from Lydia's arms and handed her to Trevor. She hooked her arm through Lydia's and guided her toward the house. "We're going to see Mama."

Another tightness overwhelmed Lydia's stomach, and she gripped Chloe's arm, releasing a long breath.

Chloe's eyebrows lifted. "It's just as I thought." She guided Lydia the rest of the way to the house. "Mama," Chloe's voice echoed through the home.

Lydia looked back to see two more of Gideon's siblings had pulled up the drive.

"Lydia's in labor."

Lydia looked back into the house. Her gaze locked with Gideon's. The look of pure terror that wrapped his face was proof enough—today, they were having their babies.

∽∾∻

Lydia opened her eyes. The labor had not gone as smoothly as she had hoped. Her body refused to progress even with the aid of a most painful medication. Soon one of the babies had gone into distress, and the doctors were forced to perform a C-section. Lydia had never seen Gideon so unglued. The nurse had given him ginger ale and crackers to keep him from passing out and being admitted himself.

Now, lying in the hospital bed, Lydia felt sore but much more at peace. The nurses had been wonderful to her and her family the two days she'd been there so far. Her gaze floated around the room until she found the figure sitting in the chair beside her. The man of her dreams held the most precious treasures she'd ever met—her sons. Lorma's brood of ten grandsons and twelve granddaughters had been made even when Lydia gave birth to two boys.

Gideon must have sensed she'd awoken as he looked up from the boys and locked gazes with her. "You are the most amazing woman in the world."

His genuine awe of her brought tears to her eyes. "We serve an amazing God who has blessed us beyond what we deserve."

"Amen to that."

"Is it time for them to nurse?" Though her stomach protested the movement, Lydia gently sat up in the bed.

"I think so." Gideon stood. "Which one first?"

"I'll take both." Lydia grinned at the look of shock on Gideon's face. "The nurse showed me how to hold them like footballs." She fluffed and situated a pillow on each side of her.

Gideon handed her one boy then the other. Within minutes, both were nursing soundly. "I can't believe I'm a dad." He pushed a strand of hair away from her face. "I was just getting used to being a husband."

"I'm that tough, huh?"

He kissed her forehead. "I've loved every minute with you."

Tears welled in her eyes again. She'd cried more the last few days than she had in her lifetime. "I love you, Gideon." She lifted her face to accept a kiss on the lips. "You're a great dad."

His stomach growled as he straightened to his full height. "It's been a while since breakfast."

Lydia looked at the hospital clock below the television and gasped. "It's three o'clock. Go get some lunch."

"Will you be okay?"

She nodded. "There's a button right beside my hand I can push if I need help."

"Okay." He kissed her forehead again. "I'll be back in a minute."

She watched as her "hero," as her phone said, walked out the door. Peering down at the fuzzy-haired, healthy boys in her arms, she exhaled a long breath of contentment.

All of her life, Lydia had longed for peace. When she finally met Jesus He'd given the fullness of His mercy and love. She finally accepted His pleasure in her, and then He blessed her with the three most adorable fellows she'd ever know.

She lifted her face toward the ceiling and closed her eyes. *Oh, Jesus, You are so good. Your delight in me is humbling, but I'll take it. Your peace is my greatest desire.*